For a long mo
though her h
a whisper, "I r
me out."

Gabe looked
want from me

"Everything. I wanted everything from you."

"Everything, huh? Well, that's what you got from Drew."

She snorted. "Sure I did."

He lowered his head and met her gaze with a look both angry and despairing. "What are you saying? That you married Drew because I wasn't there for you after Steve died?"

She rubbed her hands up and down her arms. "Don't be dense, Gabe."

He advanced on her slowly. "How am I being dense?" He stopped less than two feet from her. "Why don't you spell it out for me?"

She couldn't breathe right with him so close, knowing what his touch did to her, wanting to feel his strong arms around her, as she had eight years ago. She was torn between moving forward into his arms and running out of the room as fast as she could. "Jeremy could come in."

He shrugged his broad shoulders. "What did I have to do with you marrying Drew?"

She couldn't look at him. "What does it matter now? It's done—and he's dead."

"I want to know."

"Use your imagination, damn it."

"You wanted sex?"

Okay, now he was pissing her off. She looked up into eyes that were hooded, revealing nothing. "Yes, okay? I wanted sex. I wanted love. Is that what you wanted to hear? I wanted to be loved and made love to. I wanted to be reassured that my life wasn't over at twenty-two."

"So Franklin fit the bill."

God, he was infuriating. She shoved against his chest. "You're not paying attention. I wanted to be loved by you, you idiot. You. But you refused to talk to me or see me. You cut me off like I was nothing to you. Like we'd never even been friends, never mind lovers."

Also available from Ana Barrons and Carina Press

BETRAYED BY TRUST

ANA BARRONS

WRONGFULLY ACCUSED

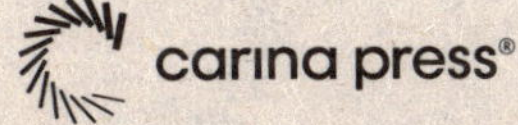

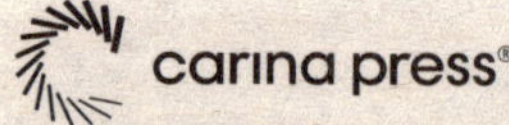

Recycling programs for this product may not exist in your area.

ISBN-13: 978-0-373-00243-6

Wrongfully Accused

This edition published by arrangement with Harlequin Books S.A.

www.CarinaPress.com

Printed in U.S.A.

Dear Reader,

Have you ever fallen for someone you had no business loving? It happens all the time. Most people hide the truth and go on with their lives, but sometimes the love is too strong, the chemistry too hot...and both people get burned.

In *Wrongfully Accused*, Kate is engaged to a man who needs her, a man she loves like a brother. But she has fallen hard for his older brother Gabe, a divorced DC cop with a young son. When Gabe is forced to shoot a teenager in the line of duty, Kate's comfort leads to passion—and destroys their tender friendship.

Gabe's guilt creates a barrier Kate can't break through, especially after his brother dies in a car accident, leaving Kate a multimillionaire. Only the affection between Kate and Gabe's son—her godson—has kept them in each other's lives.

Shut out by Gabe, Kate marries an ambitious congressman who promises her the love she so desperately needs. But it's her money and the power it can buy that the congressman loves, not her. Eight years later, he dies in a mysterious plane explosion—and Gabe is helping the police and the FBI pin the explosion on Kate.

Imagine the pain of knowing the person you've never stopped loving thinks you're capable of murder. And not just one murder—but two! Gabe has long held Kate responsible for his brother's death, believing she drove him to commit suicide after they married so she would inherit his millions.

But is that really what Gabe believes, or has he been lying to himself and everyone else to keep the guilt of loving Kate from eating him alive?

Wrongfully Accused combines my fascination with political corruption and my obsession with bringing hopeless lovers together. When I write, I lose myself in my characters' heads and hearts, leaving them in charge! As I wrote their story, even I wasn't sure Gabe and Kate could move beyond past hurts and find happiness together.

I hope you enjoy this tale of passion and heartache, politics and deception, and a love so strong it can't be denied.

Happy reading!

Ana

Dedication

For Mom

Acknowledgments

A million thanks to my wonderful critique partners and BFFs: Joyce Lamb, Maggie Hoye and Linda Cutillo, for your insight, your honesty and your humor. I love you guys!

Endless kisses to my loving and brilliant husband, for being my biggest cheerleader.

Love and xoxo to my loyal and encouraging sisters for reading those early, early drafts of my manuscripts—you two are the best!

And eternal gratitude to my fabulous agent, Laura Bradford, and my incredibly talented and meticulous Carina editor, Mallory Braus, for all your help. You two are amazing.

WRONGFULLY ACCUSED

Prologue

Washington, D.C.

Officer Gabriel Hugo pressed his back hard against the cinder block wall of the apartment breezeway, Glock pointing down between his size thirteens. Sweat dripped from his forehead and off the end of his nose, trickled down his neck and chest and soaked through his shirt. The humid night air amplified the stink of garbage, piss and marijuana smoke.

And fear.

His.

Please, God, I don't want to shoot this kid.

Kevin Brewer was sixteen at best, raised in a shit hole a lot like this one and lacking a single reasonable bone in his skinny, filthy body. If he would put his fucking gun down for one minute and hear Gabe out they wouldn't be in this standoff. But the kid was forcing his hand. If Gabe dropped his gun the punk would off him without a second thought. Not only did Kevin have a poor excuse for a conscience, he had something to prove, making him the most dangerous kind of adversary.

"You won't get out of this alive, Kevin," Gabe called. "You know there's backup coming. Even if you shoot me you won't get out of this building without a shitload of holes in you. Is that what you want your mama to see when she comes down to identify you? Her baby boy's brains coming out the back of his head? Is it worth it to make your first cop kill so your homeboys'll be proud of you?"

"I told you," Kevin called back, his voice shaky and a little breathless, like he was hyperventilating. "Throw me your piece and you walk. Otherwise you shut the fuck up."

Gabe blinked sweat out of his eyes and counted to three. "Drop the fucking gun, Kevin. Put your hands on top of your head and kneel on the floor, and nobody will hurt you. You hear me? Prove that you have a fucking brain in your head."

"Fuck you!"

"You got a death wish, Kevin? What are you, twelve? You want to die at fucking twelve years old?"

Finally, sirens in the distance. Gabe clutched his gun with both hands as he slid closer to the corner of the wall, imagining Kevin moving away from him and toward the steps leading down to the alley. Praying Kevin was moving away.

Please, God, don't make me shoot this kid.

He pictured Jeremy back at his apartment, asleep in his crib while his brother and his girlfriend kept watch. Or, more likely, while Steve worked on his computer and Kate snuggled Jeremy in her arms.

The sirens were loud, closing in. Gabe risked a glance around the corner. Kevin was coming at him, gun raised, panic and determination in his dark eyes.

No, don't let this be happening.

"Drop it!" Gabe shouted. But Kevin took aim and was about to squeeze the trigger.

No choice, no choice, no choice.

They fired at the same time, but Gabe's aim was truer and the boy dropped to his knees, then pitched forward on to his face. Gabe lowered his gun slowly, went to Kevin's side and felt for a pulse. Outside doors slammed and footsteps rang up the cement steps.

And rang, and rang, and rang…

It was nearly 4 a.m. when Gabe unlocked the door to his Capitol Hill apartment and stepped inside. No sign of his brother or Kate, so they had to be in his bed. He only asked them to stay overnight with Jeremy when he got an emergency call. They always rushed over, understanding that he didn't want to call Lindsay and let her think he couldn't handle having Jeremy spend the night. No way. He'd call the Pope to babysit if it would prove him worthy of having joint custody of his son.

He threw his keys down on the coffee table and pulled his shirt over his head. God, he stunk. The AC in the building was on but it was struggling. He peeled off his jeans and boxers and headed into the bathroom for a shower. It smelled of the girly, floral shampoo Kate used, and for a moment he stood with the lights off and inhaled. The room smelled of life and beauty and purity, not ugliness and death.

Do not think about the boy you killed back there.

He turned the jets on hard and hot and let the spray pound his chest and face, as though it could somehow batter away the pain and guilt. He lathered some generic shampoo into his thick hair, then scrubbed at his body with soap and scraped the loofah over every inch of his skin until the hot water ran out. No matter how hard he tried to empty his brain, he couldn't escape the image of Kevin falling to his knees. Kevin lying in his own blood.

Turned out the boy was fifteen.

Gabe wrapped a towel around his waist, brushed his teeth and went into the living room. He'd grab a sheet and pillow from the closet in his room and bunk on the too-small couch. Jeremy would be up in a couple of hours anyway.

But first he stepped into Jeremy's tiny room and peered into his crib. The boy was curled up, thumb in his mouth, sweaty curls shiny in the dim glow of the night-light. Safe. Peaceful. Tears pricked his eyes at the thought of what Kevin's mother was going through tonight.

He reached out to touch his son, but stopped himself. If Jeremy woke up he'd want to play, and Gabe was in no shape to play or talk or interact in any way with another human being.

Gabe's bedroom was dark except for the glow of his digital clock, which helped him navigate around all the crap on the floor when Jeremy woke during the night. At eighteen months his son slept through most nights, but he couldn't depend on it. He glanced at the king-size bed on his way to the closet—and saw one body instead of two.

Kate's long dark hair was spread out on the pillow. She was curled up on her side, like Jeremy, with the covers kicked off, wearing a tank top and running shorts. Gabe stood, transfixed, watching her sleep. Steve must have gone home to work on some project he couldn't do on his laptop. Nothing stood in the way of his Internet business, not even his amazing girlfriend.

Gabe went to the closet for the bedding, then glanced back at the bed. Kate took up less than a quarter of it. If he stretched out on the other side, away from her, she'd never even know he was there. He'd wake up as soon as Jeremy made a peep anyway, so what difference did it make? This way he'd actually get some sleep, instead of twisting his body into a pretzel on the couch.

He pulled on running shorts and a white T-shirt and

lay down on his back as far from Kate as possible. The ceiling fan was blowing warm air around, but the breeze helped. He must have drifted off because the next thing he knew somebody was shaking him and saying his name, over and over. Somebody who smelled like fresh flowers and soap. He opened gritty eyes to Kate's worried face inches from his.

"Gabe, are you okay?" she asked in a loud whisper.

He didn't answer, because he didn't know why she was there or why she thought he wasn't okay. They were lying on their sides, facing each other, Kate's hand on his shoulder, her warm, feminine scent overwhelming his senses.

In his bed.

His cock went rigid.

"What…" he finally managed.

In answer she stroked her thumb over his cheekbones, her eyes in the dim light filled with sympathy. "You were crying in your sleep," she said, and he realized she'd been wiping away his tears. He couldn't speak around the lump in his throat.

"Were you dreaming?" she asked. "Or did something happen tonight?"

He closed his eyes and it came back to him in slow motion.

Kevin raising his gun, aiming right for Gabe's chest.

Gabe raising his gun, knowing it was kill or be killed.

The bullet hitting Kevin's chest and the startled awareness in the boy's eyes that he was about to die.

Kevin keeling over, hitting the cement floor with a thud. His short, short life draining out of him in a spreading pool of blood.

Loud footsteps on the stairs.

Gabe's ears ringing as he felt for a pulse that wasn't there.

"Oh, Gabe," she whispered, pulling him to her and holding his head to her breasts as she stroked his hair. "Go ahead and let it out."

Beneath his cheek the thin fabric of her tank top grew wet with his tears. He squeezed his eyes tight and tried to stop the flow, but the fact that she was holding him and comforting him made it that much tougher. Fuck. What was wrong with him? He was a cop, for chrissake. A big, tough motherfucker who did what he had to do.

But he'd shot and killed a kid. A fucking *kid.*

He rolled on to his back and threw an arm over his eyes while he struggled to pull it together. Kate wrapped her small hand around his biceps and made gentle sweeps across his skin with her thumb. He felt that movement of her skin against his all the way to his toes.

"What happened to you tonight?" she asked, and she was so sweet and concerned it was all he could do not to crawl into her arms and let her hold him like she held Jeremy.

"It's not a pretty story," he rasped.

"No, I didn't think it would be," she said. "But you might feel better if you talk about it. I can take it, you know."

He sighed with effort. Little by little he told her the whole ugly story—punctuated by long pauses and throat clearing to hide the cracking of his voice—until he was drained of words and tears. But not of shame. Or grief.

When he finished she stroked his cheek and said, "Oh, God, I'm so sorry, Gabe. Try to sleep. I'll stay with Jeremy today."

Gabe lifted the arm covering his face and gazed into her

gentle eyes. How could Steve have gone home and left this beautiful, generous woman behind? He was always leaving Kate on her own. Even at family parties, it was typical for Steve to hole up in a bedroom with his laptop or take a separate car so he could leave early. Granted, his Internet business was growing phenomenally, so he had a lot on his plate. But where were his little brother's priorities?

If Kate belonged to him he would never willingly spend a night without her.

"Does my brother know how lucky he is?" he asked before he could stop himself.

Kate's eyes widened for an instant, and then she shrugged and gave him a lopsided smile.

No, Steve didn't appreciate what he had and they both knew it. His brother was brilliant and self-absorbed, and he took people for granted. His mother and older sisters had doted on the precocious, difficult, angel-faced toddler, and when the psychologists proclaimed him a genius they all but wrapped the kid in cotton batting. Even Gabe had put the kid on a pedestal. Steven looked up to him, always had, but he was of little use when Steven had one of his meltdowns. Only Kate could soothe him and bring him out of his funk. She completed him, Steve had said more than once. Problem was, Steven wasn't really there for her.

It was several seconds before Gabe realized he'd been staring at her, examining her face, marveling at the length of her thick lashes and the tiny freckles across the bridge of her nose. The fullness of her lips. Her breath warm against his skin.

Her breast pressed against his upper arm…

He wasn't sure exactly when her breathing changed or when her heart started pounding, only that suddenly their closeness had less to do with comfort and much,

much more to do with need. Fierce, hot need that spiked his pulse and drove all thought from his mind. There was only this moment. Only Kate.

Her lips parted slowly. Gabe rolled toward her and touched his nose to hers, and she expelled a soft breath that set flame to something deep and primitive inside him. He brushed her cheek with his, nuzzled his face into her silky hair and lowered his lips to the tender skin of her neck. She let out a long, ragged breath and he pulled her to him, gripping her hip. A voice inside him screamed to stop, but he placated it. *Just a kiss, that's all. One tiny kiss. To thank her.*

He lifted his head and cupped her face in his hand, then leaned in and brushed his lips across hers, once, twice, then kissed her gently. She opened her eyes and he waited for permission, then got it when she eased back on the pillow and ran her hands through his hair. His cock hardened painfully.

"Gabe," she whispered.

He let out a long breath and wrapped her tightly in his arms, then took her mouth in a deep, hungry kiss. Her lips were everything he'd tried not to imagine they would be—lush and sweet and hot. She opened for him and welcomed his tongue deep inside, sucking, tangling, exploring as though she, too, were starved. For this. For him.

He rolled on top of her, claiming her, then slid his hands down her sides, letting his thumbs graze the sides of her breasts. She gasped and arched her back. Oh, God, he couldn't stop. He shifted so his erection was wedged between her thighs and felt her answering response.

"Kate," he rasped against her lips before he angled his head and plundered her mouth again. Hard nipples pressed into his chest, driving him insane with desire. He ran his hands under her tank top, cupping her breasts while he kissed her. Kate groaned as he kneaded them, running his thumbs over their swollen peaks.

He pulled her tank top over her head and took one nipple into his mouth. She gasped, her hands moving over his shoulders, through his hair, repeating his name in a strangled whisper. He suckled hard, loving the taste of her, while sliding one hand down her back to her rounded bottom and into her shorts. Oh, God, she wasn't wearing panties. The discovery made his cock so hard it throbbed. He pushed one slim leg aside with his foot and slid his hand down the front of her shorts. He encountered damp curls, then reached lower and ran his fingers through her slippery flesh. Good God, she was hot and wet and he wanted to be inside her more than he wanted his next breath.

Kate arched into his hand, whimpering and begging. "Oh, God… Please, Gabe… Please…"

Something snapped inside him, and there was no thought, no will when he pulled off his gym shorts and shirt and yanked her shorts down her legs, then spread her thighs wide and pushed his cock into her tight, wet heat. He wanted to cry at how perfect, how right it felt inside her. Finally. *Finally.*

She dug her heels into his back, scraped the skin of his ass with her nails, begging him to go faster, deeper, harder. He lifted her hips and pounded into her with a mindless, primitive need he'd never known before. Though nearly blind with passion, he couldn't take his eyes off the face he knew so well, transformed by ecstasy.

She cried his name when she began to contract around him, and he came violently, throbbing inside her as she wrapped herself around him like she wanted to climb inside his skin. They rolled to one side, holding on to each other until their breathing slowed.

Reality slammed into his gut in a single, devastating blow. This was Kate. She wasn't his. She belonged to Steve. To *Steve*. The brother he'd protected his whole life.

"Fuck!" He reared up, disentangling from her. "What the hell am I doing?"

She reached for him as he backed off the bed. "No! Don't do this."

"Holy shit," he said, palms squeezing the sides of his head. He'd really done it. He'd made love to his brother's girlfriend. "Holy fucking shit."

Kate climbed off the bed and clutched at his arms. "Stop. It wasn't your fault, it was—"

He pulled away and held up a hand. "No. Don't say it. Don't say anything. Just get dressed and I'll call you a cab."

Her brows furrowed, but it was hurt, not anger he saw in those hazel eyes. "Listen to me," she said. "I know this wasn't fair to Steve, but there's a lot you don't—"

"We're not talking about this," he said. He snatched his gym shorts off the floor and pulled them on, covering the partial erection he still had. "I'm going to call you a cab. Be dressed and ready when it gets here." He left the bedroom quickly and punched in the numbers for a cab company, hands shaking. Then he stood by the kitchen window and waited for it to show up, cursing himself for giving into his desire for her. He'd worked at pushing Kate out of his mind for years, trained himself not to watch her move, or laugh too hard at her jokes, or lean in when she spoke. Or find reasons to touch her just…to touch her.

What kind of fucking Pandora's box had he opened?

He heard her behind him but didn't turn around.

"We needed each other tonight," she said quietly.

He pinched the bridge of his nose between his thumb and forefinger. "I said we're not—"

"—talking about it. I know. So shut up and listen."

"Christ," he murmured.

"Steve didn't leave because he had important work to do."

Gabe had no doubt that was exactly why Steve had gone home and left Kate in his bed. Trusting, of course, that his older brother would behave himself. "It doesn't matter."

"He called Ben for a ride so he could go home and get a good night's sleep."

"Is that supposed to be some kind of crime?"

"He prefers to sleep alone," she said.

Gabe went still. "You live together."

"Most nights he sleeps on the futon in the living room."

Gabe turned toward her slowly. She was wearing jeans, thank God, but her hair was tangled and her lips were swollen from his kisses. He swallowed and tried not to stare at the hard nipples so clearly outlined through her flimsy tank top. The one he'd pulled off her. When he dared to speak he asked, "Why?"

She hugged herself. "I like to snuggle in bed, and he doesn't. So if he's in bed with me either I feel shut out or he feels smothered, so he goes off and crashes on the couch."

What was this, *The Twilight Zone?* Steve didn't want to wrap his body around hers during the night? Did his brother ever pull his eyes away from his computer long enough to take a good long look at the unbelievably sexy woman he lived with? He wanted to ask whether Steve ever made love to her, but that was a no-brainer. His brother might be an obsessive-compulsive geek but he wasn't a moron.

Gabe turned back to the window. "It's none of my business what goes on between you and Steve," he said. "All I know is you're practically engaged, so things can't be so bad."

"I'm his best friend," she said. "I take care of him."

"You love him."

"Of course I love him."

An unexpected pain stabbed through Gabe's chest. "Great," he said, more savagely than he'd intended. "In that case, I would advise you to stay out of other men's beds."

"Oh my God, you're twisting this whole thing!"

No shit. A flash of orange on the street caught his eye. "Cab's outside."

"My car is here," she said, and he couldn't miss the misery in her voice.

He picked up his wallet off the table, plucked a ten and held it out to her. "Give this to the guy and send him away." When she didn't take it he was forced to look at her.

Tears glistened on her cheeks. "Give it to him yourself," she said. "And how do think you're going to deal with Jeremy today, huh? Just tell me that."

"I'm a big boy. I can go without sleep for a night."

"Fine," she said, then took a deep, shaky breath. "I know you're upset now and you don't want to talk, but you know you can call me to come and stay with him later if—"

"I won't need you to babysit anymore," he said.

Her mouth hung open, eyes wide with hurt. "That's not fair. I love Jeremy, and he loves me."

Gabe shrugged, even though the thought of taking her away from Jeremy made his chest ache. "I'm not a fair kind of guy. I think I proved that tonight."

She stepped closer. "Don't take this out on your son, damn it. You're pissed at yourself, and at me, that's fine. But Jeremy didn't do anything."

He heard two sounds at once. His phone buzzed and Jeremy called out, "Keke?" He grabbed the phone and Kate rushed into Jeremy's room. He told the cabbie to come upstairs and he'd give him ten bucks for his trouble, but the guy told him to fuck off and hung up.

When he stepped into the room, Jeremy was already in Kate's arms, curly head tucked against her shoulder, sucking his thumb while she cooed and rocked him in the overstuffed recliner. Above her hung a framed pen-and-ink drawing she'd done of Jeremy lying on Gabe's chest at six months. Like all of her work, it captured the tiniest details. His wispy baby hair, the curve of his chubby cheek and Gabe's big hand on his bare back. As always when he looked at it, Gabe was awed by her talent.

She held a finger up to her lips so Gabe wouldn't speak. He hesitated for a moment before he backed out of the room. Then he sat at the kitchen table with his head on his folded arms and listened to her humming a lullaby. Eventually, he slept.

The next time he heard Jeremy's voice he jerked awake, disoriented. The sun had come up. On the table lay a note in Kate's rounded printing.

No matter what happens, I will never regret making love with you.

Chapter One

Eight Years Later

"It's done." Congressman Drew Franklin settled back into the leather seat of the Learjet, cell phone to his ear. In front of him and across the aisle, two other congressmen chatted while assorted aides pounded away on their laptops. One of the congressmen raised a glass of scotch in a toast and Drew gave him a thumbs-up. To the person on the other end of the phone he added, "We'll have all the votes we need."

"We'll find out in a few days," the voice said.

Drew sighed, but he was too elated even to be annoyed. "Oh ye of little faith," he said. How could someone so intimately involved with his plan possibly doubt it would work? It was brilliant, and going off without a hitch, as though the bill's passage were preordained. "So, will I see you tonight?"

"Well, no… That won't be possible."

"Oh, too bad." He said it with just the right amount of sincerity that no one would ever suspect how relieved he was. "I guess we can wait to celebrate after the bill passes the chamber."

"You deserve everything that's coming to you, Drew."

"*We* deserve it," Drew said, loosening his tie. "This will be our victory."

The copilot stepped into the cabin and announced that

it was time for the passengers to turn off their cell phones. Drew nodded and held up a finger. "Gotta go. We're taking off."

"Okay, but Drew?"

"Hmm?"

"Don't forget to say cheese."

Drew frowned and clicked off his phone, then leaned back in his seat and closed his eyes while they taxied down the runway and lifted off. Hartford was overcast and 81 degrees, so it was probably in the high 80s in Washington. In a couple of hours he'd be home, and all of his hard work, his planning, his *genius* would finally be rewarded.

And yes, there *would* be dozens of cameras…

Say cheese. Of course.

He considered having a scotch. Lord knew, he'd earned it. It was the risks a man took that showed what he was made of. This had been a risky venture, no question, one that most men would never even imagine, never mind actually consider doing. For him, though, the degree of risk simply reflected the depth of his imagination.

He turned to the window and smiled down at the tops of trees, roofs, swimming pools… Neighborhoods full of families whose futures he would ultimately hold in his hands. Life would be so much more rewarding when he was in charge of everything. No more frustrating committee meetings with intellectual inferiors, no tiresome rewrites of bills, finding himself at the mercy of idiots whose idea of how to set policy was to filibuster. When his bill passed both houses of Congress and the president signed it, he—the Honorable Andrew Franklin—would have the power to rewrite the rules.

More power, ultimately, than the president.

The Director of Global Intelligence and Security. He

loved the sound of that title almost as much as he loved what would come with it. In an international crisis *he* would be charged with guarding the country—the world, when it came down to it—against political stalemate and those moronic decisions so often made at the highest levels. There he would be, standing before the president, the National Security Council, the Secretary of Defense and Joint Chiefs of Staff, *telling* them what needed to be done. It would sound like advice—persuasion, even—based on intelligence from every other spook agency in this country and around the world. Information no one else would be privy to.

Information on every U.S. citizen, anywhere on the globe—and any foreigner he considered a potential threat. Obtained through whatever means he deemed necessary.

That was the part he liked best.

And if for some reason the powers-that-be were unmoved, or managed to turn the president against him... Well, he wasn't one to tolerate obstacles. He had a strategy for dealing with the naysayers while carrying through with his agenda. While they were busy doing battle with one another, he would be busy using his authority to collect dirt on every single one of them, even if he had to invent it. Including the president.

Especially the president.

He chuckled to himself. The Patriot Act was a joke compared the Global Intel bill.

There would be questions—that was inevitable. When pressed he would play the responsive public servant, open to compromise. Behind the scenes was another story—he would take whatever covert actions were necessary to get the job done. The world needed his direction, and it was time he took his place at the helm.

He felt an erection building, so he grabbed his coat jacket and laid it across his lap. A good fuck was most definitely in order, but he'd have to play it safe for the time being. He certainly had no interest in any relationship that didn't further his goals. Kate had become a liability over time, but all things considered, marrying her had been the perfect move.

He opened his briefcase on his lap, too wired to just sit there. His digital camera sat on top of a messy pile of paper. What the hell was it doing in there? The last time he saw his camera it was at home, in its leather case. Had he packed it after all? He rifled through the compartments in his briefcase. No leather case. Kate was the one who was so bad about keeping her camera in the case, no matter how many times he reminded her.

The camera's sudden high-pitched whine startled him. He stared at the thing, unable to look away—and broke into a cold sweat.

Don't forget to say cheese.

He began to scream.

Kate flicked a glance at the little girl sitting on her father's lap across the aisle. Had she finally gotten the nose right? Pretty close, but the slope wasn't perfect. She moved her pencil back to the nose and altered the shape ever so slightly. Another surreptitious glance told her she'd captured it this time. Good. She used her ring finger to add shading and then leaned back to gauge how that pert nose fit with the rest of the face.

She closed her eyes. The sketch was good, and it had occupied her for most of the flight from Hartford, but it hadn't helped erase the image of Drew's scornful expression when he parted from her at the gate. She'd asked if he planned to be home for dinner and he'd given her that strange smile, if you could even call it that. He'd never smiled that way before, so phony and…ugly. Really, his expression had been ugly, as though he'd smelled something disgusting.

When had he come to despise her so?

"Mrs. Franklin?" the flight attendant said over the roar of the engines.

Kate looked up at the middle-aged woman leaning toward her. "Yes?"

"The captain has asked that you deplane before the other passengers."

Kate glanced around the full business class cabin. The plane was still taxiing to the gate. "We're the first ones off anyway, aren't we?"

"Yes, but…there are some people waiting for you on the Jetway."

Kate noted the tension around the woman's mouth and the stiff way she was holding herself. Tendrils of fear slithered through her gut. "Is something wrong?" she asked.

"Please, Mrs. Franklin."

The woman straightened and walked away, leaving Kate with her overactive imagination.

Buck up, Kate. Whatever it is, you'll handle it. You always do.

A minute or so later they arrived at the gate. Kate stood. The attendant opened the overhead compartment and pulled out Kate's bag, then led her past the curious passengers toward the door of the plane. The captain and flight attendants stood there with somber expressions on their faces. What in God's name was going on?

The flight had been unremarkable, except that halfway through the captain made everyone turn off their electronic devices and wouldn't let anyone use the onboard phones. None of this had affected Kate one way or the other, since she'd been busy sketching. She did hear some of the other business passengers gripe about the inconvenience, but the attendants brought them fresh drinks and snacks and everyone seemed to get over it.

On the other side of the door, Kate was met by three men in black suits carrying walkie-talkies and a soldier carrying a large automatic weapon.

"Mrs. Franklin?" the largest suit said. He pulled out his credentials. FBI. "Agent Richard Miller. Please come with us." The other agents were busy scanning the Jetway as though there were some hidden menace right there in the tube.

"Has there been a bomb scare or something?" Kate asked.

"Come with us, please," Agent Miller repeated.

The three agents surrounded her and ushered her up the Jetway, through the gate at Dulles International Airport and into a small office with a metal desk and four padded chairs. The soldier stopped outside in the hall. As soon as the door closed behind her, Kate said, "Will somebody please tell me what's going on?"

Agent Miller cleared his throat and offered her a chair. "Please sit down, Mrs. Franklin," he said. "Would you like some coffee or water or—"

"Just tell me what the in the world is going on!" A sudden thought struck her. "Is this about Drew?"

The other two agents shared a glance and the knot in her gut twisted. "Oh, God," she said, her voice shaky. "Is he okay? Is he hurt?"

"I'm afraid I have some bad news for you." Agent Miller took a deep breath and let it out. "The Learjet carrying your husband and several other congressmen to Washington exploded over Long Island Sound twenty-five minutes ago."

Her heart began pounding in her ears, blocking out sound. Surely she'd heard him wrong. This wasn't possible. "What?" she asked over the deafening *whoomp, whoomp, whoomp.*

"Congressman Franklin and several others..." The man swallowed. "I'm so sorry, Mrs. Franklin. The Coast Guard is searching for survivors, of course, but—"

Panic seized her then. *Survivors. Coast Guard. Water.* She closed her eyes and the room spun. "Oh, God," she murmured. Someone helped her into a chair. Nausea threatened and she bent forward, dropping her head into her hands. "Oh my God, oh my God, oh my God... Drew. Oh God." How could this be happening?

"I'm so sorry."

It was several minutes before the dizziness and nausea passed. Her insides were cold and tight, so tight. Someone handed her a cup of water, and she managed a small sip. In a dim part of her mind she thought of the people she needed to call. Drew's parents. Her family. Their friends.

Drew was dead. Just like that. Gone forever.

Like Steve.

Oh, God, how could she bear all that emptiness again?

"How?" she whispered.

Agent Miller's gaze slid toward one of the other agents but he didn't turn his head. "We won't know for sure for some time," he said. "But the investigation will be extremely thorough, I can promise you that."

She stared at him. "What aren't you telling me? What is it?" She searched the faces of the other agents, whose eyes would not meet hers.

Agent Miller cleared his throat again, then spoke in a low voice. "We have reason to believe…" He trailed off, one hand at his tie.

Kate struggled to swallow. "What? You believe what?"

He pulled his hand away from his tie and leaned back against the desk. His mouth was set in a grim line. "Al Qaeda has claimed responsibility," he said quietly.

Chapter Two

A week later

Kate ducked into Drew's study and closed the door quietly, then leaned her forehead against the cold wood. She didn't bother to turn on the light. If she didn't get some time alone she was going to flip out. It was all too much. People in the house constantly, especially today, after the memorial service at the Washington National Cathedral. The phone calls and sympathy cards. The politics. The phoniness. The press.

Her husband was dead, and the politicians were turning his death into a media circus. Some of these people had loved Drew, yes. His parents, who were heartbroken. His administrative assistant, Michael Clark, who'd been with Drew since he worked in the Connecticut legislature more than fifteen years ago.

She crossed the room to the built-in shelves behind Drew's desk. He kept a bottle of very good cognac there, as she'd discovered during one of the many nights he simply hadn't come home. Now she poured a generous snifter and brought it to her lips. How was she going to get through this? Granted, their marriage had been far from perfect, but they'd been trying to work it out. Maybe this time things would have changed.

"Goddamn it, Drew, why did you have to die?" she murmured.

"I've been asking myself the same question."

Kate jumped and spun around. Joy Stuart, representative from Connecticut's third district, sat in a tall wing chair facing Drew's massive oak desk. Kate couldn't see her well in the dim light, but it sounded like she'd been crying.

"What are you doing in here?" Kate asked. Her hands were shaking. "You scared the hell out of me."

Joy raised a glass. "Great minds think alike," she said. "I knew Drew kept this bottle in here, and I was sick to death of all those people." She swirled the cognac in her snifter, then took a long swallow.

Kate wasn't sure how she felt about Joy making herself at home in Drew's study, helping herself to his booze.

Joy's husband, Ben, had been best friends with Steven, despite the ten-year difference in their ages. Ben was a cardiology fellow at Georgetown Hospital when he'd hired the eighteen-year-old Georgetown senior to help him solve some biomechanical problems. The two hit it off immediately and developed a deep respect for one another. Kate was a freshman that year—her first time away from home—and when she started seeing Steven, Joy took her under her wing.

Steven's mother loved to cook and invited Kate and the Stuarts to numerous dinners, bringing them into contact with Gabe and his new wife Lindsay. The three couples grew close. After Steve died and Gabe had turned his back on her, it was Joy who introduced Kate to Drew.

She and the Stuarts remained close until politics drove a wedge in her friendship with Joy, who had become openly disdainful of Kate's liberal views—and her habit of expressing them in mixed company.

But maybe there was more to it than politics.

Kate stood there feeling awkward for a moment, and

then decided to clear the air with the woman who had once been her closest friend. "You saw more of Drew than I did over the past couple of years," she said. "Nights he didn't come in until after midnight, weekends I barely saw him, he was with you."

Joy sighed. "Ben said the same thing to me recently, almost verbatim." She ran her fingers through short, highlighted blond hair. "What can I say, Kate? We worked together. Fought battles, side by side, every single day. Shared the same values. We enjoyed spending time together."

Kate winced. "Is that supposed to make me feel better?"

Joy took a long sip of cognac and struggled to swallow it. Tears glistened on her cheeks. Finally she said, "Drew meant a lot to me. We were…close." She closed her eyes and took a deep, halting breath, obviously holding back a sob.

"I resent your closeness," Kate said, surprising herself with that bald admission. Well, if she didn't get this off her chest now she never would. "I resent that he cared about you. I resent all the time he spent with you instead of me."

Joy got up, came behind the desk and reached for the bottle, then poured herself another generous snifter. Her face looked haggard, like someone deeply grieving. *Good Lord,* Kate thought. *I even resent her grief.* She leaned against the desk, watching Joy pace around the office, running her hands over photos of Drew with various politicians and world leaders. Joy laid a hand on a photo of herself and Drew, as though she were feeling its beating heart.

"You loved him," Kate said. It wasn't a question. "You were in love with my husband."

"The whole world was in love with Drew," Joy threw back.

"The whole world of his party, maybe. But that's not what I'm talking about and you know it."

Joy turned to her, eyes narrowed, hand on hip. "Tell me you're not saying what I think you're saying."

Anger bubbled up inside Kate's chest, but she bit her tongue. She'd never imagined herself in the position of spurned wife confronting her husband's mistress. Humiliation burned her cheeks.

"Are you insinuating that Drew and I were lovers?" Joy pressed.

Yes, she wanted to scream. It would explain so many things. Like why Drew never wanted sex anymore. Why his rare professions of love, typically made when she suggested a trial separation, sounded insincere. She swallowed hard. "Were you?"

"I won't dignify that with an answer," Joy said. "If you really think your husband was having an affair maybe you should look in the mirror and ask yourself why, rather than accusing his female colleagues of sleeping with him."

The barb stung, causing Kate to gasp. "That was a low blow, even for you."

Joy splayed her hand over her chest. "Oh, well, excuse me for being indelicate, Kate. Was that blow lower than you rolling your eyes for the TV cameras during one of the most important speeches of Drew's life?" Her voice rose as she spoke. "Lower than undermining Drew's stand on prisoner's rights on his own front lawn? Lower than arguing the other side of every goddamn issue at every goddamn dinner party?"

Joy's words rang in the silence that followed. All Kate could hear was the pounding of her own heart. "You heartless bitch," she whispered. "I just lost my husband."

Joy took another long swallow of cognac, swaying a bit as she did. "You didn't deserve him."

The door to the study opened and Ben Stuart stuck his

head inside. “There you are,” he said to his wife. “What are you doing in here all alone?”

“She’s not alone,” Kate rasped around vocal cords that felt frozen. Joy couldn’t have hurt her more if she’d taken a stick and beaten her with it.

He stepped further into the room. “Oh. Sorry, Kate. I didn’t see you. I’ll, uh, leave you two to talk.”

“Oh, believe me, we’re done,” Joy said. She brushed by her husband on her way out.

Ben seemed momentarily startled, then moved toward Kate. She was struck, as always, by the calm he carried with him. Ben was a handsome, athletic man who seemed oblivious to his looks and appeal. His green eyes studied her from behind tortoiseshell glasses as though she were one of his heart patients.

“Are you okay?” he asked, squeezing her hand.

“I will be,” she managed. Once she recovered from Joy’s pummeling.

“What a terrible day this must be for you.”

Terrible didn’t begin to cover it. “It’s hard,” she said.

“So much harder when someone is torn away from you suddenly, the way Drew was.” He shook his head in that concerned way of his that she found so endearing. “And dealing with all these people. My God, Kate. There must be a hundred guests here.”

“It’s important to bring everyone together.” She gazed down at her black high heels, unsure what to say next. “I think you should take Joy home. She’s had too much to drink and…she’s grieving. She needs you now.”

He was silent for a moment, and Kate mentally kicked herself for saying too much. Even if Joy and Drew had been sleeping together, she wouldn’t want that knowledge to hurt Ben.

"What about you?" Ben asked. "Who's going to take care of you?"

She hugged herself. "My family is here. Friends from my charities." And then, more to herself than to Ben, "Being Mrs. Drew Franklin wasn't my whole life."

"Sorry to interrupt this little reunion."

Gabe? She had spotted him in the crowd after the memorial service, but there had been a large police presence at the cathedral so she'd assumed he was on the job. Never in a million years would she have expected him to show up at her house. Now he was standing in the doorway to Drew's den, his large frame blocking the light from the hall.

Eight years after Steve's death he still held her responsible. She knew that down to her bones, even though he'd never come out and said it.

"What do you want?" Ben asked Gabe, frowning.

"Joy doesn't look too good. You might want to take her home."

"Right. Thanks." Ben turned back to Kate and spoke quietly. "I'll come by tomorrow to see how you're doing."

"That's really sweet of you," she said. "But I'll be fine. Really."

Gabe closed the door behind Ben and leaned against it, arms folded over his powerful chest. The room felt smaller now that it was only the two of them. He had always had that effect on her. And as always when she was around him, her heart pounded and she had trouble pulling air into her lungs.

"So," he said, that deep voice steady and casual. "Already working on number three? You never were one to waste a lot of time mourning."

The shock of his words jerked her head back. Had he

really said—? Pain sliced through her heart, but hot anger cauterized the wound. She gripped the edge of the desk. "How dare you mock my grief, you son of a bitch."

"Joy would take him to the cleaners if he divorced her," he went on as though she hadn't spoken. "But then, you're not exactly hurting for money, are you? Steve took care of that for you."

She propelled herself away from the desk, stalked across the Persian carpet and reared her arm back to slap him. Gabe grabbed it just before her hand connected with his face.

"A little too close to the truth?" he asked, lowering his voice.

She raised her other arm and he grabbed that one as well, but she was fired up and shoved against him. "You *bastard*." A hard kick to his shin got her pushed against the study wall, arms over her head, his body pressed hard into hers.

"Careful, there, sister," he ground out.

She was breathing heavily, her breasts heaving against the solid wall of his chest. Beneath her anger she was aware of his heat, the way his thighs felt against hers, the closeness of his mouth. God, she was pathetic. His breath even smelled the same, like the butterscotch candies he'd been addicted to since he gave up smoking.

"Jesus," he said, dropping her wrists and backing away as though she'd singed him.

She was disgusted to feel tears welling. Why did she still let him get to her? First Joy, now him. *Go ahead and kick me while I'm down, guys.* That thought stiffened her spine. Okay, this really was the day to get things off her chest. And God knew, this encounter had been a very long time coming.

"For years it tore me apart," she said, hoping he hadn't

heard the slight crack in her voice. "Knowing you could even consider the possibility that I drove Steve to his death."

"I never accused you of anything," he said.

"I wish you would," she shot back. "You've never told me what you think I did to make him miserable enough to—" She took a deep breath to try and regain her equilibrium. None of them had ever said the "S" word out loud, but Gabe's expressions and body language at Steve's funeral, and his active hostility ever since, told her loud and clear that as far as he was concerned it was her fault his brother was dead.

"At first I told myself you were grieving," she went on, absently rubbing her sore wrists. "And that you'd get over it in time. At least for Jeremy's sake."

She saw him wince at the mention of his almost ten-year-old son. Her godson. She knew it galled him that she and Jeremy were so close.

"Get over my brother's death, huh? Like you did?"

She held his angry gaze. His face was as handsome as ever, but harder. There were new lines framing his sensual mouth. The five o'clock shadow that accentuated his dark coloring made him look more dangerous than even she knew him to be.

"I meant I hoped you'd get over blaming me for it," she said. "You're wrong if you think I was over Steve when Drew showed up. I mourned him for a long time. But I had to move on."

"Yeah," he said. "I noticed."

She rubbed her arms, cold despite the cognac, and gazed at a spot over his shoulder. "Think what you want, Gabe, you always have. The truth is I just wanted to be loved, and I was young enough to believe…" Why was she bothering? What she said wouldn't make a damn bit of difference to him. She'd allowed herself to believe that Drew would give her what she'd longed for her whole life. What a fool she'd been.

"You were everything to Steve," Gabe said. "He worshipped the ground you walked on."

She made a derisive snort. "He *needed* me," she said. "That's not the same thing as worshipping me and you damn well know it. I was the one who took care of him, and let the rest of you off the hook."

Gabe's thick brows drew together, and his mouth formed a tight line. His anger didn't surprise her. When a loved one dies, their foibles and imperfections are quickly forgotten. Gabe would never admit his perfect little brother had been as self-centered and emotionally labile as he was brilliant and charming.

But he did know, once.

"Spare me the bullshit," he said gruffly and opened the door to leave.

"If I didn't love Jeremy so much," she said before he could escape, "I would tell you to stay the hell out of my life, you self-righteous prick."

"What did you say to her?" Ben demanded when Gabe shut the door behind him.

"Leave it alone," he said. Damn it, he'd lost control in there. Like he tended to do any time he was in the same room with her for more than two seconds.

"Why did you come here? There's not even enough left of her husband to bury and you have to show up and hassle her?"

"I don't know why *you're* defending her," Joy said to Ben slowly, in the manner of a drunk trying to sound normal. "She actually had the nerve to ask me if I was having an affair with Drew."

Gabe watched Ben school his features, but he couldn't miss the flash of fury. Interesting.

"If you have any decency left, get out of her house and leave her alone," Ben said to Gabe. He took Joy's arm and tried to nudge her forward. "Let's go."

"I think he came to put the moves on his beloved sister-in-law," she said, and flashed Gabe a phony smile. "She's available. Again."

"Joy," Ben said in a warning tone.

"I wouldn't touch her with a ten-foot pole," Gabe growled.

Every nerve ending in his body reminded him that he *had* touched her. Had pressed her up against the wall with her hands over her head. And his body had reacted, damn it. He'd been all too aware of the softness of her breasts pressed against him, the light scent of her perfume. Her body had felt lush and warm against his. Just as he remembered it. And when she tilted her face up… Full, rosy lips pressed together, big hazel eyes red-rimmed and moist—and flashing with anger.

What had he been thinking, touching her? Granted, it hurt like a bitch when she nailed him with that pointy damn shoe, but Christ, did he really have to grab her wrists like that?

Joy's voice penetrated his regret-fest. "I have a major vote coming up tomorrow," she was saying to Ben, tugging at her suit jacket. "I would prefer to put off this little talk until after the Global Intel bill is passed."

"Of course you would," Ben said tightly, and gave her a slightly more forceful nudge down the corridor. They turned the corner at the end, leaving Gabe to process what he'd overheard.

Had Drew Franklin been screwing around with Joy?

Gabe turned in the opposite direction the Stuarts had gone and headed through the kitchen into the humid summer night. He ran a hand through his hair. Christ, he'd blown it in there. What the hell was wrong with him? Here was a great opportunity handed to him because of his connection to Kate, and what does he do? He goes and alienates her without even breaking a sweat. Insults her before saying hello, never even gets close to *sorry for your loss.*

He forced his mind back to what he'd learned early this morning. The FBI hadn't gone public with it yet, but the phone calls to *The Washington Post, The New York Times* and *al Jazeera* claiming al Qaeda was behind the explosion appeared to be a hoax. And no other group, domestic or international, had claimed responsibility. The Learjet had been lent to the congressmen by a wealthy supporter only hours before departure, and while the owner and his ground crew were quietly under investigation, the FBI speculated that the explosives had been brought aboard at the last minute, possibly by an unwitting passenger.

All of which led law enforcement to believe that someone with a serious and deadly grudge had paid big bucks to blow at least one passenger on that Learjet to kingdom come. Everyone knew elected officials had enemies, so sure, it could have been the work of any number of individuals or extremist groups. The FBI was casting a wide net, but if they discovered that one of the victims was having an affair, or gambling away the family savings, or abusing their kids, or doing God only knew what else, the spotlight would be on that person's spouse, lover, family and close friends.

So, had the ultraconservative Drew Franklin been cheating on his very liberal young wife?

Gabe's lieutenant had called him into his office right after the briefing and appointed him temporary MPD liaison with the FBI. "This case is going to be a bitch," he'd said to Gabe. "It's going to require us to think and act outside the box. You have some kind of family connection to one of the spouses, Mrs. Franklin. Get close to her. Shake her up, see what rises to the top."

Easy to say. How could he explain his relationship to Kate to someone outside his family? Yes, she'd been married to his brother for a month before he died. Yes, she was his son's godmother and favorite aunt. Did he ever see her socially or at family gatherings? Sure, he saw her at all Jeremy's birthday parties. He didn't add that it was the most awkward encounter of the year for both of them.

"Is there any way to see more of her, get her to take you into her confidence, maybe see you as a way out?"

After that performance in the study? Fat fucking chance. But he wouldn't tell his lieutenant about that. For one thing, he wanted in on the biggest case of the year. And maybe he would get something out of Kate if he played nice.

So how did he get her to trust him?

"Not by being an asshole," he muttered as he opened his car door. Jesus, where had his professionalism gone? Why had he lost it like that?

Because something had flipped inside him when he saw the way Ben was fawning over her. Steve had been Ben's best friend, for God's sake. Why should he give a damn that the guy Kate married was dead?

This case was going to be a bitch, all right.

Chapter Three

Kate yawned and poured coffee into the biggest mug she could find. It was still dark outside, and the wind lashed rain against the kitchen windows. A perfect day to stay in bed with the covers pulled over her head, but Bruno had to be fed and let out. And besides, she really couldn't sleep.

She carried the mug to the oblong pine table and sat. The room was dimly lit by the fluorescent bulbs over the stove and sink, and that was all the light she wanted right now. A few months earlier she'd papered the kitchen walls with cheerful yellow-and-white flowers and had painted herbs and spices on the tiles that lined the counters, all of which normally lifted her spirits early in the morning. But not today.

She rested her forehead in her hands. If only she hadn't had that conversation with Joy after the memorial service. The other woman had confirmed her worst fears about Drew's lack of interest in her, adding hurt and humiliation to the pain of losing him. Without knowing for certain that he'd been cheating on her, she could have mourned Drew the way most women mourned their husbands—by remembering the good times and keeping his best qualities foremost in her mind and heart. Apparently it hadn't been enough for Joy to insinuate herself into their marriage, she'd seen fit to deny Kate the right to grieve for her husband simply and cleanly.

Kate sighed deeply. That her old friend could be so cruel made the pain that much worse.

And then, of course, there was Gabe. After Joy had left her heart raw, Gabe had managed to pull it out of her chest and squeeze it until it bled. "Bastard," she said aloud.

"Who?" a familiar voice said, and Kate looked up. The kitchen door was still swinging closed behind her older sister Alison, who stood barefooted in silky pajamas, rubbing her eyes. Her bleached blond hair was sticking up at odd angles, and she was heavier than she'd been the last time Kate saw her, but she still looked great for forty. Kate's brown lab, Bruno, was right on her heels. He went directly for his water bowl and lapped up water noisily, then stood at the back door, big brown eyes on Kate.

"Did you sleep at all?" Alison asked around a yawn.

Kate opened the door and let Bruno into the backyard. "I got in a few hours," she lied. "It's awfully early for you to be up."

"No kidding." Alison pulled a mug out of a cupboard and filled it with coffee, then dumped three spoons of sugar into it. "Got any half-and-half?"

"In the fridge."

When her coffee was fixed, Alison sat down across from Kate. "So who were you calling a bastard?"

Kate sighed. Alison didn't miss a trick. "It's not important."

Alison studied her for a moment and then settled back in the chair and sipped her coffee. They sat in the comfortable, uncomplicated silence enjoyed by siblings and old friends. Kate fiddled with her spoon and Alison sipped and waited for the caffeine to kick in. She had never been a morning person as far as Kate could remember.

"Lot of people here yesterday," Alison said finally.

"Yeah."

"I was shocked as hell to see Gabe Hugo skulking around at the funeral," she said. Kate tensed. "Did he actually come to pay his respects?"

Kate snorted. "Not exactly."

"I had a feeling he was the bastard you were referring to. What happened?"

Kate took a deep breath and let it out slowly. "He was a jerk."

"Seriously?"

"Seriously. I still don't know why he came. It's not like we ever talk, even when I see him at Miriam's house," she said, referring to Gabe's mother's house, where Jeremy's birthday party was held each year.

"What's that guy's problem?" Alison asked, gesturing with her free hand. "His brother's been gone like eight years, for God's sake, through no fault of yours. You treat his son like gold, you—"

"That has nothing to do with Gabe," Kate interjected quickly. "I love Jeremy and nothing his father does will ever change that."

"Still," Alison said. "Where does he get off coming into your house and being a jerk? What did he say?"

Kate rubbed at her eyes with the heels of her hands. "I don't want to go into it right now, Ali. I just want to put it behind me." All of it. Yesterday and eight years ago. Especially eight years ago.

Once upon a time Gabe had been like Superman to her—strong, brave, heroic. When she started dating Steve, Gabe had treated her like a little sister, teasing and joking with her, challenging her to arm wrestle and throwing her around in the water at the Stuart's lake house. They talked easily and developed a friendship so comfortable that Kate missed him when he wasn't around. Not only was Gabe intelligent, funny and playful, he was the one person in his family who seemed to understand that loving Steve could be damn hard at times.

As Steven became more and more involved with his computers and his software he became less available to her, to the point where she could rarely keep his full attention for more than a few minutes at a time. Gabe, on the other hand, made her feel like she was the only one in the room.

And then they made love, and her world came apart.

"I swear, if I ever see him on the street..." Alison was saying.

Kate took a deep breath and forced a smile. "You run him over, call me and I'll finish him off."

"I noticed that Lindsay Hugo was here, too," Alison said. "All dolled up like she was invited to a state dinner or something. Probably came to rub elbows with the powers that be."

"It's Lindsay Martin now, but yeah, probably." Kate had no illusions that Jeremy's mother was really her friend, or that she gave a damn one way or the other about Drew's death. When Lindsay and Gabe split up all those years ago she didn't return any of Kate's calls. It wasn't until almost a year later, when Steve died, and left Kate very rich, that Lindsay reappeared in her life, Jeremy in tow. If it weren't for her fear of losing Jeremy, she would have told Lindsay to get lost a long time ago.

Alison leaned forward and covered Kate's hand with hers. "Seeing them had to bring back a lot of bad memories for you, with the funeral and all. I probably shouldn't have brought it up."

Kate squeezed her hand. Alison didn't know the half of it.

"Steve was so young," Alison went on. "And the whole thing was so damn tragic. Not that this isn't, but... You were heartbroken when Steve died, Katie. I was so worried about you. It was like you wanted to throw yourself into the grave with him. And then..." She didn't have to say the rest. Alison was the only other person in the world who knew about the loss that followed.

Kate nodded, afraid to speak around the lump in her throat. The sisters gripped one another's hands tighter and Kate felt a surge of gratitude for this simple comfort, and for a chance to be honest with the one person who would love her anyway. "It's true," she said in a raspy whisper. "This is bad, but Steve's death was so much worse. I don't think I could live through that kind of pain again."

"I know, sweetie," Alison whispered back. "And don't beat yourself up about it, because it is what it is. I know you loved Drew, but you two weren't exactly soul mates."

Kate sniffled. "I think you have to share the same values to be soul mates. And we didn't. No matter how much I wished it, we just plain didn't value the same things."

Alison reached for Kate's other hand and held on. "How were things before... You know."

Before he died. "Honestly? Not good. I was even considering asking him for a divorce." There, she'd said it.

For once Alison looked surprised. "Wow, I didn't realize..."

"It wasn't what I wanted, but I couldn't have what I wanted, and I found myself getting older with no kids and living a shell of a life with him, and... I know I shouldn't be saying these things."

"Yes, you should," Alison said. "This is just between us, and I'm actually glad to know you weren't planning to put up with that kind of life. You deserve to have it all, Katie."

Deserve it? Kate wasn't so sure, not after Steve… After Gabe. "Maybe I've gotten exactly what I deserve," she said quietly.

Alison reared back. "*What? You?* That's crazy talk, Katie. You're the kindest, most generous person I know."

Kate waved that aside. "It's easy to give money away when you have an obscene amount of it. And I'm not always kind. Believe me."

"Well, you do have that awful temper." Alison grinned and squeezed her hand, then leaned forward conspiratorially. "Did you ever throw anything at him?"

Kate couldn't help but grin back, remembering a couple of early temper tantrums when her parents went out and left her with poor Alison. "I've learned to control that impulse," she said.

"Well, thank God for that."

As they talked there were several times when Kate nearly told Alison about her conversation with Joy, but the pain was still too raw. So they stuck to safe topics like Kate's painting (she wasn't working on anything at the moment) and her oldest sister Jennifer's teenage children, whom she rarely saw, and her heart actually felt lighter by the time Alison finished her coffee and brought the mug to the sink.

"We're heading back to Philly at around ten," Alison said. "I would offer to stay longer, but I think you're probably ready to have your privacy back."

"I'm so glad you came," Kate said, trying for a smile.

Alison went to her and bent to enfold Kate in her arms. Of everyone in her family, Alison had always cared the most. Kate was ten years younger than Alison and thirteen years younger than Jennifer, and she'd always felt like the black sheep, or worse, completely invisible. Even though they'd seen each other rarely since Alison had left for college, she had always been there for Kate.

"I can be back here in two shakes if you need me, Katie," she said. "You know that, right?"

Kate squeezed her sister. "I know. But I think I'll be all right."

Neither of them mentioned their parents' quick departure after the memorial service. Her mother might have stayed if she'd had her way, but she'd abdicated her free will to her husband years ago, and Kate had learned early in her life that she came last where her father was concerned. It was a hard lesson, reinforced each time he missed a school play or a dance recital, or simply grunted when she held out the straight-A report cards she'd hoped would please him. Every bit of her father's praise and attention and love went to her older sisters. After a while Kate stopped expecting anything from him, but it never stopped hurting. Never.

"Don't be too proud to call," Alison said.

"I won't."

Alison stroked a hand over Kate's hair. "Maybe it's insensitive to say this so soon, but—"

"But," Kate mimicked, a real smile pushing through. Alison was so predictable. "You're going to say it anyway."

Alison gave a self-deprecating shrug. "*But,* you'll find someone else to love before too long. You're young and beautiful and you have so much to give. You won't be alone forever."

Kate was already shaking her head. "It's not worth it, getting involved. Falling in love. I don't want to go through it again."

"Maybe not right now," Alison said. "But eventually. When you're ready. You still want kids, right?"

Kate looked away. Yes, she wanted kids, more than anything, but on her own terms. "Maybe I'll adopt at some point," she said. Before Alison could reply she added, "But that's a conversation for another time."

"You do know that just because it happens once, there's no—"

"Not today, Alison. Please."

Alison lowered her eyes for a moment. "You're right. Forget I mentioned it," she said. "I'm sorry."

Kate pulled her sister into a hug. Oh, God, if only she could forget.

Chapter Four

By early afternoon everyone had cleared out. Kate was torn between being sad to see her sister go and relieved that for the first time in four days she had the house to herself. All to herself.

Drew was never coming home again.

She poured herself a glass of white wine, figuring it would either make her feel better or put her to sleep, and wandered through the house, trying to comprehend the fact that she was, once again, alone. The phone rang several times, but she ignored it and let voice mail pick up the calls. There was no one she wanted to talk to.

She ran her eyes over photos of her and Drew from early in their marriage, posed beneath the Eiffel Tower, on a gondola in Venice, standing in front of a pueblo in Santa Fe. They were smiling. In the earliest photos Drew had both arms wrapped around her. A year later he draped an arm around her shoulder. She frowned. In the most recent photos, from Stockholm, she was holding his arm, almost as though she were clutching on to him. Their smiles weren't as wide, and in a few she was looking up at Drew but he was never looking at her.

"How could I have been so blind," she whispered, her eyes blurry. It had been years since Drew had been actively affectionate toward her. They'd had a reasonably good first year of marriage, and it had gone downhill from there. Right after she begged him to have children. He'd refused, insisting on putting it off and giving a dozen reasons why it wasn't the right time.

The "right time" never came.

And yet he had resented the time and the millions she put into charitable causes, preferring that she spend it all hosting dinner parties and making him look good. The one thing he didn't begrudge was the time she spent in her studio, drawing or painting in watercolors.

She'd never been able to capture Drew in a way he found flattering, though.

Maybe they could have worked things out, if he hadn't died. She'd tried to convince him to see a marriage counselor on a few occasions, in the early years, before she understood that Drew didn't believe he needed help with anything. It had galled him when other representatives didn't automatically fall into step with what he knew was best for the country. She'd seen that belief in his infallibility as a fundamental weakness in his character. She'd pointed that out once—and he'd never forgiven her for it.

She drained her glass, went into the kitchen and poured another. What the hell? It was five o'clock somewhere in the world. And yeah, it was a bad idea to drink alone, but no one was watching. The slight buzz from the first glass felt pretty good, and a second glass would just make it better, right?

As she had many times over the past few days, she thought of Steve, of the friendship they'd shared before he became completely immersed in technology and business and all the money there was to be made on the Internet. Maybe it hadn't been passionate between them—not after the first several months, anyway—but he'd made her feel needed for the first time in her life. Fresh tears welled up. He'd died so young.

She was on her third glass of wine, in pursuit of a buzz that would kill some more of the pain, when the doorbell rang, followed by a chorus of loud barking. "Oh, God," she murmured. There was no way she was up to talking with one of the neighbors. They were sweet, all of them, and they'd filled her freezer with cakes and casseroles, but she needed to be alone. The bell rang again, and she pretended not to hear it—or hear Bruno barking his head off. After a while whoever it was gave up and went away. Kate brought Bruno down to the playroom in the basement and turned on the TV so he wouldn't go crazy if anyone else came to the door.

Then she went back upstairs to Drew's study and sat in the sumptuous leather chair behind his desk. When he was home he used to spend a lot of time in this room, alone. He rarely invited her in. She thought back to finding Joy in here, helping herself to cognac, and wondered how often she'd been at the house when Kate was away. Had Joy and Drew had sex in her bed? The thought elicited a groan of pain, and she buried her head in her arms on the desk.

"Kate?"

She jerked her head up. A tall, blond man stood in the darkened doorway, backlit from behind. "Who…?"

He stepped into the room. "It's me. Michael Clark. Are you okay?"

"Michael," she repeated. Drew's administrative assistant had always treated her with respect and affection. They'd barely had time to speak at the memorial service. She stood slowly and walked toward him. He opened his arms and enfolded her. "Michael. Oh, God. You must be feeling terrible."

He hugged her tightly and ran a hand over her back. "No worse than you, I imagine."

He rested his cheek on the top of her head. When had Drew last done that? "I'm here for you, Kate," he said. "I want you to know that."

The sound of clapping made her gasp. She pulled out of Michael's arms and whirled to find Gabe standing in the doorway, the ice in his gray eyes belying the smile on his face.

"That was deeply moving," he said.

"What the hell are *you* doing here?" she asked. "Again."

"I was going to ask Mr. Clark the same question," he said.

"What are you doing in my house?" she snapped.

"Just looking out for you, Kate," he said, hands shoved into his khakis as he moved closer, his gaze now trained on Michael.

"Like hell," she said.

"I was. I saw him ring your bell a couple of times, then try the knob, and finally pull out a house key and let himself in. I knew you were home, so I—"

She turned to Michael. "You have a key?"

Michael raised his palms. "Drew gave it to me a long time ago. He asked me to pick up some documents while you were out of town."

"Oh. He never told me." Did Joy Stuart also have her own key?

"Why did you use it today?" Gabe asked. "Your boss didn't ask you to pick anything up."

Michael flushed, but he spoke calmly. "There are files I'll need to take back to the office. I didn't realize Kate was home."

"Why were you watching my house?" she asked Gabe.

"I thought you might need protection."

She snorted. "The only person I need protection from

is you." She brushed by him on her way out of the room. "Go ahead and take what you need, Michael," she said over her shoulder. "Can I have a word with you, Gabe?"

"Thanks, Kate," Michael said. "I'll be quick and…uh, let myself out."

"Leave the key on the desk," Gabe said from behind her.

Kate stalked into the kitchen and went directly to the refrigerator, where she grabbed the bottle of wine she'd been working on. She filled her glass, drank deeply and carried the bottle to the table. Gabe stood silently watching her, arms crossed over his chest. His dark hair flopped over his eyebrows and curled slightly where it brushed his collar. A day's growth of beard stubbled his hard jaw. He looked big and mean and powerful…and sexy as hell. *Bastard.*

"It's three o'clock in the afternoon," he said, eyeing her wineglass. "And I get the sense you've been at this for a while."

"What do you want?" she asked, emboldened by all the alcohol coursing through her system. "Why do you keep showing up at my house? And don't give me any more bullshit about protection. You'd like nothing better than for someone to walk in here and blow my head off." She held up her glass and pretended to study it. "Or maybe you're hoping I'll use this to wash down a bottle of tranquilizers."

"I came by to apologize."

She stared at him. "Come again?"

"I was out of line yesterday," he said. "I don't know why I… Habit, I guess."

"Would that be your habit of blaming me for Steve's death, your habit of never acting civil around me or your habit of hating me?"

His brows drew together, but he didn't dispute any of it. She dropped into a wooden chair, her spirit drained. "Damn it," she said. "It doesn't work."

"What?" Gabe asked

"The wine. It still hurts."

"Losing Husband Number Two?"

"Losing you," she whispered.

Chapter Five

What the hell? Gabe thought, but he couldn't ignore the squeezing in his chest. Kate was slumped in a chair, no doubt working on a first-class hangover, although she'd always held her liquor better than most. She was barefooted, her long brown hair snarled, wearing an oversized gray sweatshirt with the sleeves cut off over a pair of well-worn jeans—and as striking as she'd been at the funeral in her elegant, formfitting black dress. He rubbed a hand over his face.

"That sweatshirt looks familiar," he said to cut through the silence. Why did he feel like a shit all of the sudden?

She looked down at it, then met his eyes. "It was Steve's."

"It was mine first," he said, then immediately wished he could take the words back.

"Oh. I never knew." She glanced down at the faded letters. "Virginia Tech. Well, I figured, you know, you got it for him when you were at Tech."

"It doesn't matter."

She shrugged. "You want it back?"

"No."

"Afraid it's tainted from touching my skin?"

"Just forget I mentioned it, okay?"

"No, seriously." She pulled it over her head and tossed it to him, leaving her sitting at the kitchen table in low-rise jeans and a red, lacy bra that barely covered her full breasts. "It's yours again."

He caught the sweatshirt, staring at her. Her body had changed little over the years, still as slim and curvy as ever. And every bit as sexy. More so, if he was honest with himself. Like then, his body tightened in response. And like then, he hated himself for it. He tossed the sweatshirt back to her.

"Cover yourself," he growled.

She balled up the sweatshirt and set it on the table, then rose and walked slowly toward him in her bra. "It's nothing you haven't already seen," she said. Her expression had gone from defeated to angry, but the hurt was still in her eyes.

Gabe felt his cock harden as she moved closer. "Don't go there, Kate," he warned.

She stopped too close to him. He could smell her distinctive scent, minus the perfume. Time hadn't changed that any more than it had changed her effect on him. "But this is how you like to think of me, isn't it?" she asked. "As the siren who came on to you that night in your bed?"

"Stop." His heart was pounding with a mix of arousal and fear.

"That relieves you of responsibility for—"

"I said *stop.*"

"—what happened."

"I was half-asleep," he said.

"You weren't too tired to roll on top of me."

He stopped breathing for a moment. All he could hear was the rush of blood pounding in his temples. When he could take a breath, he leaned into her face and said, "No more."

She opened her mouth to speak and Gabe covered it with his hand. Which was a bad move because the feel of her lips on his palm reminded him of how soft they'd felt against his. "Don't you say another word about that night. Not now, not ever. Do you understand?"

She pushed his hand away. "You weren't too tired to pull my tank top over my head. Or slip your—"

He grabbed her shoulders and shook her, his control gone. "You want to relive that night? Is that what you want? Okay, let's go. Let's get wild." He pulled her to him and took her mouth roughly. Ah, God, her lips were warm and as intoxicating as the wine. Kate returned his embrace with trembling arms that tightened as their kisses grew more frantic. He speared his tongue deep inside, over and over, dueling with hers while his hands roamed over her back, her ass.

He eased her back against the counter and unsnapped her bra, then filled his hands with her breasts. Her hips rocked against his, hardening his cock painfully. He bent to pull a hard nipple into his mouth when Kate suddenly gasped and shoved him away. Her lips were swollen and red from his kisses, her eyes wide with shock.

"Oh, Christ," he muttered, turning away from her. It was a struggle to catch his breath. What the hell had he been thinking, putting his hands on her? Would he never learn how dangerous that was?

Behind him, Kate was panting, but mercifully said nothing. He adjusted himself, tucked in his damp, rumpled shirt and ran his fingers through his hair. *Fuck.* He was no better than a horny teenager. He got the sweatshirt off the table and held it out to her, not looking. After a moment she took it.

"Why did you come here?" she asked, her voice breathy.

"I shouldn't have come." That was the understatement of the year.

"That's not what I asked."

When he had his breathing more or less under control he turned back to look at her, both relieved and disappointed that she was wearing the sweatshirt. But oh, God, her cheeks were pink, her lips red and swollen from his kisses, her hair wild. She looked like she'd been ravaged. And she didn't look happy about it.

He swallowed hard. "I wanted to be the first to tell you. The news will be carrying the story nonstop, and you're likely to be hounded by the press."

Her brow furrowed. "Tell me what?"

"Al Qaeda didn't bring your husband's plane down."

Her frown deepened as she stared at him. "Then…what happened?" Same thing she'd asked on that snowy day in December eight years ago, after he got the call from the Maryland State Police. Same confused, innocent look in those big hazel eyes.

She rubbed her arms as though she were cold. "So… could it have been an accident after all?"

He shrugged. "They've recovered what was left of the fuselage from the water, and found the black box. It'll take some time to analyze the voice and data recordings."

"Nobody from the FBI…or the NTSB…told me about this," she said, slurring the initials. "They've been keeping me informed. Me and Drew's parents and the other families."

"People came to your door today. You didn't answer. They called from their cell phones and you didn't pick up."

She blinked at him. "How long were you watching the house?"

"A while." Long enough to build up the courage to go in. If Michael Clark hadn't shown up he might have driven away like the coward he was.

"Well, if it wasn't al Qaeda, then who did it? Another terrorist group?"

"None of them took responsibility," he said. "Which is unusual. Someone usually tries to claim it to show off their 'cause.'"

"Then…who?"

He took a deep breath. "Could've been someone with a shit load of money who wanted to eliminate someone on the plane."

She nodded absently, hugging herself and staring at the floor. After several seconds she looked up. "You didn't come here to warn me, Gabe," she said slowly. "That wouldn't be like you. You wanted to watch my reaction to the news, didn't you? See if my pupils dilated, or sweat broke out on my upper lip."

Why did things never go as he'd planned with her? This was the perfect segue into his "change of heart" act. *No, Kate, I know you're innocent. Let me help you during this rough time.* But he couldn't pull it off. Maybe if he hadn't touched her, hadn't brought back all the memories, all the pain. He'd have to give up the case, all because he couldn't be in the same room with her without alternately treating her like shit and wanting her so bad it hurt.

"Busted," he said. "And since the media is likely to be all over your ass, I'd appreciate you skipping Jeremy's birthday party on Saturday. He doesn't need to be dragged into your mess, and neither does the rest of my family."

Her eyes narrowed. "You son of a bitch. I've never missed his birthday, and I'm not going to start now. You can glare at me silently from the corner, like you do every year."

He glanced at the open bottle of wine on the table and back to her. "Don't come drunk," he said.

"You *asshole,*" Kate said when the back door closed. "You cruel, arrogant piece of shit." Her heart pounded as the anger took hold. She grabbed her wineglass off the table and heaved it at the door, enjoying the sound of shattering glass, wishing only that it had shattered against Gabe's thick skull.

Al Qaeda didn't bring your husband's plane down.

Then who did? And did Gabe actually think she was somehow involved?

Footsteps sounded from the corridor and she remembered too late that she'd left Michael Clark in the study. Heat rose to her cheeks. Good Lord. What if he'd come in when she and Gabe were engaged in that…insanity?

Michael pushed through the door to the kitchen, then stood there, blue eyes wide, taking in first the shattered glass on the floor and then her face. "Are you okay?"

"Yes, I, uh, had an accident."

Michael shot her a knowing look and put his hands on his hips. "I'm going to assume your former brother-in-law pissed you off."

"You could say that," she mumbled. She ran her fingers through a mass of snarls. How must she look? "Listen, I'm sorry. I didn't realize you were still here."

He walked to where she was standing and laid a gentle hand on her arm. "Hey, no problem. I'll help you clean that up."

"No… I'll get it myself. Really. I'm so embarrassed."

He lifted her chin with one finger, forcing her to look him in the eye. "You're a wreck, Kate. Why are you here all alone? Where's your family?"

"They left," she said, stepping back. "And I'm fine, seriously."

"I think I know just the thing to fix you up," he said. "And I don't mean tranquilizers or psychiatry. Or more wine."

"A frontal lobotomy?"

Michael smiled. "I have this friend…"

Chapter Six

The doorbell rang at ten o'clock the following morning. Kate peered through the peephole to make sure the person standing there met Michael's description. Dark hair, beard, okay. She opened the door, but the man standing in front of her wasn't at all what she'd expected. He was handsome, around six feet tall and olive-skinned, with a well-trimmed beard and military short hair. Mid-to-late thirties, she figured, and fit—trim and muscular, like someone who spent a lot of time at the gym.

So this was what aromatherapists looked like these days?

"Are you…?" At the last moment she remembered to let him give his name, rather than supplying one for him. In case he was actually one of the reporters who'd been clogging the street in front of her house since early that morning.

"I'm Archer, Michael's friend," the man said with the slightest hint of an accent she couldn't trace. He tipped his head to one side as though studying her. "I know you're Kate, because Michael said you were beautiful and sad. I'm so sorry for your loss."

"Thank you." There was something warm and down-to-earth about this man that appealed to her. "Come on in," she said and stepped aside. The reporters were taking photos of them, and would no doubt try to make something of the good-looking guy she was letting into her house. Well, she wasn't going to let the vultures rule her life.

Archer picked up a large folding table off the porch and carried it inside with a tote bag emitting a wonderful lavender scent with a hint of something else.

"Mostly lavender and rose oil," he said, as though she'd spoken her thoughts aloud. He glanced at the living room through the arch to his left and the dining room several feet to the right of the long center staircase. "Where would you like me to set it up?"

"Umm…"

"Michael said you have a great sunroom with lots of plants. How about if we do it in there?"

Kate led the way down a wide corridor beyond the staircase, past Drew's office and a game room, toward the back of the house. When they reached the sunroom, with its wicker furniture, overhead fan and Oriental carpets, Archer moved to the center and turned in a slow circle. He smiled, revealing even white teeth and a dimple on one cheek. "This is perfect," he said, and pointed to a series of framed watercolors of the same spot in the Pennsylvania woods in each season. "Those are yours, aren't they? They're incredible."

"Thank you," she said, warmed by the praise.

"Do you spend a lot of time in this room?"

"Not lately," she said.

"You should," he said, and went about setting up his massage table. "Go ahead and take off your clothes. I'll have everything ready in a few minutes."

Well, this is awkward. She didn't move, and after a moment Archer looked up and smiled gently. "Don't worry, sweetie, you're not exactly my type, if you know what I mean."

Ah ha. She pretended to be disappointed. "And here I thought Michael had sent me a hot guy to run his hands all over me and leave me with a smile on my—" She stopped short. The guy was a complete stranger. "Oh, I didn't—"

Archer threw his head back and laughed, a deep, rumbling sound. "He'd have to send someone else for that," he said. "Although my masterful hands will fix most of what ails you, I promise."

Five minutes later Kate was lying naked on her stomach on a padded massage table, loving the feel of warm aromatic oil being rubbed into her skin by a man who knew *exactly* what he was doing. "I'll give you an hour to cut that out." She groaned. Archer laughed, making her smile. "I definitely owe Michael one. This is the best thing that's happened to me since…" Since when? She couldn't remember the last time she'd felt this good.

"That's the idea," Archer said.

"If you were straight I'd have to insist that you marry me," she said, knowing she'd get a laugh out of him. He didn't disappoint her. When was the last time she'd felt so relaxed with a man?

Then she realized what she'd said.

"God, I must sound so callous to you."

Archer's hands didn't cease for moment. "Not at all," he said. "I knew it was a joke. The lighter you can keep your spirits now the more quickly you'll heal."

She was silent for several minutes while Archer worked his magic on her tight muscles. It was as though by working the muscles her body expelled the sadness and the anger, the guilt and the regrets. When he got down to her feet she sighed so deeply he chuckled.

"Feels good, doesn't it?" he said.

"It feels amazing," she said.

"Better than sex, with none of the emotional crap. Let's flip you over."

She rolled on to her back and gazed up at him. He was standing behind her rubbing oil between his palms, so his face was upside down. A fluffy white towel covered her torso. "I didn't ask Michael. Do you do this for a living?"

"Not anymore," he said. "Now I only do it for friends."

"But you didn't know me from Adam."

He smiled as he applied the oil to her shoulders and began to knead. "True, but Michael and I are very close, and from what he told me about you I knew I'd want to be your friend."

"What did he tell you?"

"Oh, lots of things," he said. "For one that you're incredibly talented artistically, which I have now seen with my own eyes. You really are amazing, Kate."

"Thank you."

"And he admired your integrity. Your views on social injustice, for example, were not exactly popular in your husband's circles, but you didn't back down from speaking your mind. Privately or publicly."

Her gut loosened a little bit. "That's awfully nice to hear," she said. "I think it's safe to say that most of Drew's colleagues didn't appreciate my candor." Joy, for example.

"And at the risk of bringing up a sore topic," he said. "I saw the news footage of you rolling your eyes when your husband was talking about his Global Intel bill and how the Founding Fathers… What did he say? They didn't anticipate that the Bill of Rights would get in the way of doing what needed to be done?"

"That pretty much sums it up."

"Well, if it's any comfort, I was rolling my eyes too. And I remember thinking, wow, what an honest reaction. All those years of living with a politician and being on public display didn't turn Kate Franklin into a Stepford wife."

His words were a gift. “Thanks. I know should have been more discreet, but I’ve never been good at hiding my feelings, and I had no idea there were cameras pointed at me.”

“The media wanted a juicy news story and they got it at your expense.” He poured more oil into his hands and rubbed them together, then pressed his heated palms above her knee and pushed upward. She groaned and let the delicious pressure penetrate her muscles and ease the pain in her heart.

She smiled. “I’m so glad Michael sent you to me.”

He massaged her for a while in silence, and Kate’s thoughts moved from Drew to Gabe, to Joy, to her father, to Steve. To Gabe. As though she were looking down from a distance at her own body and mind, she watched to see which thoughts brought the most pain. It was thoughts of Gabe that deepened the ache the most. She let out a long, drawn out sigh.

“Always a good sound,” Archer said, his deep voice somehow comforting. “It means the pain is moving through you and out.

“There’s a lot of it,” she said quietly.

“Tell me about him,” Archer said, rubbing oiled hands up and down the front of her calves to her knees.

Kate said nothing while she processed the meaning of his question. “You mean…Drew?”

“Only if you want to,” he said. “Talking about the source of the pain helps to move it out of the body.”

She considered this. “It sounds like you mean *Drew* was the source of the pain, rather than his death.”

“Was he?” Archer asked quietly.

A surge of grief swamped her, forcing tears to her eyes. “Yes,” she whispered. “Some of it.” The part that wasn’t caused by Gabe.

"Don't fight the tears, Kate. They're cleansing, like the massage. You have a deep lake of pain residing here." He placed his fist just below her heart. "If you're going to heal you have to empty that lake."

The tears spilled freely down her cheeks. "How do I empty it?" she croaked. "It's so deep. So old."

"Talk about him. How did he treat you?"

She sniffled. No one had ever asked her that. "Honestly? Like I was invisible."

"Ah," he said. "That hurts more than anything."

"My...my father..." The lump in her throat kept her from speaking. Archer cradled her head in one hand and laid the other palm very gently over her throat and rubbed it in a circle. The heat and soothing scent helped more than she could have imagined.

"Your father didn't see you," Archer stated. "And I'm going to make an educated guess that both of your husbands put their own needs first. As though yours were unimportant."

She nodded, her tears salty on her lips. How was it possible that a man she'd just met could read her so well?

"It's easier to grieve for a partner you were very close to," Archer went on. "One who was devoted to you. The loss is harder, but the grieving process itself is cleaner, I guess you'd say." He laid her head back down on the table, raised one arm over her head and ran his hands up and down the underside of her upper arm. "I sense that you're having a tough time grieving for your husband."

"You're very intuitive," she said, when she could speak. When he didn't respond she asked, "Have you lost someone close to you, Archer? A partner?"

"Yes," he said, but his tone said he wasn't ready to discuss it. Kate assumed the wound was still too fresh and didn't push.

"Was your husband away a lot?" he asked.

She sighed. "Over the past couple of years I barely saw him."

Archer moved her arm to her belly and pulled the other one over her head. "What did he do when he was home? Work?"

"Mostly," she said. Then it occurred to her to ask, "Did you ever meet him?"

Archer hesitated. "A couple of times."

"Did you like him?"

"Michael was devoted to him," Archer said.

Kate arched her head back so she could see his face. His expression was harder than she'd seen it since he arrived. If he'd been wearing that expression when he first came to the door she probably wouldn't have let him in. Still, she didn't feel threatened by Archer. If anything, she felt as though maybe, just maybe, here was someone who understood.

"You didn't like him at all," she said.

For several moments Archer said nothing. Finally he sighed. "I'll be honest with you. I found him extremely arrogant. But I barely knew the man, and he was your husband so I'll leave it at that. I'm sorry if I hurt you by—"

"No," she said. "Please. It's good to have someone to talk to about him. My husband was far from perfect, but then, aren't we all?"

He held her head in one hand and began massaging her scalp with the other. "Did you love him, Kate?" he asked. "And I don't mean in the sense that he was your husband so of course you loved him. I had a brother I was supposed to love and I loathed him."

She swallowed. “I worked at loving him.”

“Ah.”

She tipped her head back and met his gaze. “You want to know if I was madly, passionately in love with him.”

“Only if you want to tell me.”

She smiled. “For some odd reason I do, even though I’ve known you for… what? Maybe half an hour?”

He smiled back. “Forty minutes, give or take.”

“I was in love like that once,” she said quietly, eyes closed, letting Archer’s hands soothe her brain, almost as though he held it in the palm of his hand. “I was terribly hurt. More hurt than I’ve ever told anyone before.”

“Hurt like your soul shrivels up inside you and all that’s left is a desert of burning hot pain,” Archer said.

God love this man, this stranger. “Yes,” she whispered. “Like that. I met Drew while I was dragging myself through that desert.”

“Ah,” Archer said simply. “Suddenly there was an oasis, with palm trees and all the fresh water you could drink.”

“Exactly.”

“But it was a mirage.”

She nodded slowly. “That mirage got me through the desert, and for a long time I refused to see it for what it was.”

“When did you figure it out?”

She gave him a wry smile. “The whole thing? Just now.”

“Then the massage has done you more good than I intended,” he said with a smile in his voice. “A good massage every few days and you’ll be at the top of your game next time.”

She rolled her head from side to side. “No next time. I’m done.”

“I know what you mean,” he said. “I’ve said that myself a time or two, but the next thing I know I'm out there looking for love."

They chatted like old friends for the next half hour, until Archer was packed up and ready to go. Kate walked him to the door, but he stopped her from opening it.

"I know why the reporters are here," he said. "But you haven't said a word about it."

"I don't know what to say, except that I don't know of anyone who hated Drew or any of the other congressmen enough to murder them."

He tilted his head and studied her. "Is that what you think it's about? Hatred?"

"I honestly don't know what it's about," she said. "I can't wrap my brain around it."

Archer laid a hand on her shoulder. "Promise me you'll be very careful. Don't give them any fodder for their witch hunt."

She blinked. "How can anyone honestly believe *I* had something to do with this? I was married to the man for God's sake."

Archer looked pained. "Oh, honey, after all you've been through, you still think people are basically good, don't you? That they tell the truth and try not to hurt other people."

"Well, maybe I do," she said, feeling a bit defensive.

"And that makes you the perfect prey." He squeezed her shoulder. "Beware, Kate. They'll leap out of the dark places and tear you to shreds. Take it from one who knows."

As he left, Kate wondered just how much her new friend knew about the dark places.

Chapter Seven

Jeremy was quiet when Gabe picked him up at Lindsay's house, which worked well considering the mood Gabe had been in since his visit with Kate earlier in the week. He'd been trying to put her out of his mind all afternoon, snapping the heads off anyone who came near him. Even Scott Bailey, his former partner and best friend on the force, had given him wide berth.

When they parked the car near the pizza place they usually went to during the week, he turned to his son. "What's up, Jeremy? You've barely said a word since you got in the car."

"I heard Mom talking to Richard about Aunt Kate."

His ex-wife was not known for her discretion around Jeremy, especially when she was talking to her husband. Even though the divorce agreement had specified that neither of them make disparaging comments about the other, he knew Jeremy picked up on his mother's attitude whenever his name came up. "What did she say about…Aunt Kate."

"You know the airplane that blew up?"

"Uh-huh."

"Well, the terrorists didn't do it. So now Aunt Kate's picture's in the paper, and it was on TV today."

"Is that right?" Gabe replied absently. He'd seen the clusterfuck in front of her house on the four o'clock news. He'd almost felt sorry for Kate when that doofus stuck the microphone in front of her face and asked her whether it was true that her first husband had also died a violent death. She'd stared at the guy, and the cameras had panned in close, watching her reaction. Just like he had when he went to her house, idiot that he was.

"Mom said Aunt Kate shouldn't come to my birthday party because the reporters would follow her."

For once Lindsay had come up with an idea he agreed with. "Well, you know, Jeremy, that's not such a—"

"But I told her I don't care," Jeremy said. "I hardly ever get to see her, and I want her to come. It wouldn't be the same without her."

"I thought you still saw her some weekends when you're not with me," Gabe said.

Jeremy picked at a hole in his jeans. "Not as many," he said. "Richard likes to take *his* kids on hikes up Sugarloaf Mountain, and Mom wants me to go with them."

Gabe hated the idea of another man spending weekend time with his son. Not that he was always free to do stuff like go hiking, but still. "Why do you have to go?"

"So we can *bond,*" Jeremy said, disgusted. "I can't stand those little brats. They're there like every weekend, and now they're coming more during the week. They follow me around and touch my stuff. And Mom says I have to learn to *share* better. They drive me crazy."

Gabe opened the car door and got out. They'd parked a couple of blocks from Listrani's on MacArthur Boulevard, and now they walked slowly up the sidewalk. "What do you do when you're with your aunt?" Now why did he ask that? He never asked about Kate.

Jeremy grinned. "Cool stuff."

"Like what?"

"Why don't you like her?" The words burst out of his

mouth, like they'd been lying in wait for the right opening—which Gabe had just given him.

Shit. "It's personal."

"It's about Uncle Steven, right? She was married to him."

Uncle Steven. As though he'd known him. Jeremy had been a baby when Steve died, and had never met the brilliant, sensitive young man who had looked up to his older brother and used him as a sounding board for his ideas, knowing Gabe would be excited for him, would encourage him and tell him to go for it, whatever it was. He could picture him now—Steve, gesturing with his hands, his green eyes on fire as he talked about his newest app, his idea for a better platform or a new operating system—

He swallowed hard against the stab of loss. "I really don't want to talk about that."

Jeremy stopped walking. "Why not? I want to know what happened."

Deep breath. "He was in a car accident."

"Yeah, but Mom said he had a big fight with Aunt Kate and that's why he got in the accident."

"Your Mom should keep her—" He stopped before he said *big fat mouth shut.* "Kate and I just don't get along, okay? That's all there is to it."

"My friends think she's pretty," Jeremy said. "Don't you?"

Fuck, yes. "Not really," he said.

"Then how come you stare at her?"

Gabe turned to his son, startled. "What?"

"You stare at her."

"No, I don't."

"Yeah, you do. Every time you're both at Grandma's

house, you stare at her and don't say anything, and she acts like you're not there. It's weird."

This kid was way too observant for his own good. "Yeah, well, sometimes adults have issues that kids can't really understand," Gabe said.

"Richard said maybe Aunt Kate paid somebody to blow up the plane."

Something cold spread through Gabe's gut. Hearing it from his son's mouth, the idea that Kate would conspire to take out an aircraft and fake a call from al Qaeda sounded completely insane. *Christ,* was he going crazy? He'd predicted that kind of reaction from people—been excited about it, because if it were true it would mean he'd been right to hold Kate accountable for Steve's death all these years.

"That would mean Aunt Kate's a criminal," Jeremy went on. "And that's so stupid."

Gabe was struck by how similar the stubborn set of Jeremy's jaw was to Steve's. His family had always said Jeremy looked more like Steve than Gabe. *Wink wink, poke poke.* But Steve would never have betrayed him that way. He'd been passionate about two things—computers and Kate—and that was all he'd ever wanted.

He, on the other hand…

"The FBI isn't looking only at her… Your aunt," he said. "They're investigating all the families of the people on board that plane." And their friends and associates and former colleagues and anyone they'd ever slept with or pissed off—the latter two often being the same people. Given that most of the passengers were politicians, the list of potential enemies was long.

Jeremy brightened a bit. "So, it's not just Aunt Kate they're blaming?"

"It's too soon to blame anyone, Jer," he said. "The news media likes to focus on people that are…interesting in some way." He'd nearly said "sexy," in the media sense of the word, but he stopped himself. Best he not even think that word where Kate was concerned. And sure, she was the perfect target. Young, beautiful, rich, as liberal as her husband was conservative. And a widow for the second time.

"Dad," Jeremy said, breaking into his thoughts. "We're here."

Gabe had walked right past the restaurant. He grinned. "Guess I spaced."

"At least you're smiling now," Jeremy said. "You had your cop face on before."

They ordered a large pizza with pepperoni and sausage, garlic bread and Cokes. While Jeremy made patterns on the table with the packages of sugar and sweetener, they talked about TV shows, computer games and the camping trip they planned to take in August.

"Mom says maybe Aunt Kate will move back to Philadelphia to be with her family." Jeremy frowned. "I don't want her to move away."

Please, God. The further he was from Kate the greater his peace of mind. "Is she thinking about it?"

"She's not sure what she's going to do."

"How often do you talk to her?" And why did he suddenly care?

"We usually just email," Jeremy said.

"A lot?"

"I don't know, like a few times a week. Sometimes we go back and forth." He grinned. "I want to teach her how to chat, but she said she wouldn't be able to keep up with me."

Gabe sat back, discomfited. "I didn't realize how big a part of your life she was."

Jeremy shrugged. "Usually when I say her name you look away and change the subject."

"I do?" As if he didn't know. Pushing Kate out of his mind, holding this grudge against her, had become a habit. He wasn't sure which alarmed him more—the fact that he'd done it for so long or the fact that she was in his head again. In his system. Like a goddamn drug.

Damn it, he never should have touched her.

Senator Felicia D'Argento pressed the button on her Saab keychain and heard the reassuring chirp and click of the locks. If only she had a remote door opener for her town house she'd be all set. After twelve years one would think she'd be past the paranoia about getting home after most of her Capitol Hill neighbors were asleep, but she was hypervigilant by nature. Anthony still didn't understand why she dreaded his business trips, given how often she came home late and worked weekends. But at least she came home at the end of the day, even if the end of one day sometimes blurred into the next.

As she headed down the sidewalk she compared the weight of her briefcase in her left hand with that of the gym bag hanging off her right shoulder. Time to wash her workout clothes. She could put them in the washer as soon as she got inside and then read through the committee report again while they went through the cycle. She'd toss in the blouse she was wearing as well. The back was still damp from leaning against the hot leather seats of her car. Mid-July in Washington, D.C., was a rotten time for the Saab's AC to punk out.

She climbed the steps to her front door, pulled the keys

out of her purse and let herself into the blessedly cool foyer. Once inside she flipped on the lights and locked the door behind her. *Made it.* As always she stood still a moment, listening for any sounds that were out of place before venturing through the hallway by the staircase and into her kitchen. First order of business—pour a glass of sauvignon blanc and kick off her shoes.

The sight of her practical, low-heeled shoes conjured a face she'd been sorely tempted to put her fist through a little while ago—Joy Stuart's. The evil bitch was close to having all the votes she needed to get the senate to pass a bill that would curtail the freedom of the American people in unprecedented ways. Felicia's heart started pumping faster at the thought of Joy in her tight business suit and spike heels, using every underhanded trick in the book to rush the bill through both houses of Congress while Drew Franklin's death was fresh in everyone's minds. Could so many of her colleagues really be naïve enough to think handing all that power to the Director of Global Intelligence would make the country safer?

"Morons," she said aloud as she pulled a stemmed glass off the shelf and poured herself a hefty amount of wine. She took a long sip, then stared at the glass thoughtfully. "Idiots."

In the next moment the lights went out.

"Fabulous," she muttered. She stood still in the darkness, glass in hand, and waited for them to pop back on. The power grids were overloaded—that had to be it. Except there were lights glowing in her neighbor's window. She swallowed with difficulty and set her glass down on the counter as gently as she could with her hand shaking.

She listened.

The cuckoo clock in the family room ticked out the seconds. *One. Two. Three...*

Damn it, Anthony, why aren't you home?

The pounding in her temples grew louder, making it hard to hear anything else.

You're being a baby, Felicia.

Okay, she was a grown woman, and she had to deal with the situation. Clearly the problem was within her walls, not throughout the neighborhood. *Flashlight. Get a flashlight.*

She took a deep breath, let it out and began to move slowly toward the dining room.

That's when she heard it.

The floorboards in the dining room creaked like they did when someone was coming into the kitchen…

A whimper rose from her throat and she froze as a shadow moved toward her.

"So long, Senator," the shadow said.

Chapter Eight

Ben Stuart frowned at his wife as she stood in the walk-in closet in a fuchsia silk robe, trying to figure out what to wear to a barbecue, for Pete's sake. With old friends.

"Why don't you just pull on a pair of shorts?" he said. "There won't be anyone at Miriam's to impress."

She kept her back to him. "Eighties today? Or hotter?"

In the past he would have come up behind her, wrapped his arms around her and made some comment about how her presence would drive up the temperature by several degrees. But not now. Not after her scene at Drew Franklin's memorial service. She'd been obviously drunk when he pulled her past half a dozen congressional colleagues and out the door of Kate's house. It would've been bad enough in front of family alone, but no one ever saw the Honorable Joy Stuart out of control in public. She was the image of sophistication and decorum.

There'd been a time when Joy lost control in bed with him, and the contrast with her usual comportment was half the excitement for both of them.

Those days were gone.

For the past two years he'd seen Joy in two modes—controlled or irritable. Maybe she had shown her wild side only to the now-deceased Drew Franklin. May he rot in hell.

She emerged from her closet wearing a yellow sundress and low sandals. Her body was lightly tanned. He hadn't questioned where the rays had come from. According to her those long weekends she'd spent working without coming home she'd been right here in the nation's capital, cloistered in meeting rooms and offices, only seeing sunlight through the windows.

If he had noticed her deepening color he had never questioned it. It had long been his way to avoid what he didn't want to see. Life with Joy, like life with his mother, was easier that way.

But now she'd rubbed it in his face, and the truth sat on his nose like pigeon shit.

"That color looks great with your tan," he said.

If she picked up on the irony she didn't show it. The woman could have made a fortune on the poker circuit. Then again, so could most politicians. "Thanks," she said without making eye contact. She rarely did these days. "Ready?"

He grabbed his keys and walked ahead of her out to the driveway, where their new Lexus, a gift from Joy's parents, sat in all its glory. "I wonder if Kate will show up this year," he said, glancing at his wife as she slipped into the passenger seat and slammed the door a little too hard. Ah. The satisfaction of knowing he could always get a rise out of her by mentioning Kate. He pulled away from the curb.

Ben had been going to Jeremy's birthday parties since the boy was a year old. His and Joy's friendship with the family had continued through Jeremy's birth, Gabe and Lindsay's split and Steve's death at twenty-three, seven months before Jeremy's second birthday. Despite her grief, Miriam had insisted on hosting the party at her house, permitting the first ray of light to infuse their mourning. He frowned as memories of that sad time filled his head.

"She's selfish enough to come," Joy said, breaking into his thoughts.

Christ, Joy was so predictable when it came to Kate. "Selfish?" he asked. "How do you figure that? She comes because Jeremy wants her there."

"She comes to lord it over everyone else that she's Jeremy's favorite aunt—not that I care. But she's not even his aunt anymore. That went out the door when she remarried."

Ben's smile was bitter. "Hard to say it, isn't it? When she married Drew." He shook his head and took the corner faster than was necessary. "You should have pushed Kate at me that summer. Then you could've divorced me and married Drew yourself. But that wouldn't have been as exciting, would it?"

From the corner of his eye he saw that Joy was staring at him, but he didn't look at her. It had to be killing her not to reply. Some perverse instinct kept him going. "Anyway, Kate's his godmother, and I for one always look forward to seeing her at these things." And thank Christ she was alive to be there. He swallowed hard. Things could have gone so tragically wrong…

"I'll just bet you do," Joy muttered, staring straight ahead.

"It'll be tough for her this year, though. Seeing you," Ben said. "Knowing—oh, excuse me, I mean *suspecting*—that you were fucking her husband." They came to a stop sign and he slammed on the brakes. Joy was jolted forward, then hit the back of the seat hard. "But now that I think about it," he went on, ignoring the look of controlled fury on her face, "that would certainly pump up your voracious ego. And here I was wondering why you suddenly wanted to join me this year."

"If you're trying to kill me," she said in a tone that sent

a chill up Ben's back, "maybe you should pull a Kate and pay somebody to—" She stopped short, her words hanging in the air.

When Ben turned to her she appeared to be looking out the side window. He slowed and drove the rest of the way in silence.

"Oh, no," Lindsay said when a cab pulled up in front of her former mother-in-law's house. "Tell me this is not who I think it is."

"Who?" Richard asked.

"Kate, that's who. Shit."

Gabe listened in silence from across his mother's spacious dining room, which was decorated with streamers and balloons for Jeremy's tenth birthday. He took a pull on his beer—the only one he was going to allow himself today. Every year he had one beer on his son's birthday, to take the edge off seeing Kate. *Damn it.* He wasn't ready to see her again, not after that…craziness at her house, the craziness he couldn't think about right now because thinking about it made his cock so fucking hard. He stayed where he was, holding up the wall farthest from the foyer, mouth shut, trying to think about anything or anyone but her.

He'd put off telling his lieutenant that he was the wrong person for the job, that he'd severed any real connection to Kate eight years ago. In answer to the lieu's questions he offered half-truths. Yes, he'd gone to her house after the memorial service, and again the following afternoon, and he would see her at Jeremy's birthday party. He didn't mention that he'd lost control the first two times and didn't expect to speak to her today.

Fuck me.

Miriam dried her hands on a dishtowel as she crossed

the dining room, eyes trained on the front windows. "Any reporters on her tail?" his mother asked in her straightforward, unemotional way. When Steve died, a vital piece of his mother died with him. The woman who used to laugh and argue with the same abandon with which she loved had turned into herself after her younger son's passing, and began to parse out her emotions as though giving too much would drain a finite well on the edge of drying up completely.

Lindsay's new husband, Richard, said, "Looks like she aged ten years since her husband died."

Yeah, sure she does. Gabe knew what Richard was doing—reassuring Lindsay that he wasn't attracted to her former sister-in-law. Even though Lindsay was an attractive blonde, she'd always been jealous of Kate. Still was, even though she pretended to be Kate's friend. No doubt that was about the big house in McLean that Kate's money had bought her when she hooked up with Richard. *For Jeremy,* Lindsay had told him.

Right.

Carolyn, Gabe's oldest sister, chimed in. "I'm surprised she was willing to come, with all the crap she's dealing with these days."

Gabe looked over at Carolyn, her curly light brown hair so like Steve's had been. Of the siblings, she had always been the least openly critical of Kate, which had annoyed the shit out of him plenty of times. But not today. Today he felt relieved by her subtle defense of Kate. Surprise, surprise.

"She doesn't like to disappoint Jeremy," Miriam said, and laid the damp towel carefully over the back of one of the dining room chairs. When the doorbell rang she brushed her hands against hips that had grown wide over the years and went to the front door. She opened it and greeted Kate, no doubt with a lukewarm hug.

"Hello, Miriam. It's so good to see you."

At the sound of Kate's voice, Gabe took another long pull on his beer. When he tipped his head back he saw the accusatory gleam in Lindsay's eyes. Just like every other year. And just like every year, Jeremy raced to the door and threw himself at Kate, and Gabe's chest got tight. Except this year his chest tightened in a way he found disturbing.

"Jeremy, let the woman breathe," Miriam said.

Gabe glanced over at the scene in the foyer, where a beaming Kate had her arms wrapped tight around his son, then quickly looked away. Why Jeremy was so attached to her he didn't know, but nothing seemed to shake it. Would the kid be more disappointed if *he* didn't show up or if *Kate* didn't show up?

"I'm so strong now I can pick you up," Jeremy proclaimed.

"I don't believe it," Kate teased.

"Okay, watch!"

Gabe couldn't resist a peek at Jeremy with his arms wrapped around Kate's slim waist, lifting her up on to her toes.

"Oh, my goodness," Kate gushed. "You *are* strong. Have you been lifting weights?"

"See what I mean?"

Jeremy put her down but didn't let go. "I saw you on the news," he said. "But my mom turned off the TV."

Lindsay rushed to the foyer before Jeremy could tell any more secrets. She embraced Kate warmly. "You shouldn't have bothered to come," she said in her best maternal tone. Gabe recognized it as a crock of shit, of course. "Not after all that's happened. Jeremy would have understood, wouldn't you, honey?"

"I'm just here to drop off a present," Kate said. "I'm not going to stay."

Jeremy hugged her tighter. “You have to stay!”

“Jeremy,” Lindsay said, “this isn’t a good time for Aunt Kate.”

But Jeremy was determined. He gazed up into Kate’s eyes with that pleading expression Gabe knew so well. “Please stay, Aunt Kate,” he said. “Pretty pretty please with a cherry on top?”

“Don’t harass her.” Lindsay tried unsuccessfully to pull Jeremy’s arm from around Kate’s waist. His attachment to Kate pissed her off royally, and Gabe had to admit he admired the kid’s tenacity.

Kate ran her hand over the top of Jeremy’s head, a small smile on her lips. “I’ll stay for a while,” she said quietly.

“Cool!” Jeremy shouted. He glanced at Gabe, but instead of leading Kate in the opposite direction like he usually did, he took her hand. “Want to say hi to my dad?”

Kate turned to face Gabe, her expression wary. For good reason. She let Jeremy pull her into the dining room but stopped several feet from where Gabe’s feet were planted and held on to a chair. He kept his expression neutral, but damn if she didn’t search his face for something more.

“Hello, Gabe,” she said.

Gabe felt several pairs of eyes on him. He lifted two fingers off his beer in a pseudo-wave, gave a tight nod and mumbled, “Hello.” Like they were strangers. Like he hadn’t had his tongue in her mouth and his hands on her breasts five days ago. Right before he more or less accused her of killing her husband.

Miriam called to Jeremy from the kitchen and he scampered off. Kate spotted Richard and his sister, Bonnie, and said hello. Neither of them had bothered to greet her, and now they threw back perfunctory hellos. Kind of like his,

Gabe thought. Had they always been this rude, or was he just noticing it for the first time?

"Oh." Joy stood in the kitchen doorway directing a cool look at Kate.

Gabe felt a twinge of sympathy. In her state she was no match for Joy. How must it feel to be confronted by your dead husband's mistress?

"Did Ben get the grill going?" Miriam asked Joy from the kitchen.

"He's already got some hot dogs on it." Joy turned her sharp blue eyes on Gabe. "I'm surprised you aren't hiding out in the yard yourself, Gabe." She didn't have to glance at Kate for her meaning to be clear to everyone. Kate sucked in a breath.

"No sense horning in on Ben's glory," Gabe said, and took another pull on his beer. It tasted flat and went down bitter. Because her hair was up in a high ponytail, he saw the flush that stained the tips of Kate's ears. He couldn't remember the last time Joy had shown up at one of Jeremy's birthday parties. Why this year? And why was she going out of her way to be a first-class bitch?

Carolyn, God bless her, glared at Joy, then came and stood beside Kate. "I'm sorry I missed the memorial service," she said quietly. "How are you doing?"

Kate let out a long breath and Gabe felt his gut uncoil a bit. "Okay," she said. "Thank you for asking."

The doorbell rang, and Carolyn went to answer it, leaving Kate standing there in her white linen capris and navy T-shirt looking impossibly young and out of place, lost in enemy territory. When no one else spoke, she pasted on a smile. "I guess I'll go out back and say hello to Ben," she said, and walked past the kitchen, heading for a side door that also led outside.

Richard threw an arm around his wife's shoulders and addressed Joy. "Hey, congratulations on getting that bill through committee."

Joy ran her fingers through her hair, dipping her chin in that way she had of pretending to be humble. "Thanks, Richard."

"Sounds like it's going to breeze through the House."

Joy chuckled. "Nothing breezes through a minority House, but I'm optimistic that it will pass. The president is pushing hard."

Lindsay splayed a hand over her chest. "Isn't it awful about that senator who was murdered inside her house last night?"

"And right on the heels of the plane explosion," Richard added.

"It really is horrifying," Joy said. "Almost too much to bear."

Horrifying didn't begin to cover it, and the MPD was looking real hard for some connection between Senator D'Argento's murder and a plane full of congressmen blowing up. But Gabe didn't think Joy was having such a terrible time bearing it, probably because—

"At least she was a Democrat."

Everyone turned and stared at Richard as though he'd grown another head. The thought *had* flitted through Gabe's mind that Joy was rid of an opponent to her bill, but jeez, who would be dumb enough to say it out loud? A glance at his ex-wife told him she was biting her tongue, probably because she didn't want to chew out her husband with Gabe there.

"Well, you know, no one wants to say it," Richard said, "but—"

"Then don't say it," Gabe cut in.

Richard ignored him. "Who's not going to vote for the Global Intelligence and Security bill after some bastard blew Drew Franklin out of the sky? Al Qaeda or no al Qaeda?"

Joy turned pale, then excused herself and went back into the kitchen.

Richard turned to Lindsay. "What? He wasn't *her* husband."

Lindsay glanced at Gabe and once again he could see her biting back the caustic retort her moron of a husband had coming. "They were cosponsors of the bill, for God's sake," she said in a low voice. "They were close."

"Have you actually read the bill, Richard?" Carolyn asked. "The director of Global Intelligence and Security's going to have so much more power than any one person ever has had, except the dictators, for God's sake. It's everything the liberals have been warning us about all these years. One thing I have to say for Kate, at least she wasn't brainwashed by that—"

Squeals and shouts from the foyer announced the arrival of Jeremy's friends and drowned out what promised to be the beginning of a prolonged political battle. Lindsay detached from Richard and started ordering the other adults around, Gabe excluded. According to the unspoken tradition, he would wait until he figured out where Kate was going to be and then be somewhere else.

He wiped a hand over his face and allowed himself to wonder how Kate had the courage to come to these parties year after year, no doubt feeling like a pariah, putting up with these people's bad manners. And his.

Jeremy zoomed around the corner and called to him. "Dad, come on outside."

"I'm coming." He set down his empty beer bottle and

went to him, expecting Jeremy to turn and run ahead. But Jeremy's expression looked pained. "What's the matter?"

"How come everybody's so mean to Aunt Kate?" He pinned Gabe with green eyes shaped so like Steve's. Gabe wished he could disappear, escape the accusation he saw there. "Why can't you ever be nice to her?"

There were few people in Gabe's life whose respect was important enough to swallow his pride for. His son was at the top of the list. He laid a hand on Jeremy's shoulder.

"I'll go talk to her," he said.

Chapter Nine

As soon as Kate started down the back steps into the yard, Ben put down the long fork he was using to spear hot dogs on to the grill and went to greet her. She was so grateful, tears prickled.

"Kate." Ben embraced her. "How are you?"

"Oh, getting by."

He stepped back and studied her. "Doesn't look like you're getting enough sleep."

She smiled weakly. "I sleep, but it isn't restful."

"The press still camped out on your lawn?"

She sighed. "Not this morning, but I took two different taxis and went a roundabout way to get here, in case someone was following me."

"It's nice that you came."

"You're probably the only adult who thinks so. I wasn't going to stay but Jeremy begged me to, so here I am."

"I'm glad you're here too," Ben said, smiling, then spotted something over her shoulder and frowned.

Kate turned and saw Gabe approaching, and he wasn't scowling for once. She was so stunned she didn't know what to say. He normally stayed as far away from her as humanly possible. Well, except for the times recently when he'd been too close. Too intimate.

Her heart started pounding as her body remembered. She wouldn't be that stupid again.

"Is this a private conversation?" Gabe asked when he reached her side.

"Why don't you give her a break?" Ben said.

"Ben, it's fine," Kate said. "I'm sure he's not going to make a scene at his son's birthday party."

Gabe held her gaze. "No, I'm not. And I think those hot dogs are on fire."

"Shit," Ben muttered and turned to the flaming grill.

Gabe took her arm and gently pulled her away from the grill. "How about a soda or a bottle of water from the cooler? It's about a thousand degrees out here and you're already sweating."

Okay, this was too much. Gabe, playing the considerate host? He had to be up to something. She swiped a hand over her upper lip and pulled it away damp. "A bottle of water would be nice."

He went to get it and she followed him with her eyes. Dressed in faded jeans that hugged his ass and a black zT-shirt that stretched over broad shoulders and muscular arms, Gabe looked little different than he had all those years ago, when Steve was still alive. Back when she and Gabe used to horse around and goof on one another. Back when she'd catch him watching her when he thought she couldn't see him. Like she had watched him. Still watched him.

Stupid, stupid, stupid.

Jeremy ran over to her, a smile lighting up his face. "Is my dad talking to you?" he asked.

Aha, so that was why he was being nice all of a sudden. To please Jeremy. "Yeah, he's bringing me some water," she said, hoping her smile covered her disappointment. That embrace in her kitchen the other day had obviously messed with her head.

"We're gonna play badminton, Aunt Kate. You want to play?"

"Maybe in a little while," she said. "I'm going to cool off with some water first, I think."

"Okay, but watch me!"

"Of course I'll watch you, dopey. I can hardly take my eyes off you." She ran a hand through his hair.

"Is that 'cause I look like Uncle Steve?"

His question caught her off guard. "No, it's because you look like such a badass," she said, and winked. "Now go kick some butt."

"I'm gonna kick Jacob Wilson's butt!"

"And don't forget about Owen Grant and Sammy F."

"Them too," he said, and ran off. This was his day. All his friends were here, running around the big backyard, raising hell and having a blast. That he took the time to come over and talk to her at all just made her love him more.

"He sure is glad you came," Gabe said as he came closer, a bottle of water in each hand. He handed her one.

"Thanks." The cap was already off, and she wondered briefly if he'd poisoned hers. Not likely at his son's birthday party.

She took a long swallow, and then pressed the bottle to her forehead. "You don't have to stand next to me," she said, looking straight ahead to the far side of the lawn where twenty kids were frantically trying to hit the birdie over the net. "Jeremy won't notice if you slip away now."

Gabe was silent for a long moment, then, "You know the kids in his class."

Okay, he wasn't going to accuse her of anything today. She let out a long sigh. "He tells me about them in his emails, and when I get to see him, which is less and less often."

Gabe nodded. "He said that's because his mom wants him to bond with his stepsiblings."

"So I gather." Wow. They were having a regular conversation. She turned to him, but the sight of him was so appealing she couldn't focus and talk at the same time, so she looked away. She reached into herself to pull out some of the anger she'd stoked since he was at her house last.

Be cool to him, Kate. Don't be drawn into his nice-guy act.

"Aren't you going to play badminton?" she asked.

"Nah."

"But you play every year."

He shrugged. "This is a year for firsts."

"Like talking to me."

"I talk to you," he said.

"Not at these parties. You don't even acknowledge me at these parties."

"Are you trying to pick a fight?" he asked.

She whirled on him, ready for battle. "Am *I*—" she began, but Gabe was grinning at her. Like he used to. An honest to God, handsome-as-the-day-is-long grin. And she couldn't help it. She laughed. It started as a small chuckle and grew into an all-out belly laugh that made her stomach ache. She wrapped her arm around her middle to ease the pain.

And the earth shifted beneath her feet as she looked at him. Just like it used to.

One minute she was laughing and the next she was crying.

Ben rushed over. "What the hell happened?" he asked. "Goddamn it, Gabe, what did you say to her?"

"I didn't—"

Miriam must have been watching from the window, because the back door slammed shut and she half ran down the steps. "Gabe? What did you do?"

"Nothing," he said, exasperated. She felt his big, warm hand on her arm. "Jesus, Kate, are you laughing or crying?"

She was trying to stop, she really was, but the tears kept coming, along with the laughter. Everybody naturally assumed Gabe had insulted her and made her cry, and for some reason that struck her as hysterical. Her head hurt. Her stomach hurt. Her whole body hurt, but she couldn't stop.

Gabe's arm came around her shoulders. "Everyone out of the way so I can get her inside. Okay? Back off."

He helped her into the house, his arm around her the whole time, then sat her down at the kitchen table and straddled the chair beside hers. Her cheeks were wet with tears and she was gulping in breaths. She had to stop this. Had to pull it together.

"S-sorry," she managed. She dropped her face into her hands and tried to focus on her breathing, but it wasn't working. The heat from Gabe's body seared every inch of exposed skin like she was one of those burning hot dogs he'd pulled her away from.

Out of the frying pan and into the fire.

The thought turned her sobs into giggles, and she really felt like a lunatic. Maybe she shouldn't have popped that tranquilizer her doctor had suggested to help her through the early weeks of mourning. It must be making her loopy.

"What's going on with you?" Gabe asked. He was so close she felt his breath on her cheek and neck, which made her breasts tingle. "I don't smell any alcohol on you."

That snapped her out of it. "I wasn't drinking, you idiot." She plucked a paper napkin from a ceramic holder to blow her nose on. "I'll never drink anywhere near you again."

He was silent, and her cheeks heated, wondering if the same memories that were running through her head were running through his. Or had he wiped the memory of their passionate kiss out of his big fat head?

"It's you, if you must know," she said, sniffling and wiping at her cheeks. She took a deep calming breath and let it out. "You make me crazy."

"Ditto," he said quietly.

She looked at him then, and felt the dizzying power of his gaze. His eyes strayed to her lips and held a second too long, and when he looked back into her eyes his lids were lower and his irises darker.

Oh, shit. She was in trouble.

Loud laughter rose from the living room, breaking the spell, and Gabe tuned in to the conversation between Lindsay and Bonnie.

"All she has going for her are her looks and her money," Bonnie said.

"Oh, that's all?" Lindsay shot back. They both laughed.

Gabe took Kate's arm and pulled her up from the chair. "Let's get out of here," he said, leading her toward the front door.

She pulled her arm back. "It's okay," she said. "I'll watch Jeremy play for a few more minutes and then grab a cab." Another burst of laughter from the living room turned her head, but she quickly straightened her shoulders and started to walk around him toward the back door. How like her to put Jeremy first, even though she had to be desperate to get out of there.

He should let her go. He knew it. Knew what touching her did to him. He grabbed her arm, holding her back. "Wait."

"Let go, Gabe," she said, not looking at him.

He led her across the kitchen and down a corridor to his mother's little sewing room, then shut and locked the door. The scent of fresh flowers was strong, but not strong enough to block out the scent of Kate. *Jesus,* he was a fool.

"Don't do this," she said.

He lifted her chin with one finger and ran his thumb over her lips. They were moist and warm, and he wanted to taste them. No, he needed to taste them. Now.

"Why are you doing this?" she whispered. "You hate me, remember?"

He shook his head slowly. "I haven't been able to get the taste of you out of my mind." He lowered his mouth to hers. Fuck foreplay. He latched on to her lips and assaulted her mouth with his tongue, desperate for the high he only got from this. Only from her. He pulled her into his arms, loving the feel of her breasts pressed against his chest, thrilling at the sensation of her hands sliding up his back, her slim arms tightening around him.

He lifted his mouth from hers just long enough to slant it the other way and devour her lips as though they were two halves of a sweet, ripe plum. One hand slid to her bottom and lifted her so that his erection pressed between her legs. Her low moan and galloping heartbeat told him she wanted more. And God knew, he wanted it all.

Gabe pushed her up against the door and ran his hands over her breasts, squeezing, kneading while their tongues tangled in a frenzy of desire. He felt drugged, out of control. Had to get her clothes off. Had to touch her skin, taste every part of her.

Had to get inside her.

"Gabe." It was a whispered confession of the same desperation he felt.

His cell phone buzzed in his pocket. He ignored it and pulled her closer, kissing her long and deep, knowing as soon as he sobered from this intoxication he would kick himself for letting this happen again. For being unable to keep his hands and mouth off this woman.

The phone buzzed again and he silently cursed as he eased away from Kate and reached into his pocket. The LED said Scott Bailey. Police business. *Shit.* He closed his eyes and willed his throbbing cock to go down

"Take it." Kate's voice was breathy, sexy. So fucking sexy. When she tried to step around him Gabe pulled her under one arm and planted a gentle kiss on her lips. And then another. And another. By the time she managed to wiggle out of his embrace they were both panting.

"We're not finished," he said, holding her arm, unwilling to let her go. "Not by a long shot."

She shook her head. Seeing how red and swollen her lips were only made him want her more. "This was a mistake," she said. "We'll both regret it as soon as we walk out that door."

He didn't answer, just stepped into the corridor, closed the door behind him and headed out to the side yard, away from the birthday chaos. He flipped open the phone.

"Your hot little sister-in-law?" Scott said by way of greeting.

Gabe looked back toward the house. "Who, Kate?"

"You have another one?"

"What about her?"

"You mighta been right about her."

Gabe's shoulders tightened. "What are you talking about?"

"Looks like she really is a black widow."

Chapter Ten

"Why in God's name did you insist on driving me home if you're going to act like this?"

Gabe stared straight ahead at the road, both hands gripping the steering wheel, his jaw clenched tight. Scott's phone call had left him furious, and not only because the FBI had evidence possibly linking Kate to the explosion. He was furious at himself for letting down his guard. If it were lust alone that had driven him to try to jump her bones he could deal with it. But it had always been more than lust with Kate. He'd let the old feelings resurface—for a short time, true—but it had been enough to show him they were still there.

And that made him angrier than he'd been in a very long time.

"I told you you'd regret it," she said. "And sure enough, now it's all my fault."

He shook his head and barked out a bitter laugh. "You're a piece of work, aren't you? Damn, you're good."

"Okay, that's it," she said. "Stop the car."

He didn't answer, or look at her, or slow down. The click of her seat belt unfastening forced him to glance her way in time to catch her trying to open the door.

"What the hell are you doing?" he shouted.

"Getting out. You going to stop the car or what?"

He grabbed her arm and pulled her toward him, causing the car to veer. "Have you lost your mind?"

"Stop this damn car!" she shouted, pushing against him, one hand still on the door handle.

"Shit!" He pressed the brake pedal and Kate thrust her arms against the dashboard. The McLean road was twisty and narrow, with trees on both sides. He pulled off on to dirt and rocks at the side of the road then stopped abruptly. Kate's head smacked against the windshield frame.

She muttered a curse and brought a hand to her head. Even then, she twisted to pull open the door, but Gabe's hand banded her upper arm like a manacle.

"Where do you think you're going?" he demanded. "Did you—"

Eyes flashing, she tried to yank her arm away. "I'm getting away from you," she said. "Let. Go. Of. Me."

Yeah, and hell was going to freeze over. "You are not getting out," he said, holding her in place. Her hair was wild, half in and half out of her ponytail, and her cheeks were red. "Now, let me see your head. Is it—"

With a grimace she whipped her arm around and slapped his face hard. It stung, and it pissed him off, but it was just another drop in the bucket. "Feel better now?"

"Shut up and let go, you bastard."

He moved his free hand toward her head and she cowered. That's when he let go of her arm. "Oh, for… Did you honestly think I was going to hit you?"

"Yes."

"Bullshit," he said. "I wanted to check for a lump on your head."

"What do you care if I have a lump on my head?" She was breathing hard, and it was obvious she'd hurt herself, but he wasn't about to touch her again. Touching her was dangerous, even when she was acting like a madwoman.

"And since I'm not going to leave you here by the side of the road, I'd advise you to buckle up."

"I can call a cab."

"Do you even know what road you're on? You're not the most spatially gifted person I know."

"Do *you* even know what a psycho you are?" she shot back. "You're all over me at your mother's house, you insist on driving me home and once we're in the car, presto! You're back to the snide comments and Jekyll and Hyde routine. I'm sick of you, Gabe. I've had it. I can't take any more."

"I know the feeling. Who did it for you?"

She blinked. "What?"

"Did you make contact with someone directly or get some lowlife from one of your charities to make the contacts?"

Her frown deepened. "What are you talking about?"

He quickly started the car and pulled back on to the road. "We'll talk when we get to your house."

After a moment she buckled her seat belt, but one hand was still pressed to her head. "You think I'm going to invite you in?" she said, then snorted. "You have got to be kidding."

"We'll see about that."

There were news vans parked on the opposite side of Kate's street. No big surprise. Neither was the black car in her circular drive and two men in suits leaning against it. The FBI was here. Gabe pulled the Honda in behind it and reporters descended on them.

"Stay here," he said to Kate, and stepped out. He was immediately mobbed. "Out of my way. Mrs. Franklin has no comment."

An attractive woman with red hair thrust a microphone at Gabe. "Can you identify yourself, sir?"

"No." He walked around the side of the car and opened Kate's door, then reached for her when she stepped out. Okay, after this he wouldn't touch her again. "Stay under my arm and don't say a word."

"Go to hell," she said, driving her elbow into his side. "Leave me alone." She stalked to her door.

One of the agents, a man of medium height with rimless glasses and a receding hairline, stepped in front of her and held up his credentials. "FBI, Mrs. Franklin," he said. "I'm Agent Jim Parker and this is Agent John Mancuso."

Kate's dog was barking up a storm on the other side of the door while she fumbled through her purse. "This man assaulted me a few minutes ago," she said, indicating Gabe, who was right on her heels, with a nod. "Can you arrest him or something?"

Both agents turned to Gabe, frowning. He didn't bother explaining. Instead he reached around Kate, grabbed her purse, pulled out the keys and shoved them into her hands. "You're welcome," he said.

It took her several seconds to get the key into the lock and open the door. When she was finally inside she squatted beside the old brown lab and wrapped her arms around his neck. "Hey, Bruno," she said. His nails clicked on the hardwood floor as he did his happy dance. For a moment she buried her face in his neck, then rose and turned to the FBI agents. "Do you have news for me?"

The taller, younger agent—Mancuso—said, "Yes, we do. May we sit down?"

"Sure." She pointed toward the living room. "Make yourselves at home and I'll be right with you."

"We have to get some ice on your head," Gabe said, and took a step in the direction of the kitchen.

Kate grabbed his arm. "I'll get my own damn ice. You're not staying."

"Actually, I am," he said. "I'm the MPD liaison with the FBI."

Her eyes widened. "How is that possible? That's a conflict of interest. You're prejudiced against me."

"Not at all," he said, knowing it sure as hell *was* a conflict of interest, but one his lieutenant was willing to overlook in this case.

"If there's a problem, Mrs. Franklin—" Mancuso began.

"There's no problem," Gabe said.

"Yes there is," Kate said. "Get another liaison. I don't want this creep in my house."

"Take it up with my lieutenant." Gabe followed Mancuso into the living room. The agents sat in wing chairs facing the couch. He chose to lean against the wall inside the arched entry.

A smug smile broke over Mancuso's face. "That went well," he said to Gabe.

Gabe's nostrils flared, but he held his tongue. A minute or so later Kate returned, head high, shoulders squared, her long hair loose around her shoulders and halfway down her back. She'd obviously freshened up. But her lips were still red and a bit swollen from his kisses, which sent an unwelcome infusion of tenderness through him. Jesus, he had to watch his step around this woman.

She sat on the couch, leaned back and slowly brought a bag of frozen peas to her head, wincing as she did it.

"Are you all right?" the shorter agent, Parker, asked her. He shot an accusing look at Gabe.

"Just a bump on the head." Kate didn't look at Gabe. "It's feeling better already. So, what do you want to talk to me about? Do you have news about the explosion or do you want to question me some more?"

"Was your husband cheating on you, Mrs. Franklin?" Parker asked.

For a moment nobody moved or spoke. Then Kate let out a long breath. "I couldn't swear to it one way or the other, but even if he had been cheating on me I wouldn't have killed him over it."

The three men were silent for a moment, and then Parker said, "Your first husband, Steven Hugo, died two and half months after he sold his software business. Five weeks after you married him."

"Yes, well, that's been all over the news."

"He left you forty million dollars. Give or take."

"Yes."

"Which you invested in real estate, stocks—"

"What's your point, Agent Parker?" she interrupted. "Everyone is suddenly focusing on how much money I have, which is surprising in a town full of exceedingly wealthy people. Many of whom are a lot richer than I am."

"Have you had any unusual expenses lately, Mrs. Franklin?" Mancuso asked. His deep voice carried a hint of condescension, which irritated Gabe as much as the man's slicked back hair, heavy cologne and arrogant expression.

"No," she said. "I can't think of any unusual expenses. Other than the reception here after my husband's memorial service."

"Did you and your husband have different accountants?"

"Yes, but Drew takes care of—" She caught herself. "*Took* care of most of the money."

"Even though the lion's share of it was yours?"

She flipped over the bag of peas and pressed it ever so

gingerly against her head. “First tell me why you’re asking all these questions about my finances, okay? Then maybe I’ll understand what kind of answers you’re looking for.”

Mancuso held up a palm. “Please, a few more questions and then we’ll get right to the bottom line. Why did your husband take care of your money?”

She sighed. “Finances are not my strong suit. Investments and portfolios and playing the market—that doesn’t interest me. So Drew dealt with all that.”

“I see,” Mancuso said, but he shot a look at Parker.

“What about your charity work?” Parker asked. “I understand you have millions invested for various causes.”

“Yes,” she said. “I give a lot of money to several underserved groups.”

“Like People for Prisoner’s Rights,” Mancuso said with that little smirk that was really getting on Gabe’s nerves.

To her credit, Kate met the agent’s gaze head-on. “Yes, I support prisoner’s rights, and the rights of lesbian and gay partners, and prostitutes who’ve suffered abuse, and their out-of-wedlock children, and any number of causes that are unpopular with my husband’s constituents.”

Gabe couldn’t help but admire the unapologetic way she’d thrown that back at Mancuso.

“So, your husband stayed out of that work,” Parker said, his tone nonjudgmental.

“Yes,” she said. “I have my own people who deal with that. They also deal with bequests and trusts and so forth.”

“What about private donations?” Parker asked. “Money for relatives, friends… That sort of thing. Who took care of that?”

“If it’s a large sum of money I generally have my accountant write a check out of a separate account he keeps for that purpose. Smaller amounts I take care of myself.”

"Personal checking accounts, credit cards… Your husband took care of that record-keeping?"

"I have my own checking account." She turned to Mancuso. "Which I manage and balance." Turning back to Parker she said, "But Drew liked to be in control of the credit cards and savings accounts and investments, and that was fine with me. I don't really care about the money. I'm not a particularly big spender."

Mancuso made of point of swiveling his head, letting his eyes roam over the deep red Persian rugs, the sumptuous white couches and chairs accented with red-and-green patterned pillows, the built-in cherry cabinets filled with gleaming crystal stemware, the elegant marble fireplace. He needn't have bothered with the obnoxious body language—it was evident in a single glance that this house was filled with high quality, expensive furnishings.

Kate frowned. "What I mean is, I don't buy a whole new wardrobe every year, or blow money on expensive jewelry." She waved a dismissive hand at the room. "And I wouldn't have bothered with all this."

Parker leaned toward her to redirect her attention. Gabe wondered if he realized what a horse's ass Mancuso was. "But your husband needed your signature to move money, isn't that right?"

She shrugged. "I guess so."

The two agents glanced at one another. "You're not sure?"

"Well, we owned everything jointly, so I'd guess we needed both signatures for some things, and just one for others. Like bank withdrawals. I can withdraw money with only my signature, and so could he."

Parker shifted in his chair, and Gabe knew he was about to lay it on the line. "Mrs. Franklin, huge sums of money have been moved out of your accounts over the past twelve months."

They all watched her face. She frowned as though puzzled. "Was it done electronically?" she asked. "He paid the bills online, so I imagine he did a lot of other financial transactions online too."

"No, Mrs. Franklin," Mancuso said. "Our records indicate that you did."

"Excuse me?"

"We have records of bank withdrawals, stock transactions and other financial dealings all bearing your electronic signature. What was done on paper generally bore only your signature."

She lowered the hand holding the bag and leaned forward, elbows on knees. "What are you talking about? I don't know the first thing about stock transactions, or real estate or anything else, and I have not moved any money around." She looked between the agents, and this time her gaze even stopped at Gabe for a moment, before she quickly looked away. In that moment, though, when their gazes met, he was struck by the accusation in her eyes. "How do you even know all this?"

"We'll get to that."

"Get to it now," Gabe said. "Explain to her why the FBI is sniffing around her finances."

Both agents shot him dirty looks. Parker leaned forward. "There is close to a hundred million dollars of your money currently unaccounted for, Mrs. Franklin."

Kate went still, and Gabe watched the color rise to her cheeks. Finally she said, "That's not possible."

"I'm afraid it is," Parker said. "It's all documented. In addition to the electronic records, we have reams of documents with your signature and initials on them." He opened a briefcase and pulled a sheet of paper out of a thick file. He placed it in front of Kate on the table. "Is that your signature?"

Her eyes followed his finger to where it pointed and studied the signature there. "It—it looks like it," she said. Her voice sounded higher. Younger. She lifted the paper and held it closer, then ran a finger over the signature. "It sure looks like it, but…where did you get this?"

"From your husband's accountant." Parker held up a hand. "I assure you we're entitled to be in possession of these documents."

"What is this?"

"It's a document authorizing the sale of two hundred thousand shares of IBM stock." He pulled out another document and held it up. "A hundred and fifty thousand shares of Google stock. And there's more. Amazon stock. Yahoo! Shall I go on?"

She blinked up at him. "But…I never signed anything like that. I was only vaguely aware of which stocks we owned."

Parker gestured at the paper. "Yet your signature tells us you did, in fact, sign all of these documents." He pulled out several other sheets from the file and passed them across the table. She took them but had begun to move in slow motion. Gabe recognized the signs of emotional shock. The glazed expression, slowed reflexes. The appearance of dullness.

She looked at each sheet of paper closely, asking Parker what each one was for, taking in the explanations with a slow shake of her head. All the while this was going on, Agent Mancuso studied her, taking in every last detail of her reaction while keeping his own expression blank.

When she handed the last one back, she pulled her knees up and hugged them.

"I don't know what to say," she said slowly. "Did Drew do this?"

"You tell us, Mrs. Franklin."

"Tell you what? I see my signature on these papers, so I guess I signed them… But I didn't know what I was signing."

Gabe was tired of biting his tongue. "Were you in the habit of signing legal documents blindly?"

She turned to him looking shell-shocked. "Drew was a lawyer. If he told me to sign something, I signed it. Usually it was first thing in the morning, when he was rushing out the door. I always asked what it was, but I couldn't have taken the time to read it if I'd wanted to. It always had to be signed right that minute." She shrugged, spreading her palms. "He was my husband, for God's sake. I trusted him. Why would I second-guess him?"

"Do you recall signing a lot of legal documents over the past several months?" Mancuso asked with an irritated glance at Gabe.

"Well…maybe. There were sometimes several things he wanted me to sign at the same time."

She pressed the frozen peas against her head. Curled up the way she was, with her hair hanging over her face, she reminded Gabe so clearly of herself as a teenager. Back when he'd first met her and considered her a sweet kid with a body and face to die for. He remembered clapping Steve on the back for bringing home such a fox. Now, she looked young and confused and a little scared.

She looked up. "So, let me get this straight," she said, glancing quickly at Gabe. "You think I hired someone to bring my husband's plane down. Is that what you're saying?"

The two agents stared at her. "Did you, Mrs. Franklin?" Parker asked after several seconds.

She opened her mouth as if to say something, then closed it, then opened it to say, "Are you serious?"

"Yes," Parker said. "We're very, very serious."

Kate turned to Gabe. "So it's not just you." They held each other's gaze for a long moment, and then, for the second time that day, she burst out laughing.

The two agents were looking at her like she'd lost her mind. She bent over, holding her stomach like she had at his mother's house earlier, tears running down her cheeks as she continued to laugh like a lunatic. Gabe pushed off the wall and went to the kitchen, poured her a glass of water, then put it down in front of her. He squatted beside her.

"Kate," he said quietly. "Stop this before you start crying again."

"Go to hell," she said, wiping tears from her eyes.

"Mrs. Franklin," Mancuso said sharply. "I know this is a lot to take in, but this is no laughing matter."

"I am well aware of that."

"Have you been drinking, Mrs. Franklin?" Parker asked.

"No."

"She gets like this when she's stressed out," Gabe offered.

"Only when you're around," she said.

"Tell us what really happened the day your first husband died."

Gabe snapped his head up and met Mancuso's triumphant gaze.

"Steve?" Kate said. "What does that have to—" She turned to Gabe. "What have you been telling them?"

"Not a thing."

"Who, then?"

"There have been reports that you drove your first husband to crash his car." Mancuso was doing a rotten job hiding a smirk. "Either as a suicide or in some kind of rage."

"That's hearsay, Agent," Gabe said, his voice harsh. "She was never a suspect in my brother's death. It was declared an accident."

She glanced between the two agents. "Am I under arrest?"

"No," Parker said. "We're simply—"

"Then I'd like you to leave." She stood. "Now."

"You're making a mistake," Mancuso said.

"No, I made a mistake by talking to you at all. From now on if you want to interrogate me you can go through my attorney." She strode through the living room and into the foyer, then held the door open for them. They nodded to her and left.

Gabe stood in the archway to the living room, arms crossed over his chest. God help him, the last thing he wanted to talk about with any of them was his brother's death.

Kate turned to him, her expression stony. "Get out of my house."

"Not quite yet," he said.

Chapter Eleven

Kate raised her chin. Her face was pale, no doubt a combination of fear and the pain in her head. "Like hell," she said. "I don't want you here, you bastard."

Gabe felt every bit as wrung out as she looked. "The reporters can pick up everything you're saying."

"I don't care."

"Close the door, Kate."

She glared at him, then slammed the door shut. "Don't even think about touching me."

"For the record," he said, "the only person in the department I confided in after Steve's death was Scott. He was my partner before I made detective. And it was years before I ever said a word to him."

She crossed her arms. "What did that agent mean about 'some kind of rage'?"

"He's speculating."

"Oh? And what about you? What do you think happened? Do you think we had a fight or—"

"No." Gabe took a deep breath and let it out. He'd put off having this conversation for eight years. "I think it had to do with what happened between you and me."

She stared at him. "Wait a minute," she said slowly. "Are you talking about *that* night? The one you've forbidden me to mention?"

And jumped her bones to make his point. "Yes, damn it."

"I never told Steve about that."

Gabe didn't move or take his eyes off her. "Well I sure as hell didn't."

She frowned. "What's your point, then?"

"Did you tell anyone else?" he asked.

"What? No!"

"Not even Alison?"

"Of course not," she said.

"So how did Steve find out?"

She stopped moving, her face suddenly pale. "He didn't. He couldn't have."

"You sure about that?"

She splayed her fingers on her chest. "I would never have hurt him like that. That was the last thing I ever wanted to do."

"You left him," Gabe said. He swallowed, knowing he'd been every bit as culpable as she had been. "That hurt him."

Kate stared at him, then said carefully, "You knew exactly why I left him. You of all people knew."

Yeah, he knew. Less than a week after that night, his mother had called him while he was working. She'd been agitated, worried about Steven's state of mind. She told him Kate had moved out of the apartment and Steven was a basket case. Gabe still remembered the overwhelming guilt he'd felt. They all knew Steve was fragile emotionally. As far as the family was concerned Kate was Steven's guardian angel, put on earth to love and protect him and keep him safe. Gabe had gone and made love to her and she'd left Steven. Great. But, coward that he was, he hadn't called his brother or gone to see him. In fact, he'd had as little contact as possible with Steven after that night, right up until the day he died.

"So why did you get back together three weeks later?" he asked.

Kate hesitated, looked away. "He begged me to come back," she said with a half shrug. "He'd already put the sale of his business in motion. He promised we'd spend more time together, that he wouldn't be so distracted all the time." She swallowed. "That's the reason I gave him for leaving, that he was too absorbed in his work. So he upped and sold his business, just like that." She finished with a snap of her fingers.

"You didn't push him to sell?" Gabe asked, hearing the accusation in his own voice. Kate shook her head no.

"I told him not to sell it for my sake. I knew how into that business he was. Everybody did. I said we didn't want the same things and it was best not live together anymore, but…" She trailed off, then lifted her hands. "He cried, he begged. He told me he couldn't live without me."

"Still doesn't explain why you married him," Gabe said. "You could have kept seeing him, spent time with him and eased out of the relationship. You didn't have to marry him."

"I know that."

"So?"

"So, what?"

"So, why did you marry him?"

She and Steve had surprised everybody—especially Gabe—by getting married three months after that night in his apartment, two months after Kate went back to Steve. They'd only been apart for three weeks, but according to his mother, Kate had already found herself an apartment. Then suddenly, *boom.* She and Steven were living together again, and announced that they were getting married.

The pain he'd felt at that announcement had been white-hot.

Kate frowned. "Why ask? You assume I married him for the money, so why bother asking me? You assume I pushed him to sell the business in return for getting back together, and that I somehow contrived to get him to go smash his car into a tree so I'd have it all to myself. Right? Isn't that your brilliant assumption?"

Gabe didn't answer. He wasn't sure he could.

They were silent for a long moment, and then Kate chuckled, joylessly. "So, Steve being Steve, he sells his business and goes right out and buys himself a Porsche *and* a Maserati. Then he spends all his time driving them, washing them, talking to other Porsche and Maserati owners online. In our time *together,*" she said, making quotes with her fingers, "he talked incessantly about cars, about becoming a race car driver, going to rallies all over the world. Showing me photos of race cars on the web. I thought I'd go crazy."

She went to a small table in the foyer and mindlessly straightened photographs. "It didn't have to be computers with Steve. It just had to be something he could lose himself in. Computers, cars, who knows what would have been next?" She turned to Gabe. "Why is it so hard to accept that he was racing around in that damn Maserati and crashed it by accident? Why do you insist on believing I had something to do with it?"

Anger surged through Gabe, and the words he'd never spoken spilled from between his clenched teeth. "Because he called me from his *damn Maserati,* that's why. Because he told me you should have married me, not him. Why did he say that?"

She went still. "He actually said that?"

"Yes, goddamn it."

She held on to the edge of the table and gazed into near space, as though remembering something from long ago. Her anger was gone, along with any remaining trace of color in her face. Even her lips looked bloodless. "What words did he use?"

"What difference does it make?" As though he couldn't remember. As though Steve's words weren't permanently etched into his brain. They had come at him out of nowhere. No greeting.

Nothing but those words…

"I need to know," she said. "It's important."

"Fine." The cat was out of the bag now, there was no sense trying to hide anything anymore. "He said, 'You're the one who should have married her, you bastard.' That's it. That's all he said."

Kate gasped and put her hand to her mouth. Tears sprang to her eyes and her face crumbled. She stumbled away from the table and walked to the wall, then leaned her forehead against it. Gabe looked away, unwilling to witness her grief or her guilt or whatever it was. He'd seen those emotions too many times in his own mirror.

They were silent for a long time, and then Kate said in a voice rough with tears, "So, the reason you've hated me all these years is that you assumed I told him we'd slept together."

Gabe didn't answer, or look at her.

"If only he'd told me what he was feeling, I could have kept him from getting into that car," she said. "I wish to God I'd known."

When he turned she was still braced against the wall as though she would fall down if she let go.

"If you didn't tell him about that night, why did he say that to me?" Gabe demanded, his chest aching. "Did you tell him you didn't love him? You knew how he was. You knew he could go over the edge with the right provocation."

"Of course I didn't tell him that," she said, sniffling. "I did love Steve. I always loved him, but..."

"But what?"

"I told you that night what it was like between us. I took care of him. He needed me, I liked being needed. You all counted on that. But it was never passionate between us."

Gabe winced. He'd never felt so intensely passionate about a woman as he had about her. "So, then, what?" he said. "You told him you weren't sexually satisfied?"

"I didn't have to."

He stared at her. "Then why the hell did you marry him, two months after... Why didn't you just keep things the way they were?" Fury exploded inside his chest, as it had all those years ago. "What you're telling me doesn't make any goddamn sense."

She whirled on him, her face flushed. "Oh, and it makes more sense to believe I wanted him to die so I could inherit his money?" she shouted back. "I didn't give a damn about his money. If that was what I wanted I wouldn't have tried to give it to your mother. Or did you conveniently forget about that?"

He hadn't forgotten, but the idea of taking Steve's money had felt repugnant to all of them at the time. "My mother couldn't take his money. None of us could. It wouldn't have felt right."

"I understood that. Your mother said Steve would have wanted me to have it, that I was young and had my whole life ahead of me." Kate moved to the staircase, grabbed the banister and lowered herself to a carpeted step. She hugged herself. When she spoke her voice was ragged and she shook her head slowly back and forth. "How could you ever in a million years imagine that I'd want Steve dead? That I'd marry him and then deliberately hurt him so he'd crash his car? That's just crazy, Gabe. Jesus Christ."

Gabe pounded his fist against the wall beside him. "Then, damn it, why did he call me? Why did he tell me *I* should have married you, and then crash his car into a tree? Something must have happened. What the hell was it?"

She was silent, tears running down her cheeks. Gabe waited, breathing heavily from shouting. "Okay, you win," she said finally. "Something did happen."

He sucked in a breath. "What?"

"I told him I was pregnant."

He fell back a step, unable to process her words. "You… what? You were pregnant?"

"Yes."

"Is that why you—?"

"Yes. That's why I married him. Happy now?"

No, he wasn't happy. Not at all. "But, what happened? Did you…?"

"No," she said. "I did *not* have an abortion. I miscarried the night after the funeral."

Gabe rested a hand on the wall to stop the dizziness. "But you just said… You and Steve—"

"I know what I said."

He swallowed. "How far along were you?"

Kate held his gaze for a long moment, then lowered her head and clasped her hands between her knees. Tears dripped off her nose and she brushed them away. "So, it looks like you were right all along. It was my fault. I thought he'd be happy, or at least happy enough. He barely reacted when I told him, just went back to his computer. I didn't expect him to… He didn't pay attention to when my periods came, or…" She trailed off on a sniffle and covered her face with her hands.

Gabe's gut was ice-cold. He'd been so desperate to get

inside her that night he hadn't used a condom. Was it possible? Could *he* have gotten her pregnant?

It wasn't hard to do the math.

It came back to him then. All the phone calls he hadn't answered… The emails begging to talk to him, that it was very important… He'd erased everything, as though by doing so he could erase the memory of their lovemaking, of the feelings he could no longer deny. The guilt had been as overwhelming as his desire for her, and he'd known he had to stay away from her or lose his fucking mind.

As he stood frozen, Kate rose, her legs wobbly, her shoulders hunched, her expression impossibly sad. She turned her back to him and trudged up the steps, clutching the banister.

"Kate," he called to her. "Wait."

She kept climbing. "Get out of my house," she said.

Chapter Twelve

The sun was going down when Kate opened the door to her accountant, Edward Lowell, who stood on the porch with a pained look on his face. As usual, Bruno was being obnoxious. “Hello, Ed,” she said, pulling the dog aside by his collar. “Come on in.”

He stepped inside without a word until she closed the door behind him. “I don’t know how this happened,” he said.

“It’s true, then?”

He nodded his balding head. “Believe me, I thought at first it was a mistake, but I spent most of the day with his accountant, and then I double-checked and double-checked again, and your assets are gone. Your accounts are empty.” He followed her into the living room and sank into a chair. “God, I’m sorry, Kate. I had no idea.”

She perched across from him on the sofa. “Where do you think it went?”

“My best guess is offshore someplace.”

She took a deep shaky breath. “When did he do this?”

“He did it gradually over the past year. Then, about three weeks ago, the withdrawals got bigger and bigger. Until it was all gone.”

“What about life insurance?”

He mopped his forehead with a handkerchief. “He was single when he met you, of course, and he…he never changed the beneficiary from his parents’ names to yours.”

Good God. He hadn't loved her enough to take care of that one small detail. Then again… "Well, he probably figured his parents could use the money more than I could if anything happened to him."

Ed nodded but didn't meet her gaze.

"So all that's left is the real estate, I suppose. Unless there are more stocks."

"No stocks left, I'm afraid," Ed said. "He sold off most of it over the past month."

Kate felt sick to her stomach. "We owned this house and the beach house jointly. He couldn't have sold those out from under me."

"Well…no. But he was carrying a huge line of credit on both houses, which depleted your equity."

"How the hell did he get a line of credit without my—?" Then she remembered. "Oh, that's right. He did manage to get my signature."

Ed opened a manila folder and flipped through the stack of documents. "Do you recall any of the documents you signed recently?"

She thought back. "I do remember some that had to do with property. He said we were refinancing the loans."

Ed looked sad. "So you didn't examine them closely."

She pinched the bridge of her nose. How could she have been such a fool? "No. I never did. He was the lawyer. I figured whatever he was having me sign was legit. It never occurred to me to question him."

"I've seen this type of thing happen before," Ed said. "But never to this extent."

She raised her eyes to his. "So where does this leave me? What do I have?"

"This house, although it's mortgaged to the hilt. Your car is paid off, and there's your furniture and personal belongings. Your husband's government pension, of course. I don't know the amount yet, but it should be enough to make ends meet, at least for a while. Less than a hundred thousand a year, I imagine."

Ed set his glasses down on the table and leaned closer. "There are millions invested for your charities, Kate. Just say the word and I can start the paperwork to move that money back to you."

She had expected this. "Those people have nothing, Ed. The veterans are disabled, and will be for the rest of their lives. Our country used them and threw them away. I can't take more away from them. And the kids in Peru?" She lifted her arms in a shrug. "Come on. Those tutoring centers are all that stand between them spending their childhoods making bricks beside their parents and learning to read."

"But—"

"I won't take that away from them. From any of them."

Ed sighed. "Then you'll have to move. You can't afford to keep up the mortgage on this house, unless you find a job that pays very, very well. And to be frank, at the moment I'm not sure…"

He didn't have to finish his sentence. As an unofficial suspect in her husband's death, the headhunters wouldn't exactly be pounding on her door. "I'm sure I can find something. If not here, then someplace else."

"I'm so sorry, Kate."

"This makes no sense."

"No, of course it doesn't. Did your husband have gambling debts? Anything like that?"

"Not that I know of, but I'm starting to realize how little I knew about my husband."

Joy, on the other hand, probably knew a lot about him.

An hour or so later, Kate showed Ed to the door and rubbed at her temples. God, she was tired. She'd cried herself to sleep after the confrontation with Gabe. She had, at the very least, upset Steven by telling him she was pregnant, even though her intention had never been to hurt him. At worst—and this was the possibility she would have to live with for the rest of her life—she had caused him to deliberately crash his car.

She sat down on the same step as last night and forced herself to think back on the events leading up to the moment Steve left their apartment for the last time.

Three weeks after the night she'd been with Gabe, she'd been at Alison's, packing to move into her new apartment, when she spotted her calendar and realized her period was late. Her breasts were more tender than they usually were at that time of the month. She remembered the thrill that had shot through her at the thought that she could be pregnant with Gabe's baby. She'd gone right out to the drugstore and picked up a home pregnancy test and voilà. It was positive. She'd cried with joy, fool that she was. There was no question that it was Gabe's baby. Not only had she and Steve not had sex in weeks, he'd always used a condom. Always.

Then came the frustration and sadness when all of her calls and emails to Gabe went unanswered. She'd considered leaving a voice mail message, or just spelling out the situation in the subject line of an email: *I'm having your baby—call me.* But she couldn't risk someone else seeing it, or hearing her message.

And oh, God, the night she'd waited outside his apartment for him to come home, and how her gut had twisted when she saw him walk up the steps of the building with a busty blonde on his arm. Even now, the memory caused her to bend over in pain. At the time she'd vomited into the bushes, then driven back to Alison's town house in Reston, Virginia, and sneaked into the basement so she could cry her heart out in private.

Sitting here now, she rubbed her eyes with the heels of her hands. Alison had found her, and assumed Kate was depressed over the breakup with Steven. Kate had broken down and told Alison she was pregnant, leaving her sister to assume the baby was Steven's. When Alison told her to face up to responsibility and marry the child's father, Kate had realized that she did want her baby to have a father. Steven might be moody and distant, but surely he'd love his own child—or a child he believed to be his.

"God," she murmured. "I thought I was such a good liar."

Once she accepted that Gabe didn't love her and she would never have a life with him, she agreed to go back to Steve. She remembered their pathetic lovemaking, the silent tears, Steve making every excuse in the book for why he couldn't maintain his erection. Still, she'd pretended to be desperate for it, to justify the pregnancy. She would tell him the condom broke and call it a blessing, and tell him not to look a gift horse in the mouth.

But she'd been miserable and depressed. She was living a lie with a man she loved as a brother while her heart belonged to a man who had turned his back on her.

Kate groaned aloud and wrapped her arms around her knees. She had been three and a half months pregnant when she finally told Steven. Her jeans didn't snap anymore. She hadn't started showing, but it wouldn't be long. Besides, she'd gone ahead and married him to give her child a father and a family, and she had to tell him sometime.

"Oh, God, Steve," she whispered. "If only I hadn't told you."

It'd been snowing that day, the first of December. The

roads were icy. She'd woken up alone, as usual, and when she went into the kitchen Steven was on his laptop. She'd gone behind him and hugged him, and impulsively said, "Guess what? We're going to have a baby."

Steven had gone still. She'd slid her arms off him and pulled out a chair beside him. He stared at her. "Did you hear me?" she asked.

After a long hesitation he said, "I used a condom."

She'd grabbed his hand, forcing a smile. "I didn't mention it because I didn't think it mattered, but that night I noticed that those condoms were expired. It could've had a hole in it."

Steven had stared at her, and then said, "I guess so."

Unable to meet his gaze, Kate had gone to the counter to pour herself some coffee. With her back to him she said, "It'll be okay, honey. I'll take care of the baby. And I won't be so lonely when you're busy."

She tried to remember how long she'd kept her back to him while he sat in silence. Finally she'd turned and found him scanning something on his laptop. She had breathed a sigh of relief and gone to take a shower. At some point Steven popped into the bathroom and said he was going out for a while, and she'd said, "Okay, drive safely."

Those were the last words they'd ever spoken to each other.

When Gabe showed up at her door a couple of hours later she'd been so surprised to see him it didn't occur to her that he'd come to give her bad news.

"Enough," she said, wiping away tears, and stood. She rubbed her arms as she made her way upstairs, then stopped halfway and went back to the kitchen for some wine. It would help her sleep, and since there was no one else around she couldn't make a fool of herself.

Ten minutes later she was lying in a hot bubble bath sipping her wine. Drew had been out late at night often, but he usually came home eventually if he was in town. Even though he'd frozen her out, having someone else in the house had made her feel safe. She'd have to get used to being on her own. She closed her eyes, letting the hot water and aromatic bubbles relax her muscles.

When she opened them again the bathroom was dark. Had she fallen asleep? Bruno was barking somewhere in the house, which probably meant he'd heard another dog or someone was on the property. That thought gave her no comfort. Through the skylight she could see a few stars through the clouds. Power outage? Or had a circuit blown?

"That's probably it," she whispered to calm herself down. The bathroom door was locked—she always locked it when she was alone in the house. She grabbed a towel and wrapped it around her, then tried the light switch. Nothing. No light leaked under the door, which meant the bedroom was dark as well. *Damn it.* She felt around for the thin terry cloth robe she always left hanging on the door, pulled it on and tied the belt.

She took a deep breath. This was probably a neighborhood power outage from some stray lightning, but she had to get to a window to see if her neighbors had lights. If it was a circuit, well…maybe she'd wait until morning to go down to the basement. The AC would be off, but she could deal with that.

She opened the bathroom door and stepped into the bedroom. Bruno wasn't barking anymore. There were no sounds at all, not even the usual whoosh of air through the vents. She looked around in the dark, barely breathing. Something felt…off.

She moved toward the window overlooking the pool,

past Drew's chest of drawers and full-length mirror—where she spotted a tiny movement at the foot of the bed that stopped her cold.

She froze, heart pounding, unable even to run back into the relative safety of the bathroom. Her mouth went dry. Even her brain seemed frozen, too shocked to think or move her limbs. The movement she had sensed stopped as well, but as her eyes adjusted to the dark she made out a crouching form dressed all in black.

It was a man.

And he was watching her.

Oh God oh God oh God...

A scream tried to break through but no sound emerged. Instinct drew her arms up and around her middle in a protective posture.

"T-take...whatever...you w-want," she croaked.

The person stood slowly, hands at his side.

Please, please, go away.

He chuckled, and it was the most evil sound Kate had ever heard. She tried to swallow but her spit had dried up. He took a step toward her, and she saw a flash of metal in his hand. A knife.

No.

"Please," she whispered, edging closer to the window. She could barely feel her legs under her, but somehow they carried her. The man chuckled again and she moved faster.

Suddenly he lunged.

She screamed, the sound loud and terrifying as it ricocheted around the room. He stepped on the hem of her robe, pulling it open, and grabbed her from behind—one muscular arm wrapped around her torso, pinning her arms. He was big and hard and smelled of alcohol and cigarettes and sweat.

I'm going to die. Oh God.

She felt the cool metal of the knife on her neck.

"Be a good girl and I won't have to cut you," he said in a low, gravelly voice that sent a violent shudder through her.

She could no more than whimper in response.

"Hear me, bitch?" he asked, pressing the knife edge closer.

"Y-yes," she whispered.

"Good." Then he wiggled against her bottom. "Mmm," he said in her ear. "I been wantin' to get me some ass."

"No." She whimpered again. "Please."

He pressed the knife deeper and she felt a warm wetness sliding down her throat. She squeezed her eyes shut.

"Did I hear you say no to me?"

I'm dead I'm dead I'm dead.

He spun her out in front of him and slapped her hard across the face, knocking her into the wall. Pain burst through her face and head, and she slid to her bottom. *The window.* She had to get to the window…

"You say yes to me," he commanded from above her. "You say I will love to spread my pretty legs for you. Say it, cunt."

"Please—"

He kicked her hard in the hip and she grunted in pain. "I didn't hear you."

"No—"

She tried to curl into a protective ball but he kicked her again. "Bitch said mess you up if I have to. Do I have to?" He grabbed her by the hair and pulled her up. "Do I have to mess up that pretty face?"

"No!" She grabbed the arm holding her hair and kicked out, connecting with his groin. He grunted and loosened his grip just enough for her pull away and run the last few yards to the window. She flung out her arm and smashed the glass as hard as she could.

"Fucking bitch!" he shrieked as the high decibel alarm pierced the night.

Chapter Thirteen

Gabe was halfway to Lindsay's house when the call came in over the scanner. Without hesitating he called in his location, stuck a siren on top of his Honda, did a U-turn in the middle of the road and raced back in the opposite direction.

"What happened?" Jeremy asked.

Gabe swallowed. "That address… It's Kate's house." What the hell had happened? "Maybe she accidentally forgot to disarm her alarm."

"Wow, we're going to Aunt Kate's?"

Gabe ran a hand over his head. "Ah, shit, I should've taken you home first. Your mother's going to have my ass." But what if something was really wrong and he got there too late? The hair on the back of his neck was prickling. Bad sign.

"It's okay," Jeremy said. "She'll understand."

Yeah, right. "I'm going to check it out. You stay in the car, you hear me? Do not leave this vehicle under any circumstances."

Jeremy grinned. "Jeez, you're such a cop. I didn't know your car could go this fast."

"Hold on."

He'd been so shaken when he left her house two nights ago that he'd picked up a six-pack of beer and downed four of them before he calmed down. Then he'd spent most of the night going back through the day, over and over. Jeremy's party and their encounter in the sewing room. Scott's call, telling him about the missing money. The scene in the car. Kate's reaction to the FBI's revelations. And the crowning glory, their showdown in the hallway.

She had been pregnant when Steve died. And had lost the baby—on top of losing Steve.

He still didn't know what to make of it all. Sure, she could be lying about the pregnancy, there was no way to prove it now. But her reaction to Steve's words had been real. He'd swear to it. And what if the baby had been his? Was that why Steve had made that phone call? How long had it been since he'd had sex with his wife?

In the wee hours he'd been struck by the staggering amount of harm he'd done to Kate over the years. He had taken advantage of her vulnerability and then shut her out as though she meant no more to him than a one-night stand. He had built a wall around himself and his family after Steve died, and the harder she'd tried to get inside the higher he built the wall. *Jesus,* what kind of hell had he put her through?

Now he had to revisit the whole sordid, tragic mess. His feelings for her, his guilt and hers. It would take more energy than he could afford right now, and there was still the question of her involvement with the plane explosion. Half the time he was convinced it was all bullshit—Kate would never even attempt something like that.

No. If he were honest, that was the way he felt most of the time.

Two minutes later they pulled up a few houses past Kate's. Her house was completely dark, even though her Prius sat in the circular drive. It was barely nine-thirty. Not even the porch light was on. This was not looking good. Gabe reached across Jeremy's lap, unlocked his glove compartment and pulled out his SIG pistol, cuffs and a flashlight.

"Whoa," Jeremy said. "You going to shoot somebody?"

"I hope not." Gabe laid a hand on his son's shoulder and looked hard into his eyes. "Do not leave this car, no matter what."

"I promise," Jeremy said, his expression solemn. "Be careful, Dad."

"Always am, sport."

Gabe hopped out of the car and flicked the lock so no one could get in. Then he ran around the back to the kitchen door… and found it unlocked. *Shit.* Not good. He made a quick call for backup, then made his way slowly through the kitchen and into the dining room, gun held tightly in both hands, listening with his ears and with his gut. His gut told him there was no one lying in wait on the ground floor. Back against the wall, he made his way up the wide steps to the second floor, stopped and listened. Someone was up here. The question was, who?

He entered each bedroom in turn, then spotted the open door at the end of the hall. That had to be the master bedroom. If Kate were here, that's where she'd likely be. He stepped inside and instantly spotted jagged window glass. That was when he heard the rapid breathing. "Police!" he shouted. "Put down your weapon."

"Here."

Her ragged whisper came from the corner of the room, close to the window. "Kate?" he said. "Are you alone?"

"Y-yes."

Gabe stuck his gun into the back of his pants and moved toward her voice, his feet crunching on broken glass. "Are you hurt?"

"Yes," she whispered.

He found her curled in a ball on the floor, her back to the wall. He squatted down. His eyes had finally adjusted to the dark, and he could see that she was naked and bleeding. A potent mix of fury and fear squeezed his chest. "Can I move you?" he asked gently.

"Yes."

He reached out to pick her up but she blocked him with her arm. "My robe," she said.

"Jesus, Kate, this is no time to be modest," he said, but cast his eyes around until he spotted a white robe a few feet away. "It'll have glass in it. Let me help you to the bed, okay? Then I'll find you something to cover yourself."

"Blanket," she whispered.

He pulled the comforter off the bed, noting that it smelled of men's cologne. Her husband's scent? Or someone else's? He held one hand out to her, but she shook her head. That's when he noticed that she was cradling one arm in the other. He pulled out his flashlight and pointed at the arm—and went still when he saw how much blood was on her.

"Oh, Christ," he said. Without waiting for permission he lifted her in his arms and laid her gently on the bed. "There's blood every— Oh, my God, your neck."

"Blanket."

He laid the comforter over her and ran to the bathroom for towels. When he came back in she had rolled to her side, away from him. He laid a hand on her back. Sirens blared in the distance and he knew the cavalry was on the way. Medics. An ambulance. "Turn over and let me see where you're bleeding."

"My arm," she murmured. "And…he kicked me…"

That son of a bitch. Gabe wanted to find the guy who'd

done this and rip his fucking throat out. "Was it just one man, Kate?"

She nodded, and rolled slowly onto her back.

"Did you get a look at him?"

"Dark skin… pretty sure…"

Gabe pulled the comforter down enough to see the gash on her neck—which, thank God, appeared to be a surface cut—and then lower, to the arm she was cradling. It looked badly cut up, but there was no blood spurting. She was making an effort to cover her breasts, but he could see her torso was covered in blood.

"I'm going to find this bastard," he ground out. "The ambulance is almost here, and they're going to take care of you."

She closed her eyes. He hesitated, then pushed bloody strands of hair off her forehead. "Kate? You're going to be okay."

She didn't react, and he could see she was fighting tears.

He ran his flashlight around the room, and what he saw gave him chills. The two walls near the window were streaked with blood, most likely hers. And there was blood on the carpet. He lifted the bottom of the comforter and saw the blood on her feet. There were probably glass shards in them as well.

"Hurry up," he muttered, hearing the sirens up close, then the slamming of car doors. He wished he had his radio on him, but his cell chirped. "We're upstairs in the bedroom. She says the guy ran away. Dark-skinned…" He turned to Kate. "Anything more you can tell me about your attacker?"

"Strong," she whispered. "M-mean."

"I know, honey. I mean, what was he wearing?"

"All black."

"Was he tall? Short?"

"B-big."

"Teenager?"

She shook her head no.

Gabe repeated her answers into the phone even as he heard footsteps pounding up the steps, and saw the glow of flashlights. "The medics will take over, okay?" he said to Kate, and noticed bruises forming on her cheeks. *That motherfucker.* "They'll fix you up."

She raised her gaze for the first time. "Happy?" she whispered.

Yeah, he'd been an asshole all right. "I want to kill the bastard," he said, past the lump forming in his throat. "What does that tell you?"

"You're… a cop." Then she went limp.

The medics rushed into the bedroom. "I think she passed out," Gabe told them. "Or she's in shock. Lacerations on her neck and right arm. Glass in her feet."

His cell phone chirped again and he read the LED. "Fuck," he muttered and flipped it open. "I'm sorry, I know we're late. A call came in from Kate's house, and—"

"Kate's?" Lindsay said. "Are you serious?"

"Yeah. She was attacked. The medics are here now."

"You brought your son to a crime scene?"

Double fuck. "I didn't know it was going to be a goddamn crime scene," he said. "I was close, and I locked the car doors and told him to stay put."

"You irresponsible ass," she said.

Gabe's blood boiled. "Look, you know where she lives. Get in the goddamn car and pick him up, okay? I want to stay and help them catch this fucker."

Lindsay hung up without answering. "Shit." He stepped closer to the bed, where the medics were working on Kate.

The lights came on, which meant the intruder had merely fucked with the circuit breakers rather than cut the wires. Gabe looked over at the corner where he'd found Kate curled up and was sickened again by the blood on the walls and carpet. His gut went cold, and it was tough to swallow. Who the hell would do this to her? And why?

"Rape kit," someone said.

Jesus, no, he thought. *No.*

A stretcher appeared and he stepped aside to let them through. One of the medics spotted Kate lying naked on the bed and murmured, "Holy shit," and Gabe had to force himself not to punch the guy in the face.

"Happy?" she'd asked him.

He had a hell of a lot of repenting to do.

Chapter Fourteen

When Kate woke up she found herself lying on a bed in a strange room that had a pale green-and-white striped curtain all around it. *Where...?* There were machines with bright lights, and her body ached all over. *A hospital.*

She moaned as disjointed memories crashed over her. *The man in her bedroom. The knife. Terror.* He had hurt her, tried to kill her. Tried to… Tears filled her eyes.

"Kate?" The voice was deep and male. Familiar.

Drew?

No, Drew was dead. She moaned again at the pain that realization brought her. Drew was dead. Steve was dead. Maybe she was dead.

"Kate?" the same voice said. "Don't cry, honey."

She turned her head very slowly in the direction of the voice and was startled to see Gabe's face. No, she must be imagining it. She closed her eyes and opened them again. It was still Gabe. He was standing over her looking rumpled and grizzly. He laid the back of his hand on her cheek and stroked. Her vision went watery again, and she sniffled. Gabe? In her hospital room looking like he was worried about her?

"Don't try to talk," he said. "You're going to be all right. Your right arm is pretty badly cut up and bandaged, and your feet…" His Adam's apple bobbed as he swallowed. "You gave us all a scare there for a while, but I guess I deserved to be scared out of my wits." He tried to grin, but didn't quite pull it off.

No. This was all wrong. She must be dreaming.

"Oh, she's awake," a nurse said, entering the room with a tired smile and a white foam cup. "How are you feeling, Mrs. Franklin?"

"Okay," Kate said, her voice raspy, as though it hadn't been used for a long time. What was Gabe saying? That seeing her hurt made him realize he cared about her? No, it couldn't be that, not after the other night. If anything, knowing what had happened with Steven probably made him hate her more.

"Any pain in the arm?"

Kate looked down at her arm and was surprised to find it lying on top of the blankets, crooked at the elbow, heavily bandaged and in a sling. She tried to move it and winced.

"There are twenty-nine stitches in that arm," the nurse said, like it was something to be proud of. "You must have put your arm right through the window."

"The alarm," Kate rasped. "Smashing glass sets it off."

The nurse produced a cold pack wrapped in a bandage. "Hold this to your face with your good hand," she said, and Kate dutifully pressed the pack to her cheek. "That's right. Hold it there as long as you can. The more we do it the more the swelling will go down, and the less colorful your bruises will be."

"Can we give her some water?" Gabe asked.

The nurse picked up the foam cup and held it out to Gabe. "You can rub a small cube of ice over her lips, but she can't drink quite yet. We don't want her vomiting."

Gabe took the cup. The nurse fiddled with the tubes running into Kate's arm through a needle, reset a couple of machines and left the room with instructions to both of them to call her if there was a problem.

Kate raised her eyes to his. Would he actually do what the nurse had suggested? He reached into the cup awkwardly, then took out a small ice cube and gave her a questioning look.

"Would that feel good?" he asked.

"Why?" she whispered.

He swallowed and dropped the cube back in the cup. "Why what?"

"Why are you being nice?"

He looked away, silent. She waited. When he met her gaze again he started to speak, stopped and looked away again. Then he made a show of checking his watch.

She closed her eyes and turned away. Best not to look at him, or talk to him, or get suckered into thinking he cared about her at all. Because the only thing about her he didn't find repulsive was her body. And that just wasn't good enough.

Then it occurred to her. "My statement."

"When you're ready. I want to catch the bastard who did this to you, so as soon as you're up to it."

"Send someone else."

"For what?"

"My statement."

He was silent for a moment. "It's my case, Kate. I was first at the scene. I saw what he did to you. I saw the shape you were in. And I'll never forget it."

She shook her head slowly. "No."

"Look, I'm not going to come on to you," he said. "I'm sorry about the party. And…the other day. I lost control, and I had no right."

She almost smiled at that. Would have, if her heart didn't hurt so badly. "No more, Gabe," she said. "I'm done."

He swallowed hard. "Jeremy sends his love. He asked if he could come and see you, and I told him maybe I'd bring him in when you're feeling better."

So now he was invoking Jeremy's name? What did he want from her? "Jeremy, yes," she said. "You, no."

Damn if he didn't go around to the other side of the bed so she'd have to look at him. "Please," she said.

He squatted so she had to look into those damn gray eyes with their thick black lashes. They were puffy and red. Like he hadn't slept. Having him this close set her heart beating faster, made her mouth go drier than it already was.

"I'm keeping this case," he said. "That's not negotiable. And it would make it a hell of a lot easier if you'd cooperate. Maybe I'd have a chance of finding this creep and making him pay for what he did to you." He glanced at her bandaged arm. "Twenty-nine stitches, plus cuts and bruises on your other arm and legs and feet, a bruised cheek, bruised hip and a slash across your neck that could have gone deeper if he'd meant to kill you."

She squeezed her eyes shut. "He wasn't working alone."

"How do you know?"

"He said *the bitch* said to m-mess me up if he had to." A hot tear escaped down her cheek. It wasn't enough that her husband was dead and had robbed her blind. Or that she might have been responsible for Steve's death. Or that Gabe still had the power to hurt her. Now she'd been attacked and beaten in her own home, and the man—

"What else did he say?"

Her stomach began to pitch, but she forced back bile. "Next time… he'll kill me."

He wiped away her tears with his thumb and she drew back. “No,” she whispered. “No touching.”

“Oh, right,” he said. “Um… I’ll pull up a chair and get my recorder out and we’ll start from the beginning. Okay? Are you comfortable like that?”

No, she wasn’t comfortable. Maybe she’d never be comfortable again. She ached and she was exhausted and she just couldn’t deal with his games anymore.

“Just be a bastard,” she whispered. “So I know what to expect.”

“How about if I decide to be a nice guy?”

Her eyes drifted closed. “So much better…at being a bastard.”

“You were a bad boy, Tyrell,” the voice said.

Tyrell took a swig of beer and wiped his mouth with the back of his hand. In the other he clutched the silver cell phone. “Yeah, well, you knew that when you hired me, bitch.”

“I told you specifically not to hurt her unless you absolutely had to.”

“Define ‘absolutely had to.’”

“If I can’t trust you to follow orders I’ll find someone who can.”

“’Sides, she hurt herself, smashing her arm through that window. Wasn’t my fault.”

“You fuck up like this again you’re going back to jail, asshole.”

“I’ll get back in there and find ’em. Don’t you worry ’bout nothing.”

“You didn’t find them?” The voice was shrill and loud. Tyrell held the phone away from his ear.

“I’ll find ’em next time.”

"Goddamn it, you have to get them before the cops get a search warrant for her house, understand? They get a search warrant, they'll take them and you'll never get your money."

"I said I'll take care of it."

"And how do you expect to get in there again, now that you've alerted the police? It was bad enough the FBI's watching, and now you assault her and get the police involved? I should have known better than to hire an ignoramus to do a man's job."

"What the fuck you know about doing a man's job?" Tyrell said. Bitch was pissing him off. "I said I'll get 'em, I'll get 'em. Back the fuck off."

"You'll have to do it differently next time. I'll come up with a plan and be in touch. And Tyrell?"

"Yeah?"

"You ever call me a bitch again, I'll cut your fucking heart out."

Chapter Fifteen

Senator Arlen Fischer rubbed his eyes with the heels of his hands. *Let this be a hallucination.* He pulled his hands away slowly and studied his computer monitor.

Fuck.

It was still there, in all its glory. How had this happened?

God, if you can just keep Nina from finding out I'll never be unfaithful again.

"How could I be so fucking stupid?" he asked himself, and drowned out the obvious answer with a long swallow of scotch on the rocks. Why was this woman doing this? And why now? It had happened months ago. Was she the one setting him up?

The woman on the screen looked like a Playboy Bunny—big tits, blond hair, full lips. Christ, he remembered what it had felt like to be inside her, to run his hands and his mouth all over her body. How could he not, when a full color photo of her sitting on his cock was two feet from his face? He scrolled back down to her message and read it, shaking his head.

Take Mrs. Fischer on a trip far, far away, Senator. Leave tomorrow and don't come back until after the recess. Otherwise, I'll send your wife and constituents one photo for each vote of yours I don't like.

Another swallow of scotch. So, whoever was behind this was trying to stop him from voting on some piece of legislation that was coming up over the next two weeks. He scratched his head. There were all kinds of votes coming up. Which one was she trying to quash?

"Who the hell are you?" he asked the monitor.

He poured himself another scotch, then stood and paced around his office. He'd heard about things like this happening, who hadn't? Was he the only senator being blackmailed like this? What was next? They had the photos. They could take him for all he was worth.

"Fuck," he said, then louder, "Fuck!"

Nina stuck her head inside the door. "What are you swearing about, Arlen? For God's sake, the kids aren't deaf, you know."

"Sorry," he said. When she tried to step inside he moved toward the door, blocking her. "I'm sorry. I'll stop swearing."

Her gaze dropped to the glass in his hand, then back to his face. "Are you all right?"

"I'm fine," he said quickly. Behind them, the picture was still up on his monitor. When had he gotten to be so careless? "Go back to the kids. I'll be out in a few minutes."

"You're acting really weird," she said, frowning. "Did something happen today?"

"No, I'm just stressed out. Really, really stressed out." He wiped the sweat off his upper lip. "I need to get away. Now. Tomorrow. Let's go away, honey. Just the two of us. What do you say?"

She stuck her hands on her hips. "I say you've lost your mind. We can't go anywhere until the recess, you know that."

He set down his glass and grasped her upper arms. "You're not listening," he said, and her eyes widened. "I can't take the stress. I can't wait for the recess. I want to go away right now. Anywhere you want. We can leave in the morning."

"What's gotten into you, Arlen?"

She would have to be difficult. "Read my lips, Nina. I'm. Stressed. Out. Okay? I need to get away. The kids will be happy to get rid of us for a couple of weeks."

Her head snapped back. "A couple of weeks? You'll miss every vote. A lot of people are counting on you to vote against that Global Security bill, or whatever it's called. How can you walk away from that? This isn't like you, Arlen."

The Global Intelligence and Security bill. Is that what this was all about? The implications chilled him. Had he been fucking a *terrorist* that night at the hotel?

No. She had to have been sent from the other side of the aisle. Not a terrorist. That couldn't be it.

Oh, fuck.

What had he done?

Tears filled his eyes, and Nina's mouth dropped open. "Arlen? My God."

He moved his hands to her shoulders and squeezed. "Please," he rasped. "I need to get away."

She stroked his face. "Okay. Okay, I'll… make it work. I'll have to make some calls, and then… Where do you want to go?"

He smiled. What would he do without her? "How about an Alaskan cruise?"

Chapter Sixteen

Kate's front door opened and Gabe was so surprised to see Alison that for a moment he didn't speak. Her silence told him she was equally surprised, but she recovered first and greeted Jeremy.

"We came to see Aunt Kate," Jeremy said, peering around Alison.

"Oh, uh…she's upstairs," Alison said, clearly unsure what she was supposed to do. Her gaze flickered between Gabe and Jeremy, then settled on Jeremy. "Well, come on in little cutie-pie, and I'll go tell her you're here."

Jeremy zipped around Alison and into the house. "I know where her room is," he called back.

Alison blocked the doorway before Gabe could step inside. "She's in the room next to it, but knock first, Jeremy," she called to him, then said to Gabe in a low voice, "She specifically told me she didn't want to see you."

He raised his brows. "Even on police business?"

"You always bring your kid along on police business?"

"I'm officially off duty," he said, tamping down his irritation over having to explain himself. Alison was nothing if not protective. "But Jeremy wanted to come and see Kate, so I figured I could kill two birds with one stone."

"Why can't somebody else do the investigating?" Alison asked, her lips pinched. "Why you?"

"It's my case." He was losing the battle against irritation. "I'm the one who found her lying in blood and broken glass on her bedroom floor. I saw the line of blood on her neck. I saw the cuts on her feet and her legs and her arms, and the bruises on her face and her ribs. There's not another detective on the force that wants this guy as bad as I do."

Alison swallowed, chagrined. Her face had gone pale. "I didn't realize…"

No, of course she hadn't. He looked over her shoulder. "Who else is here? Are your parents here?"

"No," Alison said, not meeting his gaze. He had shaken her. Good.

"Their daughter was nearly killed and they can't be bothered?" Jesus, it galled him the way Kate's parents overlooked her. No matter how hard she tried to please them she never seemed to measure up to her older sisters.

And it'd been a long time since he'd given a damn how they treated her.

"My parents are old and my father isn't well. Not that it's—"

She obviously stopped herself from telling him it was none of his damn business. He wanted to say, *They'd come if it were you or Jennifer,* but instead he said, "When did you get here?"

"I drove down from Philly this morning to pick her up from the hospital."

"Let me in, Alison." His tone made it clear he was not asking her permission. He softened it by adding, "I promise not to upset her."

Alison sighed and stepped aside to let him pass, then closed the door behind him. Jeremy's excited chatter drifted down from upstairs. Kate's responses were subdued. "How is she? Does she have to stay in bed?"

Alison crossed her arms over her chest. She and Kate

were the same height and both had their mother's hazel eyes but that was where the similarities ended. When Gabe and Lindsay split up, Steve had tried to fix him up with Alison, who was closer to his age. Gabe remembered how pleased he'd been that Kate kept insisting they had nothing in common. As though she'd wanted to keep him for herself.

That was months before Steve's death, and he'd had no business being pleased.

"It's better if she does," Alison said. "She gets tired easily. But you know Kate—she does what she wants. I just got her to go up for a nap, but I knew she'd want to see Jeremy."

"How long are you staying?" Gabe asked.

"A few days. Until Kate can do things on her own, like wash her hair. She doesn't like to be dependent on anybody."

Gabe smiled at that, earning him a puzzled frown from Alison.

"I have to say," she began after a moment. "I'm grateful that you found Kate and helped her. I am. But you know, for the past eight years you've treated my sister like a stranger. At *best.* What's with this old friend stuff all of a sudden?"

"Maybe I've seen the error of my ways."

"Uh-huh. Or maybe it's that you have an *in* with the number one suspect in the plane explosion."

Gabe held up both palms to stop her from getting wound up, and to lessen the risk of him losing his temper. "She's the media's choice for number one suspect. Not the cops'. Not the FBI's. And not mine. You want to tell me off, fine, but what do you say we wait until I solve the assault case?"

A burst of laughter from Jeremy distracted Alison, but

then she turned back to Gabe. "You know, Ben and Joy and I were the ones who were there for her when Steve died," she said. "We saw her grief. That was no act. And neither is her grief over Drew. Even though, admittedly, it doesn't run as deep."

Gabe ran a hand over his face. They were getting into acutely uncomfortable territory. "I'm not here to measure her grief, Alison."

She moved a step closer and tilted her head back to meet his gaze. "After Steve died, I also saw how she cried over you, over the way you shut her out. I think the reason she drew into herself had more to do with—"

"Alison?"

Gabe and Alison both looked up at Kate's voice from the second floor balcony. Alison moved quickly to the stairs, but Kate's gaze was trained on Gabe. Even from a distance, he could see the purplish bruising on her cheeks, the slight glaze in her eyes. Wearing only loose boxers and a tank top, and with her bandaged arm in a sling, she looked thinner, more fragile. Her long, dark hair was messy, her lips rosier than usual, as though she were feverish. There were scabs and bruises on her legs. She looked sick and hurt and vulnerable and he wanted nothing more than to take her into his arms and hold her. Why she had this effect on him he simply didn't know, but he was beyond trying to deny it.

"What are you doing out of bed?" Alison asked, as though she were speaking to a child. Gabe remembered Steve saying that Alison's "mothering" grated on him and Kate so much they didn't like to tell her when anything was wrong because her first instinct was to take over. The good news was it probably meant Alison would sense Kate's annoyance and leave sooner rather than later. In spite of her shortcomings, Alison was intensely loyal, and intuitive as hell. As their short but direct conversation had proven.

"It's okay," Kate said. "Do you know if we have the stuff to make macaroni and cheese for Jeremy?"

Gabe moved to the foot of the stairs. From there he could see the death grip Kate had on the banister overlooking the foyer. He started to climb, moving slowly, his eyes never leaving hers. "Jeez, he's hungry again? We had breakfast half an hour ago."

Kate stepped to the side, putting more distance between them. As though she had eyes in the back of her head, Alison moved to block Gabe from continuing his climb. "I'll check," she said to Kate. "But I'm pretty sure we do. If not, I'll pick up whatever we need."

"Don't you have a housekeeper to do that?" Gabe asked.

Alison turned to him, eyes narrowed. "I think we both know she can't afford one anymore. And since she won't be entertaining any time soon, and she has a cleaning lady and me here to help out, why—"

"Alison," Kate said sharply, glancing toward the bedroom where Jeremy was apparently flipping through channels.

"He can't hear me," Alison said.

"Not now, okay?" She took a deep breath and said to Gabe, "Can you leave Jeremy here for the afternoon?"

Her dismissal stung, even though he deserved it. "His mother wants him home at noon. I only brought him by for a short visit. And I was hoping I could ask you a few more questions."

"So you *are* here on police business," Alison said.

"Oh. Right," Kate said. "I guess we can do that now."

"But you're supposed to be resting," Alison said.

"Give me a minute to get dressed."

"Don't do it on my account," Gabe said.

Alison shot him a look, then said to Kate, "You can't even zip your jeans with one hand."

"I won't put on jeans."

Alison brushed by him and stalked down the steps headed for the kitchen. Gabe took a step up, then another, watching Kate's throat work. She flushed. Before he reached the top of the stairs she'd nipped into the room next to the master bedroom, grabbed some clothes off a chair and gone into the bathroom.

Jeremy lay back on several large pillows, sneakers on the puffy ice blue comforter, pointing the remote at a huge TV screen. Kate obviously hadn't bugged him about taking off his shoes—no doubt one of many reasons he loved spending time with her. Gabe sat on the edge of the bed to wait, absurdly relieved this wasn't the bed Kate had shared with her late husband—the one he had placed her bloody, beaten body on four days ago.

She came in about five minutes later wearing white drawstring pants and a man's white dress shirt that hung to midthigh, draped over her shoulders, long sleeves hanging. Jeremy spotted her. "Aunt Kate? Can we plug in the game cube in here?"

Her smile was warm. "If you can do it yourself. Miss Gimpo can't hook anything up right now."

"My dad knows how."

Kate held on to her smile but when she turned to Gabe it didn't reach her eyes. "Okay, great."

"Your mom wants you home in an hour," Gabe said to Jeremy.

Jeremy's face fell and he flopped his arm onto the bed. "Can't you call her and tell her Aunt Kate really, really wants me to stay and keep her company?"

"Are you supposed to be doing something special with her today?" Kate asked.

"No. She's pissed at my dad for not dropping me off before we came here that night the guy hurt you."

Gabe got to his feet when the blood drained from Kate's face. He reached out to wrap an arm around her, but she flinched away before he could touch her. "Kate—"

"I don't… I, um…" she stuttered, obviously shaken, whether by the memory of the attack or by Gabe's nearness he wasn't sure. To Jeremy she said, "I don't want to get your mom upset."

"But you want me to stay and keep you company, right?"

Her smile was back. "I always want that, Dopey."

Jeremy grinned hugely. "Miss Gimpo."

She was still too pale, and Gabe took her arm and led her back to the bed. She pulled away as soon as she reached it, as though his touch burned her. When she was settled onto the pillows beside Jeremy, Gabe said, "The questions can wait. Just relax and I'll get you some tea. Do you still drink it with honey and milk?"

Jeremy dropped the remote and bounded off the bed. "I'll make her tea! I know exactly how she likes it. Right, Aunt Kate?"

"Oh, yeah. You make the best tea I've ever had."

"In your whole life?"

She laid her hand over her heart. "In my whole pitiful, gimpy existence."

Jeremy laughed, a spontaneous, bubbly sound full of innocence and delight and love that raised a lump in Gabe's throat. Then he raced from the room, leaving Gabe alone with Kate. He sat down on the edge of the bed about three feet from her, staring at the doorway Jeremy had just flown through.

"Still icing those bruises?" he asked

"Yeah, when I remember."

"He really loves you," he said. After a few seconds he glanced at Kate, who was staring down at her lap. "And it's obvious that you love him."

She nodded slowly. "He's the best."

Gabe found it hard to speak. "Even though he's my son, and I've been a bastard to you for so long, you can still love him that much?"

She took a deep breath that looked painful and turned to him. The expression in her eyes spoke of love and hurt and confusion, and the lump in Gabe's throat grew. She said nothing, letting her eyes say it all.

"You—" He caught himself and bit back the words. *You would make a great mother, Kate.* He shook his head.

As though she'd read his mind, she closed her eyes and turned away.

Gabe's phone conversation with Lindsay was more contentious than he'd expected. Not only was she furious that he had brought Jeremy to "that house" where a crime had been committed, he had "set her up" to look like the bad guy by pulling Jeremy away from Kate. Gabe made a crack about Lindsay worrying that she wouldn't get any more money out of Kate—never mentioning that the money appeared to be gone, since that little tidbit was not for public consumption—and Lindsay demanded he get Jeremy home no later than noon or she'd take him to court.

Fat fucking chance.

Jeremy had tears in his eyes when he said goodbye. Kate stroked his face and kissed his forehead with a sad smile that reminded Gabe of how he felt when he dropped Jeremy off at Lindsay's. Gabe watched the glide of her fingers over the boy's skin, the familiar way she cradled his head and held him to her, and wished it were *his* skin and *his* head, *his* arms wrapped around her slim waist.

"I'm going to call your mom and see when I can get you over here for a real visit," Kate promised.

"I'm planning to take some time off to spend with Jeremy before he goes back to school," Gabe said without realizing until that moment that he was actually going to do it. He met Kate's wary gaze.

Jeremy's face lit up. "Really, Dad? So maybe we could do stuff together, the three of us?" He raised his face to Kate. "Wouldn't that be cool?"

Kate didn't even glance at Gabe. "Of course it would," she said carefully. "But I'm sure your dad wants to spend time just the two of you."

"I'm in charge of this case," Gabe said. "So I can't leave the city."

"That's okay," Jeremy said quickly. "We could come over here and go swimming and play video games and pool and air hockey. This place has all kinds of cool stuff in it."

Both Kate and Gabe chuckled at his enthusiasm. "Maybe your dad could drop you off when he's busy," she said.

"But he could come over, too, right?"

Kate wet her lips, a nervous habit Gabe remembered. And one that had always turned him on. Kind of like her breathing, and her walking, and sitting and, God help him, her laughing.

"Sure," she said. "If he has time."

"I'll make time," Gabe said.

* * *

"What was that all about?" Alison asked when Gabe and Jeremy left.

Kate knew by the challenge in her sister's tone that any answer she gave would force her to defend Gabe's presence in her house, and she simply wasn't up to it. Alison meant well, but she was a master at turning any conversation into a battle. "I think I'm going to take that nap now."

"Well, it's about time."

Kate bit her tongue and reminded herself that being a tyrant was Alison's way of showing her love.

"Are you actually going to let him hang around here with Jeremy? Isn't it pretty obvious what he's up to?"

Kate raised a hand to her forehead and headed toward the stairs. "I'm sure he was only saying that to please Jeremy."

"He acts like he's trying to—I don't know—get in your pants or something."

Kate pulled in a breath. "For God's sake, Alison. He hates me." And yeah, he wanted in her pants, but that desire seemed completely disconnected from his feelings about her.

"Exactly," Alison said, as though she'd made her point. "So now all the sudden he's trying to be Mr. Nice Guy? Please. I think he wants to poke around your house and try to find evidence that you were plotting to blow up Drew's plane."

Kate plodded up the steps. God, she was so tired. "Well, he can poke around all he wants, because there's nothing to find."

Alison followed her up. "Yeah, but cops plant evidence all the time, Kate. I certainly wouldn't put it past him."

"He's an honest cop," she said, and immediately regretted it.

"*Honest?* I can't believe you're defending him."

Kate grabbed the banister. "I don't have the energy to fight with you, Ali, okay? So let's agree that Gabe's a prick and not talk about him anymore." She continued up the steps.

"Oh, so now *I'm* fighting with you?" Alison said. "I'm here to help you, but I can't sit around with blinders on when you're defending the guy who—"

"Stop!" Kate felt herself sway. Her head was pounding and all she wanted to do was lie down right where she was and cry. "Please, just stop."

Suddenly Alison's arms were around her, stabilizing her. "Oh, honey, I'm sorry." The anger was gone from Alison's voice. "I didn't mean to get you upset. Come on, let me help you upstairs."

Kate allowed her sister to help her up the steps and into her room. The bedspread was a wreck from Jeremy playing on it, which brought fresh tears to her eyes. If only her baby had lived, Jeremy would have had a playmate. And she would have had what she wanted more than anything in the world. "Remember the night you drove me to the E.R.?" she said, giving in to the impulse.

Alison pulled back the duvet and Kate lay down on the cool sheet. "How could I forget? That was a terrible night. I still think about it sometimes."

"Thank you for staying with me that night," Kate said, squeezing her sister's hand.

"What made you think of that suddenly?" Alison asked, studying her. Was there a hint of suspicion in her voice?

Kate closed her eyes. "I was just wondering what it would have been like, you know, if the baby had lived."

The bed sagged next to her hip. "You never told Drew?"

Kate shook her head. "No. I never told anyone. Did you?"

Alison let out a long breath. "I told Jennifer, much later. We were talking about you, and wondering why you and Drew never had kids. But that's it, I swear."

Kate nodded. "Okay."

They were silent so long Kate nearly dozed. Then Alison said, "Kate?" and the question in her tone told Kate it would be safer to feign sleep. Finally she left the room, but Kate could feel her watching, wondering. Alison was nothing if not intuitive.

Maybe she wanted Alison to know, wanted to share the truth of what had happened with someone who would love her anyway. Someone besides Gabe.

Alison's whisper tingled up her spine. "I get it now, Katie." Then the door closed, and Kate felt a little less alone.

Chapter Seventeen

At eleven o'clock the following morning Gabe pulled into Kate's circular driveway and parked behind a blue Volvo wagon with Pennsylvania plates. Alison's car. He glanced into the backseat as he made his way up the walk to the front door and was surprised to see a suitcase lying there.

He rang the bell once, waited for several seconds, then rang it again. From somewhere inside Bruno was barking his head off, but no one came to the door. He rang again. Still no answer. He lifted the heavy brass knocker just as someone pulled the door open, and found himself face to face with Alison. They stared at each other, and the look in her eyes said she found him seriously lacking. Neither said a word, and Alison didn't move aside to let him in. So he crossed his arms over his chest and waited.

"All set?" Kate's voice came from somewhere behind Alison, but still, neither moved. Alison was the first to fold.

"Don't think for a minute that I don't know what you're up to," she said, her voice low and angry. "Kate may have blinders on but I don't. And if you hurt her, or use her again, or make her the fall guy for something she didn't do, I swear to God, Gabe, I'll find a way to make you pay."

He knew better than to respond directly. "I take it you're leaving?"

"My husband came down with the flu, and Kate insisted I go take care of him. God forbid anyone should put her first."

"No one ever has," he said. Steve hadn't put Kate first

either, something Gabe seemed to have forgotten for the past eight years.

Alison tilted her head to one side and studied him. “No, they sure haven't.”

“Who's at the door?” Kate appeared in the foyer, eyes widening when she spotted Gabe. “Oh.”

“I have some questions for you,” he said. “If you're up to it.”

Kate's gaze moved back and forth between him and Alison, who still hadn't moved or taken her eyes off Gabe. “Sure,” she said slowly. “As soon as Ali's on the road.”

“I'm out of here,” Alison said. She turned and embraced Kate quickly, then pushed past Gabe to her car. Kate's brow was furrowed as she watched her sister climb into the driver's seat and pull away without a sideways glance.

“She doesn't trust me,” Gabe said. Alison's parting shot had thrown him. *“If you use her again.”* Kate claimed she hadn't told Alison about that night. So why did he get the feeling she knew?

Kate stepped aside without looking at him. “Come on in and let's get this over with.”

Damn it, he didn't like her blowing him off, even if he did deserve it. “When do you get the stitches out?”

“A few days.”

“Are you in much pain?”

“Not your concern. Can we get started?”

She was wearing denim shorts and a different tank top—blue this time—with a bra underneath. Her exposed skin was lightly tanned, her waist tinier than he'd ever seen it.

Gabe stepped inside and closed the door behind him. “You look better today. Stronger.” *But too thin,* he wanted to say. He held his tongue.

She still didn't look at him. “Where do you want to start?”

He pulled out a small notebook and pen. "Can we go into the living room or something?"

"Let's go into the sunroom."

He followed her through the foyer past a small mahogany table where a pile of mail sat unopened next to a vase of wilting flowers. Dust had begun to accumulate on the wood. They continued down the corridor beside the staircase, past photographs of Kate and Drew in various exotic locales. His gut clenched. She'd certainly lived the good life with the bastard.

He'd seen the sunroom at the reception and thought it frilly, with its white wicker furniture and flowered cushions. Now, with the ceiling fan turning slowly overhead and an alluring scent in the air he found it pleasant and relaxing. He noticed a laptop sitting open on a table.

"I bet you spend a lot of time in here," he said.

Kate half reclined against a pile of pillows on the couch. "I do now," she said, and smiled in a way that sent a spark of jealousy through him. Christ, where had that come from?

He sat down in the chair nearest to her and was pleased that she didn't move away. He laid his forearms on his thighs and leaned toward her. That was when he noticed the circles under her eyes, and the slight wince when she shifted her hurt arm.

"You're tired," he said. "And in pain. Maybe this isn't a good time. You need rest."

"I'm fine. Let's get this over with."

"Tell you what. How about if I make us some tea and then we can talk for a few minutes."

She looked about to protest, then changed her mind and said, "Fine."

He left her and went into the kitchen. When he came

back a few minutes later with the tea her eyes were closed and she was slumped against the pillows, her wounded arm cradled in the other.

"You're not taking the pain pills, are you?" he asked.

She swallowed. "They make me nauseous. And sleepy. I don't want to sleep."

"Why not?"

"I just don't."

"You've gotten the locks changed, right?"

"Yes. Alison took care of it."

"Who else do you know had the old key to the house?"

Her eyes flickered open, and he saw the pain in them. Damn stubborn woman. "Violetta," she said. "My cleaning lady."

"Whoever attacked you didn't have to force their way in here," Gabe said.

"How do you know?"

"The CSI team checked every possible way someone could have gotten in and found nothing. Apparently the guy waltzed in, turned off the alarm, threw the breakers that control the lights and walked around freely. He left by the back door, but probably came in the front."

"Other people may have keys," she said. "I don't know who Drew gave them to. Maybe Joy has one." She swallowed again. "They spent a lot of time together."

Gabe couldn't miss the slight flare of her nostrils, the lowering of her eyes. "Bruno didn't freak out when you were in the tub, did he?" he asked. "When whoever it was came in."

She frowned. "He may have barked a little. I think I fell asleep in the bath."

"But if he was really upset you wouldn't have stayed asleep for long, right?"

She hugged herself with her good arm. "No, I wouldn't have."

"With Alison gone, who's going to spend the night with you?"

"I wish you wouldn't do that thing where you jump from topic to topic like you do with suspects." She paused. "Then again, that's what I am, right? A suspect."

"Not officially, and not in this case," he said. "This is about finding the bastard who attacked you. And you didn't answer my question."

"I'll be fine. Whoever came in last time won't try it again."

He moved to the sofa and leaned in, knowing it made her nervous but wanting to make his point. "Listen to me carefully, Kate," he began. "You're hurt, you're weak, you're vulnerable, and the guy who did this to you said next time he was going to kill you."

She closed her eyes and shuddered. "There's a patrol car in the neighborhood, right?"

"Not good enough," he said.

"You're saying the police presence is meaningless?"

"I'm saying you're a sitting duck for a clever burglar or rapist or whatever he was. If he didn't find whatever he was looking for, he'll be back."

"He could have been looking for valuables."

"True. Which is why the police went through the house that night, but they said there were no obvious signs of disturbance. I assume you checked your jewelry?"

She nodded. "It's all there."

"Electronics?"

"Um… Well, that was really Drew's department. I checked his study, but the only things I know for sure are missing are some of his books."

"What kinds of books?"

"His rare books collection. *Don Quixote, David Copperfield, Divine Comedy.*"

"Are they worth money?" Gabe asked.

She shrugged. "Probably, but I have no idea how much. I also don't know how long they've been missing, so it may mean nothing."

"After you rest a little while we'll go to the study and check it out." He stood. "Who can come and spend the night with you? Or better yet, where can you go to spend the night?"

She shook her head. "I don't want to stay in a hotel."

"Don't you have a friend you could call?"

"Sure, but I don't want to."

"Why not?" he asked, although a part of him was relieved that at least there wasn't a man she'd like to call.

She pressed her lips together and sighed. "Because I don't want to be around people, okay? I don't want to answer their questions, or be comforted by them, or controlled by them. I even had trouble dealing with Alison, and she's my sister."

"Then I'll stay."

Kate went still. The silence was broken only by the shushing of the ceiling fan. "No," she said finally. "You won't."

"I'll bring Jeremy along."

"Oh, right, I'm sure Lindsay would go along with that in a heartbeat."

"I won't mention it. Jeremy's going to be spending the next couple of weeks with me, and where we spend the night is none of her damn business."

She hugged herself tighter. "No. I won't do this with you, Gabe. I told you that. I can't deal with your schizy behavior."

"I won't touch you." Now, that was a bald-faced lie. It was impossible for him not to touch her.

"What I don't understand is why, after all these years, have you decided you can't keep your hands off me?"

He ran a hand through his hair, suddenly irritated. "I can keep my hands off you," he said, sounding prickly even to his own ears. "I'm not touching you now, am I?"

She ignored him. "And now that you know what…really happened that night, you're still acting like you want to…" She swallowed. "Why else would you offer to spend the night at my house? It doesn't make sense unless it's about *that.* And by the way, you're not staying."

He leaned closer. "About what happened…what you said to Steve that night—"

She held up a hand, her eyes suddenly moist and rimmed in red. "I told you," she said in a hoarse whisper. "You were right, at least about me upsetting him. But you were wrong about—"

"I know you didn't say it to hurt him," he said quickly. "I accept that." *And I was wrong to hold you accountable, when I was guiltier than you.* Somehow, he couldn't get the words out. "I've been a prick to you for a long time. You won't get any argument from me about that."

She drew back and stared at him. "What's this? That sounded like a real apology."

"It's a start."

Chapter Eighteen

Joe Marshall kissed his baby daughter's fuzzy head and grabbed his car keys. "Be back in twenty minutes," he said to his wife, Sydney. "Anything besides formula?"

Sidney's mouth twisted as she pretended to think. "Well, you could pick up some chocolate ice cream. If you don't mind me being fat a little longer."

He smiled back. "Honey, I adore your body. And I'd be happy to demonstrate exactly how much once the baby's down for the night."

"Mmm…that chocolate ice cream could get me in the mood, Senator."

"You got it."

Sidney frowned. "I still don't get where all that formula went. It's so weird, Joe."

"Honey—"

"Seriously. Are there baby formula thieves around here or what? Maybe a homeless person who slipped into the garage?"

Yeah, right. "I don't think there are a lot of homeless people in Oakton, Virginia. Maybe a homeless raccoon, though." Or a spaced-out new mother who was positive she had another case of baby formula in the garage.

"Cute."

He winked. "Be right back."

Joe hopped in his Mazda, which was perched at the top of a long driveway that wound downhill through the woods. Oakton had its share of big houses and yards, and a country feel that made you forget you were a stone's throw from the nation's capital, but it sure was a car-dependent lifestyle. Which was why he'd opted for a sports car. If he had to be in a car to get everywhere, he may as well enjoy it.

The third time he stepped on the brakes he realized they were gone. *Fuck. Time to downshift.*

Except his clutch was gone too.

He hit the trees at around forty miles an hour.

Chapter Nineteen

"Relax now," Archer said. "Drift off if you want. I'll get my stuff together slowly and make you some of my special herb tea before I leave. How does that sound?"

"Mmm."

Kate's body felt weightless. Archer had set up a separate stand beside the massage table with a pillow for her hurt arm, and he'd taken great pains to make her completely comfortable. With her arm still aching and her hip and legs sore, his treatment had focused on stimulating her skin and teaching her to breathe properly for maximum relaxation and healing. He had covered the padded table with warm blankets and alternated hot and cold packs on the sore areas of her body.

He treated her like a queen. No one had ever been so solicitous of her needs. And yet he wasn't her husband or her boyfriend—just a friend of a friend who liked her and wanted to help. He'd refused payment of any kind, insisting that his massages and treatments gave him at least as much pleasure as they gave her.

She must have drifted off, because suddenly Bruno was barking and she heard two male voices at the door. Still, she didn't move. Archer would take care of everything.

"Mrs. Franklin is unavailable right now," the man said.

After the initial shock of coming face-to-face with a guy

who looked like a centerfold for *Soldier of Fortune* magazine, Gabe held up his creds. "I'm here on police business."

The man was dressed in lightweight black drawstring pants and a black shirt that showed off his solid physique. A glance downward told him the guy was barefooted. Something ugly and violent slithered through Gabe's gut.

Deep brown eyes regarded him coolly. "She's resting. Detective."

"Well, I'll be sure not to disturb her for very long," Gabe said. "And who exactly are you?"

"A friend."

Gabe was about five seconds from shoving the guy aside. "Well, if you're Mrs. Franklin's friend you'll let her know I'm here. Now."

Amusement lit the other man's eyes. "Really."

Fuck. The guy was going to force his hand. Gabe took a step forward…and the guy stepped aside.

He turned toward the rear of the house and Gabe followed him into the sunroom, stopping when he spotted Kate lying on a raised table, covered only by a large towel across her middle. Her head was on a small pillow and a foam wedge raised her knees. Her bandaged arm rested partially on a pillow with her hand on her belly.

"Kate," the man said quietly, laying a possessive hand on her bare shoulder. "There's a detective here to see you."

"Hmm?"

Gabe watched in horror as she smiled up at the other man and covered his hand with hers.

"A… Who?"

"It's me," Gabe said coldly. "Sorry for disturbing your nap, but this can't wait."

She propped herself up on her good arm, causing the towel to slide down a few inches. Her hair was tied up in a loose knot on her head, her eyelids half closed. It had been three days since he'd last seen her, and the bruising on her face was much less noticeable.

He'd missed her, damn it.

Kate shared a quick look with the other man, then turned back to Gabe. "What are you doing here?"

"I need to talk to you," he said. "Alone."

"Oh." She turned back to her *friend.* "I'm sorry, Archer, I guess..."

Archer stepped behind her and helped move her into a sitting position. Gabe fisted his hands in his pockets and took a couple of deep breaths to help him hold it together.

"How do you feel?" Archer asked

Her smile was dazzling. "Wonderful. I can't believe what you did to me." Then she slid off the table and secured the towel at her breasts.

"I hope the effects last," Archer said with a glance toward Gabe. "At least for a while."

Gabe was struggling not to drag her away from the bastard then kick his ass for doing whatever it was he had done to her that had left her looking so goddamn happy and satisfied.

To Gabe she said, "I guess I'll, uh...get some clothes on."

"You do that," he said.

His eyes followed her out of the sunroom and then he turned to Archer, who was calmly placing small bottles in a wooden box, folding sheets and towels and shoving pieces of foam into a large tote bag. "What are you, her masseur?"

"Masseur, aromatherapist, friend," Archer said. "Kate has been deeply traumatized, and she needs someone to focus on her emotional and mental well-being."

"And that's what you're doing?"

Archer looked at him, amusement still dancing in his dark eyes. "I think you could use a massage, Detective. You're strung as tight as a violin."

"How long have you been hanging around her?" Gabe asked.

"Long enough to know what she needs."

The two men stared each other down. Gabe's jaw hurt from clenching his teeth. "And how did her dearly departed husband feel about her having a friend who knew what she needed?"

Archer's smile tightened. "He didn't give a flying fuck about what she needed or wanted."

"Sounds like you knew him pretty well."

"No," Archer said. "I doubt anyone knew Drew Franklin well."

"All set?" Kate asked from the doorway. She was barefooted, dressed in white drawstring pants and a loose, flowy top.

Archer collapsed the massage table and hoisted it under his arm, then grabbed the tote with the other. "All set," he said.

"I'll walk you out."

Gabe slumped on the wicker couch and blew out a breath. Goddamn it. Who was this guy, and what was he to Kate? Not that it was any of his business, but it irritated the crap out of him to show up at her house and find another man there. And what the hell was he doing being jealous, anyway?

The Lab, Bruno, shuffled over and lay down at Gabe's feet. He bent down and rubbed his neck until Kate reappeared several minutes later. She sat in a wicker rocker across from Gabe and said, "What's up?"

He didn't mean to blurt it out, but somehow the words were in his mouth and he couldn't hold them back. "So did you hook up with this guy before or after your husband died?"

She stared at him for a moment, then narrowed her eyes. "Don't even start."

"It's a relevant question."

"Relevant to what?"

"To the investigation."

"That's not what you came to talk to me about, because you had no idea Archer would be here. So why don't we get to the police business and not go to the other place."

"Fine." He threw the newspaper he'd been carrying inside his jacket on the wicker table so the front page faced Kate. A bold headline read Senator Joe Marshall Paralyzed in Car Crash.

Kate's eyes widened. "Oh, my God. Joe Marshall… He's a great guy." She turned to Gabe. "I've met his wife. They… She just had a baby."

"Marshall's the second Democratic senator who's been killed or disabled since the plane crash, which killed four Republican congressmen."

Kate sat back in the chair, stunned. Gabe frowned, knowing he'd upset her, but at the same time hoping the truth was sinking in. "There's something going on," he said. "And it's bad."

She closed her eyes, laid her head back against the cushion and rocked gently in the chair. He left her alone and watched her, like he used to, marveling at how beautiful she was even now when she was too pale and too thin. But it had always been more than her beauty that drew him to Kate. More than her talent, or her intelligence, or even her sense of humor. He'd always been able to relax around her. To talk to her about anything, knowing she would listen without judging or repeating what he'd said to another soul. How could he ever have—

"It doesn't make sense," she said, and leaned forward. The movement brought him out of his reverie. "Is there any evidence that terrorists are behind these latest deaths? I've been laid up, after all, so it couldn't have been *me*."

Gabe ignored the sarcasm and clasped his hands between his knees. "The FBI and the MPD are looking for a connection between Marshall's accident, Senator D'Argento's murder and the plane explosion."

"What does this have to do with me?" Kate asked. "I mean, it's awful and disturbing, but there's got to be more, or you wouldn't have come here."

"I'm worried about your safety," he said, and began ticking things off on his fingers. "Four Republican congressmen. Two Democratic senators—so far—and we just learned that Senator Fischer has suddenly bowed out to take a long cruise."

"Are you serious? Arlen Fischer? I can't believe he would leave before this vote. He's come out so strongly against the bill all along. I wonder what happened?"

Gabe shrugged. "No one knows or no one's talking. And in the midst of all this, someone breaks in here and attacks you with no obvious intent. I don't like it."

Kate wrapped her good arm around her middle and leaned back into the cushions, her expression somber. "It doesn't make sense. I'm not an elected official. I have no control over the vote. And besides, who would target both sides of the fence, assuming this all has to do with the Global Intel bill? Which is awfully close to passing in the House, thanks to Joy. Maybe it's all about something else."

"Like what?"

She tugged a lock of hair forward and twirled it around

and around her finger. Just like she used to when she watched TV with him and Steve, or played cards at the lake with Joy and Ben, or talked on the phone or just sat staring into space... Like she was now.

"You still do that," he said quietly.

She stopped twirling, and a tiny flush colored her cheekbones. "You know," she said. "Those three senators did have some things in common with Drew and the others on the plane."

"Such as?"

"Well, for one thing, they're all fiscally conservative, and they all voted against additional funding for endangered species."

Gabe snorted. "So, maybe some rabid environmental group knocked them off?"

"Why not?" she said, a little indignant. "Is it any less likely that Greenpeace did it than that *I* did it?"

Gabe couldn't miss the hurt in her eyes. He'd known her for thirteen years, even though they'd barely interacted for the last eight. But he'd spent a hell of a lot of time with her in the early days, and there was no way he would have believed then that she was capable of hurting a fly. It was only after he'd made love to her that he'd—

"If nothing had happened between us, would you still have wondered if I'd deliberately driven Steve to—" She stopped short and swallowed. "—crash his car?"

Gabe stared at her. "You a mind reader now?"

She shrugged and looked away, but the flush in her cheeks remained. "If you want I can look into their voting records," she said. "See if I can find anything that ties all those people together." She glanced at him. "But then again, I'm sure the FBI and the police would prefer to do that themselves, in case I decide to fudge the facts. I don't know what I was thinking."

Gabe rose from his chair, lifted the ottoman and set it down right in front of her. He sat so their knees nearly touched. She was giving off a delicious scent, no doubt from whatever was in the massage oil. He wished he'd been the one rubbing it into her skin. He forced himself to stop that thought before he started imagining Archer's hands on her body.

Kate inched away, keeping her torso half turned away from him. Her body language was telling him loud and clear to back off, but he couldn't. Still, he refrained from touching her. "There's something else," he said.

She turned and shot him a look over her shoulder. "What?"

"Mancuso called me this morning."

That got her to shift forward. "What did he want?"

"He told me the NTSB investigators have determined conclusively that the explosion came from inside the cabin, as opposed to one of the engines, or something that had been fastened on the outside of the plane."

Kate stared at him without blinking. "So, you're saying someone planted explosives inside the plane before it took off?"

"Or carried it on board with them."

She sat back against the cushions. They were silent while each of them thought about what that meant. "Do they know what it was?"

"They're still running tests, but it was probably PETN."

"Oh, right. The stuff the shoe bomber used, and that Christmas Day incident way back when." She turned to him, frowning. "But the passengers all went through security."

"I know."

"They didn't have to, to board a private jet," Kate said.

"They probably did it to make a point about Global Intelligence and Security."

Something about that statement niggled at Gabe, but he couldn't put his finger on it. "So if it wasn't already onboard, then someone either deliberately or inadvertently smuggled in an undetectable explosive."

"Deliberately?" Kate sounded incredulous. "That would make the person a suicide bomber."

Gabe nodded. "Well, one of the things we're looking at is whether someone on that flight was suicidal or some kind of psychopath, including possibly a political radical."

Kate held his gaze. "Or, as the media has convinced everyone in America, it could've been someone with a shitload of money who wanted to eliminate someone on the plane."

In that moment, looking into hazel eyes that held determination, pain and sincerity, Gabe was certain she was innocent. It also occurred to him that some of the pain he saw there was likely physical.

"When was the last time you took something for the pain?" he asked.

She looked momentarily startled at the non sequitur. "I had some Advil about… I don't know. Maybe…maybe this morning."

"Maybe, huh?" He rose. "Where are they?"

She sighed. "In the cupboard next to the refrigerator. I would have taken them but I couldn't get the top off."

Gabe went to the kitchen and returned with a glass of water and four brown pills, which he held out to her. "So you haven't actually taken anything since your sister left."

She took the pills and reached for the glass. Gabe watched her drink it down without stopping.

"You're dehydrated," he said. "When was the last time you ate or drank?"

She closed her eyes. "Don't hassle me, Gabe, okay?"

"You've got a ton of leftovers in the fridge."

"Alison left me well stocked. You should see the freezer."

"So why haven't you been eating?"

"Too much work," she said.

"Jesus." He went back to the kitchen and dug through a bunch of plastic containers, some of which smelled so damn good his stomach growled.

"When was the last time *you* ate or drank?" Kate asked from behind him. He turned and saw a tiny glint of amusement in her eyes.

He smiled. "Was it that loud?"

She sidled up to him and bent down. "Michael Clark dropped off some salads and Italian soda from Balducci's this morning. Let's bring over these containers and a couple of forks."

Wow. She was inviting him to sit down and eat with her. He pointed to the table with a stern expression. "You go sit your boney little butt in a chair and I'll take care of it."

She gave him a mock salute. "Yes, sir, commandant."

He pulled down plates and glasses, found the forks and carried it all to the table, then pulled out the Balducci's containers from the fridge. Kate poured herself a tall glass of grapefruit soda and took a long swallow, then put it down with a little shiver. "Bitter."

"It's grapefruit, what do you expect?"

She started filling her plate and he followed suit. After a few generous forkfuls she said, "God, I'm starved."

They didn't talk much while they ate, and Gabe managed to contain his satisfaction at getting her to take some pain pills and eat. She was letting him take care of her, as though he were still the trusted friend and brother who had helped her out when she and Steve both had the flu. Or the guy who'd brought them pizza and beer when their car was in the shop. It soothed something in his soul.

But, greedy soul, it wasn't enough.

When they were both full, he cleared away the plates and put the food in the refrigerator. Kate slumped in her chair, eyes closed.

"Tired?" he asked.

"Food coma. I think I need a nap." She yawned and ran her good hand through her snarled hair. "Yuck."

"Have you been able to take a bath or shower since your sister left?"

She made a silly show of sniffing her armpits, like she would have all those years ago when they'd been close. He couldn't have imagined her doing that even as recently as an hour ago. Some barrier had come down between them, and he was unreasonably pleased about it.

"Why?" she asked, getting to her feet. "Do I smell?"

"Seriously," he said. "Do you need help with that?"

Chapter Twenty

Electricity arced between them, leaving their gazes locked. Kate couldn't take a breath for several seconds as the image of Gabe joining her in the shower filled her mind, overwhelming her senses. Moisture pooled between her thighs, and her nipples tingled. She couldn't speak.

"I mean," he said after they'd stood there too long like that, "do you want me to run you a bath, or wash your hair in the sink or something?"

She couldn't keep her gaze from traveling down his body to the bulge in his jeans, but then she quickly shifted back to his face. He looked as though he hadn't shaved that morning, and a tuft of dark hair stuck out at the side of his head. Almost as though he'd just rolled out of bed and come over. "Um…what?"

He shoved his hands in his pockets and started toward her, slowly, like a predator. She shivered, but didn't move away. "Do you put a plastic bag over your arm?" he asked without taking his eyes off hers. He wasn't looking anywhere near her arm. "I can fix you up, and then get the water started, or…" He stopped about a foot away from her and rested his hip against a chair.

She closed her eyes for a moment, and when she opened them it felt like her lids hadn't made it all the way up. *Damn it.* "I can run a bath myself," she said. "Washing my hair is a problem, though. I kind of do it one-handed."

Gabe scooped her hair into his hand, then pulled it all over one shoulder. "Let me wash it for you," he said quietly.

Her heart was pounding too fast. "How?"

"However you want." His pupils were huge in spite of the light pouring into the kitchen. "Wherever you want."

It was hard to swallow. "In the kitchen sink."

"Okay," he said. "I'll go up and get your shampoo and whatever else you need."

She told him exactly what to bring down, then lowered herself to a chair to wait. Oh, God, she was being an idiot, letting him touch her. *Damn, damn, damn.* Gabe had to know it was a mistake. Maybe he would change his mind once he got upstairs and had gathered her things together. He was famous for changing his mind where she was concerned. If only she didn't want him so bad. If only her body wasn't screaming for him. Hadn't screamed for him for the past eight years.

Maybe they should just do it and get it out of their systems.

The one time they'd had sex Gabe had been overcome with guilt so strong he'd never recovered from it.

She had never recovered, either, but not from the guilt. From him. From Gabe. She'd been in love with him, and he'd turned away from her with a finality she still couldn't comprehend. All that was left of the passion they'd felt for each other was lust. Pure and simple. And that wasn't enough to risk going through it again.

When he touched her head she jerked away. "What happened while I was upstairs?" he asked, his voice rough.

She glanced up at him, then quickly away. "I don't think this is a good idea after all," she said. "I'll get Violetta to help me. She comes in a couple of days to clean."

"You can't stand having dirty hair," he said. "It depresses you. I can't remember how many times you told me that."

"A long time ago. My moods aren't so volatile anymore."

"Oh, no? So, how do you explain why five minutes ago you wanted me to—"

"Hah!" she said, the anger welling up inside her. "Talk about volatile. Who's the master at changing his mind?"

"I'm just trying to help."

"You're just trying to—" She stopped before saying it.

He held her gaze for several moments, then set down the towels and hair products and folded his arms over his chest. "I promise not to do anything remotely sexual," he said. "I will wash your hair while you're fully dressed, and when I'm done I'll comb it out for you. That's all." He raised three fingers. "Scout's honor."

"You got kicked out of Boy Scouts." But her anger was fading as quickly as it had risen.

"Not until after I learned the pledge." He was grinning, and it was impossible to resist him when he looked like that. Which was exactly the problem.

"Fine," she said, and went to the sink, which was remarkably clean. "Did you put all those cups and stuff in the dishwasher?"

"Yes," he said. "Do you want me to put the towel around your shoulders or what?"

"Okay, but throw it on quickly. Don't...linger."

He did as she asked, then turned on the tap and adjusted the temperature. She bent her head forward and felt Gabe's big hand on the back of her neck, positioning her so he could wet all of her hair. His body was close. Too close. He was slightly behind her and to her left side, and his heat saturated through her clothes. His arm brushed her back and neck repeatedly as he gently tugged on her hair in an attempt to get it thoroughly wet.

When he began to massage shampoo into her hair and scalp she nearly groaned. "You okay bent over like that?" he asked.

She grunted and he kept it up. After a couple of minutes of sweet torture she said, "That's probably enough. You can rinse now."

"Yes, ma'am." He held her head in his hands while he moved it from side to side. Rivulets of water ran down the back of her neck, but rather than feeling uncomfortable it made her feel…sensual. "Conditioner? Or do you want a second wash?"

She lifted her good hand and ran small clumps of hair between two fingers to make sure it squeaked. It did. "Okay, conditioner."

He massaged the thick, aromatic stuff into her hair. "Smells good," he said. "Like watermelon and lemons."

The smell, of course, was nothing compared to the feel of his hands on her head, his right arm resting on her neck and upper back. "That's probably enough," she said, her voice hoarse. He rinsed her hair for a long time, rubbing to make sure all the conditioner was out and that it still squeaked. Finally he was finished. He turned off the tap, squeezed her hair between his hands and wrapped a second towel around it.

"Better?" he asked.

She lifted her head and grabbed the end of the towel to mop her face. It felt like heaven to have clean hair. "Yes," she said. "Thanks for the help."

He smiled. "Anytime. Why don't I run a bath for you, and then you can feel good all over?"

"That's a great idea." Okay, she was handing over control, but was she really going to pass up a bath just to prove how independent she was? "It's been a couple days."

Gabe went up ahead of her and got the bath started. She grabbed a plastic newspaper sleeve from a cupboard and followed him, amazed at how much lighter she felt. Was that from having a clean head, or was it something more?

Remember, he changes like the wind.

No, she wouldn't forget. But damn it, when Gabe sent a gentle breeze her way it was so easy to block out the gales that had come before.

She waited in her bedroom—the one she'd been using since the attack—while Gabe messed around with the water temperature. The smell emanating from the adjoining bathroom told her he'd poured in lavender bubble bath. When he stepped out she was sitting on the bed, waiting.

"Can I help you get that sling off?" he asked.

"Oh." His offer surprised her. "No, I can get it."

"What about the bag? Can you manage all that?"

"Yes. The hardest thing will be keeping this towel on my head."

"Well, get undressed and I'll wrap it up good and tight."

She stared at him, but his expression was unreadable. "I think you got that backward."

"How are you going to get that little shirt off over a turban? Go put on a bathrobe and then I'll wrap your hair up."

"I have a better idea," she said. *Read: a safer idea.* "Maybe you could just help me comb out my hair and—"

"—stick it up in a ponytail." He finished her sentence for her. They used to be able to do that, once upon a time. "Yeah, where's a comb?"

She got off the bed and went to sit at an oak dressing table, which held a mirror and hair and face products. Gabe came behind her and went to work with the comb, starting at the ends of her hair and moving up, making sure all the snarls were out before he moved on. Kate was mesmerized by their reflection in the mirror. Big, tan hands holding sections of her hair, working at it gently. And slowly. He didn't seem to be in any rush, and neither was she.

When all the snarls were out, Gabe proceeded to comb through her hair from root to end, over and over, holding the damp mass in one hand while he pulled the comb through with the other. Kate tipped her head to the side, exposing her throat, unable to look away from the protruding bit of Gabe's anatomy directly behind her head. Her hand was trembling when she reached for a hair tie on the dressing table and held it out to him.

He gathered her hair up and wrapped the band around a couple times to hold the ponytail in place, then brushed the length of her neck with the tips of his fingers and brought his hands to rest on her shoulders. She shivered and he tightened his hold, then began gently kneading her muscles. She closed her eyes and let her head drop forward, giving him access, telling him without words that she wanted his hands on her, that she didn't want him to stop touching her.

He slid his hands inside the loose armholes of her thin top so he was massaging her skin. The proximity of his hands to her breasts sent lust spearing through her, straight to her already moist pussy. The expression "putty in his hands" popped into her head and pretty well described the increasingly boneless sensation in her limbs. Oh, God, how did he do this to her?

Without warning he grabbed the hem of her shirt and slid it up over her head. Her arms rose as though by some otherworldly force, and it was gone. She stared at herself in the mirror, sitting there in a plunging, black lacy bra, her chest heaving in arousal, Gabe's hands moving sensuously up and down her arms. A moan escaped her lips and she knew she was lost.

"Stand up," he said, his voice rough with desire. She stood and he turned her toward the full-length mirror on the back of the bedroom door. Her breath hitched at the sight of them—Gabe huge behind her, hands first on her arms then wrapped around her middle. They both watched as he tugged at the drawstring on her loose pants and they slid to the floor. She stood there, wearing only a sheer bra and panties, while Gabe was fully dressed in jeans and a black T-shirt.

"You're so beautiful, Kate," he whispered into her hair as he ran his hands over her belly and tightened them on her waist. His breathing sounded labored, as though he were struggling to control himself. But she didn't want his control. She wanted his passion, wanted his hands and mouth all over her. When he unclasped her bra and let it slide down her arms she leaned into him completely, hands clutching his arms, desperate to feel his hands on her naked breasts.

"Even with these," he said, running his fingers gently over the myriad thin scabs on her back. "And this." He bent down and placed a tender kiss on her bruised ribs that made her writhe with desire. "I'd like to kill the guy who did this to you."

He lifted his head and blew out a breath, followed by a muttered curse. "Into the bath," he said, and nudged her forward. "Oh, wait." He disengaged long enough to grab the plastic sleeve off the bed and pull it over her bandaged arm. He stuck a hair tie around the top to keep it in place, then gave her a little shove forward and followed her into the bathroom.

The water in the claw-foot tub was still running, so Kate bent down to shut off the tap. When she stood, Gabe was right behind her, his hard body pressed against her back, hands clutching her shoulders. They were inches from her breasts, but he made no move to touch her there. He moved his hands to her waist, and slid them slowly down over her hips, the caress so tender, so erotic, she gasped his name. He caught the elastic of her panties and lowered them, his hands staying to the sides of her thighs. His breath was coming as fast and shallow as hers, but he continued his slow trail down until the panties slid to the floor.

"Jesus Christ," he rasped as his hands began the trip back up her thighs to her hips and stopped. His fingers were so long the tips curled around to the sensitive spot close to the apex of her thighs. His face was close to her ear, his hot breath on her cheek, warming her neck and chest. Her nipples were so hard they ached. He was breathing open-mouthed, pushing bursts of air through in a way that told her in no uncertain terms that he was intensely aroused and on the edge of control.

"Gabe," she moaned, rising on tiptoes and rubbing her ass into his rock hard erection. Her limbs felt tingly, her head light.

He lowered his head and kissed the curve of her neck, and she was sure he would ease the death grip his hands had on her hips, but instead he backed away. "Get in the tub," he said in that husky voice. "Don't turn around."

"But—"

"Do it, Kate."

It took more willpower than she knew she had to step into that tub without turning to him. But if she turned around now—naked—they would make love until neither of them could stand up, and God knew where it would end. That knowledge had to be scaring the hell out of Gabe.

Holding her plastic-wrapped arm out to her side, she lowered herself into the steaming water, which covered her breasts completely. The scent of lavender added to the sensual fog that was rapidly overtaking her senses. But when she turned to see Gabe leaving the room, a frisson of panic penetrated.

"Gabe?" He stopped, his back to her. "You won't leave, will you? While I'm in here?"

"No," he said. "I won't leave."

She closed her eyes and lay back against the tub. It felt like she was sliding into a warm, delicious dream. Her mouth had trouble forming her next words. "Are you going to go back to hating me again…because of this?"

He braced his arm against the doorframe. "I'm done hating you," he said, and closed the door behind him.

Chapter Twenty-One

Gabe went to the French doors in the bedroom, flung one open and stepped out onto the balcony overlooking the swimming pool. He gripped the cast-iron rail and let his head fall forward. His groin throbbed, his pulse was racing and he struggled to get his breathing under control. How he had found the strength to walk away from her he would never know. Now the trick would be to stay out of that bathroom, knowing Kate was aroused and willing. And gloriously naked.

He shut his eyes and groaned, unable to get the image of her body, the feel of her skin out of his mind. Maybe if he hadn't pushed her panties down and felt the softness of her thighs and belly he wouldn't be suffering like this. What had possessed him to undress her? She'd been leery of letting him help her precisely because she didn't want to make herself vulnerable to him, physically or any other way.

She didn't know he was afraid for the same reason.

He shook his head, then raked his hands through his hair. He had to get this outrageous desire for her under control, which meant not doing stupid things like washing her hair and fucking *undressing* her. What the hell had he been thinking?

She's still a suspect in the bombing, even if you don't believe she did it.

He took in a huge breath, let it out and stepped back into

the room. While she was in the tub was a perfect time to look around the house. Yeah, what his lieutenant had asked him to do wasn't exactly ethical, legal or not, but people poked around their friends' houses all the time. Did that mean he qualified as Kate's friend?

As he made his way downstairs to Drew's study, he tried to think back to a time when he had thought of Kate as just a friend. He opened the study door and flipped the wall switch, then gazed around at the dominion of Kate's late husband.

A pain more insidious than jealousy speared into his gut when he remembered his reaction to the news that his sister-in-law was involved with a colleague of Joy Stuart's six months after Steve's death. Gabe brought his hand to his solar plexus and tried to rub it away. Christ, he didn't have time for this.

"Goddamn it," he said aloud. He should get out. *Now.* It wouldn't be hard. His lieutenant already suspected that he couldn't be objective, and had considered assigning another detective to the case. He could detach himself from Kate's life and move on.

Right.

He was in too deep.

He'd spent a lot of years lying to himself, telling himself it was Kate's fault Steve was dead, telling himself the fact that she had married someone else less than a year later was proof that she had wanted Steve dead so she'd have the millions to herself. But he knew it was all bullshit.

No. He deceived himself all those years because when Kate married Drew Franklin she had cut Gabe to the quick.

Never mind that he'd turned away from her months before Steve died—suddenly becoming too busy—when the truth was he couldn't stand to see the two of them together. After Steve's death his feelings had vacillated between numbness and self-loathing. Even as he had frozen her out, he'd wanted her, wanted to grab hold of her and let her heal him, bury himself inside of her and hide from the aching loss and guilt. But no sooner had he figured it all out than Joy had informed him Kate was in love with Drew Franklin and would probably marry him.

In his rage and humiliation, Gabe had created a reason to despise her that had nothing to do with hurt or jealousy. And the more he convinced himself that it was Kate's fault Steve had died, sparing himself the crushing burden of guilt, the more he poisoned his family toward her.

Except Jeremy.

Gabe lowered himself to the chair behind Drew's desk, leaned back and closed his eyes. Kate's love for her godson had never wavered, nor Jeremy's for her. The bond between those two fascinated him. It bordered on mother/son, or even brother/sister.

With an effort, he moved his fingers to the keyboard of the computer sitting in front of him. The screensaver was the U.S. Capitol. Figured. Kate's was probably a woodland scene, or a beach. Maybe a polar bear, or seal cubs. Some endangered species or other. He punched a couple of random keys and wasn't surprised when he was asked for a password. Only a moron would go off on a business trip and leave his computer unguarded.

His lieutenant had "suggested" he look through Kate's computer files. If Kate had records of some conspiracy, it was extremely unlikely that she would keep them on her husband's computer. Which meant he had to spend some time with her laptop. Jeremy said they emailed back and forth all the time. From this computer or the laptop?

Could a woman who loved a child as much as Kate loved Jeremy be guilty of conspiracy to murder her husband?

No way.

He took his time trying a variety of passwords Mancuso had suggested with no expectation of success. Drew's date of birth, both parents' first names, his city of birth, college, and so on. It was amazing how many people used simple passwords so they wouldn't forget. That's something Kate would do, he thought. So he tried her maiden name, Callahan, her birth date, Bruno…

It was Bruno's whining that finally drew his attention away. When he glanced at his watch and realized an hour had passed, he jumped up.

Was Kate still in the tub?

He took the steps two at a time and went into her bedroom, where Bruno sat before the bathroom door whimpering. "Kate?" he called through the door.

No answer.

"Kate?" he called louder. "You still in the tub?"

When she still didn't answer he opened the door. She was slumped in the tub, head lolled to one side. His heart stopped. Was she just asleep or unconscious? He rushed to her side and moved her head so she faced him. Her skin was cool, but her lips were rosy and she was still breathing. Christ, he was getting paranoid.

"Kate," he said. "Wake up, honey."

She didn't respond or open her eyes. The arm wrapped in the plastic sleeve had slid into the tub, which meant he probably needed to change the dressing. Damn, he hoped getting her stitches wet wouldn't slow down the healing.

He reached in and pulled the plug. The bath water was barely tepid. He grabbed a large, peach-colored bath towel and waited for the water level to drop so he could lift her out into it and wrap her up. The glimpses of her body through the haze of bubbles made him hard—when the water sank below her breasts, leaving frothy trails, his cock began to throb. Soon he could see all of her, the dark curls between her legs frosted with small white bubbles.

He eased her body forward, then wrapped the towel around her back and lifted her out of the tub. Her eyes fluttered briefly, but she didn't wake up. He smiled and carried her out of the bathroom and laid her gently on the bed, then wrapped the towel around her. He grabbed another towel off the rack and dried off her arms and legs, lifted her again and eased the bedclothes back.

Still holding her, he sat on the edge of the bed and inhaled her scent. She had to be exhausted to be so sound asleep. If he didn't know better he'd think she'd given in and taken a pain pill after all. She was normally a light sleeper, no matter how tired she was. Or at least she used to be.

Her body was warming now that she was dry, but he had to get the damp towel off her. He eased it off her and sucked in a breath at the sight of her plump round breasts. His lips ached to taste them. He shifted her around and set her down on the sheet, then pulled the towel away. As though she missed his warmth she curled toward him. He still had to deal with her arm. The bandage wasn't soaking wet, but it needed to be changed.

He got what he needed from the bathroom and set to work unraveling the damp bandage, drying off her arm with a small towel and rewrapping it. All the while he was aware of the softness and heat of her body, and imagined his mouth on her breasts, his tongue in her pussy, making her scream and cry out his name. God, how he wanted that.

It wasn't until he was finished that he realized she was watching him through narrowed slits. "You fell asleep in the tub," he said, his voice raspy. "Your bandage got wet so I changed it."

She nodded once before her eyes closed again. He reached out and stroked her hair and felt her shudder beneath his touch. All he had to do was pull off his clothes and slide between the sheets with her. He could hold her while she slept, and make slow, gentle love to her when she woke up. He could rid himself of all the tension and frustration and pent-up lust he'd been carrying around since the moment he first touched her again. And she wanted him. It wasn't like he'd be taking advantage of her.

As he sat there stroking her hair he heard a soft snore. She had fallen back asleep. Huh. He blew out a breath, tucked the bedclothes around her and left the room.

There was a knock on the door and Tyrell cursed and swung the telescope away from the balcony of the Franklin house. If he had his way he would slit the old lady's throat and get her the fuck out of his life. This undercover shit was for the birds. He could never be a cop. Fucking cops weren't supposed to hurt anybody. He liked to hurt people. He liked it a lot. But he had to admit that posing as an undercover detective to keep an eye on Kate Franklin was fucking brilliant. Just the right mix of truth and fantasy.

Old people were so fucking gullible.

"Detective?" the voice trilled through the attic door. "Would you like some coffee cake? It's fresh out of the oven. I could bring it up with some coffee."

"Sure," he called back, careful to keep the scorn from his voice. "That would be nice. Just, uh…leave it outside the door."

"Oh, of course," she said in that conspiratorial tone he was coming to hate. He had no patience for sweet old ladies. Any old ladies, for that matter, but sweet ones—ugh. 'Course, her rich bitch neighbor wouldn't think she was so sweet if she knew the old lady was helping him spy on her.

He touched the long cut on his cheek where the Franklin bitch had cut him with glass, and swung the telescope back toward the bedroom. She had to be out of it by now. He bet her pussy tasted like fucking honey. When he got his hands on her he was gonna take everything he didn't get last time. And take it and take it and take it—before he messed her up permanently. He wondered if the cop was fucking her while she slept.

"You wait till he leaves, cunt," he promised.

Chapter Twenty-Two

Gabe was heading back up to check on Kate when her doorbell rang. Ben Stuart stood on the stoop. "Jeez, do you have another facial expression besides a frown?" Gabe asked, moving aside to let the other man in.

Ben's frown deepened. "Why are you here? And where's Kate?"

"She's napping." Gabe glanced up at the second floor balcony. "Very deeply. I'm going up to check on her again."

"For a second there you almost looked worried about her," Ben said. "She's probably exhausted. Or depressed. Grieving people sleep a lot. And you still haven't—"

Gabe was climbing the steps. "Kate doesn't sleep that hard. She crashed in the bathtub and I had a hell of a time waking her up." He paused and fear curled in his gut. "She didn't wake up all the way, come to think of it."

Ben was right on his heels. "What the hell's going on, Gabe? If you're taking advantage of her I swear to God, I'll—"

Gabe spun on him. "What? You'll what? Kick my ass?"

Ben's jaw tightened. "If I have to."

For a long moment they stared each other down. "I'm not taking advantage of her," Gabe said finally, although it galled him to answer to another man. "We have unfinished police business."

They went into Kate's bedroom and Gabe flipped on the light. She didn't as much as flinch. "See what I mean?"

Gabe said. "She's been out like a light since about four o'clock. Did you ever know her to sleep like this?"

Ben approached the bed. "Well, she's on pain medicine, right?"

"Wrong. She refuses to take it. I gave her four Advil when I got here and that's all the pain medicine she'd had since Alison left yesterday."

Ben's sat beside Kate on the edge of the bed, pressed two fingers to her wrist and studied his watch for several seconds. The furrow between his brows deepened, and he lifted one of Kate's eyelids, then the other. "Shit," he said.

"What?"

"Her pupils are dilated." He looked up at Gabe. "Call an ambulance."

Gabe fumbled his cell out of his pocket and made the call, panic tearing at his gut. "Is she in any danger? Shit, I should have called earlier."

"And she's naked," Ben said.

"Well, don't look," Gabe shot back, and pulled a robe out of her closet. "Move and let me put this on her."

"What are you doing with her, you bastard? And don't give me that crap about police business. Last I heard you wouldn't touch her with a ten-foot pole, and now you have exclusive rights to her body? If she were awake what would she say about that?"

"Not now," Gabe ground out. "I'll explain later. But you won't like it."

Ben pressed his lips together. "No, I'm sure I won't. Just tell me you're not setting her up to go to prison."

"She'll go to prison over my dead body," Gabe said. "That good enough to get you off the fucking bed so I can cover her before the medics get here?"

Ben stood and Gabe blocked the other man's view with

his back. Kate's lithe body was like deadweight, and his gut twisted harder. "Shit," he said, when she flopped back. "Jesus Christ, Kate, don't do this to me. Wake up." He turned to Ben in desperation and found the other man coming back from the bathroom with a wet washcloth in his hand. Gabe pulled the front of the robe over her breasts and moved aside so Ben could mop her face with the cold towels.

No response.

"Oh, Jesus Christ." Gabe hadn't felt this helpless since the day Steve was killed. He pulled Kate into a sitting position. Her head lolled forward. "Kate. Wake up, honey. Please. Wake up." He started to shake her, but Ben grabbed his shoulders.

"Stop it," he said quietly. The sirens were getting louder by the second. "They're almost here. There's nothing we can do now except wait."

Gabe pulled Kate onto his lap and held her close, tucking the robe around her so she was decent. Then he raised his eyes to Ben, whose accusatory expression so closely matched what he was feeling inside.

If she didn't make it he would never forgive himself.

Gabe's name was on her lips when she surfaced, but the face peering down at her belonged to Ben. He was frowning, but then his expression cleared and he gave her a gentle smile. "Hey, there," he said. "Welcome back."

She blinked a few times, and turned her head—a mistake because it made her so dizzy. "What happened?" God, her voice sounded hoarse. And why was she in the hospital again?

Another man came up beside Ben, this one older and

heavier but with a kind face. "I'm Doctor Cohen," he said. "How are you feeling, Mrs. Franklin?"

"Um…dizzy." She tried to see past his shoulder but there was a curtain all around.

He pulled out a tiny light and held it up. "Look at my finger," he directed. "That's right." He repeated the exercise over and over with both eyes, and then said, "A Detective Bailey would like to join us while I ask some questions. Is that okay with you?"

Detective Bailey. Not Gabe. Where was Gabe? "Why?" she asked. "What happened?"

The doctor turned to Ben and mumbled something. Ben left and a nurse came in with a blood pressure cuff, followed by the detective. All three crowded around her bed. With the curtain closing them in she was starting to feel claustrophobic.

"Hello again, Mrs. Franklin," the detective said. He was a nice-looking guy with short blond hair, a goatee and unreadable brown eyes. How did cops manage to hide what they were thinking so well? Well, most cops anyway. Gabe had never been any good at it as far as she was concerned. She wanted to ask for him, but something stopped her. Had he been here earlier?

"Why am I here?" she asked, directing her question to the doctor. He and the detective shared a look.

"You were brought in an hour ago, unconscious."

She blinked. "Really?"

The doctor nodded. "Can you tell me what medicines you took over the past 24 hours, Mrs. Franklin?"

"None," she said.

The two men exchanged another glance. "Think back," the detective said. "Did anyone else give you medicine to take? A visitor, maybe?"

She tried to think back, but it was so hard to remember. "I don't think so."

"Did you have any visitors recently?"

"Was...was Gabe here? Earlier?"

The detective's smile didn't reach those unfathomable eyes. "Did Detective Hugo give you any medicine when he was at your house today?"

Gabe was at her house? Her eyes stung, so she closed them for a moment. "Um...I don't remember. What day...?"

"Do you remember anything that happened today?" the doctor asked.

"Not sure. What day is today?"

"It's Friday night. Did anyone come to your house today?"

All she remembered was Gabe pulling her out of the water, holding her in his arms. "I don't know."

"What do you remember, Mrs. Franklin? What was the last thing you remember doing?"

"I was in the water," she said. "And...Gabe pulled me out."

"Was anyone else present when Detective Hugo pulled you out of the water?"

She tried to lift her right hand to her eyes but noticed it was tightly bandaged and in a sling. Images flitted through her mind. Gabe gently touching her cuts... Kissing the bruise on her ribs... Pushing her panties to the floor...

A delicious shudder escaped her.

"Are you all right?" the doctor asked.

"Think, Kate," the detective said as though the doctor hadn't spoken. "You don't mind me calling you Kate, do you?"

"No."

"Was anyone else at your house today, Kate?"

"Today?"

The doctor turned to the detective. "I'm sure you know how to do your job, but I can tell you that her memories at this point aren't reliable. If I'm right about what I believe she has ingested, there's no telling whether they'll ever be."

"Ingested?" she repeated. "What did I ingest?"

"It's possible someone gave you a drug, Mrs. Franklin," the doctor said. "A designer drug similar to rohypnol but slower acting and more potent."

"It's a variation on roofies—the date rape drug," the detective said. "Someone could slip it in your coffee and have close to an hour to get you someplace more private before it really kicked in. And then, once you're out, you stay out longer."

"And remember very little," the doctor added. "It's a diabolical drug. Fortunately, even in high concentrations it's rarely lethal."

She went still, trying to wrap her brain around what he was saying. "Who would do that?"

"That's what we're trying to figure out," the detective said. To the doctor he said, "Look, I get that her memory is unreliable, but I'd like to talk to her for a few minutes alone, if that's okay with you."

The doctor nodded and laid a fatherly hand on Kate's good arm. "I'll be back to check on you shortly. Buzz the nurse if you need anything else."

When he was gone, the detective—what was his name again?—moved closer. He was smiling, but somehow it didn't comfort her.

"How close are you and Gabe, Kate?" he asked.

Close. Were she and Gabe close? "We used to be… close."

"And now?"

"I don't know," she answered honestly. "Sometimes… we're close." *Too close.*

"What do you mean by too close?"

Had she said that out loud? "I'm confused. What's your name again?"

"Scott," he said. "Scott Bailey. Gabe used to be my partner."

"Oh."

"Was there another man at your house today, Kate?"

Another man. "I don't know."

"A neighbor, maybe? Old friend? A colleague of your husband's… Anybody like that?"

An unfamiliar anxiety churned in her gut. Why couldn't she remember? "Was Gabe here earlier?"

Scott Bailey leaned closer. "I know this is a personal question, Kate, but it's important, and I'd like you to answer it if possible. Will you do that?"

She swallowed. "I'll try."

"Did you have sex with someone earlier today?"

She wasn't sure she'd heard him right. "What?"

"Sex. Did you sleep with a man? Gabe, maybe? Or someone else?"

"Gabe," she repeated. Did she have sex with Gabe? She wanted to.

For a moment Scott Bailey looked angry. "You had sex with Gabe, Kate? Is that right?"

She closed her eyes and felt Gabe's lips on her neck, his hands moving down her thighs, dropping her panties to the floor, then pushing her toward the tub… A memory or a dream?

"Kate?"

She opened her eyes. "He helped me take a bath."

Chapter Twenty-Three

Michael Clark appeared in the open doorway of his Dupont Circle town house wearing only pajama pants and looking like a living, breathing ad for Abercrombie & Fitch. He frowned when he saw who it was. "What do you want at this hour, Detective?"

"We need to talk," Gabe said.

A blond young man wearing identical pajama pants came up beside Michael and laid a possessive hand on his arm. He gave Gabe a thorough once-over and said, "What's going on?"

"I have no idea," Michael said, and stepped aside to let Gabe in.

The young man gazed up at Michael. "The guy's a detective, you don't know what he wants and you're letting him in?"

Gabe stepped up to the doorway. "Don't worry," he told the younger man. "He's not my type."

Michael folded his arms over his sculpted chest. "No, your taste runs more for slim, vulnerable brunettes you can bully."

Gabe's temperature rose. "You nearly had me convinced yours did as well, until I saw the two of you together."

"So, what's this about?" the young man asked.

"Police business," Gabe said, his gaze never leaving Michael's.

"I'll deal with this, Tom," Michael said. "Wait upstairs for me, okay? This won't take long."

"Whatever." Tom huffed and left the foyer.

Michael led the way into the living room. He didn't sit or offer Gabe a seat. "You'd better have a good reason for being here, Detective."

"So, where'd you get the Italian soda?" Gabe asked. "Kate said it was a little bitter."

Michael blinked. "It came from Balducci's. Why? You going to arrest me for bringing her grapefruit soda?"

Gabe shrugged, but inside he was seething. He'd tried every angle he could to get a search warrant for Michael's home and car, but the techs had found no trace of Queen of Hearts, better known as Q, in any of the food or drink Michael had brought. It was virtually invisible after a couple of hours, leaving no clear marker in the blood or anywhere else. And even if the slightest residue had been left in the glass, Gabe had run everything through the dishwasher. Only its slightly bitter taste—less detectable in an espresso than in a glass of wine—and the aftereffects of prolonged unconsciousness, very low blood pressure and dilated pupils, indicated its presence.

"Only if our lab finds traces of Q in it." He was bluffing, of course, but Michael might not know it. "In which case I'll very happily arrest your ass—after I kick it from here to St. Louis."

Michael frowned. "What the hell are you talking about?"

Gabe stepped closer and Michael took a step back. "You fucking well know what I'm talking about, you bastard. But here's what I can't figure. You probably didn't give her the Q to fuck her, considering what a hunk Tom is."

"Wait. What?" Michael did a good job feigning surprise. "Are you saying somebody gave Kate Q? Isn't that a date rape drug?"

At least he hadn't pretended not to know what it was. Gabe went on as though the other man hadn't spoken. "So that tells me you just wanted to knock her out, maybe to give you time to look around for something. Want to tell me what that was?"

"You have nothing on me," Michael said. "If you did you would have come here with a search warrant. Is Kate all right?"

"No, she's not," Gabe growled. "She's in the hospital."

"Good Lord." Michael ran a hand through his blond hair. "How bad is she? That stuff's not fatal as far as I know, but—"

"Funny how you know so much about it," Gabe said, taking another menacing step forward. Yeah, he was intimidating the guy, but so far he hadn't laid a hand on him.

So far.

"Well, well," a familiar voice said from the open doorway. "Have I walked into a domestic altercation?"

Gabe turned to the foyer and frowned at Scott Bailey. "Why are you here?"

"Neighbor thought he heard some shouting," he said smoothly. "I'm here to keep the peace."

That was bullshit, but Gabe knew he had to wrap this interview up. To Michael he said, "I'm watching you. Have you got an alibi for the night Kate was attacked in her bedroom?"

Michael had the balls to snort. "You've got to be kidding. Did you go off your meds, Detective?"

"Let's go, Detective Hugo," Scott said, indicating the door. He nodded at Michael. "Sorry to intrude, Mr. Clark."

As they descended the steps Gabe asked, “How’d you know where to find me?”

“Ben Stuart said you were ranting about Michael Clark before you left the hospital.” As soon as they were out of sight of the town house windows, Scott pushed Gabe up against the side of the corner house and got in his face. “What the *fuck* was that all about? And what the *fuck* are you doing with Kate Franklin?”

Gabe shoved him away. “Get out of my face, goddamn it. What’s your problem?”

“My problem? Think again, bro. This is *your* problem. And it’s looking bad.”

“What the hell are you talking about?”

“Wanna know what the lieutenant asked me tonight? Why he sent me to the hospital to interview Kate?”

“He sent you to the hospital?”

“He said, ‘Have you noticed that every time Kate Franklin gets hurt it’s always Hugo who’s on the scene first, and she’s always naked?’”

A sick feeling rose in Gabe’s belly. “Like I’m somehow involved?”

“Everybody knows you hate the woman’s guts,” Scott said. “You think she drove your brother to crash his car so she’d be a rich, young widow.”

Gabe wished he could slip out of his skin and slither away. “The only person I said that to was you, and it was a throwaway comment.”

“Well, don’t look now,” Scott said, “but your ‘throwaway comment’ was picked up by a lot of people. Did you really think you could shoot off your mouth about something like that after a few beers and people would just forget about it?”

Gabe winced. "That would've been a good time to knock my teeth down my throat."

"So now husband number two kicks the bucket and the al Qaeda thing's a hoax. Who tosses out another 'throw-away comment' about liking her for the plane crash?"

Gabe scrubbed a hand over his face. Jesus, he'd made a mess of it. "Tell me the lieu doesn't believe I would actually harm the woman. Go after her with a knife? Slip drugs in her soda so I can… What? Have sex with her?"

"Did you?"

"Did I what?"

"Fuck her." Scott let a couple of beats go by. "Cause she says you did. And that you made her take a bath."

"Kate said I…" He trailed off. If she had Q in her system she would be confused about what had happened, or as much of it as she could remember. "I washed her hair for her in the kitchen sink, and then I ran a bath for her so she'd be clean. She couldn't manage it by herself. I did not have sex with her." Yeah, Bill Clinton had nothing on him in the lying-by-omission department.

"And then you helped her into bed after her bath."

"She was asleep—or I thought she was. I figured she hadn't been getting enough rest, so I lifted her out and put her to bed." And then he'd let her lie there, unconscious, while that shit ate away at her brain. "I didn't freak out until Ben came by and we couldn't wake her up. He checked her pulse and saw that her pupils were dilated."

"Uh-huh. And what were you doing in her house all that time?"

Gabe couldn't tell Scott he'd been searching around, because the lieutenant had been adamant that it stay between them. "Hanging out. I didn't want to leave her alone."

Scott leaned closer and pointed two fingers at his eyes.

"Look at me and tell you haven't been in Kate Franklin's pants. Go ahead."

Irritation pricked at Gabe, even though he understood that Scott was just doing his job. "We've been over this. I said no."

"Ben said you acted like you thought she was dying, and you were freaking out."

"Yeah, well… I was."

"Which tells me either you're involved with the woman or you did harm to the woman. Or both. It tells me you're not objective about her."

"I've never been objective where she's concerned."

"So, I will ask you again. What the hell is going on between you two?"

Gabe tilted his head back, wishing for some divine inspiration. How could he explain what there was between him and Kate in a way Scott would understand and not judge overly harshly? It was several moments before he met Scott's gaze again. "It would take too long to explain it. Let's just say I was an asshole to her for eight years and I'm trying to make amends."

"Making amends, huh?" Scott said with a smirk. Gabe wanted to wipe it off with his fist. "Never heard it called *that* before."

"Drop it," Gabe said. "I know what I'm doing."

Scott shook his head. "She's trouble, Gabe. And from where I'm standing—" he nodded in the direction of Michael Clark's town house, "—your judgment is going down the toilet because of her."

"Thanks. Remind me not to ask you for any testimonials."

"For your next job?"

"Go to hell." Gabe strode across the street to his car.

"So what did you think you were doing, hassling Michael Clark?" Scott called from behind him. "You had no warrant. You had no evidence. And you were intimidating him. He could file a complaint."

Gabe unlocked the Honda and opened the door. "He won't," he said. "He's guilty. What I need to figure out is why he drugged her. He's got to be after something in that house. And if he is, maybe he's behind the attack on Kate."

"You're not thinking straight," Scott said. "If he wanted something of Drew Franklin's why wouldn't he just ask Kate for it? He worked with the guy for like fifteen years. Why would he have to knock her out?"

Gabe slid into the driver's seat but didn't pull the door closed. "I don't know yet. I need to talk it through with her. Maybe she'll have some ideas."

"I guess this means you intend to spend more time with her."

"Better move your hand if you don't want the door slammed on it."

"If it's any consolation," Scott said, his hand still resting on top of the door, "you've got great taste in women. I'd do her myself, as long as I didn't have to marry her."

Gabe slammed the door and peeled away from the curb before he gave into the temptation to ram his fist into Scott's face.

After Tom fell asleep, Michael poured himself a scotch on the rocks and carried it into the darkened living room, where he sipped at it thoughtfully. Gabe Hugo puzzled him. There was something between him and Kate, he'd bet his life on it. Hugo's behavior was more like that of an angry lover than an objective police detective. "I wonder if he realizes it," he mused aloud.

He heard the key twisting in the front door, and a moment later Archer's light tread coming up behind him. He frowned. In the best of times, sharing a town house with Archer was like living with twins, one of which was funny and intelligent and the other brooding, demanding, self-centered. Michael had expected some form of sympathy from his former lover in the aftermath of Drew's death, but Archer's repertoire was limited to repeated attempts to divert his attention, or "cheer him up." Interestingly, if it were Archer who'd died, he imagined Drew's reaction would have been similar.

Michael had loved working with Drew—had actually believed himself in love with Drew for several years, before Kate came along and Drew swooped in and married the poor girl while her head was still spinning with grief. He could be extraordinarily persuasive when he put his mind to it. One of their colleagues had joked that Drew Franklin could persuade a polar bear to buy a condo in Miami. All he had to do was convince the bear that he understood perfectly what he was going through and knew exactly what he needed.

Of course, Drew had never really understood a thing about the needs or desires of others. And he certainly couldn't relate to their pain.

Archer's strong hands worked Michael's neck. Damn it, why couldn't he leave him alone? That part of their relationship was over.

"I need a few minutes alone… To think," Michael said.

"Penny for your thoughts."

"Just wondering what a sweet, intelligent woman like Kate Franklin sees in a cowboy like Gabe Hugo."

"What makes you ask that?"

"He stopped by here earlier to ask me some questions."

"So…Kate and Detective High-Strung are involved romantically?" Archer asked.

"Apparently."

"Well, well," Archer said, warming to the subject. "It's not a surprise, is it? I mean, who wouldn't like all that hard male flesh? I bet he's hung like a stallion."

"Cute," Michael said. He should be beyond jealousy with Archer, but some habits died hard. He eased his neck out from between Archer's hands and went back to sipping his drink.

Archer dropped into a wing chair beside him. "What did he want?"

"Well, I dropped off the food this morning, like you suggested," Michael said. "And then, I don't know, something happened to Kate and now he thinks I spiked the Italian soda with Q."

Archer dismissed that bit of information with that incredibly annoying little wave of his hand, the one he used whenever the problem was Michael's and not his own. "That's bullshit. Q doesn't leave any trace. And besides, if anybody did spike her soda it was probably him. He was the last one with her."

"How did you know that?"

"Know what?"

"That Hugo was the last person with her?"

"He showed up right before I left her house today."

"You massaged her today?" Michael asked. "I didn't know." Then why hadn't he brought over the food himself? He released a long breath. This was exactly the kind of thing that had destroyed their sexual relationship. Archer's need for secrecy made intimacy impossible. Most of what he hid were little things. The times he'd come home late and made up an excuse about where he'd been, when he'd really only gone to a movie. Clicking off screens on his laptop the second Michael walked into the room. Text messages he said were from his mother, when Michael knew damn well he was lying. Thank goodness they'd been able to part amicably.

"You got the soda at Balducci's, right?" he asked Archer now.

"Hmm? Yeah, I think so. Either that or Trader Joe's. Is she okay?"

A frisson of unease tickled Michael's brain. "How can you not remember where you got it? You bought it—"

"I bought the salads this morning," Archer said. "I got the soda a while back."

Michael frowned. "I never saw it. Where was it?"

"Why are you giving me the third degree about a bottle of grapefruit soda, for God's sake?"

Michael set his glass down, then rubbed at his eyes to keep from exploding. How many times had they had stupid arguments just like this one? Well, they weren't partners any longer, they were roommates, and he wasn't going to get sucked back into that unhealthy dynamic. Finally, he stood. "Good night."

"You didn't tell me about Kate," Archer said. "Is she okay?"

"She's in the hospital, that's all I know."

"Seriously?"

"Yes." Michael walked around the coffee table to avoid getting too close. Upstairs a warm, easygoing, uncomplicated government accountant lay asleep in his bed. He didn't even glance at Archer, didn't want to remember what it was like when they'd shared a bed, all the passion and the heat and…the darkness. There was a darkness in Archer that alternately frightened him and thrilled him.

As Michael passed him, Archer grasped his hand. "Michael."

No. Michael knew that tone, felt its power all the way to his groin. No, he wouldn't give in. Not again. Tom was a nice guy, a considerate lover, maybe he could be something more. He wouldn't get caught in Archer's web.

"I think you need me tonight." That deep voice promised hot mouths and deep, hard penetration. Exquisite pain.

"That's where you're wrong," Michael said, but his voice was already husky with desire. It was too late and they both knew it.

Chapter Twenty-Four

Gabe collected Kate from the hospital under close scrutiny from the staff. The nurse asked her repeatedly, as though she were a moron, whether she was certain she wanted to leave with him. It was clear by the matron's body language and glowering looks that she considered Gabe no better than Jack the Ripper. Kate seemed oblivious of the innuendo, and was relieved to see him. The smile she gave him when he stepped into her room was bright and hopeful. She believed in him. She was happy to see him.

Gabe's gut performed some complex acrobatics when she turned that trusting face to him. He identified guilt, and regret, and a healthy dose of fear. What if he let her down again? But enveloping all the other feelings was a powerful surge of honest-to-God joy. He was doing what he should have done all those years ago—supporting her. Granted, when Steve died his guilt and grief had rendered him virtually unable to support anyone beyond his mother, and her just barely. But he had cut Kate off as though she were a stranger, which, he now understood, had compounded her grief over Steve's death.

When Gabe got her down to the lobby in the requisite wheelchair, Jeremy jumped up from the couch in the lobby and ran over to her. Gabe turned to Kate as Jeremy approached and saw the sparkle in her eyes. *She could be his mother,* he thought, *she loves him so much.*

Had she been pregnant with his brother or sister?

"Let me push her!" Jeremy said, and elbowed Gabe out of the way.

They were nearly to the door when Ben walked into the lobby. He shot Gabe a curious glance, smiled at Jeremy and bent down to kiss Kate on the cheek. Then he held out a hand to her good one and helped her out of the wheelchair. Gabe felt a sharp stab of jealousy at the look in the other man's eyes when he held her in his arms. Ben figured his wife had been screwing Drew Franklin, which was likely the death knell for their marriage. Over the years they'd been friends Gabe had often wondered whether Ben felt the same desire for Kate he felt. Joy was an attractive woman, true, but she had never been as effortlessly kind and down-to-earth as her friend.

"Oh, I'll be fine," Kate said in response to something Ben had said too quietly for Gabe to hear.

"Dad and I will take good care of her, Uncle Ben," Jeremy said. "Dad's going to help me make macaroni and cheese for her. Hey, you want to come over and have some too?"

Ben shot Gabe another look, a darker one this time, and said, "That's not a bad idea. I can't remember the last time I had homemade mac and cheese. If it's okay with Kate."

"Of course it is," she said.

Ben followed Gabe back to the house, and ran to open Kate's door before Gabe or Jeremy could get to it. Then he took her arm and walked her inside, chatting quietly with her. Something hard and ugly was growing in Gabe's gut and he didn't like it one bit.

"Do you need a nap?" Ben asked her when they got inside.

Kate turned to Jeremy and smiled. "Not when I've got some time with this guy," she said, then turned her gaze to Gabe and held it, letting him know he was included in that last statement. "I can sleep later. And besides, I feel fine now."

Jeremy tugged at Gabe's arm. "Let's go make the food, Dad, I'm starving."

Gabe didn't want to leave Kate alone with Ben. She must have realized it, because she said, "Yeah, let me go get the ingredients," and preceded them into the kitchen. Jeremy was right on her heels. Gabe started to follow but Ben put a hand on his arm.

"A word?" he said.

Gabe looked at the hand and said quietly, "Sure, when you take your fucking hand off me."

"In the living room," Ben said.

Inside the living room Gabe crossed his arms over his chest and waited for Ben to speak. Ben's expression was as angry as Gabe's was blank. At least he hoped it was.

"I want to know what the hell you're up to," Ben said. "She's hurt, she's vulnerable and she adores Jeremy. If you're playing on that to get close so you can set her up, I swear to God, I will personally make your life a living hell."

"Since when are you a fucking knight in shining armor?" Gabe asked. Ben's gaze slid away for just a moment, enough to show that the comment had rattled him. Interesting.

"This is the perfect entrée into her home," Ben went on as though Gabe hadn't spoken. "Bring Jeremy over, act all solicitous, like you actually give a shit about her, and then move around freely, trying to get the goods on her."

"Are you finished?" Gabe asked, affecting boredom. "Because I've got some mac and cheese to make in the kitchen. Although I'm not sure she has the ingredients for four."

"We saw what she went through after Steve's death,"

Ben said, his anger growing increasingly visible. "That's why Joy introduced her to Drew, to offer her some diversion. We didn't know she was going to fall for him the way she did."

Gabe's jaw clenched involuntarily, and he struggled to keep his cool.

"She spent a lot of time with us because she could talk about Steve. She couldn't spend time around your family, even though she wanted to, because you made it clear she wasn't welcome." Ben stepped closer. Gabe didn't budge. "You were the one subject we learned to avoid around her. After a while she didn't break down when we talked about Steve, but if your name came up, or we talked about a time when you were around she got a look on her face…" He trailed off, then added in a bitter tone, "Steve's death broke her heart, but it was you that destroyed her, you bastard."

Ben left after lunch. He hugged Kate tightly at the door, which made Gabe's gut constrict painfully. He insisted on doing the dishes while Jeremy got into a swimsuit, and then Kate and he sat on opposite sides of the patio, watching Jeremy swim and dive. They clapped and encouraged him, but Gabe had trouble meeting Kate's gaze. Jesus, he'd really done a number on her. If that was the only reason Ben was acting so protective toward her he could deal with it. It was the other possibility that made his skin itch and his chest hurt.

He was so fucking jealous he barely recognized himself.

"Aunt Kate, take pictures of me!"

Kate held up her bandaged arm. "It's hard to do it one-handed, but I guess I could try."

"Dad can do it," Jeremy said, giving Gabe a hopeful look.

"I didn't bring a camera," Gabe said.

"You can use mine," Kate said. "I mean, if you want." Something in her eyes told him she'd picked up on his mood and didn't know what to make of it. When would he ever learn how sensitive she was?

He rose. "Sure. Tell me where it is and I'll go get it."

"It's in my bedroom. The master bedroom. Somewhere." She started to rise. "I'll have to look for it."

"If you don't mind me looking around, I can try to find it," he said. "If I can't find it then you can come up."

"If you're sure you don't mind," she asked, lowering herself back to the seat.

He went up to the master bedroom, where he'd found her not so many days ago naked and bleeding. The investigation had stalled, officially at least, but he was going to find the bastard that hurt her if it was the last thing he did. He looked around on the dresser, on bookshelves and every other surface, but didn't spot a camera. On impulse he opened the drawers in the nightstand. There was nothing in one, but in the other he found a photograph that sucked the breath right out of him.

It was old, taken when Kate and Steve were still in college, on the Georgetown campus. Steve had his arm around her—but she was looking up at Gabe, who was grinning and making horns over her head with his fingers. The edges were ragged, especially on the right side, where he stood, as though she had gripped that side harder. He sagged, photo in hand, his vision suddenly misty.

He'd been such a fool.

He put the photo back. From outside he could hear splashes and Jeremy's excited calls to Kate. She was laughing, and he wondered how he had gone so many years without hearing that laugh. He went into the huge walk-in closet and saw that Drew's clothes were still there, suits and shirts lined up in straight lines, shoes perfectly even beneath. On the other side were Kate's clothes. He smiled. Her stuff was on hangers, but several items were hanging at odd angles, obviously by an owner who had better things to do with her time than line up her shoes and leave an identical gap between each hanger.

On a shelf against the back wall he spotted a small silver digital camera in a black case, and he picked it up. He tried it and saw that the battery was charged, so he went to the French windows overlooking the pool, opened them and took some shots from that angle. He zoomed in on Kate's face, capturing her expressions, the pride she obviously felt at each of Jeremy's feats. At one point she looked up and spotted him, and he snapped a shot. Then he rejoined them at the pool, but this time he sat beside Kate.

"Wow, I can't believe my camera's in the case," she said. "It drove my husb—" She stopped. "Drew was always bugging me about taking better care of it. But I always felt like a tourist with that thing, slung around my neck."

"You always were a bit, shall we say, free-spirited with your belongings," Gabe said, grinning.

She smiled at him, and lust sucker punched him in the gut. For a moment he stopped breathing and simply gazed at her. She was a little pale, and he knew she had to be tired, but she looked…happy.

"You love having Jeremy here," he said quietly.

It took her a moment to answer. "I love having both of you here."

He swallowed and took some more shots of Jeremy in the pool—and noticed that his son's lips were blue and he was shivering. "Okay, out for a while, sport," he yelled. "You're turning blue."

"Aw, Dad, I'm okay."

"Out."

"One more dive."

"Out."

"Aw."

Kate got up and grabbed a big fluffy beach towel, and wrapped Jeremy in it one-armed as soon as he got out of the pool. The boy leaned into her and she held him close, rubbing his back. She turned to Gabe and her eyes told him something he was afraid to let himself believe.

"Let's look at the pictures," Jeremy said. "Can we download them on your computer, Aunt Kate?"

She held up her arm. "You or your dad will have to do the honors."

"You know how, Dad."

"Which computer?" Gabe asked, rising. All he wanted in that moment was to pull Kate into one of those empty rooms and kiss her senseless. As though she could read his mind she licked her lips.

"The one in the office has a bigger screen than that little PowerBook of yours," Jeremy said.

"Never make fun of my Mac," she warned in a gruff voice that made Jeremy laugh. "We can't use the office computer because I don't know the password."

"Your laptop's right inside," Gabe said, then turned to Jeremy. "But you're wet."

"Oh, that's okay," Kate and Jeremy said at the same time, then laughed. Kate held up her good hand and Jeremy went to slap her a high five but it missed by a mile.

"Don't worry, Dad," Jeremy explained. "I'm supposed to miss."

"Yeah, yeah," Kate said, poking him in the shoulder. "You're blind, admit it."

"Miss Gimpo!"

He'd missed out on so much all these years when Jeremy had been spending quality time with Kate, bonding with her in a way he actually envied. Jeremy loved him—that much he knew—but he and Kate were buddies. Soul mates.

Jeremy ran ahead to the bathroom and Kate touched Gabe's arm. "It's easy to be so relaxed when you're the aunt," she said gently. "I don't have the hard work of parenting. I just get to spoil him and pretend he's mine."

Gabe stared. She had read him so well. He reached out and rubbed his thumb over her cheek, telling her without words not only that he appreciated the gesture but that he wanted to touch her. That she meant something. It was a risk, touching her, knowing she could refuse him. She could pull away, stay clear, not set herself up for his—how did she put it? His schizy stuff. His hot and cold act. She'd lowered her lids slightly and was studying him through those thick lashes of hers.

When Jeremy came dashing around the corner he stopped short and glanced between the two of them. "You're not fighting, are you?" he asked warily.

"No," Gabe said, and dropped his hand reluctantly. It was getting more and more difficult not to touch her. Constantly. "Let's sit down and I'll download these pictures. Got a card reader?"

"There's one in the office," she said, and went to get it.

"There are a shitload of pictures on this card," Gabe said when he'd finished downloading the memory card from Kate's camera. Belatedly he glanced at his son. "I mean, there's a boatload of them."

"Really?" Kate said. "Huh. I thought that one was pretty empty. I downloaded a whole bunch right before…" She trailed off. "But I probably forgot to clear the card. Just open the last bunch. The other stuff is from a charity event. Not too exciting."

"Which charity?" Gabe couldn't resist asking. "Foster Homes for Abandoned Lambs and Piglets?"

Kate grinned and punched him in the arm. "Yeah, go ahead and laugh. And thanks for the idea."

Gabe opened the last couple of dozen shots, and they *oohed* and *aahed* over them, and laughed at some of Jeremy's antics. But it was the close-ups of Kate's beautiful face that hit Gabe the hardest. She was genuinely interested in Jeremy, and that showed through in the range of expressions he had captured. When he got to the one of her looking up at him on the balcony, her eyes clear and direct, he had to clear his throat.

She looked like a woman in love.

"Maybe I skipped some at the beginning," he said, and moved the cursor up. He double-clicked on an icon and was hit between the eyes with a close-up of Drew Franklin's face and bare torso. Kate gasped. The man appeared to be reclining against a pillow wearing a satisfied smile and nothing else.

Gabe closed the laptop. Something hot and dangerous welled up inside his chest. Kate had given him the impression that she and Drew hadn't had a close relationship, that her husband hadn't loved her. The look on the man's face suggested they'd at least had a good sex life. Recently. That knowledge twisted his gut.

"Hey, that's your husband," Jeremy said to Kate, oblivious to the tension in the air. She didn't answer. "Did you know him, Dad?"

"No." His voice was gruff. "Why don't you go see if there's any ice cream?"

"Okay. You want some, Aunt Kate?"

Gabe glanced at Kate, who looked like she'd swallowed her tongue. She shook her head, and Jeremy bounded off to the kitchen.

"Nice shot," he said. "Are there others from the same photo session on this card? Maybe we could go through them together."

"I didn't take that picture," she said quietly. "I don't understand. I can't remember the last time I took a picture of Drew. And I never took one like that."

Gabe raised the screen and the picture zapped him again. "Oh, no? Let's try another one." He closed it and double-clicked on one above it. It was a variation on a theme. This time Drew's eyes were closed but he was smiling like he'd just had great sex. The bastard.

"I really don't want to see these," Kate said.

"Aw, come on," he said, feeling perverse, knowing that each picture was going to make him feel worse, but wanting to make her suffer with him. He double-clicked again, and this one was blurry. Drew was reaching for the camera, one hand covering an erect penis.

"Oh, God," Kate said, and stood up. Her voice sounded scratchy, like she was really upset. "I can't… You go ahead and enjoy them without me, Gabe. Enjoy whatever little head game it is that you're playing." She stalked across the room, her back stiff.

Gabe gritted his teeth. "Well, if you didn't take them, who did?"

Kate lifted her good arm without stopping or turning around. "I don't know," she said. "Ask Joy."

He watched her go, feeling like a louse and an idiot. She was upset, that much was obvious. Could she be faking it? He ran his hand over his head. For crissake, he had to decide whether he trusted her or he didn't. Believed her or thought she was a liar. The guy was dead and he was shoving half-naked photos of him under her nose. Of course she was upset.

"Jesus Christ," he muttered.

"Where'd Aunt Kate go?" Jeremy asked, carrying two huge bowls of chocolate ice cream into the sunroom. "Did you two start fighting again?"

Gabe grabbed one of the bowls and started shoveling the ice cream into his mouth. "This is good. What kind is it?"

Jeremy gave him a look. "Don't you know *anything* about her?"

"Oh, of course. Häagen-Dazs. Jeez, how could I not have known?" He glanced toward the doorway, hoping Kate would come back in. Was she too pissed off to be around him now? "Shit," he said.

"Shit?" Jeremy parroted, grinning. "You think this tastes like shit? Wait till I tell Aunt Kate you think her Häagen-Dazs tastes like shit."

"I think that's enough cussing from you, mister."

"I think that's enough cussing from you, too, Detective," Jeremy shot back.

"Touché." Gabe finished the bowl and put it down, then stood. "Wait here. I'm going to go make sure she's okay."

"I'll go," Jeremy said.

"No. I'll go. I want to talk to her for a minute."

"Do you think she's upstairs crying, cause, you know?" Jeremy nodded at the laptop.

Gabe grabbed the laptop. "I don't know. I'll be right back."

Chapter Twenty-Five

She wasn't surprised to hear the bedroom door open and close behind her. This time she was ready for him.

"Kate?"

She whirled on him. "What is your problem? Why did you act like that about those pictures? What business is it of yours if I have photos of Drew? I was married to the man."

He leaned against the bedpost, the laptop tucked under his arm. "It struck me as inconsistent, that's all."

"And you still haven't made up your mind whether I've been lying or telling the truth. About anything. Have you?" He didn't answer right away, and a familiar ache invaded her chest. She shook her head slowly. "I'm such an idiot. I let myself believe things could be different between us, but they can't."

"Could that be an old memory stick?" he asked, as though she hadn't spoken. "Could you have taken those pictures a while ago?"

She turned away and pressed a hand to her stomach. "No. I never took pictures like that of Drew. Not that it's any—"

"I know, I know, it's none of my business. Why would he have left pictures like that with your camera?"

She felt drained, suddenly, and sat down on the bed facing away from him. "You'll think I'm an idiot, but I don't even know if that's my camera. His was the same as mine. And I don't know what motivated him to do any of the things he did. Unless he hated me so much he hoped I'd find the pictures. He obviously hated me enough to steal all my money."

Gabe came around and stood in front of her, but she didn't look up. "Yeah, about that. It doesn't make a lot of sense, does it? I mean, he was sponsoring a major bill and was up for reelection in November."

She shrugged. "So?"

"So, you were bound to find out about the money eventually."

"Apparently he didn't think I was smart enough to figure it out. I signed anything he stuck in front of my nose, as you pointed out not so long ago."

"Let's say you found the pictures," he went on. "Or you found out about the money. Either one, or both. And you decided to expose him and file for divorce. That could have ruined his chances for reelection."

She rubbed her hands up and down her arms. "No. He wouldn't have seen it that way. Drew believed everything he touched turned to gold. The idea that he might be wrong about something was intolerable to him. If he planned to rip me off, or to use my camera with another woman—" she swallowed with effort, "—it wouldn't occur to him that he might get caught."

"What you're describing is extreme narcissistic behavior."

She nodded. "That's what I think too."

Gabe began pacing around the room. "Still. Let's say he stashed the money in some overseas account or whatever. How would he spend it without anyone knowing about it? That sounds unnecessarily reckless. I mean, he had complete control of your money anyway, so what—"

"He must have been planning to leave me." And here she'd been the one threatening divorce. Surprise, surprise.

"If he left you there would be a financial settlement, and you'd discover the money was gone."

"So what? He made it look like I'm the one who moved it around. He could have claimed I was trying to screw him out of his share." She closed her eyes. "You can't imagine how humiliating it is to realize you didn't know your husband at all. I feel like the biggest loser in the world." As soon as the words left her lips she realized she'd confided something to Gabe she wasn't willing to share with anyone else. Go figure.

"Why did you marry him, Kate?"

She raised her head at the anger beneath his words. "You want the whole story or the bottom line?"

Gabe raked a hand through his hair. He was standing by the antique desk that had once been owned by John Quincy Adams, looking grim. "Give me the bottom line and I'll let you know if I want to hear the whole story."

After all this time he wanted her to explain? "Okay. Bottom line? I was lonely, depressed and…unmoored. My best friend and husband was dead. Drew came along and fell in love with me." She lowered her head. "Or so he said."

"What about you?" Gabe's voice was rough, the question more of a demand. "Did you love him?"

How could she answer that? "It's not that simple," she said quietly.

"How complicated can it be? You either loved him or you didn't."

"Why are you so angry?"

He looked shocked. "I am not angry."

"Well you sure sound angry. Is it because you think I

stopped loving Steve just like that?" She snapped her fingers. "Or that I stopped—" *No. Don't go there.*

"Or that you stopped…?" he prodded.

She hugged herself and turned away from him. "I never stopped loving…anyone. But I was devastated. And Drew made me believe he understood what I was going through, and that he would be there for me." Yeah. He'd known how to play her, all right.

"You had your family," Gabe said.

She met his gaze. "I had Alison. But it was *your* family I needed. I needed to be with people who loved Steve as much as I did. That's why Ben and, well, Joy—" she nearly choked on the name, "—were so important to me. Then."

"My mother was incapable of supporting anyone, including herself. She couldn't talk about Steve. She would have been of no help to you."

Grief and fury tore through her chest. "Did it ever occur to you, or anyone, that I could have been a help to *her?"* She stood, fists clenched. "I loved Steve too. I was grieving too. Having someone else around who felt the same pain would have been a comfort, not a burden."

For a long moment neither of them moved or said a word, and it felt as though her heart would burst open. Finally, she said in little more than a whisper, "I needed you so badly I nearly went crazy when you shut me out."

Gabe looked up at the ceiling and blew out a breath. "What did you want from me?"

"Everything. I wanted everything from you."

"Everything, huh? Well, that's what you got from Drew."

She snorted. "Sure I did."

He lowered his head and met her gaze with a look both angry and despairing. "What are you saying? That you married Drew because I wasn't there for you after Steve died?"

She rubbed her hands up and down her arms. "Don't be dense, Gabe."

He advanced on her, slowly. "How am I being dense?" He stopped less than two feet from her. "Why don't you spell it out for me?"

She couldn't breathe right with him so close, knowing what his touch did to her, wanting to feel his strong arms around her, as she had eight years ago. She was torn between moving forward into his arms and running out of the room as fast as she could. "Jeremy could come in."

He shrugged his broad shoulders. "What did I have to do with you marrying Drew?"

She couldn't look at him. "What does it matter now? It's done—and he's dead."

"I want to know."

"Use your imagination, damn it."

"You wanted sex?"

Okay, now he was pissing her off. She looked up into eyes that were hooded, revealing nothing. "Yes, okay? I wanted sex. I wanted love. Is that what you wanted to hear? I wanted to be loved and made love to. I wanted to be reassured that my life wasn't over at twenty-two."

"So Franklin fit the bill."

God, he was infuriating. She shoved against his chest. "You're not paying attention. I wanted to be loved by *you,* you idiot. *You.* But you refused to talk to me or see me. You cut me off like I was nothing to you. Like we'd never even been friends, never mind lovers."

"Are you guys talking about sex?"

Kate gasped when she heard Jeremy's voice from the doorway. Heat infused her cheeks.

"Oh, Jesus," Gabe said, moving quickly toward the

door. "Who raised you, anyway? Don't you knock when you walk into somebody's bedroom?"

Jeremy's gaze darted back and forth between them. "Wow, you guys had sex?"

"That's enough," Gabe said.

"But Aunt Kate said—"

"It's rude to repeat things you overheard when you weren't supposed to be listening." Gabe took Jeremy by the shoulders and turned him around, then marched him back out the door. "Go downstairs. I'll be right behind you."

"That's what you said before."

To Kate's surprise, Gabe stepped back into the bedroom and closed the door behind him. "We haven't finished this conversation."

She dropped her head into her hands, thoroughly embarrassed. "Oh, I think I've said quite enough."

"I haven't," he said.

When he left the room Gabe's heart was beating double time. She had wanted him, not Franklin. *Holy shit.* All those years, they could have been together…

"Dad? Are you okay?"

Jeremy's voice snapped him out of it. "Yeah, why? What did I miss?"

"I asked you if we're staying here tonight. Cuz if we are I want to sleep in the room with the Nintendo Wii. Then we can play it before we fall asleep and as soon as we get up in the morning."

Hell, yes, they were staying. "If it's okay with Kate, it's okay with me." Of course, after that conversation he wasn't so sure she'd agree. "Go on up and ask her. But Jeremy?"

"Yeah?"

"Don't bring up what you think you heard, okay?"

"I won't," Jeremy said. "But I know saying lovers is about sex."

Jesus, the kid had heard every fucking word. "Let's not talk about it anymore, okay? In fact, it would be best if you forgot you ever heard us talking about that." *And don't tell your mother, for crissake.*

"How? I can't make myself forget stuff."

"Try."

"Whatever."

"What goes on between Kate and me is nobody else's business. You understand that, don't you?"

"Yeah, I guess so."

"Okay, then."

When Jeremy went upstairs to talk to Kate, Gabe sat down and opened the laptop. He double-clicked on the first jpeg icon and pulled up yet another photo of Drew Franklin, this time on a beach, standing by a very blue ocean. There were palm trees in the distance. The next shot was a close-up of his face and chest, followed by several more close-ups. Franklin wasn't looking at the camera, which may have meant he wasn't aware the shots were being taken. Whoever he was with probably used a telephoto lens. Soon Gabe was looking at shots of Franklin's anatomy—his chest, his nipples, his butt outlined in a very small, tight European bathing suit. And yep, sure enough, shots of his package.

"Jesus," Gabe murmured. Did Joy take these? If he were Ben he'd kick her ass out of the house so fast her pretty blond head would spin.

In one series of photos Franklin was dressed in a T-shirt and jeans, walking down the street in what looked like a small beach town. The passersby were mostly darker-skinned, with a few Caucasians thrown in. Franklin was facing the camera in only one photo. The shot was blurry, which suggested it was taken with the same telephoto lens—held too close to the subject—used to get the close-ups on the beach. He appeared to be saying something to the photographer.

Then Gabe spotted the photographer, reflected in the store window. “Holy shit,” he said quietly. What would Joy make of this? And more importantly, how would Kate react?

The photographer was a man.

Chapter Twenty-Six

Ben was lying on his back staring up at the bedroom ceiling when Joy came in the front door. She was making more noise than usual, which meant one of two things—she was pissed off or she was drunk. Since Drew's death and the excitement surrounding the House passage of the Global Intel bill, her drinking had accelerated. Not a good sign. But why should he care? It was only a matter of time before the marriage was officially over. If he had a shred of pride left he would already be gone. Or she would. Yet, here he was, awake in their marriage bed, his throat tight, jaw clenched, angry and hurting and wishing things could have been different.

The destruction of his marriage wasn't the only thing he wished to God he could change. He was in the business of saving lives—he knew how to listen to his gut. How many times had he rejected the safe, conventional, ass-protecting way to treat a patient and gone with his gut instead? Most of the time he was right. So why the hell had he ignored his gut when so much was at stake?

He squeezed his eyes shut. Obsessing over that question would drive him mad.

When Joy began climbing the steps he rolled on to his side. There was no point confronting her about her whereabouts or who she'd been with or how much she'd had to drink. With Joy it was all sarcasm or stony silence these days. She had important things to think about, a lofty mission to accomplish. He almost snorted at that. *Lofty my ass.* The bill she and Franklin had dreamed up had fascist undertones the extreme left-wingers would rant about and the rest of the country wouldn't bother to read or understand. If she and Franklin had adhered to any bit of political so-called wisdom it was that if you were going to lie, make it a good one.

The door opened and Ben clenched his jaw tighter. There was a time when Joy would come in late, slide between the sheets in her business suit and wake him up for sex. He would remove every bit of her clothing piece by piece, kissing and nibbling her in the process so that by the time she was naked she was begging him to fuck her. Is that how she'd been with Drew Franklin?

"Fuck," he murmured,

"I was thinking the same thing myself."

He squeezed his eyes closed at Joy's clever response, angry that he had an erection in spite of himself. "I'll bet you were."

She went into the bathroom and he heard the shower go on. If she thought he was going to fuck her she was wrong. So her boyfriend was dead. Not his problem. Soon she wouldn't be his problem at all.

His mind drifted to Kate Franklin. Lovely, kind, quirky Kate. First she lost Steven, who had alternately adored her and ignored her. Then she ended up marrying a prick who cheated on her, and now she was in some kind of screwed up sexual relationship with Gabe, of all people. That Gabe was attracted to her came as no surprise. Who wouldn't be? Ben had wondered himself what it would be like to make love to her. But after all those years of Gabe treating her like shit, how could she let it happen?

Joy slipped into bed behind him smelling of rose shower

gel and spooned him from behind. She was naked and slightly damp, and the feel of her breasts pressing into his back made his cock harden again instantly. *Damn* her. She ran a hand over his nipple, then squeezed it between her thumb and middle finger. He expelled a sharp breath but forced himself not to turn to her.

Within seconds Joy had rolled over him and positioned her head near his groin. "Damn it, Joy," he said in a harsh whisper as she pulled his cock out of his boxers and closed her hot mouth over it. Then she wrapped her legs around one of his and rubbed her pussy up and down while she sucked him, groaning deep in her throat. *Christ,* he was horny. And he wanted her. He wanted the bitch who'd been with another man.

When he was as close to coming as she was willing to push it, she slid up his body and wrapped her thighs around his neck, then stretched back on the bed, body arched, while he used his lips and tongue to bring her to a screaming orgasm. And then, because he was hurt and pissed off, he rolled her on to her stomach, lifted her ass and took her from behind. Hard. Fast. Balls slapping against her thighs as he thrust. Hands squeezing her breasts as she panted and grunted in some combination of pain and pleasure he had no interest in analyzing.

When he came he ground himself into her, holding her in place while he emptied every drop. He collapsed on top of her for a few minutes while he caught his breath, then rolled off her on to his back. Joy moved into the circle of his arms and draped herself across him. Just like that. As though nothing and no one had ever come between them.

"My God, Ben, that was incredible," she breathed into his ear. "That was best sex I've ever had."

He went still for a moment, then carefully removed her

arms and legs from his body and sat up at the edge of the bed so he wouldn't have to look at her.

"What?" she asked.

"I'm not interested in being compared to your dead lover. Thanks anyway." Christ, he'd been a fool to give in to her.

She came up behind him, but he stood before she could touch him, grabbed his jeans and a shirt off the chair and yanked them on.

"Where are you going?"

"I'm out of here."

"Ben—"

"I'll be back to pick up my things." Then he closed the door behind him, snagged his car keys and headed off into the night.

Chapter Twenty-Seven

"It's me, honey. It's okay. I'm here now. Shh, it's okay."

Kate startled awake to find herself wrapped in strong arms, her cheeks wet with tears, whimpering like a child. In the darkness she recognized Gabe's voice, his distinctive scent, the hardness of his big body. Was this real? She was sure she had gone to bed alone.

"Gabe?"

"Yeah, it's me."

"Is he still here?" she whispered.

"Who, honey?"

"The man…in black. He had a-a knife."

Gabe stroked her hair. "There's no one here but us. You were dreaming, sweetheart, that's all. It was just a dream."

"Are you sure?"

His arms came around her tighter, and he kissed the top of her head. "Yes, I'm sure. God, you're so cold." He pulled the comforter up over both of them. "You must have kicked your covers off. You were sobbing and thrashing around when I came in."

She snuggled closer, pressing her wet face into his hairy chest. "I was so scared," she whispered. "He was going to kill us."

"Who?"

"The man. He was going to stab both of us."

"You and me?"

She nodded against his chest, her palms pressing his

hot flesh. The terror was fading, replaced by a sense of well-being she hadn't felt for a very long time.

"You were dreaming about me," Gabe said, stroking her hair. Good Lord, it felt good. Everything about being in his arms felt good.

She swallowed. "It's not the first time." Not even close. Maybe she was dreaming now. She nestled in closer and he responded by holding her tighter. She let out a long slow breath and threw out a thank-you to the universe for giving her this gift. Even if it turned out to be a dream, it was the best damn dream she'd ever had.

"Cozy?" he asked.

"Mmm."

He wrapped his legs around hers and she realized he was wearing only boxers—and had a world class hard-on. She groaned before she could stop herself, and felt his muscles tighten.

"Kate," he said. "If you want me to leave, tell me now." His heart was thumping beneath her cheek. "But before you answer, you have to know something."

Was he talking about staying in bed with her. Making love to her? *Oh, God.* The surge of lust was so powerful she shuddered and let out a long breath against his skin. In response, Gabe pushed his cock into her hip and the length and heat of it caused her vaginal muscles to contract and then expand, readying for him.

"Gabe," she breathed. Her fingers found his nipple, causing him to jerk and tighten his hold on her. She tipped her head back, wanting his mouth on hers with an almost violent desperation, but he shifted back.

"Listen to me." His voice was husky, unsteady. "If I make love to you now there's no going back. Do you understand me?"

She didn't, but it didn't matter. All that mattered was having him inside her again, after all these years. Could it really be about to happen?

"Kate? Do you understand what I'm saying?"

"I don't care," she whispered. "I want you."

"You'll belong to me," he said. "Body and soul. It can't be any other way with us. It never could."

His words thrilled her, made her pussy throb with need. "I want to belong to you."

He wrapped her hair around his fist and pulled her head back. In the dim light leaking through the curtains she could see the fierce glow in his eyes. "Are you sure you're ready for that?"

She swallowed. "God, yes." He stared at her. "Please."

He moved his head slowly toward hers, eyes wide open, watching her. And then his lips claimed hers and his tongue filled her mouth and her world shifted.

Gabe wanted to possess her, body and soul. And she wanted to give it all to him.

He rolled her on to her back and covered her with his big, warm body, then began to sculpt her with his hands, running them down her sides, over her swollen, aching breasts through her thin nightgown and lower, over her hips and around to her ass. He pressed her head deep into the pillow and plundered her mouth with such intensity it was difficult to breathe. Not that air mattered. She was beyond needing anything but his hot mouth, his tongue, his hands. His thick, hard cock pressing against her pussy.

He began to rock against her and a long, slow gasp rose from her throat. She wrapped her legs around his waist and moved with him. Gabe's mouth moved over her jaw and down her neck, nipping, licking, while his hands shoved up her nightgown and began to knead her breasts. She arched into him, and he moved his lips to one hard nipple, teasing with soft licks that drove her wild with need before he drew it into his mouth and sucked.

"Gabe," she whispered urgently, wanting everything he could give her all at once. She would die if he didn't enter her immediately, would die if he lifted his mouth off her breast. He slid her nightgown over her head and held her hands there, their fingers intertwined as he moved to her other breast. She squeezed his hands as her body twisted and rocked to his primitive rhythm. Then, keeping her hands in his, he began a slow move down her body, over her belly, kissing and nibbling, licking the tender hollow of her hips.

He looked up at her then and held her gaze. "I dream of putting my tongue inside you," he said roughly. "And now I'm going to do it."

"Please," she begged. "I'm desperate for it."

He released her hands and pulled down her panties, then pushed her legs up until her knees were bent and her thighs wide open to him. Again he raised his head and gazed into her eyes. "This is all for me."

"Yes."

He lowered his head and rubbed his whole face in the wet folds of her pussy—his cheeks, his jaw, his nose. The pleasure was so exquisite she lifted her hips off the bed and pushed herself harder into his face, whimpering his name.

"Oh, God, I'm going to come," she said, and then Gabe's mouth covered her, sucking and licking with his big, hot tongue, thrusting it up inside her as she screamed her climax. The wave traveled from her center down her legs to her toes and back, up her spine and out to her fingertips, shocking her with its intensity, bringing tears to her eyes and a lump to her throat. Nothing in her life had ever felt as good as having Gabe's mouth on her. Nothing.

He slid up her body and kissed her with a hunger only he had ever shown her. When he lifted his head he said, panting, "Do you understand now?"

"Yes," she rasped.

"I need a condom."

She shook her head and reached inside his boxers to wrap her hand around his cock. It was huge and rock hard and she was desperate to have it inside her.

But not quite yet…

She pushed him on to his back and pinned his legs with hers. "My turn."

He raised his brows, his gray eyes filled with heat. "Oh, please, be my guest."

She kissed him leisurely on the lips, exploring his delectable mouth with her tongue while she stroked him, and then kissed her way slowly down his neck and chest, stopping to lick his flat nipple. He sucked in air between his teeth. When her thumb grazed the wetness seeping from the head of his cock, she brought it to her lips and gently licked it off. He groaned.

"Jesus, Kate," he said in a strangled whisper. "Do you have any idea how much I want to see my cock between your lips?"

She smiled and slid down his body, kissing his belly, running her tongue around his navel and then dipped into the slit at the head of his cock. He gasped and cupped the back of her head. She lapped up the salty pre-come, thrilled that she was tasting him at last, and then took him into her mouth.

"Kate… Oh God… It's so good."

Encouraged, she took him deeper, pumping him with

her mouth and her fist until he began to rock into her, setting the rhythm.

"Stop me if I'm going too deep," he breathed, even as his grip tightened in her hair, holding her in place. "Oh, Kate…"

As his cock grew harder and thicker his words became unintelligible, and he suddenly pulled her head away. "I want to be inside you when I come… I need to be there."

"I want you inside me," she whispered, crawling up his body. She straddled him and tried to put him inside her, but he scooted up the bed.

"Damn it, I need a condom."

"I don't care," she said. "I want you inside me."

"Kate—"

She grasped his shoulders and leaned her face into his. "Please, Gabe. I need you now. Just this once." In the back of her mind she knew it was reckless not to use a condom—again—but she couldn't risk him changing his mind when he left her bed to get one. No, she would feel him move inside her, and she would worry about the consequences—physical and emotional—later.

Gabe held her gaze for a long moment, then flipped her on to her back, shoved his boxers all the way off and settled between her legs. "No turning back, Kate," he said. "Are you sure?"

She'd never been so sure about anything in her life. "Yes."

He lifted her hips, took his cock in one hand and guided himself to her entrance. "Look at me when I come inside you." She nodded. With his hands gripping her hips and their gazes locked, he pushed inside her and groaned. "Oh, God, Kate, you're so tight."

Feeling Gabe inside her brought a lump back to her

throat and she choked back a sob. She'd wanted him for so long.

For a moment he seemed stricken. "Am I hurting you?"

She reached up and cupped his cheek, words failing her. She shook her head and whispered. "Please."

He began to move then, and she struggled to watch him through eyelids that wanted to close, as though to watch would lessen the ecstasy. The body above her and inside her was magnificent. Hard and muscular and musky with arousal, and with a look of such fierce tenderness in his eyes she fought not to weep.

Love me, Gabe. Just a little.

With each long, slow thrust she moved closer and closer to coming, and her heart was bursting with so much pent up emotion she couldn't contain it any longer. "I love you, Gabe," she whispered, wrapping her arms around his neck. "I love you so much."

His eyelids lowered and his jaw tightened. "Kate," he said, and began to move faster, pushing deeper inside her. She'd never felt this much sensation during sex, didn't know her body was capable of such intense pleasure. As he thrust, his fingers gripped her hips so tightly it was almost painful, but she didn't care as long as he kept moving.

"Kate," he said again, and his ragged tone told her he was getting close. Knowing she was going to make him come sent her over the top and he covered her mouth with his to absorb her scream. Within seconds he followed her, the sounds emerging from his throat harsh, primal. Inside her he pulsed, then he collapsed on top of her, his face in her hair, his heart pounding against hers.

Tears streamed down her cheeks as she lay beneath him. *Please don't have second thoughts. Don't regret this.* She ran her hands up and down his sweaty back, loving the weight of him on her, the warmth of his breath on her neck.

Eventually she dozed, and woke up when he stirred and rolled off her, pulling her into his arms. She tipped her head back to look up at him and he kissed her gently on the lips.

"Are you okay?" he asked.

"More than okay."

"Did I hurt you anywhere? I should have been more gentle."

"I didn't want you to be gentle."

"What about your bruises, did I—"

"No." She kissed him to shut him up. "How about you? Are you… I mean… Do you still—"

"Yes," he said, and kissed her, presumably to shut her up, then stroked her hair off her face and cupped her cheek. "I meant what I said. You're mine now."

"I was always yours," she said.

Chapter Twenty-Eight

When Kate woke the sun had barely risen, and she was nestled against a big hard body. *Gabe.* She could barely believe it. He hadn't left her during the night as she'd expected. One long arm was draped across her, their legs intertwined. The bed smelled strongly of sex, which wasn't surprising considering they'd dozed and made love twice more before falling into a deep sleep. She smiled and stroked his arm.

Mine, she thought. She'd given herself to him completely. If she belonged to him then the reverse must be true. He belonged to her. She hoped she would never have to let him go.

She didn't feel the way a woman who'd lost her husband should feel. Then again, Drew hadn't felt the way a husband should toward his wife. And she had never gotten over Gabe. She'd tried to hide the truth from herself, of course, but a part of her had always known that she would have left Drew for him. And never looked back.

"You're thinking," a deep, sleepy voice said in her ear. He pulled her back into him and she could feel his erection at the juncture of her thighs. "I hope you're thinking about me."

It thrilled her to hear him say that. "As a matter of fact I was," she said as he nuzzled her neck. Her body responded to him instantly.

"What were you thinking?" His hand moved to her

breast and kneaded, tightening the coil of desire in her belly. She pushed her breast into his hand, prompting him to squeeze harder then run his thumb round and round her hard nipple. Already she was so wet she could feel it on the inside of her thighs.

"Take me from behind," she whispered, pressing her bottom into his erection. "Mmm, now."

"Your wish is my command," he murmured into her hair, and guided his cock to the sensitive opening of her vagina and slid inside, expelling a long groan as he filled her completely. But before he could move inside her someone began pounding at the front door and ringing the doorbell, and Bruno was barking his head off.

"Good Lord," Kate said, leaning over to look at the digital clock on her nightstand. "Who could that be at six-thirty in the morning?"

"Stay put," Gabe said. He kissed her shoulder and slid out of her. "I'll get rid of whoever it is and be right back. Do not move."

She rolled on to her back and smiled up at him. His body was incredible naked. All dark hair and ropy muscles, a perfect male specimen. And he was hers. "I have no desire to go anywhere," she said.

Gabe slipped on his jeans and T-shirt and went downstairs barefooted. She heard the front door opening and then men's voices. Who in the world could it be? She waited, hoping whoever it was would go away quickly, but instead the voices seemed to be getting louder. Anxiety churned in her gut.

She slid from the bed and pulled on some clothes, then went out to the balcony overlooking the foyer. A familiar voice said, "So basically, you're off the hook." It was one of the FBI agents. The taller guy, Mancuso, the one she didn't like at all. "We've got everything we need."

"For what?" Gabe said. His voice sounded seriously cold. She knew what it was like to be on the receiving end of that voice, and she didn't envy the agent.

"To bring Mrs. Franklin in."

Kate's gut seized. Bring her in? What were they talking about?

"Could you tell her we're here, please?" Mancuso said.

"Not until you tell me what's going on."

She started down the stairs. "I'm here, Gabe. It's okay." Not really—she was nervous as hell. And why had Mancuso told Gabe he was off the hook? For what? She wanted to stand beside him and take his hand, but something in his body language told her to keep her distance.

Right. He was investigating the break-in. It might be considered bad form to have a personal relationship with the victim. Still, the look he was giving her was not the look a man would give his lover. Her gut clenched tighter.

She stood alone, several feet from the two agents. "What's going on?"

"Agent Parker, Mrs. Franklin," the shorter one said.

"Yes, I remember."

"And you remember Agent Mancuso."

Kate didn't respond or acknowledge the tall, rude agent. "What brings you here at six-thirty in the morning?" Jeremy was still sleeping, thank goodness. She'd prefer he not be exposed to this part of her life.

"As you know, the CVR was retrieved fairly quickly, Mrs. Franklin," Parker said, then held up a hand. "Excuse me, I'm referring to the 'black box.'"

"Cockpit voice recording," Gabe told her, his tone somber.

"That's right. And we've analyzed the recording."

"So now we know the source of the explosion." Mancuso smirked, and the knot in her gut pulled tighter still.

"And?" she asked.

"It appears to have come from a camera in your husband's possession."

The shock actually caused her to take a step backward, as though someone had hit her. Her pulse pounded in her temples, and she felt suddenly dizzy and nauseous. Gabe came to her side then, and took her upper arms. It wasn't a particularly warm gesture, more like he was making sure she didn't fall.

"You okay?" he said.

"What's going on?" she said. "I don't understand."

"Let them explain." After a couple of seconds he let go of her.

She wanted to tell him it wasn't only the FBI agents she didn't understand, it was also the way he was acting. As though last night hadn't happened. As though he hadn't claimed her, body and soul, for himself…

"What does this mean?" she asked the agents.

"Do you own a camera, Mrs. Franklin?"

"Yes."

"Can we see it?"

She hugged herself. "Well…I guess so, but I'm not sure it's mine."

"Is the Congressman's camera here?"

She turned to Gabe, but his expression was closed. "Yes. It's the same kind as mine. A Canon, I think. We took some pictures with it yesterday."

"I'll get it," Gabe said, and disappeared into the den, then reappeared within a few seconds. Kate followed him with her eyes, feeling helpless. Trapped. He handed the camera to Parker, who proceeded to examine it. Gabe didn't look at her.

"How could a camera cause an explosion?" she asked.

Oh, but she was cold, so cold. And so completely alone. "Didn't all the congressmen and their staff go through security?"

Parker ejected the memory card from the camera and put it in his pocket. To Gabe he said, "This is the one with the sleazy photos of him?"

"Yeah," Gabe said.

Was she hearing him correctly? "You-you told them about those pictures?" she asked. What was going on?

Parker turned to her. "We'd like you to come down to headquarters with us, Mrs. Franklin, and discuss what was inside the camera your husband took on board that Learjet."

She opened her mouth, but nothing came out. Gabe was frowning down at the floor. Goddamn it, why wasn't he supporting her? Why wasn't he holding her and telling these men they were full of it? "Gabe?" she asked, and heard the panic in her voice.

"What was on the cockpit recording?" Gabe asked Parker, still not looking at her.

"We'll share the recording once we get Mrs. Franklin to headquarters."

Kate looked around wildly. "Are you arresting me?"

"Not at this time," Mancuso said.

"I would have appreciated a little warning," Gabe growled.

Kate turned to him. "What's going on?" But she had a horrible feeling she already knew.

"We don't have a warrant for your arrest, Mrs. Franklin," Parker said with a sharp look at his partner. "Not at this point. We'd simply like to take you in for questioning."

"Oh, I see," she said. "And if I don't give you the right answers then you'll arrest me."

"For now let's just say we're taking a ride to headquarters for a little chat."

She stared at the agent for a moment and then whirled on Gabe. "Why are you acting like you don't know me anymore? What happened to you between last night and this morning? Or should I say, five minutes ago until now?"

"Let's go talk for a minute, okay?" He took her elbow and eased her toward the kitchen as he said to the agents, "We'll be right back."

Tears welled up in Kate's eyes. When they were out of earshot of the agents she turned to him and gazed into his eyes. "Was it all an act, then? Have you been hanging around here to help the FBI?"

His eyes darted toward the living room, then he took hold of her shoulders. "I have to let them believe I'm helping them, Kate, or they'll shut me out. Do you understand? I'll be of no use to you if I'm on the outside."

"They told you to spend time with me, didn't they?" *Please say no.* "Didn't they?"

He raised his eyes to the ceiling and blew out a long puff of air. "Not officially," he said. "But that's not what—"

She backed away from him. "Oh, my God," she whispered. "It was all an act. You do still hate me."

"Of course I don't hate you," he said, clearly annoyed.

She put her hands over her ears. "I trusted you. I actually thought you cared. I thought…" She trailed off, her heart so heavy she wasn't sure she could stay on her feet.

Gabe kept his voice low. "It wasn't like that, damn it. I need you to trust me on this."

Anger rushed through her. "Trust you? *Trust* you? You lying son of a bitch!" She backed farther away from him, but continued to shout. "Don't ever come near me again, do you hear me? I never want to see your lying face—"

"Kate, you don't understand."

"Aunt Kate?"

Through her tears she saw Jeremy standing there in his pajamas, wide-eyed and frightened. She leaned down and pulled him to her. "Jeremy," she said quietly. "I'm so sorry. Just remember that no matter what happens I love you, and that will never change."

Jeremy held on tight. "Why are you crying? Did my dad make you cry?"

"Kate," Gabe said. "Listen to me, damn it."

She straightened, easing out of Jeremy's grasp, and met the boy's gaze. "I'll see you soon, okay?" she said, running her hand through his snarled brown hair. "You take care of yourself, and don't let that jerk Jason K. get you in trouble, you hear me?"

"But where are you going?"

"Kate," Gabe said, his tone urgent. "Listen to me."

She ignored him and focused on Jeremy. "I have to go talk to those men in there about that plane explosion. I'm not sure when I'll be back, but I'll email you, okay?" Then, mostly to herself, she said, "I'll have to get Violetta to pick up Bruno." As if on cue, Bruno got off his bed and came to her side. She squatted and hugged him tightly, and new tears welled.

When she stood, Jeremy looked so confused and upset it made her chest ache. "Are they taking you to jail?"

"No!" Gabe shot back. "I won't let that happen."

Kate bit back a snort. If she lived to be a hundred—which was doubtful under the circumstances. Terrorists got the death penalty, after all. She would never forgive Gabe for abandoning her when she needed him most. He'd ripped out her heart and stomped on it, and she would never let him or anyone else that close again. *Never.*

She looked down at Jeremy. Well, other than this beautiful, precious boy.

She kissed Jeremy on the forehead and headed for the living room. Gabe grasped her arm, but she jerked away.

"Dad?" she heard Jeremy say as she joined the agents in the living room. "Why is Aunt Kate crying?"

Kate grabbed her purse off the dining room table and slid her feet into sandals. If she did end up in jail they'd give her a jumpsuit, right? She nodded to Parker, and out of the corner of her eye saw Mancuso's smug grin. If she got through this a free woman, she would report him to somebody, just for being a supreme asshole.

A chill ran down her spine as she left her house—possibly for the last time.

Chapter Twenty-Nine

"I appreciate it, Parker," Gabe said stiffly. He was standing before a two-way mirror looking into an FBI interrogation room. Kate sat there in her drawstring pants and yellow T-shirt, arms hugging her torso, head bowed. Every few seconds she shuddered from sobs. Goddamn it, he should be holding her. He should be in that room fighting for her. Protecting her.

"And she should have called her lawyer, damn it," he murmured, and was immediately surprised he'd said it aloud.

"You've got a thing for her, don't you?" Parker asked, his tone matter-of-fact rather than judgmental.

"I just don't think she did this," Gabe said around the lump in his throat. Christ, he felt terrible.

Parker raised his eyebrows. "When you hear the recording you may think differently. Be prepared."

"Is Mancuso going to be in there?" Gabe asked.

"No," Parker said. "It's clear that he grates on her, and there's nothing to be gained by upsetting her more than she already is."

"Thank God for small favors."

Parker nodded and left the room. A minute later he joined Kate in the interrogation room. With the microphone on, Gabe could hear him offer her water and saw her shake her head in response. After Parker went through the formalities of turning on the recorder, he began.

* * *

"Mrs. Franklin, tell me for the record why you and your husband were in Hartford on the day your husband's plane went down?"

"Drew had a seminar to attend, so we spent the weekend with his parents. They live in West Hartford."

"I see. Are you close to his family?"

"No. They don't approve of my political beliefs and… Not that we were close before I embarrassed Drew on national television, but after that…" She shrugged.

"Did you and your husband sleep in the same room at your in-laws' home?"

"Yes."

"Did you help him pack his bags?"

Kate sighed. "No. He didn't need my help. It was only the one bag, anyway. And his briefcase."

"Did you see what was in his briefcase when he was packing?"

"I don't even remember seeing it in our room."

"But it was in the house that morning?"

"I guess it must have been."

"Did you bring your camera on that trip, Mrs. Franklin?"

"Yes."

"And did your husband bring his camera?"

"I guess so, because the one I unpacked at home was his, not mine."

"The cameras were the same make? Did you buy them together?"

"Drew bought them both a couple of months ago. I already had one, an old Canon, but for some reason he decided I should have a new one. I was so happy he'd thought of me I…"

"Yes?"

She shook her head. "Nothing. I was just happy when he brought it home, because he didn't seem to spend a lot of time thinking about me."

"Did you or your husband take any pictures over the weekend?" Parker asked.

"I didn't. Maybe he did."

"Did you spend much time together?"

Kate's laugh was bitter. "No. We had dinner with his parents once, and the rest of the time he was with his aides or one of the other congressmen and women who were along for the seminar."

"That was the seminar on international relations held at the University of Hartford?"

"Yes." She sighed. "Some of those people were on the… his plane."

"Did you know the other people well?"

"Well I'd certainly been in their company, but no, the only one I knew well at all was Michael Clark, Drew's AA."

"Were you unhappy with your husband, Mrs. Franklin?"

Kate looked stunned for a moment, and Gabe found himself holding his breath. "I wasn't—" She stopped and cleared her throat. "I tried to make it work. Not hard enough, obviously, but I believed in my marriage vows."

"Did you love your husband?"

She took a deep, shaky breath. "I thought I did for a long time. But it was never…" She shook her head.

"Let the record state that Mrs. Franklin shook her head no," Parker said.

"No, that's not what I was saying. Let the record state that."

"Go on."

"What I meant was, I wanted to love him, but it was difficult."

"Did you fight much?" Parker asked.

"Not for a long time, no. That would have required us to be connected."

"You sound bitter."

"About the marriage?" She unwrapped her arms and laid her forearms on the table. "Look," she said. "I know you're hoping I'll reveal some deep anger toward Drew, and confess to killing him, but really, I was hurt, not angry. I didn't kill him or even so much as consider killing him. I mean, for God's sake, I could have divorced him. It's not like we had kids to stay together for."

Parker went on almost as though he hadn't heard her. "I'd like you to listen to this cockpit recording from the Learjet in the final moments before the explosion. You can read the transcript at the same time." He pushed a sheet of paper in front of her.

Gabe had gone still when Parker asked Kate whether she had loved her husband. She'd told *him* she loved him last night. That she had always been his. And he knew in his bones she was telling him the truth. His chest constricted.

Mancuso stepped up beside him and handed him a sheet of paper. "So you can follow along," he said, and Gabe didn't have to look at his ugly face to know he was smirking.

Below him in the interrogation room, Kate scanned the sheet and then dropped her head into her hands. "Oh, God…"

Parker pointed out the initials on the transcripts, explaining that CA meant the Captain, CO the copilot, FA flight attendant and FR Drew Franklin. Then he flipped on the tape. For the first thirty seconds or so the pilot was talking to the control tower at Bradley International Airport, and there was some light banter between him and the copilot, along with the usual altitude and other technical exchanges. Knowing what was about to happen, Gabe's gut tightened.

CA. What was that?
CO. Sounded like a scream.
CA. Damn it, who's screaming?
[Sound of knocking]
[Cockpit door opening]
FA. Captain, one of the…it's Franklin…
FR. *[faint]* Open the goddamn window!
CA. What the hell?
CO. Jesus Christ…
FA. He wants to throw his camera out the…escape hatch…
FR. *[faint]* I'm telling you…get off me! Open it! Get rid of it!
CA. What's he got?
FR. *[faint]* My wife's…That bitch!
[Explosion]

Parker turned off the recording and stared at Kate, whose face had gone pale. For a moment Gabe was certain she would throw up, but she seemed to pull it together.

"It sounded like…" she began. "I don't know, it sounded like he was going crazy."

"Yes, he sounded panicked, that's for sure."

"I don't understand. How could a little camera like that explode?"

"I was hoping you could tell me, Mrs. Franklin."

Kate threw her arms out to her sides. "How in the world… I don't even understand how cameras work, never mind how to make one explode."

"You're a smart woman."

She splayed one hand across her chest. "I'm an artist, for God's sake. I run a charitable foundation. I'm not a mad bomber. This is completely crazy."

"You've moved in excess of ninety-five million dollars over the past year. Where did it go?"

She scrubbed her hands over her face. "We've been over this. I have no idea."

"Could it have been used to pay someone to create a camera bomb that was virtually undetectable?"

"Not by me."

"Who else had access to your husband's belongings before he got on that plane?"

"I don't know. Probably no one. Drew didn't like people messing with his things."

"But you shared a room with him, you told me that. Did he get dressed in your room?"

"Yes."

"Did anyone else come into your room that morning?"

"No, not that morning."

"The night before?"

"Maybe."

"Maybe? You don't know?"

"Some of Drew's colleagues came back with him for a drink."

"Who were they?"

"Michael Clark. Joy Stuart and her husband, Ben. Maybe Congressman Jorling, others. I don't know."

"Okay," Parker said. "What time was this?"

"Late. I had fallen asleep on the sofa in the TV room."

"Okay. Where were your husband and the others?"

"Well, when I woke up I heard them talking in the living room."

"Not in the bedroom."

She shrugged. "No, but… Well, they were in the house."

"I see. Do you believe any of those people would want to kill your husband, Mrs. Franklin?"

"Not really."

"Not really?"

"No." She was clearly exasperated. "I mean no."

"What kind of idiot rolls over a babe like her?" Gabe's nostrils flared at the sound of Mancuso's voice behind him. How this asshole ever made it through the FBI academy he'd never know. Rather than risk punching the guy's lights out, he kept his eyes on Kate and didn't turn around, or acknowledge Mancuso's presence.

"Can I take it you enjoyed your assignment, Hugo?"

"You can take it however the fuck you want." So much for self-control.

"I wonder why she didn't call her lawyer?"

Gabe had been wondering the same thing. "Probably figured she had nothing to hide. Common mistake." And he hadn't had the presence of mind to insist on it. "From what I'm hearing I'd say this would be a good time for her to call someone, though."

"Hard to dispute evidence like this, huh?" Mancuso said.

Gabe whirled on him. "Evidence like what? There's no proof it was Kate's camera, or even that it *was* a camera. The flight attendant could have gotten it wrong. And even if it were her camera, and even if she wanted to kill her husband, and even if she found some undetectable explosives, why the hell wouldn't she just poison him? Or blow up his car?"

Mancuso shrugged. "Hard to understand why people do the crazy things they do. Why does a mother strangle her kids and keep them in the freezer for four years? Why not drop them off at the local church?"

Gabe realized that he was coming across as convinced of Kate's innocence, which was a surefire way to be locked out of the investigation. He was careful to temper his next words. "I'm just saying, if that's the best you've got it'll never hold up in court. You'll have to hope Parker cracks her, but from what I can see," he indicated the window behind him, "she's not about to confess to anything."

"She had to be working with someone," Mancuso said. "All that money went somewhere. The question is to who, and what kind of trail did they leave?"

"Why didn't Michael Clark take the same flight back to D.C. as your husband?" Parker asked.

"I think he said something about seeing friends in Connecticut."

"Isn't that a bit unusual? Right before a major vote I would think the congressman's AA would go wherever the congressman went."

"You'll have to ask him. Joy wasn't on the flight, either, and she—"

"Joy?"

"Joy Stuart."

"Right, the other sponsor."

"Drew wasn't even supposed to be on that flight."

"Excuse me?" Parker said.

"He was going to drive home."

"All the way to Washington?"

She nodded. "He only took the flight because Congressman Jorling called when Drew was about to drop me at the terminal and told him there was a spot on the Learjet."

Parker frowned. "Why didn't you tell us this before?"

"Didn't I?"

"What did your husband do with his car?"

"It was a rental. I guess he returned it."

They were silent while Parker shuffled through papers, frowning more deeply. "Why would your husband drive home instead of flying?"

She raised one shoulder in a half shrug. "He liked his time alone in the car to listen to his CDs, make phone calls…whatever he did, without anyone else around. He didn't like me to drive places with him even when we were both in Washington."

"Why is that?"

Her sigh was heavy. Dejected. "I guess I cramped his style."

"So, let's back up. Of the people who had been at your in-laws' house the night before, your husband was the only one who took that flight."

"That's right. Almost as though…"

"Almost as though…?"

She frowned. "Almost as though the rest of them knew the plane was going to explode."

Chapter Thirty

The look on Joy's face when she opened her door was almost comical, she was so stunned. Dressed in khaki shorts and a polo shirt and wearing very little makeup she looked younger and softer than she did in her professional garb. Not that he was fooled.

"Gabe," she said when she'd recovered her composure. She ran a hand through her short blond hair. "What are you doing here at this hour?"

"I'd like to talk to you for a few minutes, if you don't mind."

It was clear that she did mind, but it would have been hard to say that to an old friend. "You're about the last person I expected to find on my front porch."

"No," he said. "The last person you'd expect to find would be your old friend Kate."

She blinked but didn't change her expression. A few beats passed. Her hand had tightened on the door, and she made no move to let him in. "It's not a great time, to be honest. I've had a long day and I still have work to finish."

"I won't take up a lot of your time. I promise."

She huffed and stepped aside. As he passed by her into the foyer she said, "I can't wait to hear what's so important."

"I don't suppose I could bum a cup of coffee off you," he said. "It's been a long day for me too."

Annoyance flashed across her face, but she said,

"Sure. Sit down and I'll…go get it." She turned to go to the kitchen. "I'll have to make a fresh pot, so it could be a few minutes."

"No problem," he said, as though he were doing her a favor. As soon as she was gone he went into the living room and ran his cop's eyes over every surface, not knowing what he was looking for exactly, but hoping something would jump out at him. He was convinced there was something of Drew Franklin's that someone wanted, and that someone had gone after Kate twice to get a look through her house. If that someone happened to be Joy…

Joy walked into the room with two mugs of coffee. "I fixed it the way you always used to like it." Apparently she'd decided it was best to be pleasant, and handed him a mug with an American flag on the side. "Half-and-half and two sugars, right?"

"Good memory," he said, and took a sip.

Joy sat on the sofa, cradling her coffee in her hands. "So what's on your mind? Is this police business or personal?"

He remained standing. "Where's Ben?"

"Out," she said coolly. "What's going on?"

"Is he likely to be home anytime soon?"

She tilted her head to one side. "Well, now, this is interesting. You show up at—" she glanced at her watch, "—almost eleven o'clock and want to know if my husband's going to show up?" She flashed him a sexy smile. "I never knew you cared."

He sat beside her on the sofa, a little too close. Her eyes widened a bit, but she recovered. "There are a lot of things about me you never knew," he said.

She stared at him. "Should we be drinking something stronger than coffee?"

He smiled slowly. "You tell me."

Her nervous giggle told him she was off balance. Good.

"Tell me about you and Drew Franklin," he said, squeezing her shoulder as though he was about to start massaging. "How long were you lovers?"

She blinked several times. Gabe was counting on her confusion. Was he coming on to her by asking about her former lover or was this a fishing expedition?

"What makes you think we were lovers?" she asked cautiously.

"You're a beautiful woman, and he spent a lot of time with you. He also didn't much care for his wife." He was gently kneading her trapezius muscle, keeping her relaxed and unsure where the hell he was coming from.

"Is that what Kate told you?" she asked.

"More or less."

"Drew and I were close," she said. "But we weren't lovers. If Kate chooses to believe that to justify her actions, that's her prerogative. But she's wrong."

"What actions?"

She shrugged, but didn't pull back from his hand. Apparently she was enjoying the massage. He just had to remind himself not to slide up a couple of inches and strangle her.

"Oh, come on," she said. "It wouldn't surprise me at all if she had something to do with that explosion. The American people don't appreciate this, but let's face it, it's not that hard to smuggle explosives on to a plane. And there are new materials out there our intelligence agencies don't even know about. They're ridiculously behind the curve on so many things the terrorists are doing."

"And you're going to change all that when you're the Director of Global Intelligence," Gabe said.

Joy froze. It had been a hunch on his part, but he'd obviously hit pay dirt. "What are you talking about?" she asked, pulling away from him. "The bill hasn't passed the Senate yet. And even if it does, the president hasn't decided who he's going to appoint to that position."

"You'd be perfect for the position," Gabe said evenly. "If I were the president I'd pick you."

"Why?"

"Because you're smart, you understand all the intricacies of the bill and what it needs to be effective. Who else is as qualified as you?"

Bit by bit she relaxed again, but there a wariness in her eyes. "Why are you really here?"

He sat back, knees spread, arms resting on the back of the couch, like he was settling in to watch a football game. "I'm stumped," he said. "Someone's either trying to hurt Kate for personal reasons or they're trying to get her out of the way."

Joy folded her arms over her chest. She was sitting forward on the couch, away from the long reach of his hand, her body turned halfway toward him, but her closest leg crossed away from him. Protecting herself. "And you're telling me this because…?"

He shrugged but held her gaze. "Who hates her enough to do her bodily harm, Joy?"

Joy brought a hand to her throat and gave a harsh laugh. "Why are you asking me?"

"Because I can't think of anyone who hates her more than you."

In the silence that followed Gabe felt Joy's anger building, like a sudden thunderstorm that charges the air. Eyes narrowed, nostrils flared, she slowly unfolded her arms and placed tight fists on her thighs.

"What, exactly," she began, her voice low and controlled, "are you saying, Gabe? Are you accusing me of trying to kill your darling sister-in-law?" Blue eyes flashed. "Drew's loving, supportive wife?"

The fact that she'd referred to *killing* Kate as opposed to hurting her was not lost on Gabe. "You make it sound as though Drew would have liked to kill her himself."

The moment the words left his lips, Joy went deathly pale. She swallowed hard. "I'd like you to leave now," she said in a shaky voice. When she stood she was unsteady on her feet.

Gabe frowned. "Are you okay?"

"No, I'm tired and I'm…insulted." She lifted her chin and glared at him. "And disappointed, Gabe. Very disappointed. Drew was a good man, and to suggest that he would try to kill his wife is ludicrous. Why would he do such a thing? For her money? Is that what you're thinking?"

Gabe studied her for several seconds. Joy was practically wringing her hands. What the hell was that about? "Drew Franklin is dead. Why would I suggest *he* was trying to kill her?"

"That's not what I meant," Joy said. "You were referring… speaking in past tense. I was just saying… I was standing up for him, okay? It's not nice to speak ill of the dead."

Gabe rose and Joy stepped away from him. "You seem more nervous than insulted," he said. "Is there something you want to tell me?"

She wouldn't look at him. "No. I'd like you to leave."

Instead of leaving he reached out to grip her shoulders.

Joy's eyes widened. "What are you doing?"

"Look me in the eye and tell me you believe Kate has it in her to murder anyone. Go ahead."

Joy stared at him for a long moment, then covered her eyes with her hands. "Oh, God. What a mess."

Was he actually going to get a confession out of her? He gentled the hands on her shoulders. "Tell me about it, Joy. I'll do whatever I can for you, but you have to tell me everything."

She pulled away, revealing an anguished expression. "No, you don't understand. It's not about me. It's about… someone else." She shook her head as though pained. "I wanted so badly to keep his name out of it, but at this point I think it's my duty to tell someone."

So that's the way she was going to play it. Gabe took her cold hands in his. "Talk to me. Whose name are you trying to keep out of it?"

Her blue eyes were moist. "You have to understand that I don't know anything for sure. If I did I would have told you. But it's all so surreal, you know?"

"What's surreal?

"You know someone, or think you do, and then you find out…" She took a long shaky breath, and Gabe held his, waiting. "I think Michael Clark had something to do with it."

Gable blinked in surprise but hoped he showed no other outward sign. Maybe Joy would be of some help after all. "With the attacks on Kate?"

"Yes."

"Go on."

"Would you… There's some white wine in the fridge. I think I need something stronger now."

"Sure." Gabe went into the kitchen, pulled down a stemmed glass and grabbed the bottle of Pinot Grigio from the refrigerator. He moved as fast as he could, not wanting to leave Joy alone any longer than he had to. When he returned Joy was sitting on the couch, an open purse beside her. She snapped it closed as he approached.

"I thought I had some tissues in there," she said with a sad smile.

A box of tissues sat on the lamp table at the far end of the couch, and Gabe reached for it. Joy seemed surprised that it was there, then blew her nose daintily and crushed a tissue in her fist. He poured her a small glass of wine and sat down beside her again, though not quite as close as before. This time *she* turned toward *him* and moved a little closer, so that her knee was resting against his thigh.

"So," he prompted. "Michael Clark."

"He worshipped the ground Drew walked on," she said after a long sip of wine. "He would do anything for Drew. He always acted as though he liked Kate, but I'm sure he was as pissed off at her as the rest of us, especially after that awful news story. How could he not be, when you look at all the work Drew put into everything he did? Michael was always there, working right beside him. In the last two years I was there too."

"Did Michael resent you?"

She gave a harsh laugh. "Oh, yes. He tried hard not to show it, but over time it became more and more obvious that my presence in Drew's life threatened him."

Gabe settled into the couch as before, arms opened wide across the back cushions, as relaxed as could be. "Was he in love with Drew?" he asked.

Joy met his gaze. "I think he was, yes."

"Was Drew in love with him?"

Joy gave him an incredulous look. "Of course not. That was the problem. You see? That may be what ultimately sent Michael over the edge. Not only couldn't he have Drew, it killed him that the two sponsors of the bill were

Drew and me. He's a very ambitious man, Gabe. I happen to know that he wants to be Deputy Director of Global Intelligence, but not if it means he has to work for—" She stopped.

"For you," he said.

She lowered her head for a moment, then looked at him. "Okay, I admit it. But you can't say a word outside this room. The president and I have had some preliminary discussions about me being the Director of Global Intelligence if the bill passes both houses."

Gabe mimicked zipping his lips. "Mum's the word. So, what makes you say Michael had it in for Kate?"

Her eyes slid away. "I just think he did."

"Is that all you've got?"

She hesitated. "No, there's more." She took another long swallow of wine and set down her glass. "I was in Drew's office the other day—Michael has taken to using his desk. And I found some things—notes, phone numbers. I think he was involved with some rough characters."

The innocent-looking blond guy's face—Tom?—appeared in Gabe's mind as he refilled Joy's glass. "Who were these rough characters?"

"Like me, Michael worked in the Public Defender's office in Connecticut for a while."

"I remember you talking about that a long time ago, down at the lake," Gabe said.

Joy smiled. "We go back a long way."

"Yes, we do." And it wasn't going to do her a damn bit of good if she had harmed Kate.

She sighed. "Anyway, there was a guy we both defended, an alleged murderer. Tyrell King."

"You and Michael worked together on his case?"

She nodded. "He was a nasty piece of work. Liked to

use a knife on women. In the end Michael got him off and he walked. Free as a bird. I found a note in Drew's desk with Tyrell's name circled." She took a long sip of wine. "There was a phone number below it. I assumed it was Tyrell's."

"Is that all?"

She put a hand to her forehead. "I didn't want him to know I was suspicious, but I wanted to know what in the world he was doing with Tyrell's number. So I went into his office for something and, well, snooped through his cell phone calls."

"What did you find?"

"A couple of dozen calls to and from that number. And he had it listed on his phone as TK."

"There's not a whole lot I can do with that," Gabe said. "Not unless there's some evidence that this Tyrell actually did something illegal on Michael's behalf."

She fiddled with her wineglass. "There may be. In the office. I'll have to take you there."

"What is it?"

She swallowed. "A tape recorder. I set it up in the office to record Michael's conversations. It will be one-sided, but if he's talking to Tyrell I'll know it."

"Can't use that in court," Gabe said.

"And isn't that ridiculous? Under the Global Intel bill we'd be able to use covertly obtained information to confiscate his cell phone and anything else we wanted."

Yeah, and to hell with the Constitution.

"What the hell are *you* doing here?"

Anger blazed in Ben's eyes as he entered the room. Joy leaped to her feet.

"When did you get here?" she asked. "I didn't hear you come in."

"I sneaked in the back door," Ben said, eyes moving back and forth between Joy and Gabe. "Don't tell me you're starting up with Gabe now that Drew's gone? Is it just Kate's men you're interested in?"

Joy threw Gabe a dark glance but didn't respond to Ben's question. "Gabe's here on police business."

"Ah," Ben said, looking directly at Gabe. "You do have an unusual way of conducting police business with attractive women."

Gabe reached into his back pocket and pulled out a few photos. "You both might be interested in these," he said, and dropped them on the table. He watched Joy's face change from puzzled to disgusted to angry. Ben was too busy staring at the photos to see her reactions to them.

"So, your boyfriend swung both ways," Ben said after a few moments. "Be hard to ID a guy with a camera hiding his face." By the time he looked at Joy she'd managed to mask her horror, but not her anger.

"I told you we weren't lovers," she snapped, directing it at her husband. "There's the proof."

Ben studied his wife, and Gabe saw the first shred of doubt cross his old friend's face. "Actually, you never did say you weren't lovers. You didn't respond at all whenever I brought it up."

Joy raised her chin. "I didn't think your insinuations deserved a response."

"Uh-huh," Ben said, his expression impossible to read. "Well, I came by to pick up some of my things. Don't let me disrupt this little tête-à-tête."

"Actually, we're just leaving," Gabe said. He picked up the photos and stuck them back in his pocket. "Joy and I are going down to the Cannon House Office Building to check out some things."

Ben turned to Joy. "I'll be gone by the time you get back."

To Gabe's surprise, Joy moved to stand in front of Ben. In a low voice she said, "Even now that you see your suspicions were wrong? Please, honey. Just wait for me." She gestured toward the wine bottle. "Sit on the couch and have some wine, and we'll talk when I get home. I won't be long." When Ben didn't reply she put her hand on his chest. "Wait for me, Ben. There are some things… I'll explain if you'll wait, okay? If you still want to leave after we talk I'll help you pack." She moved closer and whispered, "But I can be very persuasive."

Gabe pretended not to hear.

"Where's Kate tonight?" Ben asked, and Gabe realized he was talking to him.

"Busy," Gabe said. He wasn't about to mention that the feds had taken her into custody. It was Joy or Michael Clark—or both—who belonged there, not Kate. He would prove that if it was the last thing he ever did. But right now he had to play along with Joy, make her believe he trusted her and find out what she knew.

"Ben?" Joy said. "Will you wait?"

"I'll think about it," he said.

Chapter Thirty-One

When they'd left, Ben spent a few moments staring at the front door. So Drew was gay? Okay, bisexual. That had to piss off Joy big time. No, he had no illusions that the affair never happened. He knew his wife too well. If he'd accused her falsely she would have let him know about it in no uncertain terms. Joy might be good at fooling her colleagues and constituents, but she didn't fool him. At least, not for long.

He sat on the couch and poured some wine into Joy's glass, then sat back. Something was niggling at him, like an itch he couldn't quite reach. Both Gabe and Joy had been lying, that much was clear. Gabe had been cozying up to Joy for a reason, and it wasn't sex. Ben had seen him with Kate and the chemistry between those two was explosive. He took a sip of the wine. The attraction between Gabe and Kate had never been far from the surface, not even when Steve was alive. Maybe the bullshit Gabe had put her through all these years had been about *his* guilt, not hers.

He knew all too well how insidious guilt could be.

His gaze roamed about the room, stopping at photos of him and Joy, their families, several of Jeremy. They'd had some good years together. Maybe they would've had children eventually, if he could ever have persuaded Joy that her job wasn't all that mattered. But, truth be told, the job *was* everything to her. If she'd actually been in love with Drew her grief wouldn't have run its course so quickly.

More likely the affair was an extension of the job. It was power Joy loved. How had he ever thought she would be happy married to a cardiologist?

"I don't have time for this shit," he muttered, then tossed back the rest of the wine and stood. No sense waiting for Joy to get back. She would just try to feed him more lies, and he wasn't interested.

When he got to their bedroom the door was locked. *What the hell?* Who was she locking out? The answer was clear of course—she was locking *him* out. "Bitch," he said aloud. But when had she done it? He hadn't told her he was coming over tonight, and every other time he'd stopped by the bedroom had not been barricaded. Had she locked it when Gabe came over?

He tried the knob again, pushing and wiggling, but the more he fiddled with it the angrier he became. Goddamn it, this was still his room, and he'd be damned if he let her lock him out like he was some sort of intruder. Was there something in there she didn't want him—or Gabe—to see?

Practical as always, he considered the cost of replacing the door, and decided it was worth it. He took a few steps back, then lunged at the door, throwing all his weight into it as though he were making a full body tackle. He felt something give, so he did it again. And again. Each failure pissed him off more than the last. After throwing his upper body against it five or six times he was ready to use his feet. It only took two good kicks to break the lock.

The overhead light and both bedside lamps were on, and Joy's white MacBook was sitting on the bed. A quick scan around the room revealed nothing unusual. So what was the big deal? He went to the bed and picked up the laptop, fully expecting to be denied access, since she'd never shared her password. But this time all he had to do was press a key and the screen lit up.

At first he didn't know what he was looking at. The column on the left side of the document was a list of initials, none of which registered with him. Beside each set of initials were strings of letters with numbers underneath most of them, but not all. Further down the list there were no numbers beneath the letters. His heart rate picked up and he sat down. The comforter was warm where the laptop had been.

He was looking at a code of some kind. He glanced at the spine on a thick book lying open beside it. *Don Quixote.* He reached for it, swallowing hard. The itch was back, and a part of him wanted to shut down the laptop and leave the house. Quickly. Before he figured out what was going on.

He flipped back to the first page and saw that the book had belonged to Drew Franklin. There were little scraps of paper between the pages and faint circles around some of the letters. He set the book back down and studied the Word document on the laptop. Definitely a code. He closed his eyes for several moments, then scrolled down the page until the next page came up. This time there were names of places with large numbers beside them. Belize: 14,000,000. Liechtenstein: 3,000,000. Geneva: 4,000,000. Canary Islands: 12,000,000. Costa Rica: 8,500,000. The list went on.

"Shit," he said. This was crazy. Joy was cracking codes to numbered accounts holding obscenely large sums of money. And he strongly suspected it was Drew's money—or, more likely, Kate's.

Ben closed the laptop and ran his hands over his face.

Okay, he had to get a grip. There was nothing illegal about having numbered offshore accounts in and of itself. The illegality was usually where the money had come from. Drew must have moved Kate's money into numbered accounts only he and Joy could access.

White-hot pain lanced his gut. How could she? No matter that being a successful politician required her to tell her share of lies and half-truths, make secret deals, compromise to win support for what she believed in. What he was looking at stunk of felony theft, of betrayal beyond that of the marriage vow.

"What have you done, Joy?" he whispered.

Hypocrite, his conscience whispered back.

Slowly he straightened and opened the laptop again. He leaned against the pillows Joy had left propped up and began a thorough search of her files, noting that several of the letters had Drew's name in the signature line. Apparently she'd drafted letters for him in addition to her other services. As he read, her smell surrounded him, along with the memories of all the times they'd made love in this bed. When his vision went blurry he wiped his eyes on his shoulders and called himself twelve kinds of fool for caring.

Sometime later—he had no idea how long after he'd begun—he found a document he wished to God he'd never seen. It made him physically sick to read it, and he stopped midway through. His finger hovered over the delete button, then retracted. Then hovered, then retracted. Finally he closed the laptop, set it down beside him on the bed and closed his eyes.

Someone was going to prison for a long time.

He slid one hand behind the pillow and pulled out the scrap of satin that had been there every night he'd shared with his wife, and held it to his nose. It was all that was left of the blanky Joy had slept with since she was a child. Her security blanket. They never talked about it. It shared the bed with them night after night, conferring a comforting energy Joy depended on. It had come along on their vacations, and on the rare occasions it didn't make it back into their suitcase, he had turned around without question and gone back to get it.

Could an inmate have a blanky in prison?

"Thanks, Sam," Joy said to the Capitol police officer who had accompanied her and Gabe to her office suite in the Cannon House Office Building. "I'll call downstairs when we're ready to leave."

"Good enough, Mrs. Stuart," the officer said, and strolled down the hall.

Joy unlocked her office door, reached out to her left and flipped on the overhead light. She and Gabe stepped inside the outer office, where her administrative assistant and other aides had assorted desks and tables. Six padded seats for visitors were lined up along the wall beside the door.

"It was easier not to explain why I wanted to get into Drew's office," she said by way of explanation, but Gabe hadn't asked. More likely she was nervous. They'd spoken little in Joy's car—she had insisted they take hers—on the way over. She'd been taking deep breaths, calming herself, but her fingers had gripped the steering wheel so hard her knuckles were white.

"Must have come as quite a shock," Gabe said, leaning back against the door, arms crossed over his chest.

"Hmm?"

"The photos," he said.

"Oh," she said, casual as could be. "Well, I'd be lying if I said I wasn't surprised."

"So, what now?"

"Now we wait until I'm sure Sam is gone and we go down the hall to Drew's office." She was fiddling with things on people's desks, straightening pictures, checking the soil in a couple of potted plants on the window ledge. Gabe watched. And waited.

A minute or so later she said, "Wait here. I'll be right back."

"I'd rather come with you," he said.

"If Sam comes back, or if anyone else shows up, it'll raise a lot of questions if we're both in Drew's office."

"He's dead, Joy," Gabe said dryly. "I'm a cop."

"Everyone knows the FBI is in charge of this investigation. Just… trust me, okay? It's better if I go in there myself."

He pretended to acquiesce. "Fine. I'll be waiting."

Joy left, and he gave her thirty seconds to get where she was going before he stepped out into the hallway. There were security cameras mounted discreetly near the ceilings, and he didn't want to attract attention, so he stood there for a few moments and then sauntered down the hallway in the direction of Drew's office.

Joy's scream didn't have far to travel, and she was still screaming as Gabe pounded down the hallway with his gun in his hand. He burst into the office and smelled that familiar metallic scent of blood at the same instant he saw what she was screaming about.

Michael Clark was slumped over his desk with half his head blown off, a gun in his blood-soaked hand.

Chapter Thirty-Two

"Oh, my God." Kate stood in her foyer and gazed around at the wrecked house. Pictures had been torn off the walls and smashed. Cushions had been ripped apart, lamps and tables overturned. Even the china cabinet in the corner of the dining room had been knocked over. She should care about the shards of fine china and crystal strewn about the floor, but she didn't. Frightening as it was that someone had done this, all she felt about the ruined pieces of her life with Drew was…nothing. She had never really cared about the trappings of wealth, other than those things that entertained Jeremy.

Mancuso was talking rapidly into his phone, but Kate wasn't interested in what he had to say. She headed toward the stairs and, right on cue, he said, "No, Mrs. Franklin. Don't go up there."

She turned to him and said slowly. "I am going up to my bedroom, Agent Mancuso, and I am going to pack a bag and get the hell away from this house."

Mancuso signed off and said, "I need you to wait until the cops get here. This house is a crime scene."

Right. The D.C. cops. *Gabe.* The searing pain of his betrayal fueled her determination. "I don't need to wait," she said. "I'm getting my things—assuming there's anything left intact—and I don't give a damn what you or the cops or the CIA or anyone else wants me to do. You boys can go through and have a blast picking through my life." She turned back to the stairs and continued up. He followed her silently.

Her bedroom was as trashed as the lower floor. “Holy shit,” Mancuso said from behind her. “I’m afraid I have to insist—”

“Save it,” she said, and proceeded to the bathroom. Her toiletries were strewn across the counters and the floor, and bits of broken glass glinted up at her. She spun around and nearly ran into Mancuso’s chest. It was all she could do not to slap him. Hard. She pushed past him and went to her closet. The clothes on hangers had been thrown on the floor and someone had poured something over them. It smelled like a mix of perfumes and cleaning fluid. She sighed heavily.

“Let’s go downstairs and wait for the techs, Mrs. Franklin.”

She headed for the bedroom door. No way she was going to wait around for Gabe to show up and offer more of his bullshit. He’d taken advantage of her when she was most vulnerable and thrown her to the wolves. She wouldn’t make that mistake again.

At the doorway she stopped. She turned and crossed the room, stepping over torn sheets and smashed furnishings to her bedside table and pulled open the top drawer. The picture of her and Steve and Gabe was still there. The photo was creased and worn, particularly over Gabe. Tears welled and she shook her head, remembering the hundreds of times she had stared at that face, run the tips of her fingers over it, even held it to her lips.

Careful to preserve the part with her and Steve, she tore off Gabe’s face and let that piece drift to the floor. The rest she put in a zippered pocket of her purse. At the last minute she remembered to grab her phone charger, which was, miraculously, still hanging from the wall socket. Alison had left half a dozen messages on her cell during the day, frantic because she didn’t know where Kate was. Wait’ll she heard that she'd been in FBI custody all that time. And that her house had been trashed. Their next conversation would be a long one.

She opened a door at the far end of the hallway and climbed a set of stairs to her studio at the top of the house. Before she even reached the top landing the overwhelming smell of resin and turpentine told her that her sanctuary had been breached. She stared from the doorway at the destroyed canvases, busted up easels, paint-coated walls and floors, allowing the fury to roll over her. Who could possibly hate her this much?

Numbly she went back downstairs and into the kitchen. Predictably, all the plates and glasses were smashed. Thank God Violetta had picked up Bruno. Thinking about her dog gave her the first actual pang of regret that her life in this house was effectively over. Bruno had loved the yard and the pool. As soon as she knew for sure where she was going, she'd pick him up. Of course, by the time she got him back Violetta's three children would have spoiled him rotten.

"You'll cut your feet up if you go in there," Mancuso said.

She ignored him and stepped around the worst of the mess. Stuck to the refrigerator were photos of Jeremy at various ages, starting from when he was an infant. She pulled them down and stuck them in her purse, then picked her way out of the room, down the hallway to the foyer, and pulled open the front door.

"Wait. Where are you going?" Mancuso asked.

"Don't worry. I'm not leaving town."

"You need to be in a safe house where we can protect you."

She snorted. "Please, Agent Mancuso. With friends

like you who needs enemies? I'll be safer away from you people." Gabe's face popped into her head. "All of you."

"We have to be able to reach you," he said.

"You have my cell number," she said, not looking at him.

"Yes, but—"

"I'm going to a hotel," she said, then waved a hand at him. "Feel free to follow my credit card trail."

Kate clicked the door opener for her Prius, got in and pulled away quickly. She was headed to Philly, and she wouldn't be using her credit card.

Gabe gazed down at the torn off photo in the plastic bag and felt a surge of regret so strong he wanted to weep with it. Mancuso had been jubilant when he'd handed him the bag, describing in detail how Kate had torn the photo and let that piece fall to the floor. He let the guilt wash over him—guilt that he'd agreed to use her, even though that wasn't what their lovemaking had been about. And worse, guilt that she had loved him more than she had loved Steve.

It killed him to ask the question, but he had no choice. "Where did she go?"

"Said she was going to a hotel," Mancuso said. "Told me we could follow her credit card trail. Then again, maybe she's got someone joining her there."

Gabe refused to give him the satisfaction of glaring. "I presume you had someone follow her?"

Mancuso spread his fingers over his chest. "Do I look like a rookie to you?"

No, you look like an asshole to me. "And?"

"And, she hasn't landed anywhere yet."

"Well, the last time you heard from the tail, where was she?" Gabe asked, unable to hide his exasperation.

"Relax, Detective. I'll let you know the minute I hear."

"Please do. Whoever did this may also be following her."

Gabe stuck the bag in his pocket and swept the room with his eyes. Someone had gone to a lot of trouble to make this look like an act of rage. Another woman or a furious lover would have torn Kate's clothes to shreds, not simply stopped at dousing them with a mix of chemicals. He'd thought all along that Kate's attacker had been looking for something, and this unholy mess fit his theory.

"The computer in the den was taken," Scott Bailey said from the doorway. "Not destroyed. Can't tell whether there are more books missing from the study. Kate will have to help us with that."

Drew Franklin's computer was taken. Now *that* was interesting. Probably the only useful part of this whole frustrating investigation. Whoever had broken in and trashed Kate's house had known how to avoid detection. Or, at least, immediate detection. Something would turn up if they were patient.

"What about Kate's laptop?" Gabe asked.

"We took it with us," Mancuso said. "We didn't find anything on it."

Gabe didn't bother to point out that he had already gone through Kate's laptop and come to the same conclusion, which he had shared with Parker. Clearly the FBI didn't trust him any more than he trusted them. Some things never changed.

Scott was leaning against his car when Gabe emerged from Kate's house. "Hey," he said. "Got a minute?"

Gabe checked his watch. 4:30 a.m. *Jesus.* "Make it fast," he said.

Scott scratched his blond head, a habit he had when he

had a hunch or felt uneasy about something. "Looks like I might've been wrong about her."

Gabe cocked his head back at the house. "Oh, you mean because while Michael Clark was supposedly offing himself and confessing to murder and other vague crimes someone else was trashing her house? Would've been hard for her to orchestrate both events while she was in FBI custody."

Scott gave a wry smile. "You thinking it wasn't really a suicide?"

"Forensics will be able to tell us that very soon," Gabe said.

"Meanwhile, whoever did this—"

"—may still be after Kate," Gabe said. "Believe me, I'm well aware of that."

"More likely they're after whatever they think she has in her house."

As far as Gabe was concerned Joy was not off the hook. Granted, the note Michael left took all the blame for everything. *I loved him,* it said. *He betrayed me. Tell Kate I'm sorry for everything I did to her, but now she is free to love again. I am the one who can't live without him.*

Gabe wasn't buying it. Not the suicide or the note. If Michael had written that note it stood to reason he had broken in and had torn apart Kate's house in a fit of jealousy and grief. But someone in that state would have killed himself on the spot. He wouldn't have gone back to the office—having stopped off to shower, since his body held no trace of the perfume or cleaning fluids that were all over Kate's house—written her a heartfelt apology, and then shot himself.

"Clark wouldn't have known she was in custody," Scott

said, his thoughts obviously running along the same lines. “Even the press didn’t find out until she was released.”

Gabe nodded and ran his hands back through his hair. “Yeah. But until the feds figure out Michael was murdered—”

“They won’t be looking for our guy,” Scott said.

Chapter Thirty-Three

It was almost seven o'clock in the morning when Kate climbed the steps to the house she'd grown up in. Easter and Christmas dinners had moved to Jennifer's house several years ago, leaving little reason to come here—and she'd long since stopped carrying a key. She rang the bell. Her mother opened the door and took a step back when she saw Kate. Her hand flew to her throat, as though she were looking at a ghost. "My God. Kate."

"Hi, Mom," Kate said, stepping inside. "Sorry for not calling. It was an impulse thing."

"But...but..." her mother stuttered. "We heard on the radio that you had been in custody and they were releasing you this morning."

Kate looked closely at the woman who had raised her. Dressed in loose black pants and a matching top, her blond shoulder-length hair as nicely styled as ever, Valerie Callahan looked far younger than her sixty-five years.

"I put up such a fuss that they released me sooner," Kate said. "And thanks for the moral support."

Her mother flushed. "Your father didn't think we should go," she said, then rushed to add, "But he's been very concerned. We both have. And Alison said she would let us know what was going on. I'm sorry, Kate, I—"

Kate held up a hand. "Please, don't bother apologizing. I need a place to sleep and I want to pick up some of my old things if you haven't thrown them away."

"Of course I haven't." Her mother finally stepped back and closed the door behind Kate. "Are you all right? Are you hungry? I'm making pancakes."

"No thanks," Kate said. She brushed past her mother and took the steps up to the bedrooms. She didn't want to talk to either one of them. Her father would be interested long enough to know everything was under control—and that he didn't have to exert himself—and then drift back into the living room and work on his crossword puzzles, or whatever it was that held his interest. And her mother would make excuses for him. Been there, done that.

Thankfully, her room was still mostly intact. It made sense, considering that she'd paid for them to add several rooms on to the back and sides of the house. She closed the door and locked it, then let out a sigh of relief. At least the FBI hadn't busted her when she crossed the state line. She had no illusions that she was off their radar, but given the fact that Drew had stolen all her money, she couldn't go far. Besides, they said Michael had taken the blame for all of it.

Michael. Dead. *Jesus Christ.*

She couldn't believe Michael was capable of murder, or of sending someone to her house to hurt her. A shudder rippled through her at the thought. She had to get in touch with Archer. She didn't know anything about their relationship other than they were friends, but he had to be hurting. Problem was, she didn't even have a last name for him, or a phone number.

With a long sigh she went to her closet and was pleased to find all the clothes she had left behind after college still on their shelves or on hangers. Given how much weight she'd lost, her old Levi's would still fit, and most of the T-shirts, all of the shoes. Okay, good. No immediate need to go shopping. The less contact she had to make with people the better. If the news hadn't gone out already, soon everyone would hear that she had been released, and it would be beat the press time all over again.

She sat cross-legged on the floor of the closet to pull out some shoes, and spotted a stack of her old sketch pads. Even as her gut twisted, some perverse need had her reaching for them. She swallowed and flipped over the cover of the first one, to find herself confronted by an early study of Steve's profile. Tears welled, and she ran her fingers over the boyish features. God, why had he died so young?

She closed the pad, knowing her heart would break if she forced herself to remember her time with Steve. Not now. She wasn't strong enough. Most of the pads in the stack were filled with sketches of him, years of sketches she'd made while he worked at his computer. She put them back where she'd gotten them…and then remembered. The other sketch pad. The private one. Was it still there?

She got down on her belly and crawled to the far end of the closet, beneath the shelves and rack of long dresses and coats, where no one ever looked, and lifted up the edge of the carpet. Her fingers found the spiral edge of the sketch pad, and she pulled it out, then sat with it on her lap for a long, long time, trying to get her mind to go blank, her heart to stop pounding. She should toss the thing in the Dumpster. Should have done it years ago. Why had she saved it?

Finally, after who knew how long, she flipped up the top sheet to her study of Gabe's eyes and nose. Her breath caught in her throat. He'd been much younger, less troubled, but she'd captured the shape, even the intensity of his eyes. She reached out to touch it but stopped herself and flipped to the next page. His ear and neck, the back of his head. The accuracy and detail was beyond anything she'd achieved in her studies of Steve.

She flipped through more pages, fascinated by the variations in Gabe's expressions from morose to angry to silly to contented. Just like he'd looked in her bed the morning the FBI came for her.

White-hot fury rose in her chest. "You rotten, no good son of a bitch," she spat at the drawing on her lap. "You filthy, scumsucking, lying bastard. Dirty, filthy, rotten, disgusting, lying n-no good, lying…" Tears clogged her throat and her nose, making it hard to breathe or speak. The fact that she was crying over him again stoked her rage and she began to shout. "I hate you. I hate the ground you walk on. I hate the filthy sight of you, you s-sucking, slimy…"

Somehow she got to her feet and left the closet and started slapping the sketch pad at walls, at furniture, at lamps, at pictures, all the while shouting and crying and finally just shrieking in frustration and pain. A wounded, bleeding beast had exploded out of her chest and taken over her body, and God help anyone who got in her way.

When her energy was spent and her voice was hoarse she sank to the floor and curled into a ball, shaking and hiccupping sobs and asking herself over and over what she was going to do. She didn't hear her mother enter the room, but she smelled her flowery perfume and felt warm hands pulling her hair off her face, stroking her cheek, lifting her head and laying it on her lap.

"It's okay, Katie," her mother crooned. "You've been through hell and back with no one there to help you. And I'm so, so sorry, baby. I've never been so sorry in my life."

She heard the catch in her mother's voice and cried even

harder, but this time there were arms around her, holding her together, telling her everything was going to be okay.

Her life wasn't over.

When Gabe showed up at his mother's house that evening it was closer to seven o'clock than six. His mother was stirring spaghetti sauce in the pot and Carolyn was reading the paper at the table. He gave his mother a quick peck on the cheek, which brought a smile, and sat across from his sister.

Carolyn had called him at work that morning, saying his presence was requested at dinner because Sylvia was going to call to tell them all something very important. Gabe had made her laugh by speculating that she must be pregnant, despite the fact that she was forty and divorced.

"So," he said. "Did I miss Sylvia's call?"

"No," Carolyn said. "I told her we'd call her after dinner and put her on speakerphone."

Gabe scratched his head. "Mom, do you know what this is about?"

"I'll throw the spaghetti in now," his mother said, and Gabe wondered why she didn't answer the question. Not that she was particularly interested in anything they did. It was as though all her curiosity, all her enthusiasm and vivacity had died with Steve. A familiar ache filled his chest. *Damn,* he was tired of living with that guilt.

He and Carolyn made small talk while they ate, and his mother tuned into and out of the conversation. When they were finished, Gabe opted to wait for dessert in favor of getting the phone call over with. He had to talk to Kate tonight or he'd never rest. Damn it, he had to explain what he'd done and why, and somehow make her understand how he felt about her.

And what the hell was Kate doing at her parents' house? Of all the unlikely places for her to go…

The doorbell rang, and Miriam went to answer it. "Who can this be?" Carolyn said. "Bad timing."

A loud exclamation told them whoever was at the door was a very welcome guest. Gabe checked his watch and rubbed his hands over his face. He didn't have time to talk to some family friend. He had to get out there and find Kate's attacker.

The CSI team had worked tirelessly to find prints or any evidence that could point to a suspect, but they'd found nothing. Both the police and the FBI were investigating Michael Clark's death, which they hadn't yet ruled a homicide. They knew Michael had arrived at the Cannon House Office Building alone at six o'clock that evening. Coincidentally or not, the Capitol Police, in checking their logs, discovered they were missing a visitor named Jamal Jones who had come in with a group from New Orleans that day to talk to the representatives from Louisiana. They were probably still going through surveillance tapes trying to put a face to the name.

When Sylvia walked into the kitchen with her arm around his mother Carolyn jumped up with a squeal of surprise and went to her. So much for the phone call—and getting away quickly. Sylvia let go of Carolyn and came around the table to him. He stood up and hugged her, and was surprised by how tightly she squeezed him. Her dark hair was streaked with gray strands, and her clothes were rumpled, no doubt from the flight from Chicago.

"Well, this is unexpected," he said, fixing Carolyn with a questioning look. Had she known Sylvia was coming or was she as surprised as she appeared to be? "How are you doing?"

Sylvia leaned back but held on to Gabe's shoulders.

"I thought this was important enough to show up in the flesh." To her mother and Carolyn she said, "I'm sorry I didn't tell you I was coming, but I thought it would be kind of fun to surprise you."

Gabe put his hand on his sister's belly. "So, are you actually pregnant?"

Sylvia slapped his hand away and snorted. "Is that what Carolyn told you?"

"No," Carolyn said. "I said you had something important to tell us all."

Gabe pulled out his chair and sat back down, forearms crossed on the table. "Whatever it is, if you could tell us sooner rather than later I'd appreciate it. I have to go back to work after this."

"Mom, can you make us all some tea?" Carolyn asked, and it felt as though she was trying to keep her out of the conversation. Then she turned to Gabe and cleared her throat. "Guess who I heard from today?"

For a hopeful moment Gabe thought she was talking about Kate, but then he realized how unlikely that was. "Please, don't keep me in suspense."

Carolyn turned to Sylvia, who sat beside her across the table from Gabe, and they exchanged a knowing look. "Lindsay," she said.

Gabe glanced between them. "Okay," he said. "What did she want?"

Both women leaned toward him. "Promise you won't shoot the messenger," Sylvia said.

Gabe frowned. "You know about this?"

"That's why I'm here, Gabe," Sylvia said. "Lindsay called me too."

Fuck. "About what?"

"About you and Kate."

Gabe stared at his sisters, who wore almost identical expressions of concern, except that Sylvia's lips were pressed together in disapproval. He immediately understood what had happened—Lindsay had pumped Jeremy for information and pressured the poor kid to tell her about the sleepover two nights ago. Jeremy must have woken up and seen that he was gone, then found him in Kate's bed. That information would have pissed Lindsay off royally. So she had followed her instincts and called in the big guns.

His sisters.

He leaned back and folded his arms over his chest. "What about me and Kate?" he asked.

Carolyn held up a hand. "Don't be mad at Jeremy," she said.

"I'm not mad at Jeremy," he said. "Jeremy's a kid. And most of the time he minds his own business. Unlike his mother." He didn't have to say *and you* for his sisters to get the message.

Carolyn took a deep breath and let it out slowly. "Jeremy told Lindsay you slept with Kate a few days ago, at her house."

A clatter behind him told him his mother had dropped something. They all turned to see Miriam pick up a spoon off the floor. She glanced at them, said nothing and went back to making the tea.

"Is that right?" Gabe said, forcing himself to hide his irritation.

His sisters looked at each other, then back to him. "Well?" Sylvia said. "Did you actually sleep with her?"

"And this is your business because…?" he prompted.

Carolyn folded her hands on the table. "Look, Gabe," she began. "We know it's none of our business in the sense that you can sleep with whoever you want. You're a big boy."

"I'm glad we've established that," he said.

"But we're talking about *Kate.* Who you've hated for the last eight years. Remember? Or did she drive all that out of your mind with—whatever?"

"She's probably using you," Sylvia said. "I mean, my God, up until this Michael Clark killed himself the cops were investigating her for killing her husband. What better way to get off than to sleep with one of you."

As his heartbeat picked up his gut started to burn. *Damn it.* The last thing he needed was to lose his cool. "First of all," he said, "the FBI was investigating her, not the cops, so sleeping with a cop wouldn't do jack shit for her."

"Well, don't you all work together?"

Mancuso's smug face flashed into Gabe's head and he chuckled derisively. "Only when absolutely necessary. And even then, I have no pull with the FBI. And by the way, thank you for insinuating that I would pull strings for Kate or anybody else."

"Oh, Gabe," Sylvia said.

"So we've established that you are, in fact, sleeping with Kate," Carolyn said, opening her hands for emphasis. "Right?"

"I have to assume that you've made that judgment without me, considering that Sylvia hasn't come home for anything less than a wedding or a funeral in years."

Sylvia glared, but quickly lowered her head and proceeded to play with the salt and pepper shakers.

"Did you suddenly change your mind about her?" Carolyn asked. "Or were you the one using her? To get information or something? Although, given how much you always hated her I don't know how you could do it."

"He's a guy," Sylvia said with a dismissive wave.

"I never hated her," Gabe said quietly. Sylvia raised her

head and they both stared at him. "Kate and I used to be good friends before Steve died." Damn it. He'd mentioned the unmentionable in his mother's presence. He glanced toward the sink, but his mother was pouring water from the kettle into four mugs, and didn't seem to have heard.

Carolyn leaned in further and lowered her voice almost to a whisper. "You stopped liking her even before that. You suddenly had to work the day of their wedding, and Ben stood in for you. Remember? It wasn't only that she hooked up with the congressman ten seconds after..." She trailed off with a quick glance at her mother. "For a couple months before she married Steve you were saying stuff like, 'He could do better,' and 'She'll drive him to drink.' Stuff like that."

Gabe rubbed his eyes with the heels of his hands, then leaned forward again. What he had to say would shock them, but if he and Kate were going to have any kind of future he had to clear the air with his family. "I did say those things," he said. "But I didn't mean them."

"Then why'd you say them?" Sylvia demanded, obviously still stung by his earlier barb.

"I was jealous," he said.

"Of what?"

"Of Steve."

"What are you saying?" Miriam said from beside him. All eyes flew to her. She set a mug of tea next to his arm and sat down heavily. "You wanted Kate for yourself?"

"That's not what he's saying, Ma," Sylvia said, reaching across and putting a hand on her mother's arm.

"That's exactly what I'm saying," Gabe said.

Three pairs of eyes stared at him. After several moments his mother said, "My God. All this time I wondered what on earth she had done that had so offended you, and I missed what was staring me right in the face."

Gabe's throat constricted. He laid a hand over his mother's. "I poisoned everyone against her. I was the one who wouldn't let her come over and see you." He swallowed with trouble. "It was all my fault. The whole thing."

His mother looked troubled. "What was your fault?"

She was too close. He couldn't say what he had to say with his mother looking into his eyes. He removed his hand gently and stood up and walked to the counter. Leaning back, he gripped the edge with both hands and said, "Steve's accident. It was my fault."

"What?" Sylvia gasped. "That's crazy, Gabe. You weren't anywhere near him."

He rubbed at his forehead with the side of his hand but quickly brought it back to anchor him. God, he wanted a beer. But no. They deserved to hear the truth, and he deserved to deal with the pain sober. "I thought…" he began, and cleared his throat. "I *convinced* myself that Kate had told him about what happened between us."

"*What* happened?" Sylvia asked, a touch of hysteria in her voice. "Don't tell me you were sleeping with her back then."

He shook his head. "No. But one night she was babysitting for Jeremy and I came home earlier than usual. Steve had left and gone back to the apartment."

"I hate to say it, but Steve totally took her for granted," Carolyn said, glancing at Miriam, whose gaze was still on Gabe.

"Anyway." He let out a long breath. God, this was so much harder than he'd expected. "I'm not making any excuses for myself, but I'd just shot a guy—a kid, really…" He trailed off.

His mother walked over to him and put two fingers to his lips. "I remember what happened with Kevin Brewer. You don't have to tell us any more," she said. "Whatever happened, it's okay."

"I need to," he said, his voice raspy with emotion. "You have to understand. About Kate. I won't be able to live with myself until you understand. And if you all hate me after what I have to say, then so be it."

"That will never happen," his mother said. "I'll stand right here beside you while you tell us whatever it is that's eating away at you."

It took Gabe nearly an hour to tell the whole story with no interruptions from his sisters. As promised, his mother stood next to him the entire time he was talking, silently lending her support. When he finished his sisters were staring at him.

"So, you're telling us that Kate really did love Steve, and she married Drew Franklin because she was lonely but she really wanted to be with you, and our family… And we shouldn't hate her for anything…" Carolyn took a breath. "But what about now? I mean, after all those years of all of us treating her like shit—"

"Especially you," Sylvia said to Gabe.

"You two are actually going to be a couple?" Carolyn's eyes were wide, her mouth slightly open. "You and Kate?"

"Well, first I have to find out who's been hurting her," Gabe said. "And keep her safe."

"And then what?" Miriam asked.

"And then I have to convince her that I'm not a lying piece of shit."

"Hmm, that could be difficult," Sylvia teased.

"And then…?" Miriam said, holding his gaze. Gabe couldn't remember his mother caring so much about anything in the last eight years. She'd listened to the whole sordid story without interrupting or judging. Instead, she had given him little pats on the arm or rubbed her hand over his back when he needed it. And she knew just when he did. Almost the way she would have when Steve was still alive.

"And then I guess I'll try to get her to spend some time with me."

"You love her," Sylvia said. "You actually love her."

Gabe saw only surprise in his sister's blue eyes, no censure. "Yes, I do."

Carolyn and Sylvia came to him then and wrapped their arms around him. He hugged them back, marveling at how much their love and support meant to him. "Good luck with Lindsay," Carolyn said, pulling back. "She's determined to keep you two apart, and to keep Kate away from Jeremy."

"She says Kate's a bad influence on both of you," Sylvia added.

"Lindsay always resented Kate," Miriam said, and they all turned to her. "I think she saw that you were attracted to her and it drove her crazy."

"Did you see it?" Gabe asked.

His mother gave a small shrug and an enigmatic smile. "I wasn't so blind back then."

Miriam walked Gabe to his car and held him tightly before he got in. As he was about to pull away she knocked on the window. He rolled it down.

"I always thought you would have been a better match for Kate than Steven was," she said, and stroked his cheek. "He was too absorbed in all that technical stuff to keep a girl like her happy. She took good care of him, but she had needs too and hers always came second. It was like that with her family, poor thing. Always the outcast."

"I know," Gabe said. "I never understood that." He smiled up at his mother. "You're pretty damn smart for an old broad," he said, then took her face in his hands and planted a big smacking kiss on her cheek. As predicted she swatted him away, but for the first time in eight long years her smile was wide and genuine.

She raised her face to the sky. "Will you look at all those stars," she said.

Chapter Thirty-Four

Gabe spent the next two days hanging over the shoulders of the forensics team, going through every report, every photograph from Kate's house, looking through lists of known felons in the area, lists of Michael Clark's associates and his movements over the past six months. He was beyond frustrated that he knew nothing about Kate's friend Archer, not even a last name, and she'd never told him how long she'd known him or where she'd met him.

He was on his way home midweek when his cell phone chirped. The readout said Ben Stuart. Huh. "Gabe here."

"Yeah," the voice said, so solemn it barely sounded like Ben. "Come over, okay? To the house, I mean."

The hair on Gabe's neck prickled. "What's wrong?"

The chuckle from the other end sounded defeated. "What isn't?"

"Is Joy okay?" Gabe asked.

"Yeah. For now."

"Be there in ten," Gabe said, and clicked off. He'd never heard Ben sound like that. As though someone had died. Maybe that was how *he* had sounded when Steve died. Every syllable was a struggle. Whole sentences? Not possible.

"Fuck." Something bad was going down. Or maybe it was something good for him, if not for Ben. Like a confession from Joy. That would be good and totally suck at the same time.

"Fuck," he repeated, for emphasis.

When he pulled up in front of the Stuart house it was nearly ten-thirty. The porch light was on but few lights were on inside the house. Gabe grabbed his jacket to hide his shoulder holster and cuffs. Yeah, these people were old friends, but if Joy was involved in this business he had no idea what he would find. In fact… He punched some numbers into his cell.

"Scott Bailey."

"Hey, it's me," Gabe said. "Meet me at the Stuarts', but park and stay outside. I don't expect to need backup but it's possible."

"I'll be there."

Gabe clicked off and headed up the front steps as he had dozens of times in the past, before Steve died. He knocked, and Ben answered the door without a word. Gabe stepped inside. Joy was sitting on the sofa, holding a tissue to her nose, eyes red-rimmed and wet. *Fuck.*

He stood there, waiting for someone to tell him what the hell was going on. After a long silence, Joy said, "I'm sorry, Gabe," and started sobbing into her tissue.

"For what?" he asked. Ben had seated himself several feet away on a lower step of the center staircase. Not even in the same room. His expression was grim, hands folded between his knees. The lenses of his glasses were fogged up. *Goddamn it.*

"You called me, Ben," he said. "Want to tell me what's going on?"

Ben pulled off his glasses and rubbed them on his shirt. "Yeah. Give me a minute."

Joy said, "He thinks I'm guilty, but I'm not. I swear to God, Gabe, you have to believe me."

Gabe wished he'd told Scott to come inside immediately. He didn't want to be the one to haul Joy's ass into custody. Yeah, if she had hurt Kate or had something to do with that plane going down he'd happily put her away. But Jesus, he couldn't stand seeing the agony on Ben's face. "Guilty of what?" he asked as gently as he could.

"I'm no murderer," she said, her expression pleading. "You know me. And I wouldn't have hurt Kate, whether I hated her or not. I'm not some psycho."

Gabe pinched the bridge of his nose. "Ben, I think this would be easier if you were in the same room, man."

Ben came slowly to his feet. "It's in the bedroom," he rasped as though his vocal cords had ceased working. "I'll bring it out."

"Bring what out?"

"The laptop."

Gabe knew from experience that bad things could happen when a person in the kind of shape Ben was in went into another room. Weapons appeared. Suicides happened. So did homicides.

"Joy," he said. "Come on over here. We're all going in together."

She rose from the couch. Gabe stepped aside so she could precede him into the bedroom. When they got there, Ben pointed at an open laptop sitting on the bed. A thick book lay open beside it. "That's how I found it the night you went to Joy's office."

"What's on there?" Gabe asked. He pulled out two latex gloves and moved around the bed to pick up the laptop. "Or do you want me to figure it out for myself."

"It's a code," Joy said, her voice nasally from crying. "It's for numbered bank accounts. Offshore mostly."

Gabe stared at her. "Explain."

She let out a long sigh and sat on the edge of the bed.

Her hair was sticking out at odd angles, and her face was ashen. Except where it was red from crying. “I’m trying to put together the code,” she said, sounding miserable. “So I can figure out where the money went. I thought if I could find it I could return it, somehow.”

“What money?”

She took a deep, shuddering breath. “Kate’s money.”

“So,” Gabe said, glancing between Joy and Ben, who was leaning against the far wall, gazing out the window. “You’re saying that you stole Kate’s money?”

“No. I mean, not *me* per se. Look, Gabe,” she said, an imploring tone in her voice. “I know I should have a lawyer here. I know this information is really for the FBI. I get that. But we hoped, Ben and I, that because we’ve known each other so long, that you would listen with an open mind and help me figure out how to present this in the least damaging light.”

Gabe picked up the laptop and carried it around to the side of the bed, then sat beside her. “You’re telling me that you and someone else stole Kate’s money, is that right?”

“No. What Drew did was not illegal. As far as I know.”

“Help me out here,” he said. “Drew moved Kate’s money into offshore accounts with your knowledge, is that it?”

“That’s it,” Ben said from the wall.

“But since he was on all those accounts it wasn’t illegal,” Joy said. “It wasn’t exactly ethical, but it wasn’t, strictly speaking, illegal.”

“He obtained Kate’s signature under false pretenses,” Gabe said, running his eyes down the columns of numbers. “What did he want the money for? Was it for the two of you to go off and live the high life?”

Joy flushed. “No. It was… Drew said it was for ‘making things happen.' To make sure the bill passed." She shook her head. "He sucked me right in and I was too naïve to see it."

"What do you mean by that?"

"He had big ideas about what we could accomplish. He assumed the president would appoint him Director of Global I &S and said I would be his 'right arm.'" She stopped and looked up at Gabe. "He liked to bounce ideas off me. I think he always needed someone to tell him what a visionary he was."

This was consistent with what Kate had said about him. "And he always assumed things would fall into place, right?"

Joy nodded. "There was very little possibility of failure in Drew's mind. He simply wouldn't let it happen." In a lower voice she added, "No matter what it took."

"No matter what it took?"

She inhaled, eyes closed, and let out a long breath. "The other night, when you suggested that maybe Drew had wanted to kill Kate, I was tripping all over my words because it… Suddenly it didn't sound so far-fetched, and I couldn't help but wonder… But I didn't actually believe it. Not then."

Something niggled, but he needed more to figure out exactly what it was. "If you really didn't do anything illegal, why didn't you take this to the FBI right away?" Gabe asked, then turned to Ben. "And why'd you wait three days to call me? You could have spared Kate a whole lot of grief."

Ben mumbled something Gabe couldn't make out. Joy hung her head. "I know," she said. "And I'm sorry about that. I was afraid of what this would do to my reputation. And—" she swallowed, "—I was afraid I would somehow end up taking all the blame and going to prison. I mean, look at what the media's saying now about the three Democratic senators. 'Looks like the revenge of the conservatives?' They've even speculated that *I* might have had a role in Arlen Fischer's sudden disappearing act."

How does it feel to be falsely accused? he wanted to ask. Instead he said, "Why do you have to figure out a code to get to these accounts? If you knew how to break it, why didn't Drew give you the numbers to the accounts outright?"

She raised her face to him. "I only knew about the code because he wrote himself a note about it. And I saw the note by accident."

"How's that?"

She raked a hand through her hair, then cupped her forehead and squeezed her eyes shut. "Oh, God, why didn't I leave well enough alone?"

"Because well enough just doesn't do it for you, Joy," Ben said.

Joy opened her mouth to lob something back at Ben but Gabe cut her off. "So you saw the note by accident," he pressed.

"It was at the funeral," she said. "I was in Drew's office alone for about half an hour before Kate came in. And I was, you know, touching his things…trying to find some connection…"

Ben snorted.

"Anyway, I opened his drawers…looking for some little thing I could take with me."

"Like what?" Gabe asked.

"I don't know. Like a keychain or something. And I found this little silver flash drive with an American eagle on it. I figured Kate wouldn't need it for anything and it would probably get thrown away, so I slipped it in my purse."

"Where is it now?"

"In my pocket," Ben said.

Gabe didn't object. He gestured for Joy to continue.

She took a deep breath and let it out as she spoke. "So, a few days ago I decided to see what was on it. I plugged it into my laptop and opened up the files." She blew her nose. "I was...shocked."

"I bet you were," Ben muttered.

"Can't you wait in the other room or something?" Joy said, her voice trembling. "Damn it, Ben, this is hard enough."

"I certainly wouldn't want you to be inconvenienced," he said.

Still holding the laptop, Gabe went to stand beside Ben. "You okay, pal?" he asked quietly.

"Just hunky-dory," Ben said.

"Ben, I told you everything!" Joy shouted from the bed. "Everything I told you is the God's honest truth. Why can't you accept that?"

"Why don't we turn over this little device to the FBI and see what they have to say?" Ben said, refusing to look at her.

Joy jumped to her feet. "I agreed to get Gabe involved, okay? I could have destroyed that goddamn thing, and erased those files from my laptop and no one would ever have known. But I wanted you to see that I'm an honest person at heart, even if, *yes,* I had an affair with Drew. Okay? I'm an adulteress. So crucify me."

"I prefer the term 'whore,' personally," Ben said.

Joy slapped her palms to her chest and moved toward

her husband. “Fine. Paint a scarlet W on my chest. But don’t make me out to be a murderer, for God’s sake!”

“You offered to show Ben the files?” Gabe asked.

Her adamant expression fell. Ben said, “No. She left her laptop open on the bed—behind a locked door, mind you—when she went to the Cannon House Office Building with you. I don’t like being locked out of my own bedroom—”

“You moved out!” Joy shot back.

“—so I kicked the door in. And there was her laptop.”

“No one asked you to snoop,” Joy said.

“No one asked you to lock me out. No one asked you to fuck a married man. Marriage may have meant nothing to you or Drew but it meant something to Kate. It meant something to me.” His voice cracked on the last word.

“Was the device plugged into the computer when you found it?” Gabe asked, wanting desperately to steer the conversation away from the Stuarts’ marital issues and back to the evidence he was holding in his hands.

Ben shook his head. “She’d hidden it. She pulled it out when I confronted her with what I’d seen, and told me the story she just told you.”

“It’s not a goddamn story,” Joy said. “It’s the truth.”

“Was there anything that identified the device as belonging to Drew rather than you?” Gabe asked.

Joy sagged against the footboard. “No,” she said. “And there’s more.”

“Oh?” Gabe said. As though what she already told him wasn’t bad enough.

“There’s another document on there that Ben found. I hadn’t seen it before—before we went to the office.” She raised pleading eyes to her husband, but he continued to look away from her. “Ben, please,” she said. “We don’t have to show him that one. Please. No one has to see it.

We never should have brought him into this in the first place. I don't know why I—"

"It wasn't your decision to make," Ben said.

"You may not believe this," Joy began. "But I—"

"I don't believe it," Ben interrupted. "Whatever it is. You've lied to me for the past two years, so why should I believe your excuses?"

Gabe took the laptop from her. "Pull up the other document."

Joy's hands shook, but she managed to pull it up. He scanned the open document, which was double-spaced, all caps. It was a speech, beginning with the words:

COLLEAGUES AND FRIENDS, I STAND BEFORE YOU WITH A HEAVY HEART. *[Head down, swipe at tears.]*

What the fuck?

NOT ONLY HAS THIS TRAGEDY TAKEN MY BELOVED WIFE FROM ME *[long indrawn breath, voice cracks]* AND STOLEN LOVED ONES FROM MANY OTHER FAMILIES, IT HAS, ONCE AGAIN, RIPPED AT THE HEART OF DIGNITY, OUR NATIONAL…

Gabe blinked furiously and scrolled down to where he spotted the words: THESE TERRORISTS MAY HAVE BLOWN AMERICANS OUT OF THE SKY, BUT THEY WILL NOT SUCCEED IN DESTROYING THE FABRIC OF OUR NATION. WE HAVE THE TOOLS TO DEFEAT THEM ONCE AND FOR ALL. BY PASSING THE GLOBAL INTELLIGENCE AND SECURITY BILL WE SHOW THE WORLD THAT WE HAVE THE WILL TO CRIPPLE THESE COWARDS…

Gabe raised his head slowly and locked gazes with Joy. The pulsing in his temples blocked all sound, but by the look in her eyes and Ben's it was clear that no words were necessary.

Congressman Andrew Franklin had planned to blow up his wife's plane, killing her and everyone else aboard, to ensure passage of the Global Intelligence and Security Bill.

Gabe was only sorry the man was dead so he wouldn't have the pleasure of killing the bastard himself.

Joy sniffed and said, "I'm sure someone at the FBI could tell us when he wrote it."

Gabe set the laptop carefully on the bed and crossed his arms over his chest, his eyes never leaving Joy's. "Who would have turned the tables on him?"

Joy's head jerked back. "What do you mean? I assumed he made a mistake."

"I wouldn't have taken Franklin for a stupid man, and he would have had to be pretty damn stupid to accidentally blow himself up."

Joy turned to Ben, who was staring at his shoes, and back to Gabe. "You don't think…"

"Who had the most to gain from killing Drew Franklin?"

"Gabe… Even if I wanted to, how in the world would I pull something like that off?"

"You have the codes, Joy, which means you have access to the money."

"That's crazy. I would never do anything like that."

"You have access to ex-felons."

She opened her mouth to reply and then shut it. Her shoulders drooped, as though she was deflating before his eyes. "I couldn't have done this any more than Kate could have," she said quietly.

"You've certainly changed your tune," Ben said, but his voice was shaky and his eyes held something softer when he regarded his wife. Yeah, it's one thing to be angry and vindictive over an affair, and another to imagine your wife spending the rest of her life in prison.

"I'm not like Drew," Joy said. "I… I never knew anyone like him."

"Spare me," Ben growled.

"No, Ben, I don't mean that in a good way," she said, hugging herself. "I've had time to think about him, and I see so many things in a different light now. He was completely and utterly self-centered. I don't think he ever gave a damn about any of us. Not me, or Kate, or Michael… or anyone. All Drew cared about was Drew. I can remember wondering whether it bothered him to move Kate's money." She glanced at Gabe. "Because even though I went along…it bothered me."

"He didn't have much of a conscience," Gabe said.

"No," she agreed. "And if this… If he planned to actually bring down Kate's plane…"

"When did you get the books from his study?"

Joy blinked. "Oh, you mean—" she gestured at the copy of *Divine Comedy* lying on the bed, "—I got that one and two others from Michael's office."

"Before or after Kate was attacked in her bedroom?"

"After. But I swear I had nothing to do with that. I spotted them in a box in his office and I knew how much Drew treasured them." She shot Ben a guilty look. "So I took them home. I didn't think Michael would even notice they were missing."

"When did you first see them in that box?" Gabe asked.

"I'm pretty sure they'd been there since Michael picked up the files from Drew's house."

Gabe scrubbed at his beard stubble. He had no way of knowing whether she was telling the truth. "Well, Joy, if it wasn't you, then who pulled the rug out from under Drew Franklin's master plan? Because right now, I'll tell you the truth, it doesn't look good for you."

A minute passed in which the only sounds were of Joy sniffling and the air conditioner switching on. Ben lowered himself into an upholstered chair closer to where Gabe was standing.

"I think I know who did it," Ben said.

Chapter Thirty-Five

Joy whirled to face him, her eyes wild. "What did you say?"

Ben ignored her and focused on Gabe. "The night before the plane blew up, Joy and I went back to Drew's parents' home after dinner, because she insisted she had to have a word with Drew."

Gabe thought back to how surprised he'd been when Kate had told Parker they'd been there that night. "Who else was there?"

"Michael Clark, Ed Jorling. Kate, but she hadn't joined us for dinner, and when we got back she was asleep in the TV room. And another man I hadn't met before. I didn't catch his name. Something French, I'm pretty sure."

Joy said, "He was a friend of Michael's, but I don't remember his name either."

"Think," Gabe said.

"Ben asked me that night, but I didn't know then and I don't know now." She paused. "Maybe…Philippe?"

"Go on," he said to Ben.

"I was hoping I'd get to talk to Kate, but since she was out of it I was stuck with the others. So I took my time going upstairs to the bathroom, and when I came out I heard voices coming from one of the bedrooms."

"Why didn't you tell me this?" Joy asked.

Again he ignored her. "The other man was talking to

Drew, saying something like, 'You didn't mention that this little gift was for your wife.'"

Gabe felt a chill run down his back. "Go on."

"The other guy said something about Kate being on a commercial flight."

"What did the guy look like?"

"I don't know… Sort of dark. Mediterranean-looking. Greek or something."

Gabe nodded, making a mental note to get a full description.

Ben ran his hands through his hair and his face looked pained. "So Drew says something about collateral damage."

Joy gasped and brought her hand to her mouth. Gabe swallowed and asked, "What else did they say?"

"Well, I heard one of them walking so I turned and went back toward the bathroom. Then I heard a door close and the water go on, so I figured one of them went into an adjoining bath. I walked toward the steps—and it's deep plush carpeting, so I didn't make much noise—and I see through a crack in the door that the other guy is taking something out of Kate's big brown leather purse and sticking it in his pocket.

"Oh, God," Joy whispered.

"Then what?" Gabe asked.

Ben took a deep breath and let it out slowly. "I headed downstairs before the guy realized I was there. A little later he came down and put something in the briefcase Drew had with him at dinner."

"How did you know it was Drew's briefcase and not this guy's?"

"Because Drew put it down right beside the bottom step in the foyer, and it struck me because Joy does the same thing." He did not turn to look at his wife.

"Where were you when he opened Drew's briefcase?"

"I was sitting in the living room where I could see the guy when he came downstairs. I don't think he even noticed me."

"Why didn't you report this to someone?"

Ben raised his head and looked Gabe in the eye. "I could tell you it was only because I didn't know what I'd heard or seen, which is technically true, but I'd be lying. I figured if there was something dangerous there, and I had no idea what it was… Well, when I saw the guy put it in Drew's briefcase I was pretty damn sure he was passing it along to that bastard."

"Did it occur to you that the device was an explosive?"

Ben shrugged. "Sure. I'm not stupid. But how likely was that, really? I mean, Franklin was a schmuck but he was an elected official, for God's sake. Anyway, I figured if by some crazy twist of reality he was planning to blow up his wife and the other people on her flight he deserved to blow himself up in his car."

"Oh, my God, that's right," Joy said. "Drew said he was driving back to D.C."

"What if Drew had discovered the switch and put whatever it was back in Kate's bag?" Gabe asked, his voice harsh.

"Actually, that remote possibility bothered me so much I couldn't sleep that night," Ben said. "I took a cab to the airport early so I could talk to Kate before her flight left. I tore a button off my cuff on the way over and asked her if she had a safety pin, and she went through her bag. You know how it always has everything but the kitchen sink it? Well, she started pulling things out, and I got close enough that I could see if there was anything weird in her bag. I even joked about how she'd never even know if someone slipped drugs or a bomb into her bag."

"Well, goddamn it, Ben," Gabe growled. "You should have called the fucking cops or the FBI if you overheard them talking about explosives and—"

"Nothing was said about explosives," Ben said calmly.

"Well, collateral damage and all that. You suspected that Drew was planning to blow up his wife's flight, and you saw this guy move something into his briefcase, which is exactly where the explosion originated."

Once again, Ben hung his head for a moment before meeting Gabe's gaze. "First of all," he said, "I convinced myself that it had been wishful thinking on my part. I mean, come on. I hated the guy, but I didn't really believe he was a psycho."

"That doesn't explain why you didn't report that conversation immediately after the plane exploded."

"What was there to report?" Ben said, throwing his hands up. "Before I read Drew's speech I had no way of knowing whether he, or whatever *might* have been in his briefcase, had anything to do with that explosion. So I would have been implicating myself and possibly Joy in some sick scheme with no evidence even to support my story."

"So you sat back while Kate was implicated instead."

Ben was silent. After several moments he said quietly, "If I had known she was in custody I would have contacted you right away. I would *not* have left her to twist in the wind."

Gabe was too annoyed to answer. *He* was the one who'd abandoned Kate when she needed him. Not Ben.

"And," Ben went on, "if I'd known Drew was going to board a flight with other people, I swear to you, I would have risked looking like a fool and made the report. I have to live with the fact that innocent lives were lost because I didn't alert the authorities. But you can't make me feel guilty for wanting that evil bastard to get blown to kingdom come *if* that was what he had in his possession. Neither of them identified the 'little gift' or said when he was going to give it to his wife. It was all guesswork on my part."

"Now we have to figure out who the man was," Gabe said, pulling out his cell phone. "I assume he wasn't on the Learjet."

"No," Joy said. "I knew all those people. I guess we could ask—" She stopped suddenly and stared at her husband, wide-eyed. "My God, Ben. Everyone we had dinner with that night is dead."

The Stuarts' attorney arrived at the house within thirty minutes, and the four of them discussed the situation at length with a view to exempting the Stuarts from prosecution in exchange for their full cooperation. Given that they had come clean voluntarily, there was reason for hope.

Parker and Mancuso arrived within twenty minutes of being called. Before they went inside, Gabe pulled Parker aside. "Where is she now?" he asked.

"She and her mother left Philly early this morning to go to her house," Parker said. "Our guy said they loaded up cleaning supplies into the cars."

Gabe let out a breath. At least she was in D.C. again. But with her mother? "You never did explain why you guys didn't stop her crossing state lines to begin with."

"We advised her not to leave town, but in cases like this sometimes it makes more sense to follow a person of interest. See where they lead you… Why are you shaking your head?"

"I would never have expected her to go to her parents, that's all," Gabe said. "Maybe her sister's house, but not theirs."

“People do unexpected things when they’re under stress.”

“Yeah,” Gabe said. Didn’t he know it.

Chapter Thirty-Six

"Franklin residence," the woman said.

"Mrs. Callahan?"

"Yes?"

"Is Kate there with you?"

"It depends," Valerie said. "Is this Gabe?"

Shit. "I need to know she's okay," he said.

"Oh, she's great," Valerie said, and Gabe couldn't remember ever having heard Kate's mother use sarcasm before. "Never better."

Gabe ran a hand through his hair. In the days since he'd seen Kate he had barely slept and wasn't much in the mood to do battle with a mother who had suddenly decided to become the champion for her daughter. "Is she going to be at the house for a while?" he asked.

"Just long enough to clean up the mess."

"*You're* helping her with that?" he asked, not bothering to hide his incredulity.

Valerie was silent for several seconds before answering with a clipped, "Yes."

"Huh."

"What do you want, Gabe?" she asked, her tone stern and impatient.

"I want to talk to her."

"Forget it. You've hurt her for the last time."

He winced. "That's right, I have. And I need to tell her that."

Valerie snorted. "Fat chance. Leave her alone."

"Fat chance."

The gauntlet had been thrown down. He couldn't see her, but he imagined that Valerie's expression was as tight as his own.

"Look," she said, her voice quieter but no less hostile. "My daughter has been through more than anyone should ever have to go through in their lives. I promised her I would keep you away, and I am not going to let her down."

"Are you going to keep her safe, too?" he growled.

"The man who attacked her is—"

"The man who attacked her is on the loose," Gabe said. "Michael Clark is dead, but he isn't the person who attacked her."

Valerie was quiet. "Well, we haven't been in touch with the FBI—"

"The feds are not in charge of the break-in," Gabe said. "I am. And I'm going to keep Kate safe if it's the last thing I do." When she didn't respond, he muttered, "See ya," and hung up.

Ten minutes later he pulled into the circular drive and shut off his engine. Kate's Prius was parked at an odd angle, as though she'd jumped out of the car while it was still running. He expected to hear Bruno barking his head off when he walked up the steps, but heard instead the roar of a vacuum cleaner. He rang the bell, and within seconds the vacuum was turned off and Valerie Callahan pulled the front door open.

She was wearing jeans and a loose T-shirt, and for once she wasn't perfectly made up. She gave Gabe a once-over, and he most definitely came up lacking. "Kate was right," she said, frowning. "You don't take no for an answer."

"Nice to see you too, Mrs. Callahan."

"She doesn't want to see you. I told you that on the phone."

He nodded. "And I told you I'm still investigating the break-in."

She crossed her arms over her chest. "Uh-huh. The cops have been all through this place, and so has the FBI. What more do you want from her, Gabe?"

"I need to talk to her," he said. "I need to explain."

Hazel eyes, the same color as Kate's, moved over his face, examining him. After several moments she said quietly, "I never knew how she felt about you until she came home."

Gabe's heart swelled with hope and regret. "What kind of shape was she in?"

"Bad." Mrs. Callahan looked down. "I've never seen her like that. Even after Steven died, and that was terrible. But—" her eyes welled up, "—this time it's like he died all over again and you broke her heart all over again. Only this time you stomped it into the ground. I'm not sure she'll recover, Gabe, and that's the God's honest truth."

He put out an arm to support himself against the doorframe. Jesus, he had to see her, had to put this right. "I know I hurt her," he said. "And it was the last thing I wanted to do. I know I put her through hell after Steve died. And again…this time. Please, I have to talk to her."

Mrs. Callahan shook her head. "I can't let you in, Gabe, unless you have a warrant or something. She knew you'd try to see her, and she was adamant. Desperate, really."

"Please—"

"No. She's hurting too badly. I won't do it." She pushed the door but Gabe pushed back.

"If she won't see me, would you at least give her a message?"

Mrs. Callahan sighed. "What?"

"I'll write it down." He pulled out his wallet, stuck his pinky into the tight pocket, way back in the corner and produced the tiny, worn piece of paper that had been folded and unfolded so many times the seams had ripped. He opened it now, slowly so it wouldn't fall apart, and scrawled the words beneath an old, faded message, then refolded it carefully and handed it to Kate's mother. "Give this to her. Please. It's… She has to see it."

"Fine," she said, clutching the tiny note in her fist. "Now leave."

"Who was at the door?" Kate asked. She was lugging another black plastic bag filled with ruined clothes and furnishings from her bedroom and dumping them in a pile by the railing that overlooked the foyer. She and her mother and Violetta had managed to clean up most of the house already. Her mother didn't answer. She stood at the bottom of the steps studying something she held in her hand. "Mom?"

Her mother looked up and even from the balcony Kate could see the distress in her face. She let go of the bag and went down the steps, wondering what could possibly have upset her so much. Or who.

She slowed her steps, feeling her gut tighten. "What's wrong, Mom? Who was at the door?"

Her mother glanced over at the door and swallowed. "It was Gabe," she said. "I sent him away."

Kate felt a jolt in her gut that sent a shock wave through her body and blood pounding in her temples. Gabe had been there, right in that space near the door. She could have seen him, touched him.

Yeah, she reminded herself. She could have slapped his handsome, lying face. Grabbed a brass lamp and cracked his big fat head open. So why could she only imagine being held in his arms? Would the mere mention of him torture her forever?

"Kate?"

She hadn't realized she'd stopped on the steps until she noticed her mother standing at the bottom, regarding her with an anxious expression. And then her mother was climbing toward her, stopping a couple of steps down.

"I'm sorry, honey," her mother said. "I wouldn't have told you, but… Well, he handed me this paper." She held out the tiny square and Kate reluctantly took it. "He acted like it was vitally important that you read it. And it's so old. It looks like he's been carrying it around forever."

Kate unfolded the paper with shaking hands, trying hard not to rip it further. Tears sprung instantly to her eyes when she saw what it was. Beneath the message she had left on his kitchen table almost nine years ago he had written his own.

I regretted making love to you the first time, but I'll never regret the last time.

Chapter Thirty-Seven

Gabe rang the doorbell of Lindsay's house at ten o'clock the next morning, but instead of seeing Jeremy's smiling face, Lindsay opened the door, stepped out onto the porch and closed the door behind her. Great. Just what he needed to start the day.

"I want to make something clear—" she began.

"If you're going to give me shit about taking Jeremy over to see Kate you can save your breath."

She crossed her arms over her chest. "I won't have my son exposed to your sexual escapades."

"Bullshit. That's not what you're pissed off about. You're pissed off because you're afraid Kate's not just a 'sexual escapade.'"

"Now who's full of it? What do I care who you sleep with? But I will not have Jeremy exposed—"

"Oh, like he wasn't exposed to you and Richard sleeping together when you two were shacking up. Give me a break."

"That was different. We were in a serious, committed relationship."

"This is a serious, committed relationship."

Lindsay's eyes opened wide, and she stumbled back a step. "What are you saying?"

"I'm saying that I'm in love with Kate and if she'll have me I'm going to marry her."

Lindsay's mouth dropped open. "Are you shitting me? You and...*her?*"

"Surprised? I guess you haven't talked to my sisters yet to see how the big three summit went. It was a relief, actually, getting it all off my chest. Thanks for setting it up."

If she picked up on the sarcasm she didn't show it. "And they…approve?"

"I was the one who threw shit at her in the first place. They thought they were being supportive by doing the same thing. Figured I knew her better."

"Well, Jeremy's not going anywhere today."

Gabe narrowed his eyes. "Why not?"

"He's overtired. I haven't even tried to wake him—"

Gabe pushed past her into the house.

"Hey!"

He called Jeremy from the bottom of the steps. "Come on down."

Jeremy was in his pajamas rubbing his eyes. "Dad? What time is it?"

Gabe walked right up the steps and nudged Jeremy into his bedroom. "Get dressed. We're going to go see Aunt Kate."

"Really?" Jeremy asked, his expression filled with joy. Yeah, she'd be pissed, but he had no pride left. If Jeremy was his ticket in he'd take it. There was no doubt in his mind that Kate loved his son. And even though she was hurt and angry, there was no doubt that Kate loved him as well.

He just had to get her to believe in him again.

As they headed out the front door, Lindsay grabbed Gabe's arm. "It was her money that won me full custody of Jeremy," she hissed. "I hired the best lawyer money could buy."

"I'm sure she had no idea what you were using that money for."

"Oh, no? It was in her own best interest, Gabe, which is

all she's ever been interested in. You sure as hell weren't going to let her see Jeremy, so she would've done anything to make sure I got him. And I did."

"Nice try," Gabe said, and turned his back on her.

Valerie Callahan was all smiles for Jeremy, even though she hadn't seen him in years. When she shifted her gaze back up to Gabe her expression was resigned.

"Hello again," Gabe said. From behind him, across the street, cameras were clicking away and reporters were speaking into their mikes. The hell with them.

"Who is it, Mom?" Kate called from another room.

"It's Jeremy," she said, her gaze locking with Gabe's. "And his father."

Kate appeared at the door beside her mother and immediately pulled Jeremy into her arms. "It's so good to see you."

"I'm glad you still live here," Jeremy said. He had his arms wrapped around her waist and was looking up at her. "My mom said you were probably going to move."

"That's right," she said. "I'm glad you're here, so you can at least enjoy the pool before I sell the house. Did you bring your swim trunks?"

"Yeah, they're in Dad's car."

"Go get them." Jeremy raced out the door.

Gabe hadn't said a word up to this point. "Kate, can we talk?"

Without looking at him she raised a palm. "No. I'd like to spend some time with Jeremy, if you can spare him for a few hours. I don't want to cut into your time with him, but—"

"Kate," her mother interjected. "What should I do?"

"Just go ahead," Kate said.

"Are you sure?"

"Of course."

"I'll be back tomorrow."

"Don't worry, Mom. I'll be fine."

"I'll see to it," Gabe said.

"No. You will not see to it," Kate said when her mother had gone back upstairs. She hadn't yet made eye contact with him. "I have a friend coming to spend the night."

"Who?"

"None of your business."

An uneasy feeling churned in Gabe's gut. "Male or female?"

"I repeat, none of your business."

"Look," he said. "Whoever was behind the attacks on you is still out there. And there's new information about the explosion."

She hesitated. "Like what?"

Now he was sorry he'd brought Jeremy with him. He had no idea how she would react to the knowledge that her husband had planned to kill her. The FBI was keeping the information under wraps for now, but it was only a matter of time before the press got wind of it.

"That's a conversation I want to have when we're alone," he said.

"That won't be happening. I have no intention of being alone with you."

"Goddamn it, Kate, I love you."

She turned away from him. "Don't."

"You said you loved me."

"I was in the throes of passion."

"You meant it."

This time she looked him in the eye. "It didn't keep you from betraying me to the FBI."

Gabe swallowed. Fuck, this was going to be hard. "I can explain all that."

She nodded in a way that said *uh-huh, tell me another one.* "Spare me. And if you don't mind, I have to get the house ready to sell, so…"

Gabe took a deep breath and let it out. "I need to know who's going to spend the night with you. And I can stand here all day if that's what it takes."

She huffed. "Fine. It's Archer."

Alarm bells went off in Gabe's head. "Archer? The masseur? You're going to let some guy you hardly know spend the night in your house? Have you lost your mind?"

"I know him well enough."

"What's his last name?"

"I… uh, I forget," she said.

"Are you kidding me? You don't know his name? Everything he's saying could be a lie for all you know."

"Well, it's true that I'm gullible when it comes to men," she said. "At least the ones that want to sleep with me."

Gabe ignored the taunt. "How do you know this guy, anyway?"

"He was a friend of Michael's, okay? Are you done with the third degree?"

"I don't like this guy showing up here, insinuating himself into your life. He's a stranger, for God's sake."

"No more than you turned out to be."

Jeremy whizzed through the door and ran for the steps. "I'm going to go change upstairs."

"Sure, Jer. Look," she said to Gabe, rubbing the line between her brows. "You can pick up Jeremy before he arrives if that will make you feel better."

"What will make me feel better is if *I* stay with you."

"Forget it."

Fat chance. "I'll sleep downstairs on the couch and guard the door. I won't come anywhere near your bedroom."

"I said forget it. What part of that don't you understand?"

"The part where you'd rather have some other guy spend the night in your house when you know damn well that *I'm* the one who should be here protecting you."

She narrowed her eyes at him. "Drop it, Gabe. I mean it."

"Okay, fine," he lied. "For now I'll leave you alone. What time does Archer get here?"

"He said around six or seven."

Gabe sighed. "I'll pick up Jeremy around four."

Gabe had planned to call Agent Parker from the driveway, but he didn't feel like having his picture taken fifty times so he drove back to the station and then placed the call. "What do you guys have on Michael Clark's close friends? Anything on a guy named Archer?"

"Archer, first name or last?"

"First, I guess. Kate says he was a close friend of Michael's. And he seems to have become a close friend of hers."

"Archer," Parker said. "Could it be a nickname?"

"Sure," Gabe said.

"Well, hang on." Gabe could hear him flipping pages or rustling papers for a few minutes, and then he said, "Well, the man of the hour is Pierre D'Archambault."

"It was a French name," Ben had said. *Holy fuck.* "D'Archambault. Archer. That could be him. Who is he?"

"Clark's roommate," Parker said. "Found the name on

a piece of mail. We haven't made contact yet. Hasn't been home since we found Clark dead."

The hairs on Gabe's neck stood up. "Description?"

"That's the problem," Parker said. "Nobody seems to know what he looks like. The neighbors there don't pay attention. We've got men posted, waiting for him to turn up."

"Have you run the name through NCIC?"

"Yeah, I'm waiting for results."

"I have a bad feeling about this guy."

"Sure you're not just jealous?" Parker asked in a low voice.

"Do I need to answer that?"

"No. I'll let you know what we come up with."

Gabe thanked him and hung up, then sorted through messages and spotted a group of detectives around a screen and went to see what was going on. On the screen were gruesome photos of an elderly woman sliced up in what appeared to be an attic. Scott Bailey turned and gestured to Gabe to join him.

"Practically in Kate's backyard," he said. "Her balcony overlooks Kate's pool."

"Goddamn it," Gabe said. He had to get back over there and keep her safe. Her and Jeremy. He radioed the patrol car that had been assigned to her street, only to learn it had been pulled. Every available car was around the corner at the crime scene.

"Shit," he muttered. "Hurry the hell up, Parker."

Fifteen minutes later, Parker called back. "Turns out D'Archambault was an army munitions specialist. Degree in chemistry and physics. Since his discharge he's had no known source of income."

Bingo. "Why'd he leave the army?" Gabe asked.

"Discharged for homosexual activity."

"That all?"

"And he was an unofficial suspect in the beating death of his bunkmate."

Holy shit, this was worse than he'd thought. "What happened?"

"The guy was his partner, if you know what I mean. D'Archambault was never indicted, but the army was very happy to see his back."

"Do you have a photo you can send me?"

"Yeah, I'll send it right over."

"We need to find out how much contact he had with Drew Franklin, other than through Michael Clark. Interview his staff, get records of their meetings—"

"Whoa, whoa, whoa. We know how to run an investigation, Detective."

"Also check out the Tyrell King connection," Gabe said, as though Parker hadn't spoken. "See if he had any connection to Archer." If Joy was telling the truth, and that was a big *if,* somebody was contacting the guy, and it could easily have been Archer, not Michael. "Oh, and Parker? I need this information within the next hour." Meanwhile, he would get Scott to compare fingerprints from the attic crime scene with those found in Michael Clark's apartment.

"Yes sir," Parker said dryly. "What are you going to do?"

Parker's email came up and the photo flashed on Gabe's screen. Holy fuck.

"It's him," he said, and swallowed, checked his watch. It was just past noon. "I'm going to Kate's right away." With as much backup as he could muster. "Archer is going to be there in a few hours, and I plan to be there with a welcoming party when he shows up."

Chapter Thirty-Eight

Archer was at Harry's Tap Room, enjoying baked brie with grapes, roasted red pepper-and-crab soup, and a glass of New Zealand sauvignon blanc. Michael had loved this place, this food, and this particular sauvignon blanc. They'd had some wonderful times together, but he'd known for quite a while before the breakup that Michael wasn't the one. Still, he had wanted the best for him. He certainly hadn't wanted to hurt him.

He sipped his wine, the same one he'd had with Drew the first time they had dinner. God, how infatuated he'd been with Michael's good-looking boss. Drew had sent him an email asking to meet after work, around eight o'clock, at an excellent Capitol Hill restaurant. Drew had ordered great wine and a good steak, and wasn't shy about making eye contact. He'd insisted on calling him Pierre, and said he was fascinated by explosives, that sometimes brute force really was the only way to get things done. They'd chatted about world politics and their mutual disgust with our government's inability to get things done. They needed some new blood in positions of real power, Drew had said. They needed money outside of government, power that wasn't checked by a less intelligent "leader." Dictatorships served a purpose, he'd said, but so many dictators weren't smart or sophisticated enough to run a country.

One of them brought up the question of morality. When was it was okay to take a life for the greater good? They both agreed that in a war it was okay to take lives when necessary. Archer smiled. That had been Drew's segue into the conversation he really wanted to have. His was a war to fix the world before it was too late, Drew had said. The bill he was proposing would go a long way toward making things better, creating a new order. But there were idiots standing in his way. He needed to shake people up, orchestrate something like 9/11—not killing innocent people, of course—that would make the pacifists look like morons and get the votes he needed to pass his bill. He bragged about the ways he'd already been digging up dirt on his colleagues, and said the president was ripe for the picking.

Archer swirled the wine in his glass. He'd been so hot to get Drew in bed it hadn't even mattered that the guy was a total megalomaniac. When Drew suggested taking out an empty government building or military plane, Archer had been surprised, but not shocked. Drew had told him to name his price to design the device, so he'd thrown out an outrageous number.

"Fifty million," he'd said. "Half up front." When Drew agreed he didn't believe it. How would he come up with that much money? And that's when he'd learned about Kate. How Drew had married her for her first husband's money, and his plan to move it offshore, little by little. Yeah, the whole thing was despicable, but Kate had been a stranger to him then, and for all he knew she was a first-class bitch.

He took a long swallow of his wine. He'd never expected Drew to actually come through with the money. But he'd set up an account in Barbados, and when the money showed up six months later, he knew he'd struck a bargain with the devil himself. He liked looking at all those lovely zeros, liked imagining the life he could live with that kind of money. And more. Much more. On one of the few occasions he and Drew had been intimate, he'd gotten Drew to tell him about the code he'd developed. Like some armchair cryptographer from the First World War, Drew had hidden the code in his most prized possessions—his first edition copies of the classics. *Don Quixote. David Copperfield.* Dante's *Divine Comedy.*

Crafting the bomb in a camera had taken time and imagination, both of which Archer happened to have in abundance. He'd presented it to Drew that night at his parents' house, and asked what he intended to do with it. When Drew said he could kill two birds with one stone and get the money and the votes by taking out Kate's plane, Archer knew he was dealing with a sick fuck who really had no business being on the planet. So he'd made the switch and saved Kate in the bargain. He would still be a rich man, an innocent woman would be saved and the devil would go back to hell, where he belonged.

Then he met Kate. She'd made a joke of it, but the reality was that if he'd been straight, he'd have hooked up with her in a minute.

How absurd that the FBI considered her a suspect in the plane explosion. He'd taken it upon himself to get the heat off her—and what delicious irony that he'd used Drew's own diabolical schemes to do it. So he'd killed that liberal lady senator—which Drew had planned, but for a different reason—hoping it would look as though one of the conservatives was behind it to get the Global Intel bill passed. With any luck they'd blame Joy Stuart, that two-timing bitch. Not that he gave a damn about that stupid bit of legislation. He'd blackmailed Arlen Fischer with photos of that call girl Drew had hired for this sort of thing, and let Tyrell tamper with the brakes of the third senator. Thank God the man's pretty young wife had locked the doors when her husband left the house that night.

Archer took a long swallow of the wine. He'd been a

kick-ass bomb defuser in Afghanistan before the army decided his sexual proclivities were the sum total of his worth as a human being.

And Quinn. His bunkmate and best friend. Oh, God, how he'd let him down.

When he heard the chirp he flipped open his cell. "Yes, Tyrell."

"FBI wants my ass," Tyrell said.

"What do you mean?"

"I mean, we gotta go now."

Archer took in a deep breath and let it out. "What did they say?"

"Say nothin'. I got the hell outa there I saw them at the door downstairs. They lookin' for me they gonna be on to you next, man."

"Where are you now?"

"I ain't sayin' over the phone. We gotta go today. Now. You got the tickets?"

"Yes, yes," Archer said, thoughtful. Damn it. Tyrell had gone and sliced up that nice old lady not two blocks from Kate's house. That hadn't been Archer's idea, but the FBI wouldn't see it that way. If they got a hold of Tyrell, the man would squeal like a pig.

He sighed and signaled the waiter for the check. "Well, then, you know what to do."

"I'll go get that bird right now," Tyrell said, and hung up.

Damn it. He was so looking forward to spending some time with Kate. She was a special person, a warm, accepting and beautiful women who deserved better than what she'd gotten from that lying, cheating, amoral pig, Drew Franklin. If only she knew the service he had done her, saving her life.

He hoped to God her lover would save her this time.

Chapter Thirty-Nine

Kate answered the doorbell at 12:45 and was surprised to see Archer standing on her porch. He was dressed all in black and was carrying a black backpack slung over one shoulder. His car wasn't in the driveway. "Oh," she said.

"I'm early, I know," he said. "I can leave and come back if you want, but... Well, I was lonely."

Everything he's told you could be a lie.

"It's fine," she said after a brief hesitation.

Archer stopped midway through the foyer and gazed around at the mostly empty rooms with their bare walls and surfaces. "Oh, Kate," he said. "You told me what happened, but seeing it... This must be devastating."

"It was just stuff," she said. "Come on in. Jeremy's here."

Archer perked up. "Your godson?"

"Yes. He's eating a bowl of ice cream in the kitchen."

"This is the detective's son, right?"

Something about the way he said it struck her, an emphasis that seemed a bit too knowing. "That's right," she said, careful not to show her wariness.

"Who's that, Aunt Kate?" Jeremy called from the kitchen.

Archer followed her through the swinging door into the kitchen. "Jeremy, this is Archer, a friend of mine."

"Hello, Jeremy," Archer said, with a warm smile. "I've heard a lot about you."

"Oh, uh..." Jeremy looked to Kate and she nodded. "It's nice to meet you. Want some ice cream?"

"I would love some ice cream," Archer said and turned to Kate. "What a charming young man."

"You'll give him a big head," Kate said, ruffling Jeremy's hair.

"I look like my Uncle Steve," Jeremy said.

"Oh, that's right, your dad's brother," Archer said. "'A software titan for the 21st century,' wasn't that what the media called him?"

Kate froze. How in the world had Archer heard about that?

"I'm surprised you remember that," she said as she reached into the freezer for the ice cream. Her hand trembled ever so slightly. "It was in the media more than eight years ago."

"I have a long memory," he said. "And I knew about the relationship. From Michael."

Kate let go of a breath. "Right. I figured."

She scooped ice cream into a new plastic bowl from Wal-Mart, and Archer settled in beside Jeremy, who gabbed a mile a minute while they ate. She stood at the counter with her own bowl, listening and wishing she didn't feel so uneasy all of a sudden. Granted, Gabe had put doubts in her mind about Archer, but Gabe wasn't exactly the most trustworthy person she knew.

Still, right now she would feel a whole lot better with him around.

The house phone shrilled and she reached out to answer it. It was Gabe. "Listen to me carefully," he said. "I want you and Jeremy to get into your car right now and go over to my apartment."

Kate glanced at Archer, who was watching her from the table. He seemed very interested in her phone call. She turned away. "Why?"

"It's Archer," he said. "I don't want you in the house when he gets there."

Fear slithered down her back and she wished her kitchen phone were cordless. "Care to elaborate on that?"

"He's not who he says he is," Gabe said. "He changed his name when he was discharged from the army. And he was a murder suspect, okay? So would you just grab Jeremy and get in your car right now and—"

"Um...that would be hard." She risked a quick peek over her shoulder, only to find Archer standing a foot away from her, and the expression on his face was not warm at all. She gasped as his hand came around and covered her mouth.

He hung up the phone.

Gabe stared at the phone in his hands. Did they get cut off or did she hang up on him? He pressed redial but got Kate's voice mail. He tried her cell phone but it was disconnected. He tried the house phone over and over before flicking his phone shut. He'd broken out in a cold sweat.

It was barely one o'clock, but he had a sick feeling Archer had arrived early.

"Fuck," he said, and ran to his lieutenant's office, not bothering to apologize when he bumped into someone, ignoring the curses behind him. When did this place become such a fucking obstacle course? When he finally got to the office he pushed the door open without knocking and stood there breathing hard.

His lieutenant looked up with a frown. "What the hell happened to you?"

"I need every goddamn body we can get," he said. "And I need them now."

"If we had found the books right away we could have avoided this whole misunderstanding," Archer said.

A misunderstanding. Right.

Kate had rolled over the second he threatened to hurt Jeremy and did exactly what he told her. Holding the boy's arm, he had carried two wooden chairs up from the dining room and placed them in the middle of her bedroom, side by side, separated by five feet or so. Then Kate had sat helplessly by and watched him secure Jeremy to the chair.

Tears streamed down Jeremy's red face and over the duct tape that covered his mouth. His wrists were taped behind his back and his feet were taped to the chair. It killed Kate to see him like this. Not that she was much better off, but for now her mouth wasn't taped shut.

"I have no idea where those books went," she said. "Somebody must have taken them when the house was broken into."

"No, no one took them that night."

She stared as his words sank in. "You?"

"I'm afraid so. Not directly, but—"

"Was it…did you attack me?"

He looked her in the eye. "No, Kate. I would never have hurt you like that. My associate doesn't follow orders well. Not only did he fail to get the books, he hurt you when I explicitly told him not to. And I promise you that I did tell him *not* to hurt you."

"What do you need the books for?" Best to keep him talking…

"Past tense, I'm sorry to say," he said. "I needed the code to get the money your husband hid offshore. But it's too late for that now."

"Archer, can't you please let Jeremy go?"

"I'm afraid not." His phone rang and he flipped it open. "Well?"

Kate couldn't hear the person on the other end, but

Archer seemed relieved. "Good job. Just over an hour, then." He clicked the phone shut. "This will all be over soon."

"Please, Archer," Kate said, terrified for Jeremy. "He's a child. Let him go. I'll stay here and do whatever you want."

"In this case I'm afraid Jeremy suits my purposes better than you."

Her breath seized up. "You're not suggesting…"

"Oh, come on," he said, more impatient than angry. "I'm no pedophile. How could you even think that? I need your lover's help to escape, and this little guy is my best insurance." He opened his backpack and pulled out rolls of some kind of clay. "A few more up here and then we'll be good to go."

"A few more what?"

"C4," he said. "I've already set up most of them around the rest of the house, but I didn't do these two bedrooms."

"Why… What are you going to do?" She focused on Jeremy, but he was hanging his head, sniffling, looking defeated.

"Buying myself some time to get out of the country," he said.

"What have you done?"

Archer came and squatted down beside her. "Well, I saved your life, for one."

"What do you mean?"

"We both know your husband was not a nice man. But you don't know how evil he really was."

Kate took a long breath and let it out. "Tell me."

"Your plane was the one that was supposed to explode in midair, not his."

Kate's head jerked back. "What?"

"He had me rig up your camera with an explosive called

PETN that is completely undetectable. I brought it over to him the night before the flight, but when I learned his intentions I switched the cameras. The rest is history."

She was shocked to find herself breathing heavily. "But…why?"

"Because I don't like people who go around killing innocents," he said. "Especially horrible people like him. He deserved to die and you didn't."

"Why did he want to kill me?" Good God. Had Drew really hated her that much?

Archer shrugged. "Would have killed two birds with one stone. You'd be out of his way without a messy divorce, and he'd get his bill passed."

It took her a moment to understand what he was talking about. "You mean…the Global Intel—"

He nodded. "Yes, the one that was going down the tubes in his own party. And he was right. Look at how quickly both parties jumped on it right after the—" he made quotation marks with his fingers, "—terrorist attack."

"My God," she whispered. "That's sick."

"People like that deserve to die, Kate."

"But…was it you who called the newspapers to say it was al Qaeda?"

"Yes," he said. "That was tricky, and expensive. One of the reasons he stole so much of your money. The bastard couldn't even wait until you died to get his hands on it."

"I don't understand."

"Of course you don't," he said, his expression fond. "Someone like you couldn't possibly understand someone like him. Your husband wanted to make things happen on his terms. That's why he needed your money."

"So he could hire people to blow up planes?"

"You're getting the idea. Other things too. Blackmail

people. Bribe them. Get rid of them, whatever it would take to get his own way." His voice had grown harsh. "The world was all about him, and no one else."

"Did he betray you in some way, Archer?" She made herself sound concerned, when in fact all she felt about Archer was disgust.

"Not really," he said, straightening.

"So…it bothered you that he was prepared to kill innocent people."

"That's right."

"Well…then why didn't you not plant the camera on either of us?"

He shook his head as though talking to someone slow—which she supposed she was under the circumstances. "Don't you see? He was evil. He had delusions of world domination. I couldn't in good conscience let him live."

He could still talk about conscience. "What about the flight crew?"

"Sad," he said. "But I didn't expect anyone else to die. He said he was driving home alone, and then he changed his mind. I guess that makes the others collateral damage."

"Is that what Jeremy and I are?"

"I have no interest in hurting you," he said. "I wish I could make you believe that."

Jeremy raised his head and stared at her. His eyes were round and red-rimmed from crying, his expression one of sheer terror. It broke her heart to see it, but she winked at him ever so slightly, to give him hope that she had a plan.

If only she did.

"What about Michael?" she went on. "Was that your handiwork as well?"

Archer sighed and bowed his head. "No. That was

Tyrell. I could never have done that to him. I truly cared for Michael."

Like he was "genuinely fond" of her and Jeremy? "Then why did you let Tyrell do it?"

He squatted beside her again. "You really can't see that saving your life and trying to keep you out of prison has led me to this point, can you?"

"How do you figure that?"

"If I'd let him blow you up I would have collected my money and been long gone by now. But I couldn't let that happen. I won't deny, though, that I'm disappointed not to have the other twenty-five million he promised me."

Kate gasped. "Twenty-five million dollars?"

He took her chin between his fingers. "Look at me," he said, and Kate forced herself to meet his gaze.

Please, God, let him see that this is wrong.

"Do I strike you as someone who would do this for enjoyment?" he asked, his expression almost pleading. "Or for some kind of ideology?"

"I… No, I guess not. But then, all this—" she gestured with her head to Jeremy and herself, "—is all about the money?"

"At this point it's for survival," Archer said. "I found part of the code on Drew's computer at the congressional office—God, the man was so arrogant he didn't even hide his notes—but I needed the books, and they weren't in his study like he told me. So I figured he had hidden them somewhere in the house, which is what led me to Tyrell, who Michael had been in touch with."

"Why?" Kate asked. The more he talked the more time she gave Gabe and the FBI to rescue them. But God, what if Gabe thought she'd hung up on him?

"He had this idea about rehabilitating Tyrell. I had no

doubt that Tyrell was a lost cause and I proved it when I contacted him and asked him if he wanted to make some big money." He shrugged. "He said he'd do whatever I wanted. I knew he'd been in the service and he had certain skills that could come in handy."

"I still don't see why Michael had to die," Kate said.

Archer frowned. "Michael was too smart, and he knew me too well. Both Drew and me, actually. He was beginning to put the pieces together, and once he did he would have felt obliged to go to the authorities." He shrugged. "I might have waited, but I needed him to 'confess' to get you out of jail."

Good God. Archer had actually killed Michael to save her. If he would kill his friend, what would stop him killing her and Jeremy? "What will it take for you to let us go?" she asked, pleading now.

"It's up to your lover now," Archer said. "If he does what I tell him you'll both be fine. And knowing how devoted he is to his son I imagine he'll do this my way."

"What way is that?"

Archer pulled out a cell phone and punched in some numbers. "Listen and you will learn."

Chapter Forty

Gabe picked up immediately, despite the unknown number. "Gabe Hugo."

"Listen carefully and don't fuck this up," the voice said. *Archer.* "I have your son and your lover with me at Kate's house, and their safety rests completely on your shoulders."

The words slammed into Gabe's gut so hard he was surprised he could talk. "Goddamn it, this has nothing to do with them." He gestured at Scott and they stepped outside together. The rest of the team was silent. Waiting.

"Of course it doesn't," Archer said. "That's why you will do exactly what I tell you. Otherwise they'll be blown into tiny little bits, just like those congressmen."

"I know it was you that switched the cameras," Gabe said. "Look, I appreciate you saving Kate's life, Archer. I'm counting on you doing it again."

"No, Detective, you have it backward. This time *you're* going to save her life."

Gabe swallowed hard. "What do you want?"

"I want to leave the country unharmed and without interference. I have a helicopter arriving in Kate's yard in one hour. I want you to guarantee that no one tries to stop us anywhere along our route, or meets us at the other end."

He eyed his lieutenant, who had joined them outside. "If I can even do that, what about Kate and Jeremy?"

"They'll be fine as long as you do exactly as I say."

"I can't guarantee that the FAA or the FBI won't interfere, Archer. Be fair."

"You will explain to them that your family's lives depend on their actions. Surely you have some clout, Detective."

"I want to speak to my family," Gabe said. "I want to know they're really okay."

"You can speak to Kate."

Gabe waited, his heart pounding.

"Gabe?" Her voice was pitched high, like a frightened child.

"Kate! Are you all right? Is Jeremy?"

"Yes—"

"That's enough," Archer said.

"Wait!" Gabe shouted. In the next instant he heard someone sobbing. "Jeremy? Honey, is that you?" The answer was muffled sobs, no doubt behind a strip of tape.

Archer came back on the line. "Satisfied?"

"Goddamn it, Archer," he growled. "If he's hurt I'll kill you, you son of a bitch."

"You know what you have to do."

"And if I can't pull it off, then what?"

"Well, I haven't quite finished laying the charges yet, but as soon as I—"

"What charges? What the hell are you doing?"

"Gabe," Scott whispered, a firm hand on Gabe's arm. "Calm down. Listen."

Gabe took a deep breath and forced his heartbeat to slow. He wouldn't be much good to either of them if Archer hung up before he understood what was really going on over there. "Just tell me what you're doing."

"That's better. I've got every window and door in this house wired to explode within five minutes of when I detonate. But I'll only detonate if A… Someone tries to stop me from leaving. Or B… Someone kills me or makes me unconscious. Is that clear enough for you?"

"And if you do make it out of the country, then what?"

"I'll disengage and you can go in and rescue them, like the white knight I know you are beneath that tough guy shell."

Gabe was striding toward his car, phone pressed to his ear like a lifeline. Scott was right beside him, listening in. "And if your helicopter crashes?"

"You'd better hope it doesn't."

"Fuck."

"Exactly. You'd best start making arrangements, Detective. You've only got fifty-one minutes to make it happen."

"I'm on it," Scott said under his breath and took off at a run.

Gabe tore out of the parking lot and headed in the direction of Kate's house. "Archer?"

"Yes, Detective?"

"If I lose either one of them, rest assured that I will hunt you down for the rest of your miserable life and kill you very, very slowly."

"I would expect no less of you," Archer said, and clicked off.

Chapter Forty-One

"I put Bruno in the yard," Archer told Kate. He was wrapping a charge around her ankles. "So if the house does go up, God forbid, he'll have a chance. Knowing dogs, he'll run away when he hears the first boom."

Kate stared down at him, trying to understand how a person could appear so normal—generous, even—and yet be so crazy. Chances were he hadn't always been, but he was crazy now.

Well, love could make a person crazy.

"Were you in love with Drew?" she blurted out, a second before he covered her mouth with tape.

He flashed her a wry smile. "I admit I let myself believe for a time that he found me attractive. Funny, isn't it? It was all one way with him, all about the worship. He let me—" he glanced at Jeremy and then back to Kate. "But he wasn't interested in actually doing…you know."

She knew. He wasn't all that interested in it with her, either. The thought struck her as hysterical in that moment and she began to laugh behind the tape. Tears ran down her cheeks and she began hiccupping. Problem was, with the tape over her mouth she was having trouble getting enough air, which made her panic. She tried to get off the chair but her wrists were taped together behind her back and her ankles were taped to it. Archer got the message and pulled the tape off her mouth. She gasped like a drowning person.

"Was it something I said?" Archer asked. There was real concern in his eyes.

God, the man was a total whack job.

"Please...leave it off. Screaming won't help, so I won't. I can't breathe with it on."

"Hmm. I'll leave it off for now," he said. "But remember, Kate, if people try to get into the house they'll die and so will you and Jeremy." He lowered his voice when he said Jeremy's name, but the boy raised his head anyway. "I know you have trouble believing this, but I really am quite fond of you. I have no desire to see you hurt."

"He says while attaching a charge to my ankles."

"Well, you're a clever woman," Archer said. "If you try to get out of the chair—and I have no doubt that you will—you'll think twice before touching this tape."

"Why don't you let Jeremy go and take me with you?" she said. "No one's going to shoot the helicopter down if you've got a hostage on board."

"I did consider that," he said. "But, you know, a sniper could pick me off inside that helicopter and then where would I be? This is a better plan. Less complicated. More likely to guarantee my freedom."

"If you won't let Jeremy go, could you please take the tape off his mouth?"

"So the two of you can talk?"

"Please, Archer. What's the worst that can happen? It's not like we can run out of the house." She leaned forward and looked at the charge taped to her ankles. "I can't even get out of this chair."

Archer checked the time. "Right before I leave I'll pull it off. Okay?"

She heaved a sigh of relief. "Thank you."

Bruno began barking his head off from the backyard. Archer went to the window and looked out, then left the room.

Kate turned to Jeremy. "Jeremy, honey, are you okay?"

Jeremy raised his eyes to her and shrugged.

"I know, stupid question," she said. Good God, she had to ease the poor kid's terror somehow. "He doesn't want to hurt us, so that's good. And I'm sure your dad will do whatever it takes to make sure Archer gets what he wants." God, she hoped he could, but she wasn't so sure. Still, she had to act as though they were going to get out of this. "Your dad loves you so much, Jeremy. He'll pull out all the stops. You know how stubborn he is when he wants something."

Unfortunately, talking about Gabe got the tears flowing, so she sniffed and turned away. Gabe had been right about Archer. How could she have been so stupid and careless? He'd finally told her he loved her, and she'd dismissed it. But, if the worst happened, those words would be what she held to her heart.

Gabe loves me.

If only fate were on their side.

Gabe couldn't believe his eyes when the van pulled up and stopped in the middle of Kate's street. Parker jumped out of the passenger seat. "Goddamn it, Parker," he roared. "I told you not to bring a SWAT team here."

Parker put up a hand. "They're not going to shoot him. I told you, as soon as his helicopter takes off we're going to send the bomb squad in to try to disable the charges. That is nonnegotiable."

"The guy was an ammunition specialist for eight years," Gabe said. "He rigged up a camera with a timer detonator that took down a plane. He knows damn well you're going to try to disable the charges and then take him down. Do you honestly think he hasn't figured that into however he designed this? You may have to disable the whole house at the same time for all we know. That's my son inside. And Kate. Do not screw this up."

"Listen."

There it was. The sound of distant rotors getting louder as Archer's means of escape approached Kate's house. When the helicopter came into view Gabe's cell phone rang. He opened it, knowing it would be Archer. "I'm here," he said.

"What is that SWAT team doing here?" Archer shouted.

"I was just giving the FBI shit about it, okay? They have orders not to shoot."

"You know what will happen if they do."

"Yes."

"The detonator is taped to my chest and responds to the beating of my heart," Archer said. "If I die, your son and your lover die, Detective, and no one wants that."

"Of course not," Gabe said. *Please God, don't let them die.* "I've got clearances all the way up to the president that you're not to be intercepted or attacked in any way, at any time."

"See that no one decides to be a hero," Archer said. "Oh, and one more thing. If they're planning to disable the charges on the house, they need to be aware that at the slightest disturbance the charge taped to Kate's ankles will explode and take out both of them."

"Jesus," Gabe said, imagining the horror. "Please, Archer. I only have so much control over these guys. Take that damn thing off her, would you? I'm begging you. Please."

"Sorry, but it stays."

"How will I know when we can go in after them?"

"I'll call you," Archer said, and hung up.

"Good luck, you two," Archer said. "Let's hope your savior comes through. I have every confidence that he will."

"Please let Jeremy go," Kate said, knowing her words meant nothing to him. "Please. Gabe loves me. He wouldn't do anything that would get me killed, I know that for absolute certain. You don't need both of us."

"Ah, Kate, still so trusting, even now. The government needs a child to stay their hand. Besides, you're a controversial figure. You were a suspect in your husband's murder, for God's sake." He shook his head. "How ridiculous. But, the public wouldn't crucify the feds if you were killed, no offense. The boy… Well, he's the best insurance I've got." He smoothed her hair gently and she forced herself not to jerk away. "I am truly sorry I've had to resort to this. With any luck I'll be where I need to be in about eight hours, and they'll be able to come on in and set you free. You shouldn't get dehydrated between now and then."

"At least take the tape off Jeremy's mouth," Kate pleaded. "You said you would."

"I know I did, but I don't think I could bear to hear his little voice begging." He stopped at the bedroom door and stood there for long moments as though thinking. He raised his face to the ceiling, then blew out a long breath and turned back to her. "The five-minute delay is to give you a chance," he said quietly. "If you haven't gotten the tape off by then, find a way to get into the bathroom and shut the door behind you. There are no charges in there."

"Please," she said again, but he left the room. She listened for the sound of the back door opening and closing, and prayed she didn't hear a shot follow it. Within a minute she heard Archer go out and saw the helicopter lift off in her backyard. The clock on her bed stand read 2:13. So much had happened in the last hour and a half.

"Jeremy," she said. "I need you to wiggle your way over here so I can bite off the tape on your wrists."

Jeremy's eyes grew wide.

"Easy does it," she said. "Try not to tip over."

Jeremy shifted his body weight so that his chair moved about half an inch on the carpet.

"Try not to fall over, just try to make the chair walk, one side at a time. That's it. Easy, honey." She directed him as he made his way, so slowly it was painful to watch. But he'd stopped crying, and a determined light shone in his eyes. *God, please, keep him safe. Take me if you must, but spare him.*

Seconds later, he tipped.

"So, the pilot is Tyrell King," Gabe said.

"We have a positive ID," Parker said.

"You're tracking them every step of the way."

"Of course."

"No one's going to interfere with them."

"No. We, uh, also have confirmation that it is theoretically possible to detonate from very long distances via satellite."

"Fuck." Gabe had hoped to God Archer was bluffing about being able to detonate from outside the country. Still, they had to find a way to disable the charges so they could get Kate and Jeremy out of the house alive. Drilling a hole through the roof and plucking them out that way was definitely under consideration.

"If Kate can figure out a way to get one of them free at least we'll know where they are and hopefully what Archer's done to the house."

"If there's a way, she'll figure it out," Gabe said, hoping and praying he was right. Hoping and praying like he'd never hoped or prayed for anything else in his life.

Chapter Forty-Two

Jeremy slid on his side to Kate's chair and looked up at her in mute anguish. "It's okay," she said. "Try this. Use all that good strength you've built up and try to roll on to your stomach… I mean, so your head and knees are touching the floor."

Jeremy grunted as he pushed and heaved, and finally made it.

"That's great. Now try as hard as you can to lift your head on to my lap." After several tries he did it. "Beautiful. Turn your head so your cheek is up toward me. That's right. Okay, I'm going to lean over and try to tug that tape off with my teeth. It will be awkward, so the more help you can give me the better, okay?" He nodded his assent.

It was a huge stretch for her back, and she felt bad for all the scraping she was doing on Jeremy's tender cheek, but finally she pulled the tape off. He shrieked at the pain.

"That hurt," Jeremy said. Tears streaked his cheeks, which were flaming red from the tape.

"I'm sorry. Now you can hurt me."

"Why would I?"

"Because I'm going to bend my torso forward like a pretzel so you can bite at the tape on my wrists. Can you do that?"

"I'll try," he said. "Can we escape?"

"We're going to do our darnedest."

Jeremy went to work on her tape with his teeth while

Kate coached him through it, her eye on the clock. Only half an hour had gone by. Every minute that nothing happened the more likely they were to make it out alive.

Or at least that's what she kept telling herself.

Archer was wound tighter than a spring. He knew they had a big fat target painted on the bottom and sides of the bird. He only hoped for all their sakes, including Kate's and Jeremy's, that no one got stupid and tried to take them down.

"You got the tickets?" Tyrell asked for the twentieth time.

"Yes, damn it," Archer said. "I have the tickets. Relax and fly this thing."

"Lemme see them."

"There's no point in that."

"Yes, there's a point," Tyrell said. "I want to see my ticket."

How to finesse this? There was a plane waiting for Archer in San Juan to take him—singular—into the mountains of Brazil, where he would hide out until he could get safe passage to Argentina. Or New Zealand. He didn't really care. He had a lot of money even without the rest of it, and as long as he eluded the authorities he could change his identity and his looks, and live a good life. He'd earned it, goddamn it. The government had used him and cast him aside like he hadn't saved their asses more times than he could count. He was only sorry it was Kate's money.

"I want to see it now," Tyrell said. "Or I'm gonna put this bird down in that field over there.

That might not be a bad idea, Archer thought. He couldn't very well overpower Tyrell in a moving helicopter, and so far nobody was shooting at them. Or... "It's in my bag," Archer said. "I don't feel like getting it."

"Why the fuck not?"

"Look, I'm wound up, you're wound up. Let me fly this thing for a while and you can go through my bag, grab a Coke or something—"

Tyrell's hand struck him so hard his head hit the windshield. "You didn't get a ticket for me, did you, motherfucker?"

Blood welled on Archer's lip. "Watch what the fuck you're doing, Tyrell, or we're both going down in this thing. Holy shit, I didn't know you were so emotional or I would never have—" *Whop!* Archer's head exploded with pain.

"You show me the goddamn ticket or I'm gonna throw your ass out the side door, you cocksucking piece of shit."

"You're…you're going to crash!" Archer shrieked as the bird began to plunge downward. "I'll give you my ticket. Just pull this thing up!"

"You lying piece of shit," Tyrell said, but he pulled the bird higher. "You were gonna leave me in San Juan. After all I did."

"I could only get one ticket," Archer said. "I'm going to get the other one in San Juan, I promise you. You have to trust me on this."

"Yeah, right. Trust a queer?"

"Shit," Parker said into his cellphone.

Gabe didn't like the sound of that. The house was surrounded by members of several law enforcement agencies—including a couple of fully suited bomb specialists, pointing and gesturing to various points in the house. Their attempts to hold back the media had been futile, and local cops were pushing people away from the perimeter they had set up. Talk about a clusterfuck.

He walked over to where Parker stood talking on his cell. "What's happening?"

Parker pulled the phone off his ear. "The helicopter is behaving erratically. Looks like they're arguing in there. King has struck Archer twice and it looks like he's holding a gun on him."

"Fuck," Gabe growled. "Archer can fly that thing. Get a sniper to take out King before he shoots."

"That's the plan," Parker said and returned to his call.

Gabe's heart jumped around so hard it felt as though he would blow apart any second. It was a gamble to take out King, but at least Archer would see that the government was on his side. Out of the corner of his eye he spotted a blonde trying to push her way inside the barrier, and recognized Lindsay's shrill cry. He stalked in her direction. As if things couldn't get any worse.

"This is all your fault!" she screamed when she spotted Gabe. "You go get him out of that house right now!"

"It's the boy's mother," he explained to the cop holding her back. To Lindsay he said, "I'm going to get him out if it's the last thing I do." His voice cracked on the words. "I promise you, Linds, we're doing everything we can—"

"Why aren't you in there?" she shouted.

"Because we can't do it that way," he said. "If we could I'd be the first one in. You know that."

"Well I hope she was worth it," Lindsay spat. "She'll be the death of everyone you love. Oh, God, Jeremy!"

Gabe caught her before her legs gave out, and held her while she sobbed. After a few moments he handed her over to the uniform. "I've got to get back, Linds. I'll let you know—" Spittle hit him in the face, and he wiped it off with his sleeve.

"If he dies it'll be on your head," Lindsay said, her eyes wild. "You and that bitch you love so much."

Chapter Forty-Three

Tyrell had pulled a gun from somewhere and was pointing it at Archer. "You gonna die, faggot. And I'm going to watch you bleed."

Archer drew back, heart pounding, and held his hands up in front of him. "Don't do this, Tyrell," he shouted over the roar of the rotors. God almighty, was it really going to end like this? "I know you're upset, but I've got a ton of money in a bank in San Juan, and I'm going to split it with you."

"What money?"

"Twenty-five million dollars."

"Yeah? How do I get it?"

Archer took in a long breath and let it out. "I have to go to the bank personally to get it. You come with me and—"

"Bullshit!" Tyrell spat. He leaned sideways and stuck his gun into Archer's neck. "You're a fucking liar. You had no intention of ever giving me nothin'."

"Watch what you're doing!" Archer shouted. A radio tower loomed ahead and Tyrell wasn't looking where he was going. He had to do something or they were going to crash and die. He pointed to a spot over Tyrell's shoulder and said, "Shit! Look at that!"

Tyrell turned his head and Archer wrenched the hand holding the gun upward. Tyrell pulled the trigger and launched himself at Archer. "Motherfucker!" he shrieked.

A meaty fist smashed into Archer's teeth and the helicopter wobbled drunkenly.

It was over—he was going to die. As his bowels went liquid he thought of Kate and hoped she could cheat death in the five minutes he'd given her.

He screamed as they crashed into the radio tower and burst into flames.

"I'm sorry," Jeremy sobbed. He'd tipped over again and was back on his side.

"It's okay, honey, don't cry. Please." It didn't feel as though he'd made a lot of progress on the tape binding her wrists. Time to try something different. "Stay put, okay? I'm going to try tipping my chair instead, and then I can gnaw on your tape."

"But what if you blow up?"

"I'll be careful not to bump it." Good God, what if she did bump it and exploded? What if she got both of them killed unnecessarily? What was she supposed to do?

"Wait, Aunt Kate," Jeremy said, echoing her own thoughts. "I'll try to get back up again.

"Okay, we'll try that first." Sounds from the street wafted up. It must be a circus out there. Where was Gabe? Did her mother know what had happened? And Lindsay, oh, God, she had to be going nuts.

"Got it," Jeremy said. "Put your hands out."

Kate twisted her arms back to where his teeth could reach the tape. "What would I do without you around? Mr. Smarty Pants."

A few minutes later she heard a rip. "You're getting it, Jeremy. Oh, my God." After another minute her hands were free. "You did it!"

She leaned down and hugged Jeremy to her. "Okay, let's get you free." She worked at the tape on his wrists and finally got it off. Together they tipped his chair upright and he bent over to work the tape off his ankles. He stood up immediately and nearly fell down.

"My legs feel funny," he said. "I gotta pee."

"Go pee," she said, feeling the tears spilling down her cheeks. Jeremy was free! "Pee for me too, while you're at it."

"Okay," he said.

There was shouting down below, unlike what she'd been hearing. Had something happened? "Jeremy, hurry up and look out this window."

He raced out of the bathroom and ran to the window. "People are running away and stuff. There are guys down there in big puffy suits."

"What are they doing?"

"They're like pushing their arms out, telling people to run." He turned to her. "Does this mean the house is going to explode?"

Five minutes, Archer had said. From when to when? She couldn't remember, but the situation had just gone from bad to worse. "Listen to me," she said to Jeremy, who was starting to breathe heavily. "I want you to go down to the kitchen and see if the basement door is locked. Do it right now, Jeremy."

"Why?"

"Because if it's locked then Archer probably didn't go down there and you may be able to get out through one of the windows."

"What about you?" he said as tears began running down his cheeks.

"I'll be fine. Please, honey, do this for me. Run down and see. Quick!"

Jeremy raced down the steps. Kate glanced at the clock. When had the countdown begun? The shouting had grown louder. Oh, God. Jeremy had to get out.

“It’s locked!” he called up to her.

Thank God. “Get on a chair and reach above the doorframe. The key’s up there. Do it now!”

She heard him drag a chair, heard the key hit the floor, heard Jeremy sobbing. “Run, Jeremy!” she shouted. “Stand up on something and smash open one of the windows. Hurry!”

“Aunt Kate!” he wailed.

“I love you, Jeremy. You have to get out of the house *now.* Do this for me, and for your mom and dad. Please!”

A moment later his footsteps rang on the wood steps leading to the basement. And, God willing, to freedom.

If she was lucky she had about another minute to live.

She twisted her body until she had walked the chair close enough to open the bathroom door, and then she held on and walked it into the bathroom. She shut the door behind her and, using all her strength, pulled herself and the chair over the edge and into the tub.

Chapter Forty-Four

Gabe stood frozen in the front yard, unwilling to believe this was really happening. Archer's helicopter had crashed into a radio tower and burst into flames. Now it was only a matter of time until they learned whether the house would really explode. If it did, he was going to have a ringside seat. He wouldn't let Jeremy and Kate die alone.

The sound of smashing glass drew his attention and he ran to the side of the house. "Over here!" he shouted to whoever would listen. Then he saw the most beautiful sight of his life.

"Dad!" Jeremy shrieked. "Hurry up!"

Gabe bent down, ignoring the shards of glass, and reached inside for his son. "Jeremy," he managed through the lump in his throat. When he finally had his son through the window and in his arms he let the tears fall.

"Run, Dad," Jeremy shouted. He squirmed out of his father's arms. "It's going to blow. Run!"

He grabbed Jeremy's arm and pulled him, running away from the house. "Where's Kate?" he shouted.

"Upstairs. She's taped to the chair and the—"

The front door exploded outward. "No!" Gabe shouted.

Tears streamed down Jeremy's cheeks but he tugged at Gabe's arm, forcing him to keep running. "She doesn't want us to die, Dad."

Windows blew out as though synchronized. The fire companies that were already in place leaped into action, dragging hoses from every direction toward the tragedy that was unfolding before their eyes. A news helicopter beat loudly overhead. People shouted through bullhorns. Lindsay shoved her way through the crowd and grabbed Jeremy, crying and repeating his name and God's name over and over between sobs.

"Dad!" he called, but Gabe was running toward the house. "Dad! He told us to hide in the bathroom!"

The bathroom. "There's a woman on the second floor!" Gabe shouted to the firefighters. "Please. You have to get her out."

Hoses were trained on the house, beating back the flames that engulfed it. "The second floor collapsed, pal," one of the firefighters shouted back to him. "Sorry."

He ran around the side of the house, jumping over hoses, drawing angry shouts from some of the firefighters. She had to be alive. She had to. He'd know it if she wasn't, wouldn't he?

"Kate!" he shouted into the roar of flames and water. "Kate!"

The agonizing fear that he would never see her again racked his body, stealing his breath, twisting his gut so fiercely it took every bit of reserve strength he had to stay on his feet.

"Get back!" A firefighter shouted at him. "It's burning too hot to get this close."

But the heat of the fire was nothing compared to the anguish that blazed inside him. If the fire was close to searing his skin out here and she was in there somewhere, helpless to move…

What if he stopped searching for her and she was still alive and in pain? Even now she could be shouting, but would they hear her?

No. He wouldn't give up until he found her. Even if it killed him.

It took almost two hours to beat back the worst of the flames, and Gabe continued to shout her name the whole time. He was streaked with grime and ash, coughing from the smoke, but if someone dared to touch him he pushed them away with such force that the firefighters gave up and let the lunatic be.

About a hundred yards away he spotted Bruno sniffing and whining around a particular pile of debris in the midst of the rubble. Had some instinct drawn Kate's old Lab toward the spot? The hair on the back of his neck prickled and he moved toward Bruno, picking his way around barrier after barrier until he saw it—a claw-foot bathtub, the same one he'd pulled Kate out of days earlier, lying on its side.

He wanted to run to it, wanted all of this smoking, busted material out of his way. He was desperate to know if Kate was there—and terrified of what he would find. As he drew closer he could see huge chunks of drywall nearly covering what appeared to be piece of wood furniture inside the tub.

She's taped to the chair.

"Kate!" His shouts were hoarse as he slogged across the yard, his entire being focused on getting to that bathtub. *Be alive, Kate. Please, God, be alive.*

From several yards away he saw the arm slung over the edge of the tub. Kate's arm. "Oh, God," he moaned and rushed over to her, his heart in his throat. Her skin was warm. "Over here!" he shouted at the top of his lungs. "Get a stretcher! Hurry!" He felt for a pulse. It was thready, but it was there.

"Kate," he said, lifting and tossing chunks of drywall onto the ground. He was well aware of the risks of moving her without knowing the extent of her injuries. "Kate," he repeated. "Honey, answer me if you can."

Her hair and clothes were covered with ash and plaster. Archer's words came back to him. *"At the slightest disturbance the charge taped to Kate's ankles will explode."*

So far it hadn't, but what if it could? "Get a bomb specialist over here!" he shouted. "She's got a charge on her ankles."

He couldn't see the front of her body. Her beautiful face. What if she'd been burned? Her bones crushed? He stroked her arm. "Whatever happens, Kate, I'm going to be here for you. I love you. If you can hear me, honey, I want you to know that no matter what happens, all that matters is that you're alive." His voice cracked. "Oh, baby, I was so afraid. I thought you were dead."

The hand on his shoulder was gentle but firm. "Move aside, Detective, and let me take a look at her. And take this damn dog with you."

Gabe grabbed Bruno by the collar, rose and stepped back to let the bomb specialist near the tub. "Keep everyone back," the man told him. There were medics standing by about twenty feet away from them. Gabe didn't want to move aside, but it was clear that the bomb specialist wasn't going to begin until he got out of there.

The next few minutes were some of the longest and most torturous of his life. Finally, the suited man rose to his feet, pulled off his helmet and said, "We have to move her before I can get in there." He pointed to the medics. "Go get one of my team over here." To Gabe he said, "Tell the cops to clear the damn street."

They did as they were told, and within minutes another man in a blast-resistant suit approached the bathtub. Gabe followed.

"Get back, damn it," the lead guy said.

"I want to see her."

"Then go stand by the ambulance. If she makes it out in one piece you'll see her there."

Gabe's gut twisted painfully. If the bomb exploded when they tried to remove the charge…

"Be real careful with her," he rasped, then picked his way through the wreckage to the ambulance and watched the two bomb specialists lift Kate, still attached to the chair, out of the tub, and lay her on her side on the stretcher. Gabe held his breath as they cut the tape and carefully, oh so gently, lifted the charge away from her body. Holding the charge out in front of him, one bomb specialist walked slowly, slowly over and around the debris to a waiting van and placed it carefully inside. Then the two medics ran back to the stretcher. They spent some time checking Kate over, then lifted her and headed for the waiting ambulance.

She was all in one piece.

Chapter Forty-Five

Kate cracked her eyelids enough to see where she was. For the longest time she'd been aware of the beeping and whining of medical equipment. The sight of striped curtains confirmed that she was in a hospital. *Again.* Why?

Jeremy.

Panic rose inside her. "Jeremy," she whispered.

"I'm here, Aunt Kate." And then her godson's beloved face was close to hers, grinning like the little imp he was. "I made it out just in time, and my dad grabbed me by the arms and pulled me through the window. I broke it with a golf club and it made a big mess, and I got some cuts on my forehead, see?"

Kate saw stitches on Jeremy's forehead and smiled. He was okay. *Thank you, God.*

"We thought you were dead, but then Dad found you in the bathtub and the bomb guy pulled off the tape and it didn't blow up. Good thing, huh?"

"Yeah," she rasped. Her body ached all over. She drifted back into sleep, even as a deep voice said her name.

"Kate?"

She cracked her eyelids open again, and this time the face before her was older, impossibly handsome, with dark circles under his eyes and beard stubble that had to itch like crazy. Her heart filled. "Gabe?" she whispered.

Tears filled those beautiful gray eyes. "It's me," he said, and kissed the hand he was holding. "How do you feel?"

She squeezed his hand and tried to smile. "Tired," she said. "Achy."

"Yeah, I bet. You fell fourteen feet in that bathtub, right through the floor. And then pieces of the ceiling fell on top of you." He stroked her cheek tenderly. "But you're okay, honey. Bruised as hell, but no broken bones. A little internal bleeding but they have that under control."

"Do I… My face…"

"Is as beautiful as ever." His smile told her he spoke the truth. "You're more beautiful to me than anyone in the whole world. You always were."

So were you. But she didn't say it. Not now. Not yet.

"I know I've given you plenty of reasons not to trust me, but—"

"Gabe," she interjected, and pressed a finger to his warm lips. "Later."

He pressed a kiss to her lips. "I'll wait until you're ready. But I won't give up, Kate. This is too important."

She smiled and let herself drift back to sleep.

The next time she woke there were two women talking in her room. It was several seconds before she realized one was her mother and the other was Miriam Hugo. It had been eight years since those two had spoken.

"He came for dinner a couple of days ago and told us everything," Miriam said. "And you know, I remembered how I used to think, years ago, that Kate and Gabe seemed more suited to each other than she and Steven did."

Okay, she had to be dreaming. Miriam never said Steven's name, never mind in the context she'd just imagined.

"I think Kate has loved him for a long time," her mother said. "It's too bad she wasted all those years with that insane bastard, pardon my French. My God, I can't believe none of us saw him for what he was."

They were talking about Drew, obviously. By now the

whole world probably knew he'd planned to take down her plane, to kill her and all those other passengers, to get his bill passed. And get rid of her, of course. She groaned at the hideousness of it.

Her mother was instantly at her side. "Honey? It's Mom. I came as soon as I heard. Thank God… Thank God…" She dissolved into tears.

"I'm okay," Kate whispered.

Miriam came around the other side of the bed and leaned down to kiss Kate on the forehead. Then she stroked her hair. "I'm so relieved," she said. "I don't think Gabe could have survived losing you again."

Tears sprang into Kate's eyes. "He…told you?"

"Yes, he told us everything, honey. And I only pray that you can find it in your heart to forgive him. He loves you so much."

Kate closed her eyes but the tears leaked out anyway. "I'm afraid," she whispered.

"I know, honey," Miriam said. "I don't blame you, and neither does he. He was cruel to you, and to be honest, his sisters enabled him by blindly taking his side. We all hurt you, and I deeply regret that. Sylvia and Carolyn feel the same way."

"Thank you," Kate whispered. "That means more than you can imagine."

"You just take your time with Gabe, and if it's right you'll know it. If not, well, then he blew it and you'll both have to move on."

Kate gazed up at her. "I never imagined I'd hear this from you."

"No," she said. "I was dead inside for a lot of years. I wasn't much of a mother to my other children. And men, no matter how old they are, they're still little boys inside."

"I loved Steven, Miriam, you need to know that. And I mourned him for a long time, even though—"

"I know all that, honey. He wouldn't have wanted you to be alone."

A sob burst from Kate and her mother squeezed her hand. "I tried to make him happy. I'm so sorry…"

"Shhh," Miriam soothed. "I know you did."

"Did Gabe tell you—"

"Yes, and no one is judging you for that. Either one of you."

Kate swiped at tears. "I'm terrified of him. He can hurt me so easily."

"He's really a marshmallow inside."

"I don't know how to get past everything that's happened. And I don't mean only with him. I mean Drew, and… My God, I let Archer into my home, with Jeremy there." She sniffled and her mother handed her a tissue. "How did I stay married to a man like that for so many years? What's wrong with me? Am I really that naïve?"

"Your father messed with your head," her mother said, regret plain in her eyes. "I think unconsciously you found yourself a father figure quite a bit like him—emotionally unavailable—in an attempt to get it right this time." When both Kate and Miriam stared at her she said, "Couples counseling. We've just started, at my insistence."

"The men you've loved have all let you down in their own way," Miriam said. "Gabe knows that, and he wants a chance to redeem himself. But you've got to be ready to let him, honey. There's no point rushing into something if you're still carrying a lot of baggage."

"If he loves you enough he'll wait," her mother chimed in.

"Oh, he does," Miriam said.

Chapter Forty-Six

Three months later

It was dark when Gabe and Jeremy pulled up in front of Lindsay's house. "You've been wearing your cop face an awful lot lately," Jeremy said. "Mom says you're not happy."

"Where did that come from?" Gabe asked. "We just spent the whole day at Kings Dominion having a great time."

"Yeah, but as soon as we got off the rides you stopped smiling. Every time."

"Seriously?" He hadn't thought he was so obvious. "I'll have to work on that."

Jeremy opened the passenger door. "Oh, and Mom said she wants to talk to you." He ran ahead of Gabe.

"Swell," Gabe murmured. "That ought to make me smile."

Jeremy ran into the house and Gabe took his time walking up to the porch. Lindsay stepped outside and closed the door behind her. Uh-oh.

"What's up?" he asked before she had a chance to throw any shit at him.

"I wanted to tell you that I've decided to change our agreement to joint custody. All you have to do is sign the papers and I'll give them to my lawyer."

Gabe took a step back. "Wow. Really?"

Lindsay nodded, a slight smile on her face. "I've been a jerk to you, and I'm sorry." She laid a hand on her abdomen. "I'm pregnant again."

Gabe felt a pinprick of regret in his gut. It wasn't that he still loved Lindsay, or that he wished they were still married. But there was something about Jeremy's mother carrying another man's baby… "Congratulations."

She tilted her head to the side. "You're a tiny bit jealous. Admit it."

He shrugged. She always was too intuitive for her own good. "Maybe a little. But it'll be nice for Jeremy to have a brother or sister that's really his."

She nodded, and it was hard to miss the satisfaction in her eyes. "Maybe you and Kate will have kids someday."

"Wow, you're full of surprises tonight." He tried to smile. "I appreciate the sentiment, I really do, but there's nothing happening on that front." Nothing at all. She hadn't called, or asked to see him—other than when he dropped Jeremy off or picked him up. She was living in a rented condo in Foggy Bottom and he had no idea whether she even planned to stay in the area.

"Kate was prepared to die to make sure Jeremy got out of that house in time," Lindsay said, her expression sober. "I'll be grateful to her every day of my life. And…there's something else."

Uh-oh, here it comes.

"I was so angry that day…of the explosion."

Gabe held up a hand. "Please. You had every right to be angry. And believe me, if Jeremy hadn't made it…" Tears welled every time he thought about how close he had come to losing his son. A glance at Lindsay told him she had the same reaction. "It's over. Whatever you said or did is water under the bridge."

"No, I mean before, when you picked him up. I said something that wasn't completely true."

"What?"

"I told you Kate gave me the money to get full custody of Jeremy." She looked down and slid one foot along the slate walkway, back and forth. "But she had no idea that I used any of that money to fight you in court. She never would have given me a dime if she'd known."

Gabe hadn't believed it for a moment, but said, "Thanks for telling me, Linds. I appreciate it."

She nodded. "I'm sorry I lied about that. It wasn't fair. If you love her, well... Go get her. Don't let her walk away." *Like you let me* was the unspoken message.

If only it were that easy. "Thanks," he said.

He drove back to his apartment and climbed the steps wearily. *Go get her.* Right. Everybody else said, *Give her space.* That's what she seemed to want, so he'd been gritting his teeth for three months, forcing himself not to call her unless he found a reasonable pretext that involved Jeremy, emailing her only occasionally, and only driving by her condo three or four times a week when he simply couldn't stand being so far away from her. Fuck. He was pathetic.

Once inside he sighed so deeply he almost missed the quiet voice saying his name. He spun to the living room, where Kate sat on the sofa, knees pulled to her chest, watching him. In that moment something warm and joyful pushed through the pain in his chest, stopping his breath. He couldn't speak.

"Sorry if I scared you," she said with a shy smile.

"You nearly stopped my heart," he managed, though his mouth was dry as dust. "Other than that no harm done." He dropped his keys and his gun on the kitchen table and then stood there, heart pounding with a mixture of hope and fear, unsure what the hell to do or say.

"How'd you get in?" he finally asked.

"I borrowed Jeremy's key and made a duplicate."

He moved toward her cautiously. "Does that mean you plan to use it again?"

"Depends," she said.

"On what?"

"On whether I can trust you."

He stopped and raised his face to the ceiling, then blew out a breath. "How can I prove it to you, Kate? Tell me. I'll do anything."

"Come and sit down first," she said.

He sat on the other end of the sofa, knowing that if he touched her he would pull her into his arms and never let her go. But he didn't want to scare her off. Again. "I can't believe you're really here," he said.

"I can't either." She glanced up at the photo over the couch, the drawing of him and Jeremy that he'd kept on his wall all these years. "And I can't believe you didn't throw that out a long time ago."

"I would never have thrown that out."

Her body language told him that she was frightened. Well, he couldn't blame her. Here she was with a guy who had hurt her, insulted her, betrayed her…and who was desperate to pull off her clothes and drive into her with all the pent up lust he'd been carrying around since the last time they'd made love.

"Stop looking at me like that," she said.

"How am I looking at you?"

"Like you're a cat and I'm a plump little mouse."

"I'd say you're a skinny little mouse, but you'd probably hit me."

"Hitting you would require me to unwrap my arms, and then you'd pounce." She grinned.

He grinned back. "There's nothing I would rather do more right now than pounce on you, but I'm fighting it."

She took a deep, shaky breath. "I need to understand… all those years. How could you have thought the worst of me for so long?"

He leaned forward and clasped his hands between his knees. "Guilt," he said. "Anger. Stupidity. Selfishness. Immaturity. Want me to go on?"

"Was it only me you were angry with?"

He shook his head. "I was angry at you, at me, even at Steve… And then when you hooked up with Drew, I was also humiliated. And that really pissed me off."

"I get why you were angry, but why humiliated?"

Gabe closed his eyes. "Because I wanted you."

"Why didn't you tell me?"

"I planned to. I went over to Joy and Ben's place, and I asked Joy how you were. You were spending a lot of time at their lake house on the weekends then. I knew you were hurting and I knew I was being an asshole, but I was too much of a coward to call you."

"What did you think I would do if you called?"

He shrugged. "Tell me to fuck off. It was what I deserved."

"I wouldn't have," she said.

"So, I more or less poured my heart out to Joy, telling her that I wanted to spend some time with you, trying to get a sense of whether it would be uncool for us to be together."

"She never told me any of that," Kate said, sounding outraged. "Damn her."

"She listened very carefully and then informed me that you were in love with a very good friend of hers—a congressman." He spread his palms. "She took such satisfaction in telling me that I felt like a complete asshole for opening up to her."

"What a bitch," Kate said. "I never, ever loved Drew as much as—" She laid her head on her knees.

Gabe reached over and lifted her chin with one finger. There were tears in her eyes. "As much as…"

Her voice was a harsh whisper. "As much as I loved you."

His heart soared. "I love you, Kate," he said. "I loved you then and I love you now. And I'll never stop."

Kate sniffed. Very gently, Gabe pulled her arms away and lowered her legs to the floor. Then he pulled her on to his lap and held her close. They stayed like that for a long time, and nothing had ever felt so right.

"Even though Joy's been a bitch to me for years," Kate said minutes later, "I'm glad the DA backed off charging her with conspiracy. People want their pound of flesh, and the real villains in this are all dead."

"Well, she'll have a tough time in next year's elections," Gabe said. "As will most conservatives in light of what's happened. But her in particular. Thank God that bill's dead in the water."

"Arlen Fischer's career is over."

"No great loss as far as I'm concerned. Hey, did you read about Joe Marshall? He's out of the coma and expected to make a full recovery."

"Oh, I was so happy when I saw that," Kate said. "Thank God. His family can get their life back together. And speaking of families, Ben doesn't seem very happy with the separation."

"No," Gabe said, loving being able to hold her like this and just talk. "But I think he likes all the begging Joy's doing for him to come home."

"I don't blame him," Kate said, smiling. "But you know, in spite of everything he loves her, and I think he'll forgive her over time."

Gabe twirled a lock of her hair. "How long will it take you to forgive me?"

She lowered her head and spoke quietly. "I've been working on forgiveness for the past few months. Not only forgiving you, but myself."

"For what?"

She took a deep breath and let it out. "For marrying Steve even though I was in love with you and carrying your child."

Gabe felt a stab of regret for the child they had lost. "Kate—"

She held a finger to his lips. "For allowing myself to be deceived by two dangerously disturbed men. Seriously, what does that say about me?"

He stroked her hair. "Men like Drew and Archer are masters of deception, honey, particularly with someone like you who's kind and trusting and always looks for the best in people."

"But I let Archer into my house when Jeremy was there, even though you warned me not to trust him. Jeremy could have been killed, Gabe. I don't know how to forgive myself for that."

Gabe pulled her closer. "You had no way of knowing what he was capable of. And you're human. *And* you had reason not to take my word for anything at the time." He paused. "The question is, do you feel you can take me at my word now? Because if you don't..."

She tipped her face up and he saw the answer in her eyes. "I do," she whispered.

His gut uncoiled at her words, releasing a huge sigh of

relief. "Thank God," he said, and wrapped her tightly in his arms. "I need you in my life." Her hair smelled like spring. He nuzzled her neck and felt her muscles tighten, heard a small gasp escape from her lips. Oh, yeah. Then he turned her head and rubbed his lips against hers.

She pulled his head down, and their kiss was electric. He plunged his tongue into her mouth, pulled her closer, grabbed a fistful of her hair and clutched. He wanted to touch her everywhere at once. "I need to make love to you," he rasped.

"Yes," she said. "Please."

He slid his hand inside her shirt, unclasped her bra and pulled both of them over her head, then bent his mouth to her breasts. Holding them, sucking, kissing, licking her nipples into tight peaks while Kate writhed and bucked, wanting more.

"Gabe," she said, her tone pleading.

He slid out from under her and Kate raised her hips so he could pull her jeans and panties down her legs. She was stretched out on his couch, naked and panting, hair wild, eyes heavy lidded with passion. He knelt beside the couch and lifted one smooth leg over his shoulder, then kissed behind her knee, up the underside of her thigh to her cheek, then nibbled on it, driving her wild. He moved his lips to the inside of her thigh and continued his nibbling.

"Oh, Gabe," she breathed. "Yes."

He shifted back on to the sofa and laid her other leg over the back, opening her completely to him. Then lifted her to his mouth. Her pussy glistened and he set about licking every bit of it.

"Gabe, oh God, oh God."

"You taste like heaven," he said, then lowered his face and continued to run his tongue through her folds while she tugged at his hair and begged him for more. He sucked and licked and pressed his face into her until she screamed her release, and still he continued until she lifted his head away and lowered her hips to the couch.

He stood and pulled his shirt over his head, then stepped out of his jeans and kicked off his shoes. "I need to be inside you," he said.

Kate sat up and took his cock in her hands. He groaned. "Not yet," she said, and took him into her mouth. It was hot and wet and he thought he would die of pleasure.

"Ah, God, Kate. Stop or I'll—"

"Shhh," she said and ran her tongue around the tip of his cock.

"I'm about to explode," he said. "I want to be inside you when I do." Using his remaining willpower, he pulled out of her mouth and pushed her back on to the couch.

"I've missed you so much," she said, wrapping her legs around his back and pulling him to her. "I need this."

He entered her as slowly as he could—it would be over much too quickly if he rushed. "Don't move for a minute," he panted. "Okay?"

"I'll try not to."

But he had to move, he had to. "I wanted this to last," he gritted.

"I don't care," she said. "Just move inside me."

"Look at me," he said. He wanted to see her eyes change as her passion rose and peaked.

"I'm looking."

He pulled most of the way out slowly, then plunged in. Kate tightened her legs around his back, matching her inner muscles. He tried to pull away slowly again, but damn it, he was too excited, and found himself moving faster than he wanted to. "Can't…help…it."

"Harder," she gasped.

He grasped her hips, raised her higher and pounded into her for as long as he could, even after he felt her contract around him, before he allowed himself the release he needed so badly. Right into her, with no barrier whatsoever.

Still connected, he lifted her into his arms and carried her to his bed, then pulled her to him and kissed her with all the love and tenderness he'd been dying to show her all these months.

"Kate," he said. "I didn't use anything."

"I noticed."

"What if I got you pregnant?"

"I'd be happy."

His chest grew so full he could barely contain his joy. He pulled her on top of him and kissed her soundly. "I guess now you'll have to marry me. I don't make a whole lot of money, but we'll be okay, I promise."

Her smile was dazzling. She folded her hands on his chest and propped her head up so they were face-to-face. "I get widow's benefits, so even if I couldn't work, I mean, if I had a baby…"

He kissed her. "You don't mind that you may never get all that money back?"

"The cryptographers are still working on the code, so we'll see."

"But they're missing a critical key," Gabe said. "Which probably went up in flames with those two bastards." He avoided saying Archer's or Tyrell's name. Dead or not, his anger about what they had done to Kate and the others stirred up violent feelings he couldn't afford in his line of work.

She shrugged. "The important thing is that Jeremy's

trust is intact, so we won't have to worry about paying for him to go to college." She smiled. "Or buying him a car, or his first house."

He kissed her again. "Thank you for doing that for him."

"I love Jeremy. You don't have to thank me." Her smile deepened. "There is one other thing."

"Hmm?"

"When I set up the trust for Jeremy, I…um…set up one for you."

Gabe stared at her. "Me? Why?"

"Because you wouldn't take anything from me, even though it was Steve who made that money, not me. And I knew he would want you to have it. So I thought that maybe there would come a time, you know, when you might need it for something."

He swallowed. "You did that for me? Even though I was such a jerk?"

She raised one shoulder in a half shrug. "It's not as big as Jeremy's."

"Okaaay…"

"When I set it up it was worth around two million. And that was eight years ago."

"Wait…two million *dollars?"*

She kissed the tip of his nose. "No, silly, two million goldfish. What do you think?"

He ran a hand through his hair. "Holy crap. I don't know what to say."

"How about, 'Let's buy a big old house with a lot of charm, near good schools and walking distance to shopping and the library?' Oh, and a garage or attic I can convert to a studio."

He kissed the top of her head. "How many bedrooms?"

"Let's see, two or three more kids, so…four? No, five. And at least three extra bathrooms."

He laughed. "And a big kitchen."

"A *huge* kitchen. And a mudroom."

"And a pool, a big one."

"Of course. And a big backyard, with lots of trees."

"Formal dining room?" he asked.

"Nothing formal will be allowed in our house," she said. "Ever."

He rolled so he was on top and kissed her. "Do you have any idea how much I love you?" A thought struck him and he grinned. "Even if you are marrying me for my money."

She gave him a slow smile. "Show me," she whispered.

* * * * *